Praise for *The Silenced Women*

"Weisel delivers sensitive and well-developed portrayals of the beleaguered detectives, without skimping on the action."

—*Booklist*

"In this propulsive debut, Weisel writes evocatively about a detective in crisis, a complex crime, and a city pushed to the edge by a killer's grip. With *The Silenced Women*, you're in for a smart and gritty ride."

—Zoë Ferraris, author of *Finding Nouf*

"Weisel's debut thriller is a crackling how-to-catch-'em, stacking equally intelligent and tenacious adversaries on both sides of the law, then setting them loose on each other."

—Joseph Schneider, author of the critically acclaimed LAPD Detective Tully Jarsdel mysteries

"The debut of a promising new series, *The Silenced Women* is a timely and compelling police procedural."

—Jeff Abbott, *New York Times* bestselling author of *Never Ask Me*

THE
SILENCED
WOMEN

A VIOLENT CRIME INVESTIGATIONS TEAM MYSTERY

FREDERICK
WEISEL

Poisoned Pen
PRESS

Published by Poisoned Pen Press, an imprint of Sourcebooks
P.O. Box 4410, Naperville, Illinois 60567-4410
(630) 961-3900
sourcebooks.com

Library of Congress Cataloging-in-Publication Data

Names: Weisel, Frederick, author.
Title: The Silenced Women / Frederick Weisel.
Description: Naperville, Illinois : Poisoned Pen Press, [2021]
Identifiers: LCCN 2020020055 (trade paperback) | (epub)
Subjects: GSAFD: Mystery fiction.
Classification: LCC PS3623.E432475 S55 2021 | DDC 813/.6--dc23
LC record available at https://lccn.loc.gov/2020020055

Printed and bound in the United States of America.
KP 10 9 8 7 6 5 4 3 2 1

For Meg, Chelsea, and Steven

PART I

Chapter One

The dead woman possessed a rare beauty, Eddie Mahler thought as he looked at the thin, sculpted face and the soft down of her skin—the handsomeness spoiled now by an uneven line of dried blood falling loosely around the throat like a necklace come undone.

The victim lay on her side on a park bench, the body wrapped in a red woolen blanket from shoulders to feet. Mahler guessed her to be nearly six feet and in her mid-twenties. Streaks of red dye had been inexpertly applied through the bangs of brown hair. The eyes were closed, the lips slightly parted, as if she were about to speak. For an instant he imagined the sound of her voice, a word or two left behind, hanging in the air.

Then a car door slammed behind him, and Mahler's attention went back up the hill to the parking lot. The crime-scene techs had arrived, and two members of his Violent Crime Investigations, or VCI, team were waiting for him with a park ranger.

The bench sat on a hillside in Spring Lake Park, Santa Rosa's largest public park, beside a stand of oaks with a view of the water. Below the bench, the slope dropped sharply to an access road before falling all the way to the lake's edge. Valley fog diffused the early light and muted the sounds of the ghostly joggers and dog walkers traveling through the mist along the lakeshore.

An hour earlier, a call from Detective Martin Coyle had brought Mahler to the park. Now Coyle and a new investigator, Eden Somers, were "giving him his space" but checking every few minutes for his signal to join him. Beyond the crime-scene tape, a small group of spectators had gathered to peer down at the bench.

Mahler was short and powerfully built. He had close-cropped hair and wore a flannel shirt, jeans, and a golf jacket. A takeout coffee cup kept one hand warm, while his other hand was shoved in a pocket of his jeans.

He had awakened the night before with a migraine, the pain concentrated behind his eyes. For ten minutes he lay without moving, all his attention focused on the intense headache. Then he rose carefully on an elbow to get an Imitrex from the bedside table. He slid the tiny pill onto his tongue and waited for its bitter taste to spread across the front of his mouth. When the pill was gone, he dropped three Advil in his palm and swallowed them with water. He eased back into bed and was nearly asleep when his cell went off with the call from Coyle. Now, here in the park, the migraine's intensity lessened, leaving him with a dull ache and sore neck muscles.

He turned again to the woman. Without touching the body, Mahler knew from the blood trail on her neck that a deep wound would be found on the back of her head. He could also tell from the absence of blood on the bench and ground, and the body's position, that the woman had been placed on the bench postmortem. He thought of the line at the end of the old film *Sunset*

Boulevard, when William Holden says, "Funny how gentle people get with you once you're dead."

Closer up, he could see the top of her shoulders and the edge of a dark silk blouse. In the left earlobe, a pierced earring in the shape of a hollow star. The heavy fabric blanket covering her had traces of blond fibers. Animal hair. Maybe a dog.

Mahler had viewed the bodies of homicide victims for a dozen years but never got used to it. He felt how his presence invaded the victims' intimacy with their death. He had taught himself to see what he needed, to focus on the manner of interruption— the large-caliber bullet opening on the side of a gang member's head or the knife wound on a farmworker's chest that left no other trace than an uneven, pencil-thin line across his flesh. At the start, a veteran homicide cop named Tommy Woodhouse had told him, "When you feel like looking away, that's when you should look." Now Mahler bent close to the victim and studied the dried blood on her neck. Beside the blood, he saw the dark shadows of bruised skin.

The sight staggered him. As he rose, his legs weakened, and he held out an arm to balance himself. He looked as far from the body as he could, toward the distant lake, its quiet surface just visible in the fog. He thought of the other two times he had been called to this same park, to places across the lake, and stood beside the bodies of young women. The first in jeans and sweater, the second in running gear. Both facedown and so perfectly still among the native ryegrass and manzanita they seemed like something new and terrible growing there.

Mahler drank more coffee and felt his hand squeezing the cup. He waited to recover his balance. Then he looked up the hill and nodded. He wanted to be alone, not to have the conversation that was to come.

Coyle, Eden, and the park ranger worked their way down the

hill. Coyle introduced the ranger as Officer Hadley. The ranger had a few inches on Mahler, with the chest and upper arms of someone who spent a lot of time in the gym. He wore a gray uniform, parks department baseball cap, and a pair of deep-black, rimless sunglasses that Mahler figured cost him half a paycheck. He stood stiffly with his hands folded in front of him.

"Dog walker found her about six." Hadley addressed himself to Mahler. "Older woman with a bunch of corgis. One of the regulars who come in every day before the park officially opens at seven. Entered at the Violetti Road gate at the top of the hill. She was making her way down to the lake when the dogs pulled her over to the bench. Made a call on her cell at six ten. We sent her home, but we have contact information if you want to talk to her."

Mahler could tell Hadley was speaking in a way he had heard on cop shows. The guard was probably also conflicted. On the one hand, he was in the middle of something important. On the other hand, he was already wondering how this was going to come back to bite him in the ass.

"Mind taking off your glasses, Officer?" Mahler saw Hadley's face color as the younger man removed his glasses. "How'd the dog walker get in before the park opened?"

"The gate here at Violetti Road is a steel-tube barrier. Closed from seven p.m. to seven a.m. It'll keep out a car, but people on foot have worn a little path around it. Not much we can do to stop them."

Mahler looked away. Eden was writing in a steno notebook; Coyle watched a spectator leaning over the caution tape to shoot photos with a cell phone.

"What's your routine after seven p.m.?" Mahler faced Hadley again.

"Two rangers on duty. We spend most of our time with the

overnight campers on the other side of the lake. Every two hours one of us does a patrol in the pickup. We make a loop around the whole park on the paved road, over by the West Saddle Dam, in front of the swimming area, and back to the campground. There's a ranger hut in the campground where we can get out of the weather. The patrol takes about twenty-five minutes."

Mahler pointed to the road that passed the parking lot two hundred yards away. "So last night you or your partner drove down that paved road over there?"

"That's right. Every two hours after seven."

"You see or hear anything unusual?"

"No, sir."

"You shine a light over here when you go by?"

"No, sir."

"Ever vary the route?"

"No, sir." This last answer was slower than the two previous.

"Ever get out of the truck?"

Hadley looked confused. He turned to Coyle for help but was met with a blank stare. Hadley shook his head.

"You listen to music when you drive?"

Hadley hesitated. "Sometimes I take my phone. But, you know, just one ear."

Mahler hated everything about the young ranger now—his self-importance, his phony military bearing, and the carelessness with which he wasted their time. He knew the ranger wanted to move but was standing still as a show of strength. "What's the purpose of your patrol?"

"Sir?"

"The purpose. Why're you doing it?"

"It's part of the standing order."

"Part of the standing order," Mahler repeated. "Someone— probably at least two people—carries a woman's body into the park and leaves it here, and you and your standing order don't see anything. Is that right?"

"Yes, sir. As I said, we run the patrol every two hours. So it could've happened between them."

"Or while you're driving past listening to Brad Paisley."

Hadley's fingers were pressed white around his sunglasses. He looked at his shoes.

"All right," Mahler said. "I'll send a couple uniformed officers over to the ranger hut. They'll get statements from you and your partner and talk to the campers. No one leaves until they've talked to an officer. Not even to go on patrol. Understand?"

"Yes, sir." Hadley replaced his sunglasses and walked up through the oaks toward the parking lot.

Coyle smiled as the ranger reached the top of the hill. "Well, that was fun."

Mahler finished his coffee. "He'll get over it. Right now he's thinking about what it would feel like to punch me in the mouth." He turned to Eden. "This your first?"

"Seeing a body?" She looked startled at being addressed. "I mean, a victim. No, I've seen …others."

Mahler saw fear trapped in her eyes before she retreated to the notepad. He realized they had spent little time together since he hired her two weeks earlier. She was smart, young for the team, but with a couple years' experience as an FBI analyst. "You okay? You don't have to be here."

"I'm fine." Eden straightened. "You should do…whatever you normally do."

"You think this is Partridge again, Eddie?" Coyle asked.

Mahler wondered if Coyle had noticed his unsteadiness a few minutes earlier. "Could be. Last I heard, he's still in town." He managed to get the words out but didn't trust himself to say more.

Coyle stepped close to Eden and gestured at the lake. "Two years ago, a young woman named Michelle Foss is killed in the park, over by the water tanks. Strangled, body left beside a footpath. Small town, public space like this, it's a huge deal. Chief puts on extra patrols, cars at the gates. We look at locals with a record of assaults on women, and right off the bat, we question a guy named Irwin Partridge. Matches a witness description of a man seen on a park trail the night Foss was killed. But the witness is shaky, and we've got nothing to connect Partridge to the killing."

Eden wrote in her notepad. "So you had to let him go."

"Yeah, he walks. Three days later, another body's found in the park. Susan Hart. Middle-distance runner at the junior college. This time down near the boat launch, but same type of victim, same strangulation pattern. It's as if the killer figures he won't get caught. The media start calling him the Seventy-Two-Hour Killer."

"Which scares people." Eden nodded as she continued to write.

"It's a circus. San Francisco TV stations have news vans at the park gates. A neighborhood watch is organized on the perimeter. One night our guys find a pickup by the dam—four heroes in the truck bed with deer rifles. Some knucklehead in a house above the park hears a noise outside and shoots his own dog."

Mahler stood apart. He disliked a lot of talking at a crime scene. The migraine pain now existed as an echo. He closed his eyes and pressed his fingertips on the lids. He remembered the crime-scene techs waiting in the parking lot. He waved at them. A dozen more spectators stood behind the yellow tape.

"What about Partridge?" Eden asked.

Coyle backed her away from the bench to give the crime-scene crew room to work. "With the Hart killing, we look at

Partridge again. Hold him on an old failure-to-appear warrant and take his life apart: house, car, job, family, past arrests, the works. All of which comes up with nothing. DA declines to indict."

"Then what?"

Coyle shrugged. "Then what? Nothing. We work a bunch of leads that go nowhere. But the murders stop, and the public and the media move on to the next tragedy."

"Unusual for a successful killer to stop. So the cases were never solved?"

"No." Coyle looked at Mahler. "No, they never were."

"So, if our victim here was murdered by the same killer," Eden said, "he could be starting again."

"Maybe, but this one seems different," Coyle said. "Someone bashed her head. The victims two years ago were killed by ligature strangulation."

"This one's strangled as well. There's bruising on her throat."

Coyle frowned. "You're kidding. You saw bruising under all that blood?"

"Yes. Just now. Want me to show you?"

"That's okay. Hear that, Eddie? Did you see it, too?"

Mahler looked back without speaking.

"But this bruising doesn't look like ligature strangulation," Eden said. "It's on the front of the throat, consistent with manual strangulation. Statistically, front-side strangulation is rare, usually committed by someone known to the victim."

Coyle snorted. "Statistically? Someone's studied it?"

Eden's face reddened. "Sorry. Was that the wrong thing to say?"

"Just not used to it, is all."

Mahler had had enough. He stepped between Eden and Coyle. "Detective Somers, tell the techs I want an initial crime-scene report by ten thirty." He heard his own voice, as if it were outside of him, talking too loudly. "And we need to find out who this woman is. Call Kathy Byers. Now. Tell her to put out a press release. No photos—physical description and clothing. Email it to the press, and put it on the public website. Have Kathy get tech support to set up an independent phone line for the public to call in."

He swung around to Coyle. "Where're Rivas and Frames?"

"With Gang Crimes, picking up Peña. They'll be back in a couple hours."

"Text them. Say they're on this. We're all on round-the-clock."

Coyle nodded. "You okay, Eddie?" When Mahler didn't reply, Coyle started typing on his phone. "The other thing is, the earlier victims weren't wrapped in a blanket like this one."

Mahler looked up the hill to the spectators behind the yellow caution tape, who were holding up phones. "You know what else is different from two years ago? We didn't have as much social media crap as we do now. By the time we get back to our cars, the photos from those phones are going to be on Instagram and Snapchat."

He turned back to the crime-scene crew, kneeling beside the body on the bench. "Once people see the pictures of this crime scene, all they'll care about is we found a dead woman in the park, and it could happen again in the next seventy-two hours."

Chapter Two

"Numbers don't lie. I looked it up. Eighty-eight percent of Hispanic pitchers in the majors are right-handed." Frames talked fast, as he always did with a new theory—this time fueled with an espresso shot and two Red Bulls. "With Anglos, that number's only, like, seventy. I mean, your culture has that Catholic thing, which—let's be honest—is all about conformity. Who knows how many naturally left-handed kids your religion turns into righties? Then you've got the younger players coming up from the Caribbean and all that voodoo about left-handedness being bad luck. The Spanish word for 'left' is *sinistra,* isn't it, like sinister?"

"The Spanish for 'left' is *izquierdo.*" Rivas pronounced the last word carefully, aware the correction would piss off Frames. But he also knew from experience facts were no match for one of Frames's theories. "'Left-handed' is *zurdo. Sinistra* is Italian."

Rivas was at the wheel of an unmarked Crown Victoria driving through Roseland. It was still early, and the streets were quiet. The car ahead was a red Explorer that held Mike Daley and three officers from Gang Crimes. He and Frames were part of a joint operation to arrest a Sureño dealer named Arturo Peña, suspected in the murder of a rival dealer three days earlier.

Frames turned in his seat. "You sure? No offense, bro, but being a native speaker doesn't make you an expert on the whole Spanish language. Maybe your mother, or whoever, taught you the wrong word and never had a chance to correct it."

Rivas let that one go and kept his attention on Daley's car.

It was a working-class neighborhood of closely spaced, one-story houses built in the fifties. Rivas knew the euphemisms from the city reports—ethnically diverse, high density—and he was familiar with the trouble hidden by those words. The graffiti on the highway abutments and sides of empty stores marked the territory for the VSL, the Varrio Sureño Locos. The Sureños meant drug sales, street crime, and drive-bys.

Rivas had grown up here forty years earlier and had ridden the streets on a BMX bicycle as a boy. What he saw every time he drove through were the first homes, the front yards of six-by-ten mown grass, and the daily, hard-won battles to keep them paid for.

"Hispanic guys always throw cut fastballs. Now don't tell me that's not true." Frames was into it, pedal to the metal. "Case in point: my man Mariano Rivera. His out pitch was always a cutter, thrown with an off-center, four-seam grip, pushing the middle finger as the ball's released. He could do it because you guys have unusually long second and third fingers. Weird hands, period. Who's that guy pitched for the Marlins, Antonio Alfonseca? Guy had six fingers on each fucking hand."

Rivas saw Daley, half a block ahead, and slowed down. They'd been tipped to the address the night before by an informant named Arlen Waters, a meth dealer facing ten years on his second strike. Waters put Peña at the house with his girlfriend and her two children, Peña's cousin, and an uncle. The plan was to park out of sight and go in on foot. Daley and his guys would go in the front, Rivas and Frames in the back.

"A cutter drops as it reaches the plate," Frames said. "You know this, man. So hitters are forced to settle for ground balls. Half the time, you get a cutter on the inside corner, it shatters the bat."

Rivas smiled and nodded. "What you're saying is, Hispanics are involved in a conspiracy to break bats?" His favorite part of Frames's rants was spoiling the endings.

"Come on, Rivvie." Frames sighed. "Why're you always being sarcastic when I'm trying to have a serious conversation? You know it messes with our rapport. What I'm telling you is, you're up to bat against some hot-shit Hispanic reliever, the odds are he's right-handed and throwing a cutter. And you should be able to hit it, because knowing what's coming is half the battle."

"Hey, I'm with you, partner," Rivas said. "You need to make an instructional video: *Improve Your Batting Average with Racial Awareness.*"

Frames shook his head in frustration. "You don't even try, man. You know that?"

Daley pulled to the sidewalk three houses down, and Rivas parked behind him. The street was empty. For a moment, they sat looking at the house three lots ahead. The windows were dark.

Rivas's phone buzzed. He dug it out of his pocket and read a text. "It's Coyle. We've got a homicide in Spring Lake Park. Eddie wants us back as soon as we're done."

Daley appeared at Rivas's car door. "Driveway's on the left. Let's keep them in the house."

Rivas climbed out of the car and joined Frames on the sidewalk. They wore Kevlar vests, with POLICE stenciled across the front and back. Rivas unsnapped his Sig Sauer from its holster.

Frames already held a Glock in his right hand. They jogged quickly behind Daley's team. When they reached the property, Rivas and Frames ran past the place and turned down a cracked concrete driveway to the rear of the building.

The drive led to a detached one-car garage. Between the garage and the house lay a small patch of dead Bermuda grass. The back entrance to the house was an aluminum screen door, its bottom screen flopped open with a large, frayed tear. Rivas and Frames positioned themselves on either side of the concrete steps beneath the door and waited.

A minute later, they heard Daley and his officers go through the front door, shouting orders. From inside came the sound of a dog barking. Then a large black-and-tan Doberman flew through the broken screen, past Rivas, and hit Frames in the chest. The impact slammed him backward onto the ground. Turning toward his partner, Rivas reached on his belt for his OC, the pepper spray. The screen door banged open again, and before Rivas could react, a man leaped over the steps straight at him. The collision dropped Rivas to his knees, and he smelled the man's sweat as he ran by.

An angry Rottweiler raced out of the house, barking and snarling. Rivas shot OC into the dog's face. Then he scrambled to Frames, who was lying on his back, holding on to the Doberman's collar with both hands. The dog lunged again and again, digging its paws into Frames's torso. Rivas shoved the OC canister in front of the animal's head and sprayed. The Doberman pranced wildly, whining in agony and rubbing its nose in the grass.

Rivas pulled slowly to his feet. He felt his body's early morning stiffness and the accumulated weariness of a hundred suspects wrestled to the ground. He looked behind him at the garage. The man who had knocked him over was gone.

Frames jumped up and watched the two dogs paw frantically at their faces. "Man, I hate dogs."

Rivas pointed for Frames to take the right side of the garage while he ran left. He followed a concrete sidewalk as wide as his shoulders between the garage and a broken fence. Overhead, a grape arbor supported a tangle of thick vines and yellow and brown leaves and cut visibility to a few feet.

Holding his Sig, Rivas moved slowly in the dim light, stopping every few steps to listen. Behind the garage sat a low wooden shed and, between them, a passage covered with a panel of sheet metal.

At the back of the shed, the walkway dead-ended at a seven-foot-high concrete block wall. The smooth face of the wall was impossible to mount. The alley offered no way out. Rivas's mind went back over the path. *Where'd this asshole go?* He turned around to see Peña pushing aside the sheet metal to stand twenty feet away in the center of the sidewalk, leveling his gun at Rivas's head.

Tall and thickly built, Peña wore a ragged tank top and boxer shorts. His shaved head stood on a neck and shoulders covered in prison tattoos—black spirals curling up to the base of his cheeks like swollen angry snakes climbing out of his shirt.

The two men looked at each other across the dim corridor. Rivas's gun was in his right hand, beside his hip. Peña's was at head level, pointed straight ahead.

"There's a shitload more cops back in the house," Rivas said.

"*Bésame el culo,*" Peña said. His voice was low and toneless. The hand with the gun stayed dead still.

Rivas stared at the large figure before him, at the blank face and the empty gaze of his eyes. He weighed the odds of moving out of the line of fire and raising his own gun. What part of a second would it take Peña to squeeze the trigger? The Sig Sauer in his hand suddenly felt heavy.

Is this my story?

The question rose in him before he could stop it, just as it had again and again since he turned fifty a year ago. He saw time, which moved like the air, and his own history suddenly racing toward him out of the future.

In his mind, he heard his grandmother, Maria-Elena, telling his story. The old woman lived in his house when Rivas was a boy. Small, uneducated, always bent over a floor mop or dishpan, she was the *cuentista*, the storyteller. He followed her from room to room while she cleaned, and listened to her tales of the Moreno family, his mother's lineage. Cameos of long-dead relatives she'd learned from the women before her. Arcadio Moreno, the *ganadero* killed by his favorite horse. The songbird, Maria Isabel Moreno, who bewitched three men in the same family. Eduardo Moreno, the tallest son of Rafael, who went north to Texas and was killed by a train.

Now Rivas heard his own story in the old woman's dark, slow voice. Daniel Rivas, she said. The policeman, stabbed one night while arresting a seventeen-year-old Sureño. Or, killed by an unknown assailant in a passing car. Or, shot under a grape arbor by a drug dealer named Peña.

Is this my story?

Peña's skin was olive-brown, almost black under the eyes. In the placidity and defiance of the man's expression, Rivas saw something sad and timeless, like the shadow of an ancient *campesino* lost in a new land. How far had he been hollowed out by the gangs, the years in prison? Was it possible to calculate what was left inside a man's soul? Had this criminal been sent here by the legends to kill him?

He thought of Teresa. "*Vuélvete,*" she told him every morning in the dark before he left. "Come back."

Grandmother, is this my story?

Behind Peña, Rivas noticed a slight, soundless change in the shadows under the arbor. It happened so quickly that Rivas doubted what he had seen. Then he saw it again—the darkness silently moved. Rivas tried to keep his eyes on Peña's.

The third time, Rivas caught a glimpse of Frames's face in the dark walkway space, twenty-five feet behind Peña. He was moving forward, without a sound, gun held in two hands, pointed at the back of Peña's head.

Although Frames had not made a sound, Rivas could see Peña sensed something, a change that must have flickered for an instant in Rivas's eyes. Peña still did not move.

Then Frames said, "Drop the weapon. *Suelte el arma.*"

Rivas was surprised at the power of his partner's voice. It seemed to come from a different source than the prattle a few minutes earlier in the car.

Frames's command had no visible effect on Peña. The dealer continued to hold Rivas in the sights of his gun and to grip the gun steadily. He blinked once, slowly like a prehistoric reptile.

"*Suelte el arma,*" Frames shouted again.

For a few long seconds, they all stood unmoving, a silent tableau. Then Peña's gaze narrowed at Rivas, and he raised his chin. His lips pursed in a kiss. Keeping his eyes on Rivas, he slowly bent his right arm and brought the gun to his shoulder.

Frames reached out and grabbed Peña's gun without moving the Glock he still held at the back of the man's head.

This isn't it, Rivas thought. *Death will come another way.*

He stepped forward to Peña and shoved him against the garage wall. Holstering his gun, he cuffed Peña's wrists. As he worked the cuffs, Rivas noticed for the first time his partner's shoeless feet and his ridiculous socks—sky blue with yellow soccer balls.

"Why'd you come back here?" Rivas asked. His hands started to shake.

"It was quiet," Frames said. "Quiet's never a good thing, right?"

Chapter Three

Thackrey had been awake for three days—or was it four? He couldn't remember.

With just the Adderall, it was easier to tell. Thirty milligrams of extended release in the morning, another sixty in the afternoon. But once he switched to doing stacks of Ritalin and Provigil and mixing in the new crank, the hours and days blurred together. He wiped a wooden coffee stirrer on his sleeve and poked it into the plastic bag on his lap. Balancing a tiny pile of powder on the end, he snorted it and felt a sharp sting in the back of his sinuses.

The Mercedes sat parked at a twenty-four-hour Quik Mart in Santa Rosa—Thackrey in the front seat, Russ and Vic in the back. The store's morning customers looked like admins and techs going to work at Brookside, the medical building across the street. He and the boys had started out drinking coffee to get their hands warm, but now they were bored and were playing rounds of Phone Invader.

A silver Mazda roared into the lot, swerved toward a spot,

and missed, parking two wheels over the line. A young woman emerged in black slacks and jacket, a paisley scarf knotted at her neck. She pressed a remote lock, and the car blared. Her boots clicked across the lot toward the entrance.

Thackrey whistled. "My turn. Her name's Leslie. She's in Sterile Processing, and she's just had an all-nighter with the new urology resident."

He handed the bag to the back seat and picked up his phone. Flipping through the screens, he found the jailbreak app the boys made for getting through the firewall of the California Motor Vehicles Department database. He tapped it open and looked across the lot to type in the Mazda plate. While the phone did its job, he licked the rest of the powder off the stirrer.

A file opened: Stacie Singer. Thackrey sighed. "How does anyone end up with a name like that?"

Russell leaned forward to see the screen. "Guessed the wrong name. Minus five points." He bobbed in time with the techno in his earbuds.

Thackrey opened Facebook and typed in the name. "Shouldn't I get something for guessing a name ending in 'e'?" As the search ran, Thackrey turned in his seat. "So, Victor, my faithful hadji, have we thought about how to remove the blood from the trunk liner?"

Victor's head rested against the window, eyes closed. "I think we need to talk about what just happened. Do you know what you've done, 'cause it sure seems like you don't."

"No hurry, of course. But eventually steps will need to be taken. It's a liner. Can't it be removed?"

Russell looked thoughtful. "Too bad we didn't put down plastic."

"Do—you—know—what—you've—done?" asked Victor, louder this time.

Thackrey reached behind him and tapped the phone against Victor's knee. "Hey, man, I know exactly what *we've* done. Now let's focus on what we do about it."

Victor opened his eyes. "Two options. One, I remove the liner and wash it in a large-capacity machine at a laundromat."

"That's going to attract a lot of attention and be remembered later," Russell said. "Besides, the blood's in the fibers now."

"Or, two, I replace the liner with a new one. I order it online and request overnight. Have it by tomorrow."

"You always were the smart one," Thackrey said.

"Thank you, sahib." Victor bowed his head.

Thackrey lowered the driver's side window. Victor could be trusted, although trust, like many other things, would require effort and attention on Thackrey's part. Outside, the sky was dark and leaden. Along the western horizon, coastal fog blew inland to blanket the rooftops like the folds of a shroud. "By the by, chums, as grateful as I am for your assistance tonight, you're not done. The bell tolls three times for betrayers. You're helping me with two more things concerning my late friend."

"You're joking," Victor said. "After the risks we just took, Russ and I are packing up and getting out."

"Before you skulk away, you're going to help me clean up this mess. Otherwise, I call the locals about a certain vintage Mercedes in the park tonight. We used your car, didn't we?"

"You're a shit, you know that? This is your problem, not ours."

"You played a role, too. Without young Russell's big mouth, we're not here."

Thackrey looked back at his phone. He read out loud. "Stacie only shares some of her profile information with everyone." He swiped a finger across the screen, scrolled to a key app, and tapped it. "Sorry, Stacie. In we go."

Thackrey watched the screen open. "Ouch. Someone needs new friends."

Russell looked over Thackrey's shoulder. "Minus five more. She's a business manager at Brookside." He took out a comb and ran it carefully through his short, stiff hair.

"I'll make it up in the call round." Thackrey scrolled through the profile. "In a relationship with Brian Conover. Look at the poor bastard's ears. Interests: Pop-Tarts. Quotations: Cyndi Lauper: 'God loves all the flowers, even the wild ones that grow on the side of the highway.' Could anything be sadder than this?"

The hit of Ritalin and speed scratched and burned in Thackrey's nostrils. As the drugs found his bloodstream, he felt the popping rush he'd been waiting for. His hearing burst open: the East Asian techno pop inside Russell's earbuds, Victor drumming his fingers on an empty coffee cup, and, outside, the sizzle of the mercury vapor lamps above the parking lot. He caught himself. "Where's the phone with spoofing?"

Russell handed Thackrey a phone.

"Am I old boyfriend or eager suitor?" Thackrey asked.

Russell jumped to answer. "Old boyfriend."

"Don't encourage him," Victor said. "Haven't we resolved enough of Ben's issues with women for one night? Let's just get this over with."

Thackrey peered at the phone screen. "Do I need to enter one of your Hong Kong prep school passwords? Which one was it? The King George School?"

"Give it a rest, Ben," Russell said. Checking his reflection in the car window, he pinched a wave in his hair.

Thackrey typed Stacie's number on the keypad and tapped the phone icon. The call was picked up on the third ring. Thackrey put it on speaker.

"Hello?" The voice was high and impatient.

"Hey, Stacie." Thackrey balanced the phone in his fingertips. "How's it going?"

"I'm sorry. Who's this?"

"It's me. The one who was shtupping you before Brian."

"What'd you say? Jerry?"

"I miss our nights listening to Bruno Mars and watching Sandra Bullock movies."

The voice was more cautious now. "Do I know you?"

Thackrey consulted the Facebook page. "How's Mister Tingles?"

Russell laughed. "Is that a pet?"

"What is this?" Stacie asked. "Who else is there?"

Thackrey mugged a look of surprise. "You look great, by the way. Is that scarf a Fendi?"

"In her dreams," Russell said.

The phone went silent.

"If this is supposed to be a joke, it's not funny," Stacie said after a few seconds.

Russell held up one hand. "No joke. Five points."

"But you really should take better care of yourself, young lady." Thackrey wagged a scolding finger in the air. "You drive that little Mazda way too fast."

Across the parking lot, they could see Stacie come out the front of the Quik Mart, looking at the other cars. "Where are you?"

Thackrey watched Stacie through the windshield. Women amused him, until they bored him to death. And there always seemed to be something that needed cleaning up. "And how really safe are River View Apartments? Every time I was there, I worried about the deadbolt. Come on—all it takes is a couple of tweekers following you home one night. With a tension wrench, they'd be inside. I could be in there right now, for all you know."

"Listen, you sick jerk…" Her voice rose. "I'm calling the police right now and have them trace this call."

Russell's hand went up again. "Police. Ten points."

"Do you still look under the bed before you go to sleep?" Thackrey put his mouth close to the phone. "You really should from now on. We'll be there next time."

"Fuck you," Stacie said.

Russell slapped the seat-back. "F-word. Five points."

"The problem is, you need to be less stupid if you don't want to get hurt. That's going to be a problem for you, isn't it, Stacie?"

"Fuck you." She hung up and shoved the phone in her pocket.

"Five more," Russell said.

Stacie pointed her remote lock at the Mazda, and the horn blared again. She jumped in and gunned the car out of the lot.

"Fifteen, love, front seat," Thackrey said. "Second set."

Victor watched Stacie's car roar down the street. "Now can we stop screwing around and get out of here?"

Thackrey held up the phone for Russell and exchanged it for the plastic bag. "We'll talk about what comes next. First let's order that trunk liner."

Chapter Four

(i)

Mahler walked into the VCI room and took his usual spot on the wall where he leaned against the filing cabinets. The other detectives turned their chairs to face a whiteboard.

Taped to a corner of the board were two color photos of the latest homicide victim, one showing the length of her body on the bench, the other a close-up of her face. Under the photos in red marker was: *Jane Doe, Spring Lake, Violetti Gate, 10/19.* Beneath that, someone had written: *Connection to 2017 Homicides? Next Victim = Time of Death Plus 72 Hours.*

In the past year, without being fully aware of it, Mahler had begun to doubt the business of detection—crime-scene evidence, eyewitness testimony, database patterns—the things that were supposed to identify a suspect. The two earlier homicide victims took with them to the next world not only every trace of their killer but also Mahler's belief that any killer could be found. Facts, he discovered, were useless without faith in them, and he'd lost his, as another man might lose faith in his religion or his god.

He looked across the room. For a major homicide investigation, the group was an untested squad. Rivas and Coyle had been through important cases before, but Eden and Frames were new to VCI. This would be the first major case he'd lead with his new agnosticism. How long before one of them noticed he was racing the clock with tools he no longer trusted?

Rivas took a file from his desk and handed it to Mahler. "Two pounds of meth in Peña's house. A nine mil that looks like a match for the weapon used to kill Castillo Saturday night. Mike took in the cousin and uncle for possession. Arraignment on Thursday. Gang Crimes is waiting to see if they want to talk."

Mahler scanned the first page of the file and handed it back. "If Peña talks, make sure Mike gives you a call. We might clear a few other cases while we're at it. Any problems?"

"Peña pulled a gun." The room went quiet. Rivas shrugged. "We took care of it."

Mahler waited to see if Rivas would say more. Threatening situations brought out different reactions. Some officers responded with bluster; others kept it to themselves. Rivas was usually a joker, underplaying the gravity with a wisecrack. A year earlier, when a teenage drug dealer had fired two rounds during an arrest, Rivas had said his weight-loss regimen made him a smaller target.

Now something new in his manner caught Mahler's attention. He made a mental note to talk to Rivas when they were alone. "Do we have a crime-scene report on our Jane Doe?"

Coyle looked at his laptop. "Shoe prints on the path from the parking lot to the victim. Still trying to sort them out. No usable fingerprints on the wooden seat or seat back. No indications the body was dragged. Blood on the bench and the ground under it. We're waiting on analysis, but it's probably the victim's."

"Blanket's a Pendleton brand." Coyle scrolled further down the screen. "What the company calls Eco-wise wool. Southwestern Red. King size. Can be purchased at a store here in town, in any of five other retail outlets in California, or online. They sell about five thousand a year. Hair fibers on the blanket are canine."

"Does everyone in this town have a dog?" Frames asked.

Coyle smiled. "I'll bet Animal Services would let you adopt those two puppies you were playing with this morning."

"Tell me about the victim," Mahler said.

Coyle looked back at his screen. "Five ten. One thirty-two."

"Which makes her a little taller than the girls two years ago," Rivas said. Nicknamed Señor Database, he was renowned in the department for his memory, able to recall MOs, known associates, and crime-scene details from twenty years before.

"Some makeup—eyeliner, eye shadow, lipstick." Coyle read the words as if they were in a foreign language. "No tattoos or body piercings. Evidence of old scarring on her forearms and ankles."

"She was a cutter," Eden said. "What about her clothes?"

"Navy silk blouse," Coyle read on his screen. "Blood on the back, probably her own. Sixteen-inch black skirt. Black underwear. No shoes."

"It's an aggressive look."

Frames turned in his chair. "So what're you saying there, Eden? She's a pro?"

"No, I didn't mean that. But that's a short skirt. It's a look."

"You mean for the East Coast?"

"I mean for anywhere. With the makeup and clothes, it's like she's dressing up for something."

Mahler watched the intensity with which Eden leaned

toward the whiteboard. *Maybe this is what you get when you hire a former FBI analyst.*

"It was Monday night," Rivas said. "Who dresses up on Monday?"

"*Viejo.*" Frames laughed. "Not all of us go home to watch *Wheel of Fortune.*"

"And one weird thing," Coyle said. "Techs found something written in black ballpoint ink on the inside of her left calf. Difficult to read, but it looks like eight words: *To take into the air my quiet breath.* Whatever that means."

Eden raised her hand. "Wait, I know it. It's a quote. One of those things we had to memorize at boarding school. What's-his-name, you know, Keats." She worked the screen on her phone. "Yeah. 'Ode to a Nightingale,' verse six."

Frames whistled. "Narrow the search to English majors."

"No, but the quote's about death, losing your breath. If she was strangled, it might tell us something about that."

"We don't have cause of death," Coyle said.

"We also don't know if it was written by the victim herself, whoever killed her, or someone else," Rivas said.

"Okay, okay." Eden sighed. "But if the victim wrote the words, it could tell us something about how she was killed or who she was. Habitual skin-writing might be a symptom of depression or bipolar disorder."

It was always like this at the start, Mahler thought. Lots of ideas. No one knowing which detail would turn out to be important. In most cases, the veteran homicide cop Woodhouse once told him, you find a shell casing or fingerprint and you're done. Makes you think the answers will always be there, leaves you unprepared for the ones that are nothing but being lost in a dark woods. "I think we're getting ahead of the real evidence." He looked at Eden. "Did you do what I told you with the press release?"

"Yes, sir. A physical description of the victim went up on the department's website at eight fifteen." She handed him a paper copy. "Press release to the media at the same time. Phone number and email address for anonymous tips. So far, we've got twelve hits on the website and five calls."

"Get through the tips as fast as you can. Keep a log of everything. I'll arrange for some patrol officers to start on it."

"I don't suppose anyone's found what was used to hit her?" Frames asked.

Coyle shook his head. "Nothing at the crime scene yet. When Trish does her exam, we might know more."

"Why's the victim there?" Rivas asked. The others turned to look at him. "It was a lot of work, right? Carrying the body would take two strong men. They have to get past the locked gate. I mean, there are a million easier places to leave her."

Frames pointed to the photos on the whiteboard. "Whoever did it wanted her to be found there."

"If it's Partridge, he's showing us he's starting again in the same place," Coyle said.

Mahler frowned. "Partridge's a thin guy. He couldn't have carried her. In 2017, we figured both women were killed where we found them."

"Maybe he had help," Frames said. "Or he's changed his pattern."

"Serial killers don't change patterns," Eden said.

"How do you know?"

"Statistics."

Coyle rolled his eyes. "Here we go again."

"What do you have against data?" Eden turned in her chair to face him. "You don't think data can help solve cases?"

"Maybe for the FBI. Maybe for national cases. We're a small town. We don't have a lot of *data*."

Eden looked back at the victim's photo. "Anyway, what's interesting here is the killer's arrogance. It's like someone's saying: Look, I can do this. I can put this woman here."

Mahler stood in front of the whiteboard. "All right. Let's find some facts. Martin, talk to the parks people and get the video feed from the surveillance camera at the Violetti Gate. We should also have something by now from the uniforms' canvass of the campers and neighbors. Steve, talk to whoever's in charge of that. Daniel, take a look in ViCAP for any similar homicides like this in the Bay Area. Check Missing Persons, and look into that famous memory of yours and tell me if any of the guys we've picked up in the last couple of years for assault and sexual offenses might be good for this."

"What about Partridge?" Rivas asked.

"His lawyer's bringing him in at one thirty." Mahler looked around the room. His gaze settled on Eden. "Eden and I'll talk to him. Let's meet back here at five, and I want to hear something new."

(ii)

(TUESDAY, 11:38 A.M.)

Police Chief William Truro stood behind the desk with his back to Mahler, looking out the broad windows that wrapped around his corner office. He wore a stiffly pressed white shirt and dress trousers. The window faced a busy intersection, and the chief appeared to be watching something on the street below. Only three months into the job, Truro was young for a chief, ten years younger than Mahler. He had been recruited from a department in a Seattle suburb.

Mahler shifted in his chair and waited.

Truro, still referred to as the "new chief," was a departure from his predecessor—an ex-Army MP, up-from-the-ranks officer named Frank Stone. Stone's hair had been chopped in a buzz cut, and his face had held a permanent flush of frustration. He had been a desk pounder with the same loud bark in a public auditorium as beside you in the hallway. By contrast, Truro was contained, cautious, and given to long pauses in conversation.

Mahler checked his watch. How long was he supposed to wait? He was wasting time. He felt again the churning sensation that awakened him in the night. Adrenaline charged through his veins. If he had any doubt about his nighttime experience, he was sure now. His doctor called the sensation pre-migrainous excitement, an early symptom of an impending migraine. You'll get to know the signs, the doctor said. Once you do, that's a signal you're about to have another one.

"Still getting those headaches, Eddie?" Truro asked without turning.

"Sometimes," Mahler said, not wanting to get caught up in a conversation about headaches when he knew the meeting's agenda.

"I've never had one, but I understand the pain is tremendous. Jen says you should try magnesium supplements. Apparently magnesium relaxes the blood vessels in the brain."

"Yes, sir." No sense disagreeing. Men hated for another man to challenge their wives. Mahler stared at the polished, empty surface of Truro's desk. Was Truro a next-generation no-paper guy? Everything stored on his phone, in the cloud?

Truro swung around to look at Mahler. "Mayor Ransom was just in here. Very intense woman. Do you know Marsha?"

"I've met her a few times." *Here comes the message*, Mahler thought.

Truro smiled. "I like her energy. Great to work with, gets things done." He sat and pulled himself to his desk. "Marsha's concerned about this murder in the park. Thinks we should let the public know we're on top of it. Press conference, community meeting, special task force—allay the public's fears. That sort of thing. What do you think?"

"A press conference is probably a good idea, at least to confront the misinformation on social media, but we'll need to be cautious. I don't think we need a special task force. I could use a few more officers, on a temporary basis, to look at back cases and follow leads."

Truro did not seem to hear him. "You know, Eddie, a crime like this—a homicide in a park—does a terrible thing to a community. Breaks the social compact. Takes away the sense of safety the public feels entitled to."

Mahler nodded. This was the reason he was in the room. Truro was trying out a speech on him. He thought again of the early symptoms of migraine. He could buy himself a few more hours with ibuprofen. Four hundred milligrams every six hours. A bottle of pills sat on his desk, which, unlike the chief's, was cluttered with folders and uneven piles of paper.

"This kind of case defines a department and its leaders," Truro continued. "I've seen it in other cities. It's what they all remember years afterward, no matter what else you do. What's your caseload like?"

"We suspended all other cases. We're on round-the-clock."

"On this kind of homicide, what's your average time-to-arrest?"

Mahler shrugged. "Varies. Sometimes it happens right away, other times longer."

"On average. Realistically?"

"Couple of weeks, maybe longer."

Truro studied Mahler's face. "You all right? You look a little pale."
It's called white migraine. "I'm fine."

Truro seemed to accept that. "I understand you were the lead investigator on the homicides in the same park two years ago. You get all the support you needed from this office?"

Right up to the betrayal. In his mind, Mahler saw the TV4 reporter waiting in a chair outside the chief's office. "Chief Stone took an active part."

"How about you? No judgments in hindsight, of course. But all of us can learn from the past. Anything you'd do differently?"

"I don't think so, sir." This time Mahler felt the shortness of his answer. He remembered Coyle's two columns on that whiteboard, one for each girl. The spontaneous memorials at the crime scenes: candles, construction paper hearts, stuffed bears. The news footage of Susan Hart's father, a thick, doughy-faced man, climbing to the podium at the funeral, unfolding a single sheet of paper, looking out at the faces, and the first thing from his mouth a cry of pain like an animal sound.

Truro broke the silence. "How's the new girl, Eden Somers?"

"All right. Little young. Seems spooked."

"Spooked?"

"You know, frightened."

"Of what?"

Mahler shrugged.

"There's so much in the world today to be frightened of, isn't there? Maybe she's afraid of you, Eddie. You've got a pretty stern demeanor." Truro smiled at his own remark. "Well, she impressed the heck out of me when I interviewed her. Smart, well spoken. Bit unusual, though, for you to recommend someone outside the department, wasn't it?"

"Not unprecedented. I thought we might get a fresh perspective."

"Her FBI work was in serial killings. You see a need for that on your team? We average fewer than five homicides a year."

"Apparently, she knows how to analyze a crime. I think we can use that."

"You're not being cagey with me, are you, Eddie? Some hidden agenda?"

"No, sir."

"You wonder why someone leaves a position like that to come to a small city police department?"

"Could be a lot of reasons. What's important is she might be able to help us."

Truro peered at Mahler. "Speaking of backgrounds, I saw in your file you graduated from Princeton, joined the Army Rangers. Came back home to become a police officer?"

"Yes, sir. A long time ago."

"Princeton's a fine school."

"I believe so."

"You find this work fulfilling?"

"It has its rewards."

Truro frowned and considered the empty surface of his desk. Mahler wondered if he was supposed to leave.

Truro looked up again. "I remember what I was going to tell you. Last month, when you were out to our house, you mentioned the de Young Museum down in the city. Sunday, Jen and I saw the Goya exhibit there. Francisco Goya. Know who I'm talking about? Eighteenth-century Spanish painter?"

"I've seen his paintings."

"I had, too. But not close up. One painting caught our attention. '*Corral de locos*.' *Yard with Lunatics*, I think is how it translates. Dark cell with mentally ill patients. In the foreground, two male patients wrestling each other."

Mahler nodded. *Where the hell was this going?*

"Anyway, we're in front of this painting, and Jen starts talking about the light. Apparently, you can understand what eighteenth-century artists were trying to represent if you pay attention to the quality of the light on the canvas."

Truro leaned back in his chair. "It's funny. I've been going to art museums for twenty years. I never know what I'm supposed to see. Heck, it's that way in life, isn't it? We look at something and don't know what we're seeing. But on Sunday, Jen says this one thing, and, *boom*, I get it. In this Goya painting, the light looks cold and hard, and it illuminates just part of the cell's inhabitants. The point of the painting is the quality of light." Truro shook his head and smiled.

Mahler felt he should say something. Should he say, What the fuck does the quality of light have to do with the dead woman in the park or the killer who's going to do it again in three days? He rose from his chair. "Guess I'll have to see the exhibit."

Truro beat a little tattoo with his fingertips on the edge of the desk. "Okay, Eddie. Feel free to reassign a couple of officers to help you out. I'll schedule the press conference for three. Let's do this thing."

While Mahler watched, the chief stood and, as if he had forgotten Mahler, turned back to look out the window, his silhouette framed in the pale October sky.

Chapter Five

(i)

Coyle stared at the grainy digital images on his laptop. The recording came from a tree-mounted surveillance camera at Spring Lake Park's Violetti Gate. It showed the paved entrance to the park, a canopy of trees above the road, and one side of a ticket booth. A streetlamp made a cone of light over the booth and spread long shadows to its edge. Visible at the top of the screen was the tubular-steel gate that blocked access at night.

Coyle quickly mastered the software controls to accelerate or slow the recording, freeze a frame, or print a still image. The recording ran from 8:00 p.m. Monday to 6:00 a.m. Tuesday. With a motion-sensitive camera, the captured scenes were not continuous but a jumpy series of film clips whenever the sensor was tripped. A timer ran across the bottom of the screen.

A twentysomething hipster from the county IT department had delivered the recording. The kid wore black-framed Buddy

Holly glasses, skinny jeans, and a T-shirt that said "Roadkill Diner." His short hair was moussed into a hard ridgeline that ran down the center of his head like a tiny mountain range.

"You okay with this?" Mountain Head asked as he handed Coyle the flash drive.

"Yeah, I'm good." Coyle decided he didn't need to prove his geek credentials to some stoner with spots on his face. At thirty-five, did he already look out of date? What constituted a generation in geekdom? Should he share with Mountain Head his theory that the way each person uses technology is like a signature? Not now. This guy was working too hard at looking bored.

"You watch it?" Coyle asked.

The kid shook his head. "I watched a feed a year ago when someone was breaking into the snack bar. The thing mostly picks up animals, which is kind of cool and creepy at the same time. Once in a while, you see teenagers sneaking into the park to play hide the salami. Some of them even wave at the camera."

In the beginning, Coyle watched the recording, not certain what he was seeing. The digital capture had no audio track, just a silent, dimly lit picture. The timer's numbers flickered: 20:32.34, 20:42.07, 20:56.13. Gradually, he figured out the camera's motion sensor could detect the movement of very small animals. He ran the software on fast-forward.

At 2:10:23, something appeared. Coyle slowed the recording. A raccoon walked out of the underbrush on the right side of the screen. It stood for a moment in the center of the drive, smelled the air, and walked slowly offstage. Six minutes later, the raccoon returned with something in its mouth. Or, at least it looked like the same raccoon.

Coyle sat up and rolled his neck. He thought of Adrienne.

An hour earlier he had texted to say he wouldn't be coming home tonight. She just wrote back "kay." Although they had been living together for a year, he still didn't know what she was thinking. Lately he thought their sex was better than before, but they didn't talk about it. *Was it normal not to talk about it?*

He never knew what was normal. In his job, he was around a lot that wasn't normal. And he had no one to ask. The guys in the unit only talked about work. When he told Frames his girlfriend's name, Frames did an imitation of Sylvester Stallone from the first Rocky movie, screaming Adrienne's name from the boxing ring.

Coyle clicked to fast-forward again, and the nearly identical images skittered by—ticket booth in a pool of light, ticket booth in a pool of light. Suddenly something darker. He stopped the tape. 4:02:16. A figure in a hooded sweatshirt stood next to the tubular-steel gate, facing away from the camera. The figure bent over the structure, working at something on the chain lock. "Hidy-ho, motherfucker," Coyle said out loud.

At 4:06:10, the hooded figure released the chain and swung the gate away from the drive. Coyle reversed the tape and played it again. This time he could see the person had a tool, probably a screwdriver, to dismantle the lock. The figure, who was short and appeared to be a man, walked out of the picture back toward the entrance. Coyle enlarged the best image and printed a picture. He made a note on a legal pad to check the lock for prints.

He picked up his phone to call Adrienne. But before he hit speed dial, he stopped. *If she was in a meeting, what message would he leave? Say he missed her? Whenever he said things like that, she looked embarrassed. Should he remind her to cook the chicken they bought yesterday, or did that sound like they were married?*

He couldn't talk about the case. Besides, she would think it weird he was sitting in a dark room spying on someone. He had spent so much of his life not knowing what to say. "Use your words, Martin," his mother had told him when he was little and couldn't speak. What he really wanted to tell Adrienne was he missed hearing her voice. Or did that make him a stalker? Coyle put down his phone and looked back at his laptop.

Maybe the problem with Adrienne was he came across as too techie. Is that how everyone saw him? Why did Eddie always assign him the tech stuff? He was as good as the others in the field. Six months ago, he had run down and cuffed a parole violator. Rivas couldn't have made that run. But now the new members of the team, Frames and Eden, were being assigned interrogations ahead of him.

Coyle hit forward on the recording software. A car appeared, driving through the entrance and out of sight. What was that? He reversed the tape and ran it again. The car was an older model sedan. Too dark to see the color. No license on the front. The driver was nothing but a shadow. Coyle stopped the tape at 4:09:50 and printed an image. He made a note to see if the image could be improved to reveal more of the driver or the car.

He now ran the tape slowly. Fourteen minutes later, at 4:23:14, the car came back into view, driving out the same way it had come in. Coyle reversed to replay the tape several times. The angle of the streetlamp made it impossible to see the license plate. But on the trunk he could see a three-pointed star emblem distinctive of a Mercedes, and the round taillights of an older model. Late fifties, he guessed. He printed an image of the departing car.

The hooded figure reappeared, replaced the chain and lock, and walked out of sight. It was 4:29:27.

(ii)

Thackrey stood on the open balcony, looking over the waist-high glass wall. Thirty-seven stories off the ground, the air was cold and blew open his shirt until it flapped like a sail. To the north, he saw San Francisco's Financial District, Chinatown, and the Transamerica Pyramid. To the east, the two spans of the Oakland Bay Bridge appeared out of the fog. The view straight down was the Embarcadero waterfront, with toy cars weaving in and out of traffic on Beale and Fremont.

The view filled him with a sense of mastery. It was his city—his streets, restaurants, clubs. He had made his fortune here, succeeded beyond the dreams of the creatures scrabbling on the ground below.

"What's the name of this place?" he called inside.

Victor sat on a leather sofa. "Empyrean Towers. All the units sold out before the building was even finished."

"And they let two gay wogs move in?"

"They welcomed us." Russell opened a bottle of wine at the kitchen counter. "In the new millennium, the Chinese are on top."

"And without my Indian brothers, you'd still be using eight-bit microprocessors," Victor said. "You're the face of the past, white boy."

"How much you pay?" Thackrey joined the others inside.

"One point seven." Russell handed Thackrey a glass of zinfandel.

"Lot of money."

Russell used his fingers to count off. "Two bedrooms,

twenty-four hundred square feet, Viking appliances, Poggenpohl cabinets."

Thackrey tasted the wine. "You sound like a drag-queen real estate agent."

"And now we lose it because of you," Victor said.

Thackrey watched Victor across the room on the sofa. He wondered if Victor would turn out to be a problem. "Don't get bitchy. You only ever had it because of me, because I let you buy shares of BluFish."

"We're leaving, Ben. Flying out of the country, right after we do this thing for you."

"Where to?"

"None of your business."

Thackrey walked slowly around the living room. "This where you practice your martial arts, Vic-tor?"

"It's Muay Thai," Victor said. "Thai boxing. Useful for breaking bones. Want me to show you?"

"Another time." Thackrey slipped off his shoes and flexed his toes into the thick carpet pile. "The apartment came like this?"

Russell picked up his phone and tapped an icon. "We made a few upgrades." Across the room, a sixty-inch TV came on, with nine separate windows. "For security, we put a webcam in each room. We can monitor what's going on throughout the apartment from our phones. Even if we're downtown on Market Street or up at your place in Sonoma County." He waved at himself in the middle window of the bottom row.

"I don't know whether to be impressed at your technical skills or just creeped out." Thackrey sat beside Victor on the sofa and smiled genially at him. From a pill bottle, he poured different colored tablets on the coffee table and picked out half a dozen oblong pink pills. Raising his glass, he swallowed the pills with a mouthful of wine.

Victor leaned close to the table and studied the pills. "Provigil?"

"Yeah, mostly."

"Was that two thousand milligrams? Isn't that, like, ten times recommended? You have anything else in your stack to slow it down?"

Thackrey drank the last of the wine. "Ever hear of the white-crowned sparrow? Tiny bird. White band on the top of its head. Each fall it flies from its home in Alaska to Southern California—twenty-seven hundred miles. Flies at night. Three hundred miles at a clip. Goes from sleeping nine hours a day in its habitat to an hour and a half in migration. The rest of the time it's awake, its little beady eyes open. No one knows how it does it. Awake for ten days."

"When's the last time you slept, Ben?" Russell asked. "The stimulants in those things can build up."

Thackrey smiled. "Bleaching your hair again, Russ? It looks even lighter than yesterday. What's your thing now? The only blond Asian?"

"You used to be a good guy." Russell looked at Thackrey. "What happened to you?"

"I got rich. I don't need to be good."

"You helped me." Russell stood his ground. "You remember that?"

"I kept you from shooting yourself, you drama queen."

"You stayed with me for three months. No one else would. What happened to that guy?"

"Let's not get off subject here." Victor spoke evenly. "We're concerned about the pills, Ben, because you and your late friend got us into this situation. It would be nice if you weren't lost in space for the next few days."

"If you'll recall, I'm not the one who caused it. Ask your buddy Russell."

"Really? That's how you're going to play this?"

Thackrey faced Victor. "How about you just tell me why you brought me here?"

Russell stood in front of a laptop on the kitchen counter. "An investigation's under way by part of the Santa Rosa Police Department called Violent Crime Investigations. VCI."

"What do we know about them?"

"Website says they investigate seventy-five cases a year: homicides, violent assaults, robberies."

"So who are they?"

"Not much about them on the public page," Russell said. "So we hacked through their crappy, government-issued firewall and got into the personnel files. The team is a lead investigator and four detectives."

Russell scrolled down the screen. "Lead guy is Lieutenant Edward Mahler. Been with the department eighteen years. Head of VCI the past twelve. Graduated from Princeton. Go Tigers. Served in the Army Rangers. Hobbies, reading and travel. Likes classical music."

"Let me see." Thackrey walked across the room and peered at the laptop photo of Mahler. "Guy's wound tighter than shit. Do we know anything about their success rate with homicide investigations?"

"Website doesn't have any data on clearance rates." Russell worked the keyboard. "But they average about five homicides a year. Mostly gangs or domestic violence. Pretty straightforward stuff. In-house forensic techs and a county coroner. Basically, they clear most of what shows up. Except for the occasional anomaly."

"Anomaly?" Thackrey walked back across the room and sat next to Victor again.

"A couple years ago, two girls were found strangled in the

same park where we left your friend. An arrest was made, but no charges filed. The cases are still open. And here's the thing. According to the online press reports, this VCI team is trying to figure out if our little business is related to the earlier cases."

"How confusing for them." Thackrey winked at Victor. Provoking him was always good sport.

Victor kicked the coffee table. "Christ, I hate it when you do that, Ben."

"Do what, Vic-tor?"

"Assume everyone else is an idiot. And stop saying my name like that."

Thackrey sighed. "Russ tells me you're named after a famous Indian actor—Victor Banerjee. How did I not know this until now? Would I have seen him in anything?"

"*A Passage to India*. 1984. Directed by David Lean."

"Oh, I saw that one. So did he play Dr. Aziz or Mrs. Moore?"

Victor shook his head. "For chrissakes, you're like a child. You could have left her. You could have left both of them, like a normal person. You didn't have to kill them."

Thackrey watched Victor's eyes while he spoke. At some point he was going to have to shoot Victor. He turned to Russell. "What do we think the cops are working on?"

"The blanket. It may have something they can trace."

"Fucking dog hair," Victor said.

Thackrey shrugged. "We'll deal with it."

"Blood in your living room."

"At this point I don't see the cops making it to my living room. But we can take care of the blood, too."

"The KelTec."

"My gun?" Thackrey feigned surprise. "What about it?"

"You might not want to have it with you if they arrest you."

"You have yours?"

"Yeah, but mine hasn't been used."

Thackrey looked at Victor and wondered if his earlier thought about shooting him had somehow been telegraphed to the other man. "I think it's best to keep the gun. Discourages the riffraff."

"Couple hours ago," Russell said, "I figured out my scarf must have fallen off in the park when we were carrying the body. But I doubt it can be traced back to me."

Thackrey smirked. "Can't be too many other men with your taste in Northern California."

"We've got Elise's cell," Victor said. "But we have to assume they'll find her laptop and her office computer, maybe a tablet."

"Which tell them what?" Thackrey asked.

"That's just it. We don't know."

Thackrey poured another glass of zinfandel. Holding the glass to the light, he slowly swirled the wine. "I think it's time we invoke the spirit of the late Dr. Wheeler. Remember the computer science history I taught you boys?"

"Wheeler?" Victor sat up. "The Princeton physicist? John Archibald Wheeler?"

"You two were always such good pupils. Wheeler was the guy who talked about how all matter is based on information. What was that famous thing he said?"

"It from bit."

"That's right! It from bit. Give that boy highest marks. The bit is the fundamental particle, the irreducible kernel. Every particle derives its meaning from bits, binary choices, the answers to yes-or-no questions. At the root of all things is a one or a zero. We just need to turn off the bits, change them from a yes to a no, from a one to a zero."

Thackrey went back to the kitchen countertop and turned the laptop toward him. He scrolled through the screen and silently read. After a few minutes, he pointed to the screen. "This guy here. Martin Coyle. Associate's degree in computer science. He'll be the information guy. Get into his database. Attach a keystroke logger. See what they know and where they're going."

"You really think we can erase evidence?" Russell asked.

"Not all, but enough. Elise was a very busy girl. In a day or two, these cops are going to have so much useless crap on their hands, they'll get tired."

"Tired?"

"Yeah, tired. But not us." Thackrey winked. "We'll be up here in Empyrean Towers. As wide awake as the white-crowned sparrow."

Chapter Six

(i)

Mahler turned to Eden in the corridor outside the interview room. "Look—his lawyer's Jordan Everest. He represented Partridge two years ago. Guy specializes in criminal defense and being an asshole. He's trying to make a name for himself, get noticed by a firm down in the city. Don't say anything you don't want on the news tonight."

He waited for a sign of agreement, but Eden pushed her glasses tight and watched him silently. He realized he couldn't read her. Did she not understand? Or was she so far ahead of him that she was waiting for something better?

"But what about Partridge?" she asked. "He's really the one, right? What do you want me to do? If you don't want me to say anything, I won't."

He resisted an impulse to sarcasm. "Yeah, Partridge's the one. What I want is for you to meet him. Sit across from him, watch him, smell him, whatever. If you're going to work this case, you need to know the guy. I don't care if you say anything or not."

As they walked in, Jordan Everest stood. He was a tall man, dressed in a dark suit, white shirt, and silk tie. His thick hair was combed straight back and looked wet, like he had just stepped out of a shower. He nodded at Mahler and reached his right hand toward Eden.

Eden hesitated and then shook his hand and introduced herself. She sat next to Mahler with a steno notepad in her lap.

Beside the lawyer, Partridge had not moved. He stared vacantly ahead without acknowledging the others. He had an unshaven face and deep-set eyes and wore a short-sleeved sports shirt open at the collar.

Mahler switched on the room's recorder. Out loud, he noted the date and time and identified those in the room. Mahler spoke Partridge's name last and glanced across the table at the man. He reminded Partridge of his voluntary presence in lieu of a reading of his Miranda rights. It was the first time in two years that the two men were in the same room. Seeing Partridge now, Mahler remembered the man's ordinariness and the way he smiled triumphantly when answering a question. Mahler picked up a pencil and rolled it in his fingers.

"At the outset, Detective," Everest said, "I'd like to make the point that we're here at your invitation and that my client is taking time off from his employment, at his own expense."

Ignoring the lawyer, Mahler addressed Partridge. "Where were you last night after 10:00 p.m.?"

Partridge turned to face Mahler. "I had a few drinks at the Tap Room and went home around eleven."

Partridge's mouth closed on the answer. It was a practiced reply, with just enough detail to be possible. Mahler had known other career criminals like Partridge who learned the art of interrogation. They fell into a groove of apparent cooperation. They learned to relinquish just enough information to force the questioner to verify meaningless facts. He wondered what Eden was making of Partridge.

"Can someone confirm that?"

"My girlfriend can tell you what time I got home. Name's Lorin Albright. Call her and ask her."

"Meet any women last night?"

"I just told you I have a girlfriend."

"Were you at Spring Lake Park?"

Everest rested a hand on Partridge's shoulder. "Don't answer that." He looked back and forth at Mahler and Eden. "I assume this interrogation has to do with the recent homicide? Is it your department's policy to question my client for every death in the park?"

Mahler kept his focus on Partridge. "Actually, we're going to question your client every time anyone is injured in any way in the park."

"I'm going to interpret that remark as sarcasm." Everest leaned forward. "Because, if any part of it were true, it would constitute harassment."

"This is like last time," Partridge said. "You guys are so fucking lost. You don't have a clue."

Mahler saw a smile form on Partridge's lips. He felt his fingers tighten around the pencil. He imagined reaching out and jamming the pencil into Partridge's forehead.

"Where's that old guy who questioned me?" Partridge's voice rose. "What was his name? Woodhouse? Man, you guys are embarrassing."

Mahler remembered the hours he and Tommy Woodhouse had spent across the table from Partridge, the self-satisfied smile never leaving his face.

"Irwin," Everest said, "we're here to answer their questions. It's not necessary to make any statement."

"Except, of course, you, darlin'," Partridge said to Eden. "You seem smarter than the others. And cute, too, in a steel-rod-up-your-ass kind of way."

Eden looked back at him.

"You're interested in this, aren't you? Did you study it in college? Want to write a paper about me?"

Eden's face flushed.

"Oh, my goodness. Did I hit a nerve? Yahoo! Something really did happen in college. Get too close to the fire?"

Mahler watched a sudden shift in Partridge. In his attempt to provoke Eden, Partridge lost his cool detachment. He hunched forward.

For the first time Eden spoke. "It's not relevant to your... situation."

"You sure?" Partridge asked. "Maybe you should get to know my situation. When it comes to men, I'd guess you're innocent."

Mahler heard the edge in the words. *What was going on?* It was as if Partridge was so intent on his prey, he'd forgotten where he was.

Eden straightened in her chair. "What you're doing is called misdirection. Because you're uncomfortable with these questions, you're trying to shift the conversation away from you to me. But your subconscious is unable to separate the content, so you ended up asserting my innocence, not your own."

Partridge smiled and sat back. "I was wrong about that steel rod. It must be titanium."

The moment was over, but it was enough. Mahler turned to Everest and smiled. "We're going to reopen the investigations into the Foss and Hart murders."

Mahler felt Eden looking at him but did not turn away from Everest.

The lawyer shook his head. "I assumed this latest murder would be a high priority for your squad. I wouldn't think you have time for two old cases."

"We have time to do whatever we want."

"Oh, good," Partridge said. "Is it going to be dumb-and-dumber again, or college girl?"

"Let's just be clear," Everest said. "Over the next few days, if you hinder my client in any way or violate his right to privacy, I'll file for sanctions against this department."

Mahler switched off the recorder as he stood up. "Counselor, your problem is you're playing too shallow. You're in on the ball. In a day or two, we're going to find evidence connecting your client to three murders, and then you'll want to be deep, or this thing right here is going over your head."

(ii)

(TUESDAY, 2:04 P.M.)

Two uniformed officers sat in the plastic molded chairs beside Frames's desk. They were large men, their duty belts jammed with the tools of their trade: handgun, spare magazines, OC, Taser, radio, handcuffs, and baton. The small chairs and limited space crowded the men. They sat uncomfortably, legs splayed, their feet shoved under the desk.

Pruitt, the one closest to Frames, looked around the room. "Not exactly the *CSI* set, is it?"

The other officer, Timsen, peered into his paper coffee cup and searched for a space on Frames's desk to discard it. "It's what we get for working in a time of tight money."

"A few more rounds of budget cuts, and they'll move our offices to an abandoned middle school."

"No. They'll put us in one of those empty big-box stores. Discounts on city services—that's us."

Frames tried to bring the meeting to order. "Can we talk about what you got from the canvass?"

The two officers seemed to notice Frames for the first time. "How'd you get in here anyway, Steve?" asked Pruitt. "You didn't exactly distinguish yourself in Field Training."

Before joining VCI, Frames had worked four years as a uniformed officer. He was comfortable knowing, as Pruitt pointed out, he was not the best young officer in Field. But he believed he had something in his favor. Because he was confident in his abilities, he never acted blindly to prove them to himself.

"Mahler as much of a hard-ass as everyone says?" Timsen asked.

"He is when guys like you jerk him around," Frames said.

"Then you can tell him we caught kids with weed in their tent," Pruitt said. "They'd just lit up a doobie when we showed. Scared the shit out of them. One started crying."

"We don't care about that now. What we need to know is, did anyone see or hear anything connected to the murder of the young woman at Violetti Gate."

"That's the trouble," Pruitt said. "You get up here, and you forget what real police work is."

Frames did remember. Once part of a task force on neighborhood break-ins, he had spent three days knocking on doors on Coffey Lane. House after house with no one home or frightened faces looking out at his uniform. Then a young Hispanic woman opened her door and told him about driving home from a late shift and seeing in her headlights the face of the suspect. "I can say in my report you fucked me around."

Timsen sighed and pulled a notepad from his shirt pocket. He paged through it. "A couple of the campers said a homeless guy was walking around early in the morning, saying stuff."

"What stuff?"

"I don't know," Pruitt said. "None of it made sense. But he said he saw a body."

"That's what he said? He saw a body?"

"Yeah." Timsen read from his pad. "Some old fart in an RV, Arnold Lester, was outside before dawn, screwing around with his gray-water valve or some shit, and this homeless guy comes through the campground, talking to himself."

"Who was he?"

"Probably a transient named Donald Lee. We found a supplemental report for someone fitting the description." Timsen returned to his pad. "Mr. Lester described him as having hair in dreads, wearing an overcoat, and carrying a trash bag filled with clothes."

"I'm sure he'll make an excellent witness," Pruitt said.

"Did anyone else see him?"

"Yeah. The kids with the weed said he stood next to their tent, but they couldn't hear what he was saying."

"The park guards had a Field Interview card for him on file," said Timsen. "Guy's a regular. No matter what they do, comes through three or four nights a week. He's harmless, so they leave him alone."

"What else?"

"We knocked on the doors of the houses across from the park gate on Violetti, Pepperwood, and Bader Roads," Timsen said.

"I think it's pronounced 'vee-o-letti,' not 'vi-o-letti,'" Pruitt said.

"Do you say 'vee-lence' or 'vi-lence'?" Timsen looked at Frames. "This is why I don't get invited to join VCI."

"Maybe it's because you pronounce it 'Vi-CI' instead of 'Vee-CI,'" Pruitt said.

Frames hated this kind of chatter. When he and Rivas talked, it was about important stuff, how the world worked. "Can you stop fucking around?"

Timsen read again from his notes. "The owner at 2905 Pepperwood, Mrs. Dennis, said she heard a woman scream at two a.m. But then she thought it was a raccoon. According to Mrs. Dennis, an adult raccoon and a human female scream at the same pitch. She learned that on the Nature Channel. Anyway, that's why she didn't call the police. And she said the last time she called us, all the responding officer did was grunt."

"Probably Paul Johnson," Pruitt said. "That guy grunts a lot."

"The resident at 3701 Bader said she heard a car door slam about five in the morning. I asked if there was anything else, and she said the door sounded like a large European car with darkened windows. I'll bet if I talked to her for a few more minutes, she'd have told me it sounded like a blue car. We also had three other houses mention the car door sound—at three thirty, four, and nine thirty. That last one was probably our car."

Frames pushed his chair back. Having the two officers so close made him feel claustrophobic. "Did you talk to the woman with the dogs who found the body?"

"That was a scene. Mrs. Edna Jarman at 3704 Bader. She's got six mutts, all Corgis, all named after Italian-American pop singers from the 1960s. Dean Martin, Frankie Avalon, Bobby Rydell, Dion DiMucci..."

"Strictly speaking, was Rydell Italian?" Pruitt asked.

"You're kidding me, right? The guy's hit was 'Volare.' That sound like a German song to you?"

Frames held up his hands. "Just tell me what this dog lady told you."

"She said she entered the park at about six. Gave us a whole song-and-dance about how she should be allowed to go in before the gates open, because she lives in the neighborhood and her late husband was a Pearl Harbor survivor, which apparently entitles her dogs to take a crap before everyone else. Anyway, one of the dogs, Frankie Valli, I think, led her to the bench. At first, she thought the victim was sleeping, which disgusted her and dishonored the family who donated the bench. But then she realized the woman was dead, which, in Mrs. Jarman's eyes, was a legitimate use of it."

"So all she did was tell you the same thing she already told Officer Hadley?"

"Basically, but there was one other thing. When they were leaving the bench, the oldest dog, Paul Anka, pulled her toward that group of oaks next to the parking lot. After seeing the dead woman, Mrs. Jarman was afraid to go over there. Anyway, you guys might have one of the police dogs check it out."

"Probably a used condom," Pruitt said. "Every time I've been out with those dogs, it's the first thing they find. I'll bet you twenty bucks."

"That's it?"

"We pulled up security camera footage from two residences. Nothing on them so far, but we're still looking."

"Anything else?"

The two men shook their heads, and Timsen stuffed his notebook back in his shirt pocket.

Frames stood up behind his desk, encouraging the officers to leave. For a few seconds, they sat still, looking at him.

"We get some kind of lunch voucher?" asked Timsen.

"Are we on for that condom bet?" Pruitt asked.

Chapter Seven

(i)

Mahler stood beside Rivas and Eden in the conference room. On the table in front of them lay a pile of homicide binders, the top one open to a close-up of a young woman's face. Her eyes and lips were closed. A pool of white light, meant to locate bruises or marks, burned out the woman's features. An irony of a homicide investigation, Mahler thought, is that it unmasks the victims, already exposed by murder, and lays them bare to strangers without the mercy of shadows.

"She looks young." Eden broke the silence.

Mahler nodded. "She *was* young. Twenty-one. The other girl, Susan Hart, was twenty." He waved at the binders. "Two years ago, Daniel and I worked these with a senior investigator, Tom Woodhouse. I'm hoping you'll see something we didn't."

Mahler replayed the words. Had it really been two years?

He saw the victim's face, eyes closed, lying still as the minutes ticked past.

"What happened to Woodhouse?" Eden asked.

"Got old. Retired."

Rivas picked up the top binder and held it toward Eden. "Michelle Foss. First one killed in the park. Riding her bike on the trail near the water tanks. We believe she reached the steepest part of the trail and stopped to catch her breath. The killer came from behind, pulled her into the brush, and strangled her. She took the same trail three times a week and rested at the same place. Our theory is the killer saw her and noticed the pattern."

"How was she killed?" Eden wrote notes in a steno pad. "Was there a weapon?"

"None was ever found. ME thought it was a thick, smooth cord. No fibers or cuts."

"And you never got anything when you looked at Partridge?"

"No marks on his hands. He might have worn gloves."

Mahler only half-listened to the other two. Rivas's voice ran in slow motion, as if his well-known memory of local homicides was filled to capacity, burdening his speech under the weight of too much history. Mahler remembered he had meant to talk to Rivas about Peña's pulling a gun. *Had something spooked the man?*

Rivas pointed to the next binder. The woman in this photo had a thin face and long, brown hair pulled into a ponytail. "Susan Hart. She was a runner. Set some county records in the high school quarter-mile. Had just joined the junior college team. She was running on Fisherman's Trail on the west side of the lake. Same method of strangulation. Body found in a heavily wooded section of the trail over by the boat launch."

Eden wrote in her notebook. "You think she stopped like the first victim, and the killer was watching her, too?"

"Could be. Or maybe he just got lucky. That trail isn't used much."

Mahler grew impatient with these questions. *Would they identify a killer?* What he needed were new questions.

Eden turned a page of the file. "Who made these notes in the margin?"

Rivas smiled. "Tom. He was old-school. Never stopped asking questions."

Mahler watched as Rivas put the Hart binder aside. Since her murder, the dead girl had visited Mahler once a week, telling him stories of middle-distance running in the bubbly, fresh voice of a twenty-year-old still new to her death. He saw her now jogging on Fisherman's Trail, through the winter-bare trees, back toward the boat launch, on the stretch of muddy trail she never reached. With each stride, her ponytail bounced back and forth. The way her hair moved was not in the file. For a moment, he thought of telling Eden about it.

Rivas picked up the next binder. "Irwin Carlton Partridge. Thirty-seven at the time of the last killings, forty now. In and out of the system since he was a teenager. Started out with theft, vandalism. Arrested for assault in his twenties and put on probation. Then attempted rape. Another attempted rape. No charges filed. Finally did eighteen months in Mule Creek for assault. Beat up his girlfriend, broke her eye socket."

"What was the weapon?" Eden asked, writing.

Rivas frowned. "A bottle."

Mahler felt himself suffocating. At this rate, it would take them hours to finish talking. None of this accumulation of detail would work. He and Woodhouse had gone over the same ground a thousand times, each new scrap holding promise until it didn't. Had he really expected this untainted young woman to bring new magic to the case, to reach into the old file and discover the error, the slipup the killer had left behind two years earlier? The migraine, which lay momentarily quelled in the back of his head like a waiting wild beast, left him feeling for its onset, sensitive to every sound. Beside him, Eden's pen slowly scratched across the page.

"The assault on the girlfriend—the broken eye socket—was that local?" Eden asked.

Mahler's hands squeezed into fists.

"No," Rivas said. "Vallejo, where he grew up. He moved here in—"

"STOP WRITING," Mahler shouted.

Eden jumped and dropped her pen.

Mahler faced her, his voice still loud. "You don't need to take notes. This isn't a class."

"Yes, sir. I didn't know the...practice." Eden's face flushed. She looked down at the table.

"I'm sorry I raised my voice." Mahler spoke quietly. "But your job here is to listen. You shouldn't have any trouble remembering this."

"Yes, sir," Eden whispered. She fumbled with the steno pad, her hands shaking.

At Mahler's outburst, Rivas had backed away. "Eddie, can we at least talk about whether we should go back to these cases right now?"

"You want to talk?"

Rivas took a deep breath. "I just want to be sure this is the right thing. We didn't discuss it in the briefing with Martin and the others."

"You want to take a vote?" Mahler watched the detective shift back and forth. Rivas was a follower, unused to speaking up. Maybe the encounter with Peña had shaken something loose.

"No, Eddie. Listen, we've got some good stuff on this latest victim. The car and the guy on the surveillance camera. The things from the canvass. We've got a shot—it's different from the last time. But we all have to work it. There's not time for these other cases."

"So you know the latest one wasn't Partridge? You decided that?"

"No, of course not. But shouldn't we wait for the evidence to take us to Partridge and then come back to these cases?"

"I'm not waiting for anything. I'm going after the son of a bitch."

"That's just it. It's not you. It's us, the whole team." Rivas weighed his words. "Does the chief know we're doing this?"

Mahler smiled. "Is that what this is about? I guess you've got a choice, Daniel. You can do what I tell you, or you can talk to Truro. Go ahead. Talk to Truro. Tell him you think I'm screwing this up. Maybe he'll offer you my job."

"Eddie—"

His anger spilling out, Mahler felt the words racing ahead. "He likes you, thinks you're the salt of the earth. You be the lead investigator. Bump in salary, another week's vacation. I'll retire and go home and read that shelf of books I've been staring at for twenty years."

"Eddie, for God's sake—I just wanted to talk about this."

"Does it sound like I want to talk?" Mahler bit off the words.

Rivas glanced at Eden. "All right, Eddie, you want to do this? Okay, then tell me. When did you really decide to work these old cases? You hired Detective Somers two weeks ago. She's a specialist in serial killings. You knew before this latest homicide you were going to go back to these old cases, didn't you? That's why she's here. Isn't it?"

Mahler studied Rivas. "You want to make decisions for this team, apply for the job. But if you want to work for me, do what I tell you or get the fuck out."

The men faced each other. Mahler stood still until Rivas slowly turned away and went back to the table of binders. Mahler felt the silence in the room. In seven years of working together, he had never spoken to Rivas that way. Something new had happened, something that had overtaken Mahler before he could stop it.

At the table, Rivas looked at the binders without speaking. Then he addressed Eden in a quiet voice. "Partridge didn't move to Santa Rosa until 2006. Lived with his stepmother for a while and then got his own place. He came to the department's attention once. A domestic dispute with his latest girlfriend. She declined to testify."

Eden instinctively looked at her notepad and remembered her pen was somewhere on the floor. "Martin said you had evidence connecting Partridge to the Foss and Hart cases?" Her voice was hesitant. Behind her, she was aware of Mahler moving away from them and standing by the door.

"Yeah. A female cyclist saw a man matching Partridge's description on the trail to the water tanks thirty minutes before Foss was strangled. In the Hart case, we had two things. A dark Nissan like Partridge's was seen parked on Newanga Avenue at the time of the murder. And we had a muddy shoe print, matching his shoes, on the back calf of the victim."

"Any evidence of him coming into or leaving the park on the days of the murders?"

Rivas shook his head. "No. We looked at that. The gate guards didn't remember him, and the surveillance camera had nothing. But the park borders are fairly porous."

"And you questioned him?"

"Yeah. Eddie and Tom mostly. Tom's one of the best interrogators I've ever known. Went at him for two days."

"So in the end he was never charged? The shoe print wasn't enough?"

Rivas looked behind him at Mahler until their eyes met. "No."

"And after that, no more killings happened?"

"No. We worked both cases as long as we could. Tom especially. DA encouraged us to look beyond Partridge—to boyfriends of the two girls, family members, park regulars, locals with previous assault records. In the end we looked at two guys in particular. Both had priors and lived in town. One looked promising, and then he didn't. Tom spent months on them. I think it's what burned him out in the end."

"So what now?"

Across the room, Mahler felt his breath return and gritted his teeth against the headache. He walked slowly back to the table. "One idea is, the guy had some experience before this. The killings were quick and neat. In daylight. No witnesses. No evidence left behind."

"Which brings us to these three victims." Rivas picked up the last binders. "The first one is a local case. MaryEllen Reese, killed a year before the park killings. Her body was found along Santa Rosa Creek near Highway 12. The other two are similar unsolved cases from Vallejo, during the time Partridge lived there: Beth Hunter and Amanda Smith. I just pulled them off ViCAP. As far as I know, Tom didn't look at these."

"But why'd Partridge stop after two? Studies show a serial killer doesn't stop until he's caught."

Mahler lifted the stack of binders and laid them in Eden's arms. "It's not always like the research. We don't know why our killer did anything. Your job is to find evidence that tells us who killed these young women." He turned to walk out the door.

Eden struggled to balance the binders. "I guess I don't know what I'm looking for."

Mahler paused in the doorway. "Look at the quality of light."

(ii)

The city council amphitheater consisted of rows of steep, stadium-style seating looking down at a stage with speakers' table and microphones. Mahler sat at the table with Mayor Ransom and Chief Truro. A dozen reporters faced them in the stadium seats. The mayor suggested they wait a few minutes, to see if any more members of the media would arrive.

The dulled migraine lingered behind Mahler's eyes. His nerves were still frayed from shouting at Eden and the run-in with Rivas. But impatient as he was with the pace of the two murder investigations—the latest Jane Doe and the earlier park victims—for the first time in his career, he could not see the path forward.

He looked out on the reporters—fewer and less professional than in years past. He recognized only three of them. Still, they made Mahler wary. Following the Hart murder, several news organizations had reported innuendos about his own culpability. Also, he had little to allay public fears, and the less the press and the public knew about his investigation, the better.

Mayor Ransom finally stood. She was a tall woman, with old-fashioned big hair and a speaking style that put special emphasis on the obvious. She started by saying that the press conference's purpose was to keep the public informed of the police investigation. The city and police department were committed to making themselves available to the press in the coming days. Mahler watched a reporter in the front row drawing what looked like large loops on his pad.

Truro went next. In his Class A dress uniform, the chief spoke with a stiff military bearing. He gave an outline of the investigation, several times glancing at Mahler for confirmation. He noted the steps taken to ensure the public's safety: coordination with the county for increased park patrols, enforcement of the park admission hours, and temporary suspension of overnight camping. At the end, he introduced Mahler and handed him the microphone.

Mahler ignored the microphone. "I don't have a statement. If you have questions, I'll try to answer them."

A reporter at one of the alternative weeklies spoke up. "When do you expect to identify the victim?"

"We've received dozens of leads, and we're hoping one will result in identification in the next few days."

A tall man on the aisle who Mahler recognized as a San Francisco TV reporter raised his hand. "Do you know how the victim died?"

"We haven't established cause of death yet."

"Can you say *if* she was murdered?"

"The medical examination is not complete."

"Was she killed in the park?" someone shouted.

"We don't know that."

For a few minutes, questions were called out so quickly from around the room that Mahler lost track of the questioners.

"Is it possible this was a suicide?"

"That hasn't been ruled out."

"Was any evidence recovered at the crime scene?"

"I can't comment."

"Some of the weblog photos show the victim was wrapped in a blanket. Do you know why?"

"No comment."

"Is there any connection to the family who donated the bench?"

"Probably not, but it's part of our investigation."

"Is there any significance in the location of the body?"

"We don't know."

"When was the body discovered?"

"About six this morning."

"Who discovered it?"

"A member of the public who entered the park and contacted the police."

"How did the body get there if the park is closed after dark?"

"The exact method is unknown, but it's possible to enter the park even when the gates are closed."

"Was more than one person involved?"

"That's under investigation."

"Do the circumstances match any other cases?"

"Obviously we're looking at that."

"Eddie," a voice called out, "are there similarities with the killings two years ago?" Mahler recognized Rob Christie, a veteran local crime reporter.

"It's too early for us to say, Rob. We're still collecting evidence."

"Is the same individual you questioned two years ago a suspect this time?"

"We cannot release any information about a suspect at this time."

"Has anyone been questioned in connection with the case?"

"No comment."

"Chief Truro, is it safe to use the park?" a woman in the back asked.

"Yes," the chief said. "With the measures we've initiated, we believe the park is safe."

"What's your position on the Violence Against Women protest set for tomorrow night in Courthouse Square?" the same woman asked.

"We support the public's right to freedom of speech."

"Lieutenant Mahler, do you feel a special urgency to find the suspect this time?" asked a reporter on the far aisle. The voice was new, and Mahler took a moment to locate the questioner. Dressed in a dark suit with an open-collar shirt, the reporter slumped in his seat, his long legs draped over the seat in front of him.

"My team and I feel the same urgency to identify the suspect in every case."

"Can you assure the public you won't make the same mistakes as two years ago?"

A sudden silence fell over the chamber. Mahler saw every audience member look up. He faced the reporter. "I'm not aware of any mistakes made two years ago by my team or the department."

"Really? So the second homicide wasn't caused by delays in your investigation?"

Mahler waited a beat. "I think we're done." He pushed back his chair and stood.

Chief Truro whispered, "Where're you going?"

Mahler walked around the council table and up the steep stairs at the edge of the amphitheater. Passing the reporter who asked the last question, Mahler slowed to meet his eyes before continuing up the stairs.

The room was quiet. Mahler felt the reporters watching his back. As he reached the top of the council chambers, the theater erupted, and three or four reporters called out questions at once. Mahler turned to look down at Truro, standing with his arms above his head, as the noise flooded toward him.

Chapter Eight

(i)

"We started without you," the female officer announced as Eden walked into the conference room on the second floor of police headquarters. The woman, who introduced herself as Gina Cipriani, was broad-shouldered and had the erect bearing of many of the uniformed employees Eden had met.

Across the table, a large man with a smoothly shaven head sat peering into a laptop screen. "That imposing figure over there," Cipriani said, "is future Officer-of-the-Year Bob Pace. He's my partner, in the professional sense only, thank God."

Pace waved at Eden without looking away from his screen.

Joining them, Eden felt small and underdressed. She wondered how much the uniformed officers knew about her. Did they know she was from the FBI? Would they care she was assigned to detectives from outside the department?

"You're VCI, right?" Cipriani asked. She smiled. "Just how new are you?"

"Two weeks."

"Well, welcome to the SRPD, Eden Somers. You're fortunate this afternoon to be working alongside two of this department's elite crime-stoppers." She gestured toward the telephone in the center of the table. "That's the public tip line for the homicide in the park. I'm transcribing the voicemails, and handsome Bob is hunting-and-pecking his way through the web replies. We're transferring the information to standardized forms and posting them to the department database."

Cipriani pushed a spare laptop across the table. "You may as well start reading what we've done so far and flag those we should follow up on."

Eden peered at the screen. "What're they like?"

"Mostly local. People think it's someone they know. A few sound worthwhile. But we're also getting the usual weird shit. Guy in LA thinks it's that actress from the soaps who went missing a year ago. A Seattle psychic told us to check for a rosette tattoo on the left shoulder."

Eden read the logs. Two callers knew someone with the same physical description. One caller said he'd seen a woman matching the victim's description in the park the day before. A website reply asked for a photo.

The tip line phone rang. Eden looked at the others.

Cipriani nodded toward the phone. "You want to take it?"

"How do I answer?"

"Just say Santa Rosa Police. Put it on speaker."

Eden clicked on a blank log form on her laptop and picked up the phone. Before she could speak, a woman's voice said, "Is this the call-in line for the girl in the park?"

"Yes, ma'am. This is the Santa Rosa Police Department. What information do you have?"

"Are you really with the police? You sound like a young girl."

Across the table Cipriani snorted.

"Yes, ma'am. I'm a police officer. What information do you have?"

"I live in the Redwood Apartments on the western edge of the park. The young woman who lives across my courtyard might be the dead girl. I haven't seen her since Monday."

"What's your name, ma'am?"

"Why do you need my name?"

"We're keeping a record of everyone who calls."

"You're not going to publish it or anything, are you?"

"No, ma'am."

"Could I be anonymous?"

"If you wish."

"Okay. Just put me down as anonymous."

Cipriani and Pace shared a look across the table.

"What's the young woman's name?"

"I don't know. I've never spoken to her."

Eden stared at the blank form on the laptop. Her mind raced. "Have you knocked on her door?"

"No, I wouldn't want to... Something funny might be going on inside there."

"Is her car still there?"

"How would I know which car is hers?"

"Is there an apartment manager we could call to get the name and number of the young woman?" At this, Cipriani flashed Eden a thumbs-up sign.

"You're not going to tell him I called, are you?"

"No, ma'am."

The caller gave Eden the manager's name and phone number.

"If this girl's the one in the park, is there a reward for my calling in?"

"No, ma'am."

"I guess, with all the budget cuts, everything's on the cheap now, isn't it?"

Before Eden could speak, the line went dead. She glanced across the table and met Cipriani's eyes.

"You get all kinds." Cipriani puffed out her cheeks and exhaled. "I took calls for a homicide tip line in Fresno before I came here."

As she typed in the log form, Eden wondered about the two officers at the table. She hadn't spent much time around street cops. Their size and posture were intimidating. But she was curious about something. "What was it like two years ago when the other girls were killed? Were either of you here?"

Cipriani shook her head. "Not me. Transferred in last year."

Pace looked at Eden without speaking.

"Bob has issues," Cipriani said.

Pace shrugged. "I don't want to say something that gets misinterpreted and ends up with my commanding officer."

"You, misinterpreted?" Cipriani made a face of mock surprise. "Future Officer-of-the-Year Bob Pace? How could that happen?"

"I won't repeat what you say," Eden said.

Pace sat silent for a moment. Then he said, "All right. It was fucked. No other word for it. Fucked and fucked. Two murders in daylight, and they can't get the guy. Really? What would you call it? It was fucked."

Cipriani leaned toward Eden. "I'm not sure you understood all that technical lingo, but if I understand Bob, I think what he's trying to say is that it was fucked."

Eden smiled and turned to Pace. "I was told the DA didn't believe he had sufficient evidence."

Pace shrugged. "What I heard...somebody screwed up. I don't know if it was you guys or somebody else."

"If Bob was involved, he'd have caught the guy." Cipriani raised a fist. "Nailed the bastard by his *cojones*. Wouldn't you, Bob?"

"I don't see how I could have done worse. I mean, no offense, but it's not like you Violent Crime guys—sorry, and gals—aren't paid enough. You're not on shifts. Your cars are paid for. You're not doing domestic calls on Saturday night, keeping the assholes from beating each other's brains out, drunks puking on your shoes."

"Not to mention the bad stuff," Cipriani said.

"And I'm not saying this myself. But I've heard other offices say your boss, Lieutenant Mahler, is a bit of a head case. Hasn't been right since the murders."

Cipriani's face reddened. "Gee, Bob. Why don't you tell us what you really think?"

"I just said that's not me. It's what I heard."

"A head case?" Eden asked. It was odd to hear what other officers thought of her boss.

Pace pulled his laptop back in front of him. "I've already said too much." Then he looked back at Eden. "You have kids? It's different if you have kids. A murder like this makes you worry about them. I have two girls, and believe me, you can't help thinking it could be them. Anyway, you asked me, I told you. I'm not the only one, either. Talk to other uniforms. They'll tell you. It was fucked."

Cipriani looked at Eden. "I wasn't here two years ago, so I can't speak to it. But this time, right now...you talk to people out there; they're scared. We better figure this out and find the guy before it happens again."

(ii)

(TUESDAY, 5:12 P.M.)

Mahler leaned his back against the wall of the VCI room. He had spent the past hour in his office replaying his answers at the press conference. Checking his phone, he saw that the website of the *Press Democrat*, the local paper, already had a story on his walking out. The investigation was barely under way, and in the absence of any news, he was again becoming the story. "Do we know who our Jane Doe is?" he asked.

"No," Eden said. "Forty-three calls and hits on the website so far. We logged them all and are doing callbacks or sending units out to a few of them. We can expect more calls when the description comes out in tomorrow's paper."

Mahler nodded. Homicide investigations without an initial victim identification were not uncommon. Bodies were discovered without wallets or purses. Their identity had to come from the world noticing the space they left behind—a family member not arriving home, an empty office chair. This, Mahler knew, took time—time they didn't have in this case. "I want her identity tomorrow morning. Get through all the callbacks tonight. If they sound promising, have them come in and look at photos."

He approached the detectives' desks. "What else do we know?"

Coyle scrolled through a document on his laptop "Trish sent over the initial report from the field techs. Looks like evidence of strangulation. Bruising on the neck."

"Was it a cord?" Rivas asked.

"No. Hands, probably, from the front. But Trish said she won't know for sure until after an autopsy."

"What about the head wound?" Rivas asked.

Coyle read on his screen. "Cut on the occipital artery on the left side of the skull. Five centimeters long. Trish thinks strangulation was the cause of death, but the cut was concurrent. But she's not willing to say definitively yet."

"So someone strangled and cut her at the same time? How's that happen?"

"Does anything make sense? By the way, Trish puts time of death at about eleven Monday night. Which means, if the car on the surveillance tape at four in the morning is connected to this, the killer had about five hours to get to the park."

"Which doesn't tell us much," Rivas said. "He might've spent five hours trying to decide what to do and ten minutes driving there."

Listening to this back-and-forth, Mahler thought of the elusiveness of usable information in a murder investigation.

Rivas handed a printout to Mahler. "MUPS, the Missing Persons Database, has fourteen females. None matches our victim's physical characteristics."

"How far'd you go?"

"North Bay. You want me to include San Francisco?"

"May as well, until we start getting something from the call-ins."

Coyle stepped up to the whiteboard, where he had taped the black-and-white printouts from the park's surveillance camera. One showed a man in a hooded jacket, the other a car's trunk and bumper. "This guy appeared at the Violetti Gate about four and removed the chain across the roadway. Which took some planning. We had our guys go back up there and go over the lock and chain. No prints, but there's evidence he was somehow able to dismantle the padlock."

"It's not Partridge," Rivas said. "He's taller."

"Can we estimate height and weight from the video?" Mahler asked.

"I'll try. It's not a great film."

Coyle pointed to the car photo. "Vintage Mercedes. Plate's not visible. I'm working on narrowing down the year, and then I'll try to match it with the California state DMV database."

"What kind of car does Partridge drive?" Frames asked.

Rivas shrugged. "Two years ago, a Nissan 240Z."

"We should look at his friends' cars," Coyle said.

"Does a guy like that have friends?" Frames asked.

"Martin, check names of associates in Partridge's file," Mahler said. "While you're at it, you might look at probation reports to the court for sentencing, and you can pull reports of stolen cars."

"The security camera footage from the two residences in the Violetti neighborhood was a bust," Frames said. He held up a plastic evidence bag. "Also, we sent a canine team back to the trees where the dog walker said she was pulled. They found this scarf. Obviously, we don't know if it belonged to the victim."

Eden took the plastic bag from Frames. "Color matches her outfit. And it's got a label we can check."

Rivas laid his hand on a pile of folders in front of him. "Eddie, I started pulling files, like you said, of guys we picked up the last couple years for physical assault. I've got six. You remember Robert Temple? He's out again."

Mahler took the folders. "Okay. I'll go through them." He stared at the photo of the victim on the whiteboard.

"By the way," Rivas said, "Peña's lawyer emailed me. Apparently Peña wants to see me. Tomorrow morning, first thing."

"Be careful with that. Let one of the ADAs know you're going."

Mahler took down the photo of the victim's body from the whiteboard. "There's something odd about this. This morning Daniel asked why she was left in the park. But it's more than that. She was killed somewhere else and left here. Normally, if you laid a body on a bench, you'd put it on its back, right? Or, maybe facedown."

Mahler held the photo toward the others. "Look at this. She's lying on her side."

Coyle shook his head. "What're you saying?"

"She was arranged," Eden said.

Mahler looked at her. "Yes. It was intentional."

"I don't get it," Frames said. "What's it accomplish?"

"I don't know. But someone wrapped her in a blanket and laid her on her side."

"It might have been done for her or for whoever found her," Eden said.

Frames snorted. "How's it help her? She was already dead."

"It's called 'undoing.' It's where a killer tries to psychologically undo a crime, to return the victim to a normal state."

Mahler retaped the photo to the whiteboard and stood for a minute staring at it. "Steve and Eden," he said without turning around, "go up to the park and see if you can talk to this homeless guy who says he saw a body."

"You mean like tonight?" Frames asked.

"Afraid of the dark, Stevie?" Coyle said.

"Hey, man, seven years ago I was taking point on night patrols in Diyala Province. What were you doing?"

Walking across the room, Mahler saw Truro in the doorway. The chief was back in his white shirt and Dockers. "We need to talk," Truro said.

Truro led Mahler a few feet down the corridor from the VCI room door and out of earshot of the others. "You know, after you walked out," Truro said, "one of the reporters asked if it was unusual for the chief investigating officer to leave in the middle of a press conference. She wanted to know if I thought you were having a nervous breakdown."

"The investigation's just getting under way," Mahler said evenly. "I think we covered everything."

"That's your answer? Really?"

"I don't want to waste my time when I don't have anything to say."

The two men faced each other.

"You have any idea what this town's going through?" Truro glared at Mahler. "Have you been out on the streets lately? Talked with anyone outside this office? They're waiting for the other shoe to drop. City Council wants me to put an armed patrol around Spring Lake. The newspaper asked me to comment on a story they're running about a barista wearing a Glock to work."

"We're working this thing as fast as we can."

"It's your job. For any other case, that might be okay. But this is a murdered girl at the lake, and another one may turn up in three days."

"My job is to find this guy. I can't change what the public thinks."

"We work for the public. It's all about them. So, okay, you don't want to talk to reporters. But you ever disrespect me again like you did this morning, and I won't hesitate to go after you. We clear on that?"

Mahler looked at Truro and, without answering, walked past him back to his office.

Chapter Nine

(i)

Dorothy Knolls had ruddy cheeks. Around her lips radiated the deep lines of an inveterate smoker. In her late forties, she was dressed in sweatshirt and jeans, her hair combed into a bun snatched together by a plastic claw.

She had called the incident tip line an hour earlier, saying she might know the victim's identity. She asked to see Mahler in person; she'd found his name in an online news article—one describing him walking out of the press conference.

Mahler met her in the lobby of police headquarters. He led her upstairs to the second-floor offices and through the card-key lock. The hallway was quiet and dark. From the open door of the VCI room came the sound of a quiet conversation.

In the interview room, Mahler seated Knolls across the table and pulled a notepad and pencil toward him.

"I saw you found a dead girl at the lake," Knolls said. "I want to make sure it's not my Chloe." The woman's voice had an edge, as if used to making complaints that were unaddressed. "She ran away eight days ago. We had an argument. It wasn't a physical thing. I didn't hit her or anything. You probably have a record of that other time. Anyway, she walked out, and we haven't heard from her."

Mahler's headache was back, a stabbing pain behind his right eye. He wished he was at home with an ice pack on his forehead.

Knolls opened her purse and pushed through the contents. "I don't think the dead one's my Chloe, but I couldn't be sure. Detective Somers said the body's taller than my daughter."

She found what she was looking for and slid a small color photo toward Mahler. In the picture, Knolls stood beside a younger, heavier version of herself. The younger woman looked reluctantly yanked into the frame, her eyes glaring back at the camera. Mahler wondered what moment of special unhappiness was captured in the picture.

"The victim's not your daughter." Mahler handed back the photo.

Knolls gave no indication she'd heard Mahler. "Your kids never think bad things can happen to them." She looked at her photo. "You can tell them, but they always know every goddamned thing."

"Pardon my language." She smiled crookedly, with what seemed to Mahler like artificial demureness. She put the photo away and sat with her hands resting across the top of her purse.

They were finished now, Mahler thought. He should stand and escort Knolls downstairs, but he knew she had more to say. Within his migraine, Mahler braced himself for the woman's abrupt, cracking voice.

"Two years ago, when those other girls were killed in the park, I remember thinking, why on earth were they out there alone? Why weren't they home?"

She seemed to consider these questions about the last mistakes of the dead. Then she said, "Chloe didn't use to go out alone. She was a smart girl, smarter than some."

As Mahler listened, tiny, brilliant flashes suddenly shimmered around the woman's head. He blinked his eyes, but the flickering lights floated in space, swarming together until they coalesced into an oval bubble in front of his eyes. Inside, it was an area of total blindness.

Somewhere behind the glaring object that obscured his vision, he heard Knolls still talking. "Then it was like Chloe outgrew us. Whatever we said or did, it wasn't enough."

Mahler understood the thing in his line of sight to be a hallucination brought on by his migraine, and he knew from experience that this thing, this scotoma, would last a minute or two. He could not see past the dancing aura to the woman's face, but he sensed Knolls watching him.

As he looked down, the aura tracked his field of vision. He reached with his right hand through the blind space for the pencil and picked it up, grateful for the reality of touch. He squeezed the pencil tight.

"We tried to talk to her, but all she wanted was to be with her friends, not us. Chloe had friends. It wasn't like that girl didn't have friends."

The aura faded. The dead space slowly filled with the woman's face, her eyes searching him. The tiny, sparkling stars flashed and disappeared.

"She started going out at night. Coming home at three and four in the morning. Wouldn't say where she'd been. She said it wasn't any of our business. Whose business was it? That's what I want to know."

Mahler's pain slowly subsided, and he watched his vision restore itself.

Knolls leaned forward. "Are you listening to me?"

"Yes, ma'am. I'm sorry your family is going through...this."

"Do you think another girl will be killed like last time?"

"We're doing everything we can to find whoever killed this young woman." Mahler could not tell whether Knolls heard him. She continued staring at him, as if she expected something more.

"You have children?" she asked.

"No...I don't."

"You've no right to judge me then, do you?" Her face reddened.

"Excuse me?"

"You heard me. I'll bet when a girl's killed like this, the first thing you think is, this wouldn't happen if it wasn't for the parents. You wouldn't have this terrible work if people weren't so careless and stupid. People like us get what we deserve, isn't that right?"

"Mrs. Knolls, please," Mahler said. "I'm sorry your daughter's missing. I'm afraid I can't do anything at this time."

"You can't do anything at this time? What is this, some kind of a joke?"

"There's a procedure—"

"I'll bet there is."

"Have you filed a Missing Person Report for your daughter?"

"Yeah, yeah. What difference does it make? You'll find her when she's dead."

Mahler took a business card from his shirt pocket and wrote on the back. Feeling the intensity of being so close to the woman's unguarded rage, he watched his hand make an unfamiliar scrawl. "This is the direct line for Dennis Beech. He's the officer in charge of missing person investigations. I'll call him right now and tell him to expect your call."

Knolls dropped the card in her purse without looking at it.

She pushed back her chair and stood. "You cops. You sit here and you don't say anything. And we're supposed to be grateful. But I've heard about the way you look at these girls' bodies when you find them. What you do is dirty and shameful." She swung her purse strap over her shoulder and walked out of the interview room without waiting for Mahler.

(ii)

(TUESDAY, 11:37 P.M.)

"We're being tested, you and me," Frames said. "Like right now. This is a test."

"What do you mean, tested?" Eden asked.

"We're the new kids. They rotate in new detectives every few years. Try them out. Some make it, some don't. And they give them tests. That's how law enforcement works. It's not what you know—it's about proving yourself, not fucking up."

They sat in the front seat of a Crown Victoria parked below the overnight campground in Spring Lake Park, hoping to find the homeless man who told the campers he had seen a body. The canopy of oaks made the world so dark they could see no more than twenty yards in any direction. For the past hour, they'd taken turns standing outside the car to listen for a man walking up through the trees. But now, for a few minutes, they'd agreed to sit inside to get warm. The only sound coming in the half-open windows was a deep chorus of frogs from the lake's marshy edge.

"I think we've just got different jobs to do." Eden poured herself a cup of chamomile tea from a thermos. There was something uncomfortably intimate about sitting next to Frames in the dark car—he in the driver's seat, she in the passenger's. In her two weeks on this job, they'd been alone together only once, in the break room, for a few awkward minutes. Maybe this was part of the test—being alone with another officer. "Lieutenant Mahler spreads the work around, tries to match the job with our talents."

"Talents? So you and I have what? A talent for sitting outside in the fucking cold?"

"Maybe not, but we're a team. We each do our part." She was surprised at the assuredness in her voice. She found herself talking just to fill the silence.

"Well, I'll bet two members of this team couldn't be more different than you and me. Where'd you go to college anyway? Harvard?"

"Mount Holyoke. An all-women's college in Massachusetts."

"All-women's, no kidding? Didn't know they still have those."

"I majored in clinical psychology. Sophomore year, I took a course in criminal psychology and kind of got hooked."

"Mind of the criminal, right? I got some of that in the courses I took."

"Senior year, we had to do a thesis on a real case. I wrote mine on the Highway 60 murders. The case is sort of famous. Serial killer on this highway that runs from Virginia to Arizona. Nine girls, all of them—" Eden looked out of the car. *Why was she talking so much? She hated talking about the case. It never came out right—like something anyone should be interested in.*

Frames waited to see if she would say anything else. "Rivvie says you were in the FBI?"

"Yeah. I did that special agent course at Quantico. Then I got hired as an analyst with this thing called the Behavioral Analysis Unit. We worked with local law enforcement to analyze evidence." *Did it sound like she was bragging? Would Frames think she was bragging?*

"Like profiling?"

"Sometimes. I worked on a bunch of things."

"And you left that to come here?"

"Yeah. It was—I don't know, I guess I wanted to try something else, in the field." Her voice dropped off. She wondered if Frames was buying this answer. "How about you?"

"Me? I'm a jarhead, Marine. But I always wanted to be a cop. When I got out of the service, I took my degree at the junior college. Did four years on patrol."

Frames would be better at this job than her. Better at sitting in this dark car, knowing what to say. He'd pass the test. "Did you like it?"

"It was okay. It's not what you think. Mostly you have to know how to talk to people, defuse a situation. I had the skill set. Work under command, familiar with firearms."

"That's what I mean." Eden tried to regain her voice. "Lieutenant Mahler put together the team, recognizing our different backgrounds."

Frames checked the time on his cell. He leaned back and yawned. "You think he's losing it? Mahler, I mean."

She wasn't sure what to say. Could she trust Frames? "Losing it?"

"Going after Partridge, instead of focusing on this latest murder?"

"I think he's trying to look at every possible thing to see if they might be related."

"What I heard is, the last time, two years ago, he choked. Waited on evidence, and it led to the second girl's death."

Eden found herself wanting to defend Mahler. "We don't know that. It's not really—"

Suddenly something crashed onto the Crown Victoria's hood with a force that rocked the car.

"Jesus fucking Christ!" Frames yelled.

Eden threw herself backward into the seat, dropping the cup of tea.

In front of them, a large dark thing raised itself like an animal and leaped at the windshield.

Frames braced himself on the steering wheel. "Fucking shit!"

The thing on the hood rose up. For a moment it stood over them. Then it dove off the car, vanishing into the darkness, toward the trees.

Frames pulled his gun from his holster and jerked open the car door. "Let's go," he whispered.

Eden had stopped breathing when the thing hit the hood. Now she gasped for breath, her lap burning from the hot tea. Holding a gun in one hand, she stepped outside. The oak grove was dense black.

Frames was gone. *How was she supposed to back him up? Was she too slow? Why didn't he wait?*

She listened for Frames. Once she heard someone running. Then it was quiet. Her heart pounded. She slowed her breathing and listened. Close by, small creatures moved in the dry leaves.

She walked around the car, keeping one hand in contact with its body. She thought of going back inside for a flashlight. She thought of calling for Frames. But she did neither. She pictured the dead woman on the bench across the lake. *Had her last minutes been like this?* She pushed the thought away. *They're being tested, Frames said. This is a test.*

As she stood beside the passenger door, facing the front of the car, she felt a change in the air behind her. It made no sound. She had a faint sense of a solid thing in the space at her back where, a moment before, the air had moved. She tried to breathe slowly and check her senses. She felt it, still there. She thought of the cord used to strangle the girls two years earlier, how it had come from behind before they knew it. *Where's Frames?*

She turned.

Beside the car's rear door stood a large black figure, a foot taller and looming over her. In the darkness, she could not see what it was, only the outline of something darker than the woods and sky. The shape looked like a man wrapped in rags, smelling of mold and rottenness. The figure had not moved since she faced it.

Eden stepped back a few feet and raised her gun. *Where's Frames?*

The instincts of her firearms training kicked in: keep your shooting finger off the trigger until you're ready to fire. Her hands shook too much to feel the guard. Pointing the wobbly gun toward the thing, she said, "Police officer." The words came out in a child's high, thin voice.

The black thing stood still and silent. Then, from the top of the rags came a deep, growling sound. It said, "Faideela."

Chapter Ten

(i)

Coyle sat upright in his chair and massaged his neck. He was alone in the dark Violent Crime room, the only light coming from the two laptop monitors in front of him. By now, he had been sitting in the same spot for twelve hours, with just a break at six for an Arby's melt. Tired as he was, he also felt inside a zone of concentration. For the past hour, his earbud had been playing a mix of Irish rock—Thin Lizzy and, after that, the Boomtown Rats—and he had been eating jalapeño-flavored trail mix that had orange-powdered his fingers and the keyboards.

He read the paragraph on the Mercedes website for the third time. It described how the so-called "Ponton" sedan, like the one in the Spring Lake Park surveillance film, had been manufactured from 1953 to 1962. Year to year, the main differences were in engine size, not body design.

Coyle had loaded a photo of the car from the surveillance

video on a second laptop, and now he panned slowly across the image. The trunk shape and taillights were clearly the Ponton style, but the car might be from any of nine years. The color could be dark blue, green, or even black.

He toggled from the Mercedes website to the Department of Motor Vehicles database. More than two hundred owners of Mercedes models dated 1953 to 1962 were registered in California.

Coyle stared at the spreadsheet. Who were these people, and why did they want these dumpy-looking cars? He clicked on 1959 at random and scanned down the alphabetical list of names: Marilyn Aldrich, Kenneth Ashby, Steve Baab. One of them, he thought, is the owner of the car that drove through the Violetti Gate and deposited the body of Jane Doe.

An alarm on the right-hand laptop suddenly beeped, and Coyle jumped at the sound. He had set the alarm to go off every thirty minutes to remind him of the time.

Coyle felt some satisfaction in his progress. A two-dimensional plot analysis of the hooded man in the video, using known heights of other objects in the surveillance film, indicated the man was about five feet, four inches. Based on the way the hooded figure disconnected the gate lock, the man also appeared to be left-handed.

The scarf that the search dog found in the park turned out not to be a woman's—surprising to Coyle—but a brand sold in the men's department of a chain store. The label indicated it was a Sheer Danger brand, with an Ardent Autumn design, and in stock in six Northern California outlets. Coyle had a note to check with Mahler to see if he wanted to pursue trying to get a court order to track barcode sales.

A new ME report indicated the bruising around the victim's head wound probably came from the base of the skull under the left ear contacting a sharp surface, not from use of a weapon. Checking the regional ViCAP database, Coyle found no similar causes of death in homicides in the past three years.

The database also showed no similarly "staged homicides," with a victim wrapped in a blanket, in seven western states for the past five years. Other staged homicides recorded in the data base included males in two separate cases arranged with folded hands, a female with photos, and a female with flowers.

Coyle closed the database and saw his reflection in the empty screen. *I'm a grind*, he thought. Who else would be alone in a room in the middle of the night, using five-year-old computers to search crap government databases? The point was, he was good at it—the best in the department, for what that was worth. Other cops knew his reputation. "You Coyle?" they'd say before they pulled out their phones to show him a data search. It wasn't just tech skills, it was doggedness. He always liked that word—blunt, unadorned. He remembered sitting on his bed as a child, day after day, with a Rubik's Cube. In his time in VCI, his work had led to arrests and convictions for assault and armed robbery, even if he was never in a car chase or fired his weapon. He had no reason to be jealous of Frames and Eden, or to wish for other assignments.

He clicked on his screen and found an online regional record of stolen cars. The listing showed no 1950s-era Mercedes in the past twelve months.

Still, the car in the video was the best single piece of evidence, and Coyle needed to see if it could tell him anything else. He went back to the Mercedes website. The trunk and tail-lights were unchanged over the production run, but what about the rear bumper? For twenty minutes, he looked at photos of Ponton bumpers. Then he found it. From 1958 to 1960, the rear bumper's vertical upright bars were positioned closer to the middle of the car.

Coyle switched his music to the Pixies' "Where Is My Mind" and used a finger to lick the salt out of the trail mix bag. He reopened the surveillance photos. The right side of the bumper in the photo was dented, and the left side had a parking sticker. But the bumper bars were clearly closer to the middle. He now knew the car to be a 1958, 1959, or 1960 Mercedes. Looking back at the state DMV database, he found fifty-four registered owners.

Coyle thought of narrowing the search to males. Could he assume the figure in the video was male? Or was someone with a height of five four more likely to be a female? Was it possible to imagine a woman involved in this kind of murder? Last year they had worked a case where a soft-spoken, thirty-two-year-old woman, dressed in a silk blouse, pleated skirt, and cardigan, walked into the police department lobby and confessed to beating her husband to death with a roofing hammer.

The alarm went off again.

Coyle looked at the two computer screens. A recent source of pride was his theory of programming signatures. In the past year he'd noticed his programming had its own style—a kind of signature—based on the software he used and the choices he made. He liked to think his signature was edgy. Only he had no one to tell. Adrienne said, "If it's all just coding, how can yours be different?"

With that thought, Coyle decided to do some coding. He'd promised Eddie he would create an open-case file to track progress. He reached for his phone and scrolled until he found the Kings of Leon. In a new file on the right-hand laptop, he typed in everything they knew so far about Jane Doe. He worked quickly, listing facts and probable future lines of inquiry. When he finished, he posted the file to an FTP site and programmed a firewall around it. He set up an IPtable for Linux systems, which restricted access to a single port and defined the type of traffic to accept. Then he established public and private encryption certificates. All he needed to do was to set the private key password. The Kings of Leon started on "Use Somebody." He thought of Adrienne. He set the password.

By the time Coyle finished, another thirty minutes had gone by. He stood up and walked out of the team room. The hallway was quiet. A light was on in Eddie's office, but no one was there. At the end of the hallway, Coyle turned into the common room, where the team members had storage lockers. He felt nauseated from the trail mix and lack of sleep. The first twenty-four hours of the investigation were nearly over, and Eddie would take it out on them if they didn't have something soon.

Coyle opened his locker. He smelled the sleeve of his shirt and was hit with an odor of something like sour milk. He hadn't changed since Sunday. He pulled off his shirt and threw it inside the locker. In the locker mirror, he turned his naked upper body in profile and saw his weak chest and thin arms. He flexed his right bicep, which made an almost imperceptible rise in the upper arm. He looked around the room to make sure no one had seen him. In the bottom of the locker, he found a fresh shirt like all his others—a severely wrinkled oxford with button-down collar. He put it on and, leaving it untucked, walked back to the dark team room.

At his desk, he stared again at the alphabetical list of names on the motor vehicles website. Something flashed across his memory. The parking sticker on the bumper. He looked again at the surveillance photo. The parking sticker read "San Francisco Residential Parking Permit." The motor vehicles database did not list addresses. Finding the San Francisco owners among the remaining fifty-four names would require fifty-four separate searches. He looked at the list again. The first owner was a male named Banerjee, Victor.

Coyle leaned back in his chair. *It's a start,* he thought.

(ii)

The furniture in the living room of the San Francisco condominium had been cleared to the walls. Victor and Russell bounced on the balls of their feet in front of each other. They both wore large boxing mitts. Victor shot his right leg high and kicked at Russell's head. Russell blocked the kick, swiveled round, and clipped Victor's neck with an elbow.

"Who's better at this…thing?" Thackrey sat at the kitchen counter with a highball glass of wine.

"Muay Thai," Russell said. "It's not about winning. It's about staying fit."

Russell hit Victor with two quick punches. Victor rotated his hip and used his left shin to kick Russell.

Thackrey winced. "Anything's legal?"

"The art of eight limbs." Victor bounced a few steps away from Russell. "Fists, elbows, knees, and feet. Most effective of the mixed martial arts." Victor jumped forward and kicked Russell with his right knee. Russell punched at Victor's head. They broke and backpedaled away from each other.

Russell danced toward Thackrey. "Your turn. We'll teach you."

Thackrey raised his hands. "No, thanks. I don't believe in violence."

Victor snorted. "Your ex-girlfriends would be surprised to hear that."

Thackrey glared at Victor. "Let's just get back to work."

Victor and Russell pulled off their mitts and shoved the sofa and chairs back into place.

Thackrey lay on the sofa, with the glass of wine resting on his chest. "The first time I met Elise, we hit it off."

"At a party, wasn't it?" Russell sat cross-legged on the floor with a notebook computer propped against his knees.

"No. Starbucks. She was painting a picture on an iPad."

"If you'd ordered a takeout, we wouldn't be here today." Victor stood at the kitchen counter, leaning into a laptop.

"A couple of tables were between us," Thackrey said. "I couldn't see much of her, just the tablet's screen. But even at a distance, it was amazing. She wasn't making the picture in a linear, additive way, with elements drawn one by one. The painting looked like it was exploding outward, with animals and faces and pennant-like things all tumbling on top of each other. It was like Chagall on steroids."

"Speaking of your girl…" Russell rapidly worked the keyboard. "I'm into her office computer. I found her work files and emails. You want me to erase it all?"

"No. Just delete the work she did for me. It'll be under a file with my name."

"And the emails?"

"Just mine."

"Consider it done," Russell said.

Thackrey sat up, leaning on an elbow, and drank some of the wine. "In one corner of the screen, a palette kind of thing held a wheel of colors and tints. She touched it with a finger and used her fingertip like a brush. And she worked at this twitchy, high speed, her finger zooming back and forth across the screen."

"You saw all this from a couple of tables away?" Victor asked. He had an earbud in one ear, with his phone dialed to the Velvet Underground and loud enough for the others to hear.

"Yeah. Couldn't take my eyes off her screen. I was staring. I think it made the people at the next table uncomfortable, because they left. After that, it was easier to see."

"If you're interested, I'm inside the Santa Rosa Police website," Victor said. "The city firewall was crap, but Violent Crime has its own firewall, and whoever made it has some intelligence."

"Her face, or at least as much as I could see, had this blank expression," Thackrey said. "It was as if she was just observing what was happening. Then she must've felt me watching, because she turned around. She looked for a second and went back to the tablet and worked on the images coming out of the screen. A minute later she looked back, and this time she smiled and shook her head, as if she knew I'd be staring at her."

Victor stopped typing. A new window opened on his screen. "Oh, come on, you little fuck," he said to the screen. "You're driving me crazy. Maybe we need to listen to some Clash." He tapped his phone.

"The thing is," Thackrey said, "in the beginning, I was staring at the picture, not her, but I ended up looking at her. When she caught me, I asked what she was going to call the picture, and she gave me this look. She said, 'What makes you think everything has a title?'"

"And that sort of crap was attractive to you?" Russell asked.

"For the first time that night, I saw the way her face changed. Ever notice how the same person can look different? With Elise, if you looked at her once, her face had that dumbbell prettiness, like a cheerleader at a big midwestern college on a Saturday afternoon, where you knew it was the best she would ever look. But if you looked again, her face had this other thing going on. Leaner, grown up, in a way you would never be smart enough to understand. Something French maybe. A little Jeanne Moreau. Isabelle Huppert."

"Exactly how many whites had you taken that night?" Russell asked.

"That's just it," Thackrey said. "I wasn't high."

Victor typed for a moment and watched the screen. "Password required," he said out loud.

"Why don't you try listening to your boy Coyle's music instead of your own?" Russell winked. "Go on Facebook. Get his tunes."

Victor stared at him. Opening Facebook, he found Coyle's page. "Top band is Kings of Leon."

"Try 'Taper Jean Girl,'" Russell said. "Maybe the password's there."

Victor typed a line on his keyboard. Then a second and a third. "Okay, genius, let's try 'Sex on Fire.'" He tapped his phone and typed again. He stared at the screen and waited.

"After she worked on the painting some more," Thackrey said, "she put down the tablet and looked at me. She said, 'You don't have to talk about the art, you know. It actually makes you seem ordinary.' She said I reminded her of her father, who she said was a poet. She asked if I had any Ecstasy or Oxy. I offered her a few base, but she said she wanted something that would cause more trouble. It was like whatever play I had wasn't enough. She didn't need me or anyone else."

"We're getting closer, you and I, aren't we?" Victor said to his screen.

Russell came to the kitchen counter and stood behind him. He picked up Victor's phone. "Here, try 'Use Somebody.'"

Victor listened to the music. He typed in a word. Then a second, a third, a fourth.

"It was all there the first time," Thackrey said. "Everything that was to come—the art spilling out of her like a lunatic savant, the daddy thing, the step ahead of me, the crazy risks, the part of her always wanting to leave. She said, 'You seem like someone who's used to getting his way. Why don't you tell me one thing a guy's never said to me before? I'll give you three chances.' Then she smiled, and right there, if I'd only seen it, was all the misery we were going to make for each other."

Suddenly Victor's screen changed. The lines of white type on a black screen gave way to a website. Across the top were the words "Violent Crime Investigations." Russell laughed. "I don't fucking believe it."

Victor read the screen for a moment. "Hey, Ben," he called across the room. "Good news—I hacked into the VCI website and I'm planting the keystroke logger. Bad news—they got a video of my car entering the park, and they're running a database search on it right now. Russ and I need to get on a plane this morning. Remember our agreement. We help you with this, and we leave."

Thackrey drank the rest of his wine and lay down on his back. "Calm down. One more thing to clean up first. Then you can leave."

Chapter Eleven

(i)

Mahler parked on the road's gravel shoulder. Above him lay the earthen dam that marked the northern perimeter of Spring Lake Park. The parking spot, in the shadows of an oak grove, would not be visible to Officer Hadley's patrol along the top of the dam. After chewing out the young guard a day earlier, Mahler didn't want to see the kid again.

Mahler lifted himself over a four-foot chain-link fence and climbed the steep hill to the rim of the dam. He stood for a moment on this high ground. Below him lay the valley and the lake, black and smooth in the new-moon darkness. Even without light, Mahler could see where he was headed, the footpath that descended into the trees.

He jogged down the paved trail. For the first hundred yards, he would be vulnerable to the park's patrol. But the sound of their truck could be heard across the valley, in enough time for him to duck into the brush.

Reaching a meadow, he found the route called Fisherman's Trail. It forked through the trees along the lake and led to the boat dock and the lower parking lot.

The path was muddy after several days of rain. Mahler walked slowly, picking through the mud and the dark, uneven surfaces. Several times he slipped but kept his balance. Suddenly, where the trail turned sharply, his left foot caught on something, and he fell forward into the darkness.

His arms, extended to break his fall, sank to the elbows in cold mud. He landed in a shallow, marshy edge of the lake. He pulled out one arm and tried to raise himself. But before he could stand, his feet slid out from under him again. This time his face went into the water and his mouth filled with foul, slimy muck. He spit it out and, bracing himself above the surface, pushed backward in a squat. His shoes, under water, found a solid base. Rising cautiously, he climbed back toward the trail. With the back of his hands, he wiped the mud from his face and walked along the footpath, shoes sloshing with every step.

He felt like an idiot. *Why did he keep returning?* If it was to punish himself, as the department therapist said, he'd certainly managed to do that tonight. But that explanation never felt true to Mahler—more like something the therapist formulated so she could close out their sessions. But he also couldn't kid himself that these journeys to the park were related to any ongoing homicide investigation. No clues awaited him here.

After a hundred yards, he found the place. The trail opened to a clearing, with a large, flat rock on one side. Two years ago, the second victim, Susan Hart, had been murdered here. The evidence indicated she stopped and, with music in her earbuds, had not heard the killer's approach.

Mahler eased onto the rock, stuffing his hands in his jeans pockets to ward off the cold. He visualized the victim's body, facedown, at the base of the rock. Susan Hart's right arm was stretched out, the left under her chest. The awkward, unprotected, face-forward landing of an unconscious person. Tank top, running shorts, sweatshirt, ankle socks, sneakers. A bruise on the left side of her face where it struck the ground. A small, tight pattern of loose soil and dry leaves made by the feet of the girl and her attacker in the last seconds of her life. One of the techs said it looked like a dancer's box-step diagram.

As Mahler pictured the victim, Susan Hart's now-familiar voice sounded in his ear. "Ever figure out what song I was listening to when I was killed?" the dead girl asked.

"No," Mahler said. "Your phone kept playing after you died. You had something like four hundred songs."

"What's your guess?"

"Kenny Loggins. 'Footloose.'"

She laughed. "Good song but old-school. No—Katy Perry. 'Waking Up in Vegas.' All-time favorite running song. Perfect for middle distance—sixteen hundred meters. You know I won leagues my senior year? At the junior college, I took four-tenths off my best time. You ever run, Eddie?"

"Little in high school. Cross-country."

"Figures. Cross-country runners are brooders. No time for brooding in the sixteen hundred. Three and a half times around the track. Basically a prolonged sprint. Difficult, mentally."

"I thought all races were mental."

"Each distance is a different thought process." Susan Hart's voice sounded mature. At twenty, she was the youngest of the park victims. But the voice in Mahler's ear was that of a mature woman. "In the sixteen hundred, most runners slow down at the first split. I did the opposite—went for the lead after the four hundred. My father said I was like a car with an extra gear for overdrive."

"Your coach said you had one of the strongest kicks he'd ever seen."

"It made me fast but also got me in trouble. After I won a few races, I stopped eating because I thought it would make me lighter. That's when I got anorexia."

"Yeah, I know. My sister was a runner and developed anorexia. She…died."

Susan Hart waited to see if Mahler would say more. Then she said, "A bunch of us girl runners have health issues. Lack of consecutive menstrual periods, for one. And there's a certain body type. Small breasts."

"I don't feel comfortable talking about this."

"Oh, come off it, Mister Detective. You saw my breasts. Anyway, I outgrew the issues. I'm healthy. Or, at least I was."

"Why're you telling me this?"

"You wanted to know who I am. I'm a runner. Running's all about breathing, Eddie. Knowing how to breathe. Coach taught me that. It'll be important in your new case, too—the girl you found across the lake."

"You mean that quote on her leg?"

"You'll figure it out."

"Will I? I don't see how. Nothing helps us. Look at your case. We've been over the evidence a hundred times."

"It's all there. Believe me, it's there."

"So what do I do?"

"Let me tell you a story." She spoke cheerfully, as if she was enjoying herself. "I once did a training run in the dark. Down in Santa Cruz. I was on a paved road at night. In the beginning, the moonlight was enough. But after a few minutes, the moon went behind the clouds. It was so dark I couldn't see my feet."

"What happened?"

"Best time ever."

"How's that help? Tell me what you want me to do," Mahler said. "What do you want?"

"What do you think the dead want, Eddie?"

"I don't know. I know what the chief wants, what your father wants. But what do you want?"

Mahler waited. An animal rustled in the trees. He shivered. She was gone.

As usual, he knew the wrong things. The forensics filled a thick binder, listing the articles of clothing Susan Hart wore the day she was killed and the names of the bushes and trees that watched her die. He remembered the color of the victim's bedroom walls, the nickname her mother had given her, and the salad that was her last meal.

And trapped in his memory were the concentrated details of the last minute of her life.

"It's impossible to determine how long she was conscious," the medical examiner, Trish Armstrong, had told him the day after the murder. "Besides, how could it possibly help your investigation?"

"Just tell me," Mahler had said.

They stood under the lab's bright fluorescent lights. Trish, who had just finished an examination for another case, was still in her scrubs.

"Jesus, Eddie, where's this coming from?"

"Just tell me."

"Look, I get it. The whole thing with this girl, it's awful. But we've been through a hundred of these things. It's our job."

"Tell me."

"Honestly, I don't know. And what difference does it make?"

"You don't know, or you won't tell me?"

"No one knows," Trish said quietly. She leaned against a stainless-steel table and looked at Mahler. Under her eyes were dark shadows. She took a deep breath. "It's just guessing. With ligature strangulation, you don't know if asphyxia was caused by compression of the larynx or if strangulation compressed the carotid arteries. You also don't know if the occlusion of the arteries was complete or incomplete. Which would affect the loss of blood flow. Which would determine time to unconsciousness. We'd have to make assumptions and—"

"Tell me."

"I can't."

"Tell me."

"Stop it, Eddie."

"Tell me."

"Is this about the case or you?"

"Tell me."

"Tell you what, exactly?" Her voice rose, her face up close to his. "Do you want to know this girl fought to get her fingers under the cord or whatever the fuck was around her neck? Do you want me to tell you the fingertips on both hands were cut, two nails broken off? Do you want me to tell you that hanks of her hair got caught in the cord and were torn out at the roots? That, at some point, the killer put something, probably his knee, in the small of her back to get more leverage? Do you want to know that? Do you want to know that once the doer got the cord tight, it probably compressed the carotid, not the larynx? So it cut off blood flow to the brain. Carotid compression causes unconsciousness in seven to fourteen seconds. But, in this case, the victim struggled, so it probably took longer. Does that help you in some way, Eddie? Come on, I want to hear you explain it to me."

Mahler wanted to explain it. He even had a thought of apologizing to Trish. He wanted to say he knew it was out of line for him to ask, that after fifteen years of working together, he understood the boundaries of what they did. The weight of a loss was for someone else to measure. But he also wanted to tell Trish about all the wrong things he knew, how none of them explained what happened to the girl. He didn't know why this victim was different from the dozens of other bodies that ended up in the ME's room, only that he needed to know one thing that wasn't in the files. The girl was a runner, so he thought the missing thing must be time, seconds. But he didn't explain himself, didn't apologize, because the words were trapped in his head, past his own understanding. Instead, he looked back mutely and waited.

"Twenty seconds," Trish said.

She started to walk away. Then she turned to face Mahler. "You know what, Eddie? Don't come back. I mean it. I don't want you in my lab anymore. You have any other questions, don't come in here. Send one of your team."

Then she said, "And one more thing, go fuck yourself."

Later that day, in his office, Mahler had pressed the stopwatch function on his phone and watched the numbers tick off twenty seconds. He forced himself to watch to the end.

He did it again and again. The numbers slowly climbing: 13, 14, 15—What did she think in twenty seconds? Enough time for: *Who's doing this thing? Why me? I'm just a girl! Please, please stop.* The seconds clicking on: 16, 17, 18—At the end: *I'm alone. I'm scared.*

Now, at the place on the trail where the murderer had left Susan Hart, Mahler was suddenly aware of the darkness around him. He looked at the starless sky and heard the quiet stillness of the night. The chill air blew through him. Then, as the space closed in, he thought of the answer to his own question—what the dead want, what this girl wants, is to breathe.

(ii)

"What was that word the homeless guy said?" Coyle was typing and looking at the screen of his laptop.

Eden looked at Frames. "It sounded like 'fi-dee-lay' or 'fi-dee-la.'"

Frames nodded. "He said it again in the car. I thought he was saying fiddle-de-dee or something. Guy's a nutcase."

"Do we know who he is?" Mahler's voice was louder than he intended.

The others had not heard him enter. They turned to him, and he felt them taking in his change of clothes.

"Donald Michael Lee, the man with three first names," Frames read from his laptop. "No fixed address—big surprise. Five arrests in the past six months: intoxicated in public, threatening behavior, intoxicated in public, intoxicated in public, and the ever-popular intoxicated in public. He's been on his own since 2007. Lives in the park. Has a tarp set up in the hills above the campground."

"Any weapons on him?"

"Not that I could tell. But he's wearing, like, twenty-seven sweaters and carrying a trash bag filled with all kinds of shit."

"What'd he say about the victim?"

Eden looked at her notebook. "He said, 'I saw the mummy lady.' He repeated it over and over."

"Did he see how she got there?" Mahler asked.

"He said he saw three men. They took the body out of a car trunk and carried it to the bench. He called them 'little men.'"

"Little men?"

"It sounded like that. It's not easy to understand what he says. He's missing a lot of teeth. We asked him to describe who he saw, and he just kept saying he saw the mummy lady and the little men."

"Where's he now?"

Frames rubbed his eyes and yawned. "Social Services. We drove him over this morning. You're going to have to hose out the back seat of that car or buy a new one. The guy smells like a barnyard."

"In Cantonese, the expression *fai-dee-la* means 'hurry up.'" Coyle read from his laptop.

"What the hell's Cantonese?" Frames asked.

"It's a Chinese dialect." Coyle looked up. "I watch Chinese movies sometimes, and I've heard the word 'la' before. It means hurry. I put *fai-dee-la* into an online translation site, and it says 'hurry up.'"

"So you think a homeless guy in Santa Rosa, California, happens to speak Chinese?"

"I don't know. We don't know much about the guy. But why's he say that one word?"

"Maybe it's what he heard," Eden said. "Maybe one of the men carrying the body said it. It would make sense, right? Whoever it was, they were in a hurry."

Frames snorted. "How many people speak Cantonese?"

Coyle looked on his screen again. "It's the official language of Hong Kong and Macau. Seventy million worldwide."

"Well, that narrows it down."

"I checked Partridge's statement." Rivas opened his notepad. "The bartender at the Tap Room said Partridge came in around nine thirty, stayed until ten forty-five. Came in alone, didn't talk to anyone. Left alone."

Frames pointed to the photo of the car on the whiteboard.

"But if he's inside that Mercedes at four a.m., that still gives him lots of time to meet up with the victim somewhere else and end up in the park with the hooded guy."

"There's no evidence in Partridge's file of his ever using an accomplice." Mahler shook his head. "We're just guessing." He turned to Rivas. "I read the files you gave me on local guys with similar assaults. None stood out, but let's keep them for when we know more."

"Autopsy results on Jane Doe." Coyle looked again at his screen. "Had a full meal before she died: lamb, maitake mushrooms, Yellow Finn potatoes, and green beans."

"What kind of food is that?" Frames looked over Coyle's shoulder at the screen.

"Expensive," Mahler said.

"She also had a fair amount of wine." Coyle continued reading. "Blood alcohol was point-o-eight. Traces of OxyContin in her respiratory tract, and she also tested for quetiapine, whatever that is."

"Treatment for bipolar." Everyone looked at Frames, and he shrugged. "I got a nephew on the stuff."

"Might explain the old cut marks," Eden said.

Mahler paced in front of the whiteboard. "Any evidence this was an overdose?"

"No, the level was consistent with a small dosage." Coyle bent close to his screen. "Trish says the wine on top of the quetiapine and Oxy wasn't a great idea, but it's not what killed her. Something else, too. She had soap on her face."

"She washed her face after dinner," Eden said.

"Trish said it looks like someone washed her face. The makeup was reapplied, but by someone who wasn't very good at it."

Frames grimaced. "Okay, that's just creepy."

"And just to make things more confusing…" Coyle paused for dramatic effect, "a gunshot residue test on the victim's right hand shows she fired a gun recently."

"Now you're just making things up," Frames said.

Coyle shook his head. "No, I'm serious. On the plus side, we know the Mercedes is from San Francisco. We're collecting information on each registered owner."

"Have the uniforms help you with that." Mahler turned to Eden. "Where are we on the identity of Jane Doe?"

"Cipriani and Pace did all the follow-up last night." Eden looked at her laptop. "Two callers came in and looked at a photo, but neither identified the victim. We got a guy coming in this morning. Craig Lerner. Runs a local ad agency called Lerner and Meier. He says the description sounds like his graphic artist. She didn't show up for work Tuesday. He's coming in at nine. Do you want me to talk to him?"

"Let Steve do it. Get going on the homicide case files Daniel gave you."

While the others worked at their desks, Mahler turned to the whiteboard. Someone had written across the top "72 Hours = Thursday 11 p.m. 43 Hours Before Next Victim." He looked at the photo of Jane Doe, her eyes closed, a perfect stillness in her face.

Chapter Twelve

Eden sat at her desk with Mahler's stack of homicide binders. An arm's length away on either side, Coyle worked on a laptop and Frames talked on his phone. Years of studying in dormitories had taught Eden to block out noise. She'd been awake more than twenty-four hours, and the experience of working around the clock reminded her of finals week at Mount Holyoke College, except in this case she had spent the night in a park and pointed a gun at a crazy homeless man.

The stack included seven cases: the chief suspect (Irwin Partridge), the latest Jane Doe victim, the two girls killed earlier in Santa Rosa's Spring Lake Park (Michelle Foss and Susan Hart), a victim killed in a different Santa Rosa location (MaryEllen Reese), and two victims killed in Vallejo during the time Partridge lived there (Beth Hunter and Amanda Smith).

Eden looked at the victim photos. In the back of her mind, she heard the voice of her thesis advisor, Professor Hiatt: *Never forget the victims were real people with families, favorite foods, career plans, boyfriends.* The remembered admonition brought back another memory—Hiatt's glare across the podium whenever she suspected her lecture hall audience of inattention, her old teacher's manner always a blend of the endearing and the threatening.

The victims were girls just a few years younger than Eden. They could have been her college friends. Beth Hunter had freckles like her first-year roommate, Chrissie. Amanda Smith wore glasses like her best friend, Marie. Eden imagined herself shopping with the girls. *Eden Somers and six homicide victims go to the mall.*

Eden took a deep breath. She decided to read the binders in order: crime-scene report, medical examiner's report, lead investigator's notes, and transcripts of interviews with relatives, friends, and "interested parties"—those who found the body or who provided the police with information.

The cases involved three different lead investigators and two medical examiners, so the write-ups varied in level of detail, organization, and style. The effort required to track parallel information was frustrating. It wasn't like a spreadsheet, which lined everything up and highlighted variables in red. This time, the voice playing in Eden's mind was that of her FBI supervisor, Aaron Kinsella: *Focus on the data patterns. Find the common thread.*

Eden opened a spreadsheet program on her laptop and listed the victims.

VICTIM   CITY   CRIME SCENE

Jane Doe	Santa Rosa	Spring Lake Park
Michelle Foss	Santa Rosa	Spring Lake Park
Susan Hart	Santa Rosa	Spring Lake Park
MaryEllen Reese	Santa Rosa	Santa Rosa Creek
Beth Hunter	Vallejo	Dan Foley Park
Amanda Smith	Vallejo	I-80 Rest Stop

In other columns, she listed age, height, weight, location of body, posture of body, items found at crime scene. By the time she finished the spreadsheet, an hour had passed. She thought about the way Mahler had yelled at her to stop taking notes. Was he mad at her? If she was being tested, as Frames said, would she be the one dropped from the team? What if nothing was to be found in these old cases? What did Mahler mean when he told her to look at the "quality of the light"? Was it some kind of joke he played on new hires?

Eden went through the Irwin Partridge file chronologically. The documents captured a life through the lens of the justice system: arrest reports, indictments, pleas, and appearances before the court. After she finished, Eden paged through her notes. What did it mean? *Remember your history.* Professor Hiatt tapped the knuckle of her forefinger on the podium. *We build cases on the discoveries of those who came before us.*

From her Advanced Forensic Psych course, Eden knew researchers used systems for classifying the personality types of serial killers. Holmes and DeBurger recognized four types: visionary, mission-oriented, hedonistic, and power/control. The evidence in the current cases seemed to indicate the killer, or killers, fit the hedonistic type—someone who killed for pleasure and regarded his victims as objects for his own enjoyment.

According to the literature, hedonistic-type killers choose their victims selectively. Their "*ideal victim type*" is someone they find sexually appealing. In their text on serial murder, Holmes and Holmes wrote that Ted Bundy picked his victims based on how they walked and talked.

Eden looked at her spreadsheet. Foss, Hart, MaryEllen Reese, and Beth Hunter were about the same age and body type.

VICTIM	AGE	HEIGHT	WEIGHT	LOCATION
Jane Doe	?	5.10	132	Spring Lake Park
Michelle Foss	21	5.7	138	Spring Lake Park
Susan Hart	20	5.8	110	Spring Lake Park
MaryEllen Reese	21	5.7	132	Santa Rosa Creek
Beth Hunter	21	5.6	140	Dan Foley Park
Amanda Smith	26	5.4	115	I-80 Rest Stop

The next column on the spreadsheet was *location*. Eden remembered studies in the 1990s showed the significance of geographic location in serial murder cases. Serial killers usually prefer specific locations and rarely vary from them. Geographic profiling had even been successfully used in tracking killers. In three of the cases Eden studied—Foss, Hart, and Hunter—the victim had been killed in a public park. Jane Doe had been found, not killed, in a public park.

Studies also showed serial killers use specific *methods of killing*. Fox and Levin at Northeastern found the dominant motive for the killer's behavior is to exert control over another person's life. To exert that control, serial killers prefer strangling or stabbing instead of a firearm. All the victims in Eden's spreadsheet had been strangled, and all but Jane Doe had been strangled with a smooth object, probably a cord.

Eden looked at the names of the six victims on the file folders. If she ruled out Jane Doe and Amanda Smith on the basis of ideal victim type, and MaryEllen Reese on the basis of location, that left Foss, Hart, and Hunter. But such sorting is based on academic profiling theory, which is disputed by some investigators in the field.

Eden pushed away from her desk and followed the hallway to the restroom. At the sink, she ran cold water in her cupped hands and splashed her face. Water dripping, she stared in the mirror. *Why am I here? What sort of job is this? I could quit tonight. Write a letter of resignation. Be back home in Connecticut tomorrow. Lieutenant Mahler would be relieved.*

She was hired straight into VCI detectives, without time as a uniform officer, on the strength of her work on the unsolved Highway 60 murders—first as a college thesis and then in the FBI. Chief Truro mentioned it during his interview. "You really dug into that one, didn't you?" he said with a conspiratorial smile. By which he really meant, *just how twisted are you?*

What would you know about it? Eden thought. But all she said was, "Actually, it started as an assignment."

"This one's for you, Eden," Professor Hiatt had announced at the beginning of her senior year as she held out a large accordion folder stuffed with paper on the Highway 60 case. Later Eden wondered: *What sort of case was it for a twenty-one-year-old student? Was Hiatt crazy? Or, with the pashmina wrapped loosely around her neck and the eyes that crinkled whenever she smiled, was she wearing just the sort of disguise that waited at the gates of hell?*

The case was notorious: nine women in five states, all killed the same way. Asphyxiation from dirt stuffed in the mouth. Duct tape sealing the lips, limbs bound with strips of cotton sheeting. The only suspect: a truck driver named Albert McKinley Jory. Middle-aged, large acne-scarred face, hair pulled into a ponytail. Arrested and released.

Eden researched in a study cubicle in the dark basement

stacks of Williston Hall, the campus library. But the book titles and crime-scene photos attracted the attention of other students walking past her desk. After Christmas she moved to her dormitory room, a single on the second floor of North Rockefeller Hall. She worked at night, when the other rooms on her floor were quiet.

The trouble arrived in the final semester. First, in the dining hall, esophageal spasms choked her until she ran to the toilet to throw up. Then she heard noises in the dark, imagined fingers on the latch outside her dorm window. Once, at three in the morning, when she was in the shower at the end of the hall, a girl coming home from a party accidentally turned out the overhead bathroom light. Eden screamed until a campus safety officer arrived. During finals week, the dead women from the Highway 60 murders crawled into bed beside her, hollow-eyed from the loneliness of their deaths, dirt sucked to the back of their throats. Eden woke tangled in the covers, knees jammed to her chest, shaking.

After graduation, Professor Hiatt pulled some strings with a former student working at the FBI. Just like that, Eden became the youngest analyst hired in the Behavioral Analysis Unit, or BAU, sitting in seminars beside gray-haired men with lifetimes of experience staring at human remains. She got used to photos on the conference room's large-screen TV of throats cut open, and casual lunch-table conversations on blood coagulation, entry-wound angles, and why serial killers always have three names.

She started on a murder in Baltimore, then a drive-by in Miami, and later a string of prostitute disappearances in Phoenix. At the end of her first year, Kinsella called her into his office and assigned her to a re-examination of the Highway 60 killings. "Take advantage of the BAU resources. This could be

your big one, your Bundy." Two months later, she was sleeping with a gun. Six months after that, she was back in Kinsella's
office with her resignation, watching the shy man struggle as
embarrassed disappointment spread across his face. Later she
learned the FBI, which had a name for everything, called it a
flameout.

Now in the police department restroom, Eden leaned against
the sink and closed her eyes. *Why does this keep happening? Why
do I think I can do this work?* She feared the look on Mahler's face
when she quit, the exasperation over his wasted time. Just like
Kinsella. But she needed to leave. She decided to finish reviewing the files and then resign.

In the Violent Crime room, Eden made a mug of mint tea and
picked up the victim binders. *Start again. Look at the data.* She
reread the information on Michelle Foss: crime-scene report,
medical examiner's report. Then she noticed a handwritten
note in the margin of the medical examiner's report—one of the
notes Rivas told her were made by the now-retired investigator
Tom Woodhouse. She remembered Rivas saying Woodhouse
was "old-school."

Eden went back to Woodhouse's handwritten note. The
mark looked like two cursive letters—"cv" or "cn." If it was
"cm," it might mean centimeter. Eden scanned the typewritten
text beside the note. The cord burns on Michelle Foss's neck
measured one centimeter wide. She opened the file on Susan
Hart and found the same note: cord width, one centimeter.
According to the medical examiner, the marks on MaryEllen
Reese's neck were wider and uneven, suggesting an irregular
material. The reports on Beth Hunter and Amanda Smith contained no measurements. Eden searched all the desk drawers
until she found a metric ruler. On the close-ups of Hunter and
Smith, she measured the widths of the neck bruises. Smith's

were 1.25 centimeters, but Hunter's were exactly one centimeter. Eden added a column to her spreadsheet:

CORD WIDTH

Jane Doe	no cord
Michelle Foss	1 cm
Susan Hart	1 cm
MaryEllen Reese	1.55–2.10 cm
Beth Hunter	1 cm
Amanda Smith	1.25 cm

She picked up her mug. The tea was cold. One page further in the Foss file, a handwritten note said, "three and a half." Eden read the text beside it, describing the bruise patterning around Michelle Foss's neck, which suggested the way the cord had been wrapped. The close-up photo of the young woman's neck showed dark lines wound three and a half times. Eden raised her hands and moved them as if she were looping a cord. She looked around the room. Bent over their laptops, Coyle and Frames had not noticed her. She moved her hands again, winding them three and a half times. It was a difficult, awkward movement. *Why three and a half? Why not three or two? Someone had done it purposefully. What did it mean?*

Eden looked at the four other victim photos. On MaryEllen Reese's neck, the marks were crisscrossed, as if the cord had been wrapped front to back. The marks on Amanda Smith's neck had a different spiral shape, as if the wrapping had begun on the side. Susan Hart's and Beth Hunter's bruises were a mirror image of Michelle Foss's—three and a half times around.

She paged through the rest of the reports on Michelle Foss without finding any more handwritten notes. She stacked the folders and reopened her laptop. On her spreadsheet, she added notes on the cord width and bruise pattern and used yellow highlighting to mark the consistencies.

CORD PATTERN

Jane Doe	No cord
Michelle Foss	3½
Susan Hart	3½
MaryEllen Reese	Front to back
Beth Hunter	3½
Amanda Smith	Spiral

Staring at the spreadsheet, she wondered if the similarities were a coincidence. How many possible widths of cord are there? How many ways of wrapping a cord?

Eden suddenly remembered Woodhouse had also reviewed the Hart case. She went back through the file slowly, page by page. The first time through, she didn't see any notes. When she looked a second time, she saw a single word on the backside of the medical examiner's report. Small, cursive letters in the same handwriting: "cnt" or "cvt." *Cunt? Probably not.* Crude language is only found in investigation reports when it's critical to a case, such as provocation for an argument. Also, such words are unlikely because police reports become official records and are subpoenable and discoverable by counsel. *Container? Converter?*

She flipped the page and reread the report. The text described other identifying marks found on Susan Hart's body. Scrape on left side of face, presumably made when the victim fell face-forward to the ground. Broken skin on fingertips as the victim clawed at the cord. Bruise on her lower back where assailant braced his knee to tighten the cord. Near the bottom of the page, a single entry: "Two-centimeter cut near base of spine, made with sharp-bladed instrument." The handwritten word was "cut."

Eden found the photo of Susan Hart's back. The cut was difficult to see, and Eden might have missed it if she were not searching for it. The pencil-thin line had darkened in the hours and days after death. How would such a wound occur? Had the assailant threatened her with a knife or cut her from behind when he approached? If that were true, the wound would contain clothing fibers noted in the medical examination, which it didn't, according to the forensic report. Besides, both the assailant's hands would need to be free to use the cord.

She remembered Kinsella talking about Robert Keppel, who interviewed Ted Bundy and wrote a book on what he called "signature killers." These killers leave behind a distinctive mark or object that goes beyond what is necessary to commit the crime. Keppel called them "psychological calling cards," or signatures, and noted they were sometimes left *after* the murder was committed.

Eden checked the medical examiner's reports for the other women. None contained mention of a similar cut. Getting up from her desk, she went to the supply closet, where she remembered seeing a magnifying glass. She returned to her desk, picked up the victim files and laptop, and walked down the hallway to the interview room.

Closing the door, she set to work on the table. She found photos of the backs of each of the victims and laid them side by side. With the magnifying glass, she searched the spot just below the base of the spine in each photo. No marks appeared in the photos of MaryEllen Reese and Amanda Smith. But on Michelle Foss and Beth Hunter, a line was visible. Eden measured the lines and found each to be exactly two centimeters. Opening her laptop, she added the information to the spreadsheet.

SIGNATURE MARK

Jane Doe	No cut
Michelle Foss	2 cm cut, base of spine
Susan Hart	2 cm cut, base of spine
MaryEllen Reese	No cut
Beth Hunter	2 cm cut, base of spine
Amanda Smith	No cut

She studied her spreadsheet. What had she learned? At a time when Partridge was living in Vallejo, one of the victims there had been killed in the same way as *both* victims two years ago in Santa Rosa's Spring Lake Park and had the same distinctive signature. The latest Jane Doe victim was killed in a different way, maybe by a different killer.

Eden carefully replaced the photos in their respective binders, stacked them neatly, and closed her laptop. In the hallway, a world away, a phone rang. Sitting alone in the interview room, she noticed her hands shaking; she folded one hand over the other to steady them. She thought: *Maybe I don't have to resign.* Then: *Did I just find the quality of light?*

Chapter Thirteen

(i)

In his dream, Rivas gripped the steering wheel of a speeding car. The road rushed forward, oncoming cars swerving across the centerline, roadside tree limbs scraping the trim off the doors. Was he moving toward something, or was it coming at him? All the while, an old woman sang "Rock-a-Bye Baby"—with new words about the death of a policeman named Rivas.

He woke in the parking lot of the county's adult detention facility, his face bathed in sweat. For a moment he forgot where he was. He blinked and checked the time on his cell. Thirty minutes had passed since he closed his eyes. Above the hills on the eastern side of the valley, the sky had lightened. The early morning sun spread across the parking lot, climbing the jail's brick walls and dark eyelet windows.

Rivas stared at the building's looming facade. On any given day, he could recognize more than half the men inside, shuffling the corridors in their baggy cotton jumpsuits. He knew in perfect detail their crimes, victims, and arrest records. The department's memory, Eddie called him. But Rivas also knew them like a man knows the members of his extended family— their girlfriends, ex-wives, and children. It was the special gift his grandmother, Maria-Elena, had taught him.

For the past year, Rivas heard her voice two or three times a week when he closed his eyes. The singsong voice recounting the deaths of relatives—and more and more his own dying. *How was it possible for memory to foretell the future, and to be remembered before he died?*

Near the end of Maria-Elena's life, her stories mixed reality with illusion. She had once begun each tale with its date, solemnly announced, the only legacy of a poor family. But, in her old age, the dates changed—across days, then years, and later centuries—so that memory and prophecy contended in the same story. It was as if the decades piled one on another in the old woman's mind until history, the weakest of the arts, could no longer bear all she remembered. Something more supple, like magic, took its place and let her loose to follow the flights of the ghosts who crowded her dreams.

As he looked at the lockup, Rivas felt the weight of memory as it must have burdened Maria-Elena in the end. Week by week, the space around him filled with more history: interrogations, arraignments, sentencings. A body facedown on a bedroom floor. Kids watching from a doorway. Third generation of a family cuffed in the back seat. Women together on a bench outside the courtroom. New nicknames, tattoos, and cheap guns to remember. Each name and date added to others before them, links in a chain that bound Rivas to the criminal justice system no less than it trapped the men inside the jail.

Rivas sat up and wiped perspiration from his forehead. He

had come to meet with the drug dealer Arturo Peña and his law-yer. Climbing out of the car, Rivas walked stiffly across the lot to the jail entrance. Inside, he turned over his handgun and went through the security gate. A guard escorted him to the visitor area. The place had a smell Rivas never got used to—the musti-ness of steel and concrete and the stink of men crowded together.

The accommodation for visitors to the lockup consisted of six dark booths in a narrow hallway. Each had two chairs, a coun-tertop, and a window with a speaker-box facing the common room of the general population. In the third visitors' booth, Rivas found Peña's public defender, Maricela Hernandez. Rivas had known the lawyer for five years—from when she passed the bar and began taking cases.

Hernandez wore a tan suit and balanced a briefcase on her lap. When she saw Rivas, she smiled. "*Buenos días,* Daniel. How's Teresa?"

Rivas shrugged. "High blood pressure. But I guess everyone with teenagers has high blood pressure."

Hernandez squeezed his hand. "Better to have girls, Daniel. Boys are trouble."

Rivas sat in the second chair and smiled back. "Too late now." He looked into the commons room. "What're we here for?"

Thirty feet away, Peña hunched over a table in the common room, his chest and upper arms stretching the fabric of his jail clothes.

"I don't know." Hernandez motioned for Peña to come to the window. "Arturo asked to speak with you."

Peña moved with the disinterest of a tiger at the zoo, only his eyes sharp and focused. He took his place across from them, arms folded across his chest.

"Arturo, *qué quieres*?" Hernandez bent toward the speaker. "What do you want?"

Peña lowered his head at Rivas. "You're late, *pendejo*."

"I'm here now. What do you want?" Rivas said.

Hernandez leaned on the counter in front of the glass. "Don't mess with us."

Peña's eyes didn't leave Rivas. "You got lucky yesterday, *viejo*."

"Arresting you?" Rivas said.

"No, I let you live."

Hernandez hugged the briefcase against her chest. "What do you want, Arturo? The charges so far are drug possession, possession of an unregistered firearm, resisting arrest, and threatening a police officer." She turned to Rivas. "And I understand the DA will file additional charges?"

Rivas nodded. "First-degree murder. Filed later today or tomorrow."

"You understand this, Arturo?" Hernandez asked.

Peña ignored her. "*El Viejo* and I are talking."

"Arturo, you asked to see Sergeant Rivas." The lawyer sighed with exasperation. "What do you want? Do you have something to say?"

Peña unfolded his arms and spoke quietly. "The girl's body you found. I know something about this."

"What girl?" Rivas asked, sensing a trick.

"The one you found in the park."

Rivas looked at Hernandez, who shrugged. He leaned closer to the divider. "What're you talking about? This something to do with the Sureños?"

"No. But I know how she got there."

"How do you know?"

"Because I saw her."

Rivas took a deep breath. "You waste our time, we can add charges. You understand? Your lawyer can tell you."

Peña waved a hand dismissively. "I saw this girl before you

found her. She was alive and with three boys—a whitey, an Asian, and a brown one. If this is worth something to you, we can talk about my cousin you arrested yesterday."

"How do you know it was the girl in the park? We don't have an identity. We haven't issued a photo. It wasn't even in the newspaper until today."

"I tell you something. In her ear, she has a star, is that right?"

Rivas fell back in his seat.

Peña smiled. "Now you're interested, aren't you, *viejo*? And I know because this one, the girl I saw, she looked like she knew she was going to die."

(ii)

(WEDNESDAY, 9:02 A.M.)

Frames sat across the table from Craig Lerner. The thirty-something owner of Lerner and Meier Creative Marketing wore a pressed white shirt, wool blazer with upturned collar, and jeans. A fashionable two-day stubble dirtied his chin. On the table in front of him, he pressed a tall Starbucks cup with his fingertips.

A *Venti*, Frames thought. Probably something fussy like an espresso shot, soy milk foam, and cinnamon. He watched Lerner trying to find a place to focus his attention. Twice Lerner glanced at the plain file lying between them, but each time he quickly looked up again. *Boy's on his best behavior. Seen enough episodes of* Law & Order, *he's acting the part of the upright citizen.*

"So you told our officer the description of the victim sounded like your graphic artist?" Frames asked.

Lerner nodded. "Same height and weight. General features. Of course, it's hard to tell from a few sentences."

"And she didn't come to work yesterday?"

"Didn't call, either—which isn't like her. She usually comes in at nine, along with my admin. We're a small company, just the four of us. My business partner, Ken Meier, and I come in at ten. We come in later because we work later." Lerner smiled and took a sip of his drink.

Wanting me to know he's not a slacker. "You try to call her?"

"My admin did. Talked to her roommates. They said she didn't come home the night before. That last part's none of my business, really. You can't ask too many questions these days. That whole privacy thing." Lerner rolled his eyes.

Why are guys with education and money such terrible liars? What do they imagine lying looks like? "It takes a hole in your heart to lie, Stevie," his mother used to say. In Frames's experience, the best liars were definitely guys with holes in their hearts. Like Tyler Cates, the redneck in the next bunk during basic training in the Marines. They spent every hour together for three months, but Frames never knew when Cates was telling the truth or lying. Same dead look in his eyes.

"She come to work on Monday?" Frames asked.

"Yes, she did," Lerner said. "She does our graphic design— layouts, illustrations, Photoshop stuff. On Monday we finished a print ad for a client."

"You remember what she was wearing?"

Lerner's face turned thoughtful.

What is it with this guy? Has to turn every question into a puzzle.

"Jeez, what was she wearing? You know how it is, you work right next to someone, and you never notice. Let's see, I remember she came into my office once with some proofs, and she had on a silk blouse. Dark colored. I'm not sure about anything else. She's always well dressed."

He's not going to mention the short skirt. "How about jewelry?" Frames was starting to enjoy himself.

"Jewelry? I know she doesn't wear big rings. Says they interfere with the keyboard. But you know what? She always wears the same earrings. They're shaped like a star, like a hollow star."

Frames put his hand on the file in front of him. "We have some photos here of the victim in the park. I'd like you to look at them and tell me if this is your graphic artist. Just so you know, it might be rough to see her this way."

Lerner swallowed. "I understand."

Frames slid two close-ups of the victim's face across the table.

"Oh, boy." Lerner stared at the photos. He slowly shook his head. "Wow. That's Elise. I mean, shit, it really is. What happened to her?"

"We're still working on that. But I need you to tell me for certain. Is this your graphic artist?"

"Yes, it's Elise. No question. What do you want me to do? Do I sign something?"

No tears, Frames thought. *Interesting choice.* "Let's start with her full name."

"Oh, sure. Elise Durand."

"Could you spell that?"

Lerner spelled it out. "The first name is French for Elisabeth. I think her father was French or something."

"We'll need to get any personal information you have on file for her. So we can notify the family."

"Yeah, yeah." Lerner's attention locked on the photos. "Poor Elise." Finally he pushed the pictures back to Frames.

Lerner took a phone from a blazer pocket and began tapping at the screen. After a moment, he handed the phone to Frames. "That's Elise's address and the phone number for her apartment. I'll have my admin look up her family's contact information. She moved here from Pennsylvania. Her mother still lives there, I think."

"How'd she act on Monday?" Frames wrote down the address and phone number.

"I'm not sure what you mean. Normal, I guess. I didn't notice anything."

"Did she happen to say where she was going that evening?"

"Not that I remember."

"Was that unusual?" Frames asked.

"Not really. We try to keep it pretty professional."

"Did she have a boyfriend?"

"Boyfriend?"

"Someone she saw regularly."

"You know, I think so. But we didn't really talk about that kind of thing." Lerner's face reddened.

Frames watched him. *Of course you did, you lying son of a bitch.*

Lerner straightened and tried to recover himself. "You should know Elise was an unusual young woman. Very attractive, but high-strung."

"High-strung?"

"Yeah. I probably shouldn't say this now, but in some ways, I'm not surprised something happened. She had this side to her that was—I don't know, sort of—unpredictable."

"In what way?"

Lerner puffed out his cheeks and exhaled. "Oh, man. Look, I am...or was...her employer. We didn't really socialize outside the office. So I may be talking out of school. Maybe you should talk to my admin. It's just, it was my impression that she liked... you know, in a sexual sense, what you might call—" He searched the walls for the right word.

"Mr. Lerner," Frames said, "I realize this is a difficult time. But this is a murder investigation, and we need any information you have on this young woman."

"You know what? I'm really not comfortable saying anything

else." Lerner pressed his fingertips on the table edge and stared at them. "I don't mean to be opaque, but I don't want to commit myself to anything else."

For a moment neither man spoke.

"So, are we, like, through?" Lerner pushed back his chair and grabbed the Starbucks cup.

"For now." Frames waited a beat. "At some point we'll want a full statement."

Frames let Lerner walk out the door ahead of him and then pointed him toward the stairs at the end of the corridor. As he watched Lerner walk away, Frames thought: *You can be opaque or whatever the fuck you want. But we are definitely not, like, through.*

PART II

Chapter Fourteen

(i)

Mahler leaned against the wall in his usual spot in the VCI room watching Frames. He saw a wariness in the other detective's eyes. "Where's Lerner now?"

"He left," Frames said.

"You let him walk out?"

"He didn't seem like he was going to say anything else."

"So, in your interview, this guy says the victim was high-strung and unpredictable. And he's not surprised she was killed. She liked some version of sex he declines to tell us. Any of this sound like something that might be important?"

Frames held up his hands. "Okay, okay. I knew we had to bring him back in, but I was thinking, this guy's just found out his employee's been murdered. He needs some time to—"

"To what? Figure out what his story's going to be? Go find him, and take Daniel with you." As he spoke, Mahler already regretted the anger in his voice. He disliked calling out an officer's mistakes in front of others. He took a deep breath.

Rivas broke the silence. "You think this guy Lerner was involved with the victim?"

Mahler pushed himself off the wall and walked closer to the other detectives' desks. "I don't know. But he's withholding something."

"If the victim was being treated for bipolar, that could be what Lerner means by 'high-strung,'" Eden said.

Mahler shrugged. "Yeah, but why did Lerner say he wasn't surprised she was killed?" He turned to Coyle. "Get a warrant for the victim's apartment, car, phone, the works. Once you've got it, go out to the apartment. Her roommates might be able to tell us where she was Monday night. And get a search warrant for her room."

"You want me to go?" Coyle asked.

"You have a problem with that?" Mahler sighed.

"No. It's just that I don't usually… Never mind. By the way, the men's scarf that the dogs found in the park is probably a dead end. We have to get a court order to check the store sales, and even then we have no evidence to connect it to the victim's body."

"Put it on the back burner," Mahler said. "We'll revisit it later if we need to."

"What about the victim's mother?" Coyle asked.

"I contacted the police back in Montgomery Township, Pennsylvania, and asked them to notify her in person. If I don't hear back in a couple hours, I'll give them a call."

Mahler walked back to the whiteboard. "Elise Durand" had been written in red marker under two photos of the victim. The countdown to another possible homicide now said thirty-seven hours. Beyond that, a second whiteboard was set up with photos of three earlier victims: Michelle Foss and Susan Hart, killed in Spring Lake Park, and Beth Hunter, killed forty miles away in Vallejo. Beneath each face was a close-up of a small knife cut in the flesh at the base of their spines. Mahler felt the others watching him as he studied the photos. "I understand we may have another possible match with this Vallejo victim?"

Eden opened a file. "Yes, sir. All three girls have the same signature cut at the base of the spine, and all were killed when Irwin Partridge lived in the area."

"You figured this out by yourself?" Mahler asked, without turning to face Eden.

"Yes, sir. But Daniel pulled Beth Hunter's file off ViCAP, and Sergeant Woodhouse noticed the cut on Michelle Foss."

Mahler turned to face Eden. "But you put it together. It's good work, Detective Somers. Now go back on ViCAP and see if any other cases show up with this new signature thing and—"

"I already looked on ViCAP. No other murders show up with the signature cut. It might not mean anything. The signature wasn't even mentioned in the ME's report on Michelle Foss and Beth Hunter. I only saw it because Sergeant Woodhouse made a note. Maybe it's been overlooked in other cases."

"Call the investigating officer in Vallejo, and tell him—"

"I talked to Officer Dennis Jermany. He said their leads in the case didn't pan out. Also said Partridge's name never came up. But Partridge's file shows that at the time of the Hunter murder, he had a job in Vallejo. Worked for Mare Island Rigging. So Jermany's calling the company this morning to see if they have a record of Partridge's schedule on the day of the murder."

Mahler stopped listening. The information about the signature cuts was like a new door opening. Maybe the way into the Partridge case wasn't through the local murders but through a matching case in Vallejo.

"Eddie, you saw my report?" Rivas asked. "Peña says he saw our victim Saturday night with three individuals. Probably a drug buy. If it's true, we should find those guys."

Mahler nodded. "Get the ADA on it. If Peña has something more to tell us, I want to hear it this afternoon. And, Martin, ask the roommates about the three men."

Coyle abruptly stood and approached the whiteboards. "Eddie, listen," he said, startling Mahler from his thoughts. "The new information Eden found is important for the Partridge case. But it also puts our latest victim, Elise Durand, even further outside the pattern of the other killings. We can't ignore that. Everything's different."

"Except it's a young woman strangled and left in Spring Lake Park." Mahler turned back to the photos.

"Yes, but the way it was done is different. You know, we all know, these guys have a pattern. They almost never vary from it. It's how they're wired. It's what allows us to do what we do."

"Almost never?" Mahler faced Coyle. "Is that what you want to go with here? You want to lead with that? You want to tell the press and the city we're not going to find another girl's body up there tomorrow night? And when a twenty-one-year-old's left on a dirt footpath, or under some bushes, and we put her photo on this board, you want to tell her parents that, according to the latest research and the best analysis, this *almost never* happens?"

Coyle held his ground. "All I'm saying is I think this new information on the signature cut changes things."

"Let's just do our job." The room fell quiet. Mahler walked back to his spot on the wall. For the second time in five minutes he regretted his words. *Did he think Coyle and the others needed reminding of the consequences of the case? Did he know anything they didn't? Should he tell them a few hours ago a dead girl told him the key to the latest case was the victim's breathing?*

After a minute, he said, "Daniel, make a timeline for this girl. Lerner says she was at work on Monday. Talk to the admin. Find out exactly when Elise Durand left work. The building where she worked may have security videos. When Martin talks to the roommates, we'll find out if they saw her after work. We need to know where she went and who she saw Monday evening."

Frames, Rivas, and Coyle left the room.

Eden packed her laptop into a carrying case. "I'd like to talk to former Sergeant Woodhouse, the one who worked the earlier cases."

"Tom?" Mahler frowned. "What for?"

"Ask some questions on his case notes."

"Okay, but this isn't a research project. We don't have a lot of time."

Watching her walk away, Mahler spoke again. "Detective Somers, remember in our interview with Partridge, he mentioned his current girlfriend, Lorin Albright?"

Eden nodded.

"Go and talk to her. Let's see what she has to say about Partridge."

"You want me to take Daniel or Martin with me?"

"No. Go by yourself. She's more likely to talk to you alone."

(ii)

(WEDNESDAY, 10:45 A.M.)

Mahler recognized the voice on the phone as the police officer in Pennsylvania he'd spoken to a few hours earlier—Detective Sergeant Joseph Warringer of the Montgomery Township Police. "Lieutenant Mahler, I'm getting back to you on your request for a death notification."

Out of habit, Mahler tried to picture the man. It was not a young man's voice. "I appreciate your taking the time."

"We're a small department, but we try to get right on something like this."

"Thanks. It's an active homicide investigation."

"Sure thing. After your call, I drove out to the address for your victim's mother, Carol Durand. I'll email you a report, but I thought you'd want to hear this."

Mahler knew he'd given the officer a crap assignment. Based on a murder investigation that wasn't his own, three thousand miles away, Warringer had to deliver news to a stranger that ruined her life. If she asked questions, he had very few answers.

Mahler saw Warringer in his mind. Late forties, sitting straight, both elbows on the desktop. "You spoke with her in person?"

"Yes, sir. I guess you could say it was lucky. She works in an office a few miles away, and she came home for lunch. Otherwise, I'd still be chasing her."

"Yeah, that was lucky."

"Soon as I identified myself, she knew something was up. Right away, she had a kind of fearful look. Times like that, I wish I wasn't as big as I am. Scares women. Not much you can do about that, is there?"

"No, there isn't." Mahler saw the other man's height and broad shoulders.

"Anyway, I got her to sit down and informed her of her daughter's death. I tried to keep it simple. Told her what I know, which isn't much."

"We're just at the beginning of this thing."

"I told her that. Said it appeared to be a homicide, and the local police were involved. She broke down pretty good then."

"Was she alone?"

"She was. Just the two of us there. I did my best. Asked if someone could be with her, but she said no. She lives alone."

"We only had contact information for the victim's mother," Mahler said. He heard papers rustling on Warringer's end. Paper-and-pen man, Mahler thought. Not using a tablet yet. He was starting to like Warringer.

"Speaking of that, your victim's father, Carol Durand's ex-husband, is Sebastien Durand. Divorced more than fifteen years ago. French citizen. Lives over there. I got the idea he's way out of the picture. But I have contact information I can put in the report. Couple had no other children."

"Did Ms. Durand know where her daughter was Monday night?"

"Let's see. I asked all the questions you requested." More pages being turned. "She said she did not know where her daughter was Monday evening. Last time she spoke with the girl was two weeks ago. Everything sounded okay then. Job, money."

"No mention of a boyfriend, anyone she was seeing?"

"Asked that question, too. The mother didn't know."

"Didn't know if she had a boyfriend, or didn't know who he was?"

"The second. When I asked if she had a boyfriend, she said, 'I'm sure she does. She's very pretty.'"

"Very pretty?"

"Yeah. When I asked if she knew the boyfriend's name, she said, 'No. I guess I should. She's dated several boys.' I got the impression her daughter didn't share much in that way. It's that way with a lot of kids. My own daughter won't tell me a thing."

"We're just hoping for a place to start."

"Ms. Durand said a few other things. Said she thought her daughter was well liked at the company where she worked. Apparently, your victim was an artist."

Mahler waited to see if Warringer would say more. Then he asked, "Did it sound like the mother's coming out here?"

"We talked about it. My impression is she'll try to take a flight tonight. Probably a red-eye from Philly. Be out to you tomorrow morning."

"That's good. We'd like to have a longer talk with her."

"By the time you see her, she'll have had a little time to get used to it. Be readier to talk. I don't know about you, but I find they do better the next day."

"Yeah. Shock's worn off a bit."

"One other thing, if you've got a minute—"

"What is it?"

"Ms. Durand said this thing that raised a red flag. When she told me about her last call with her daughter, she said, 'As far I could tell, Elise wasn't in any trouble.' When I asked her what she meant, she said her daughter suffered from bipolar disorder. In the past, Elise didn't always use good judgment, went out with the wrong kinds of men, took drugs."

"But the mother thought that wasn't happening now?"

"In the phone call, her daughter sounded as if everything was going well. But now, with this…homicide, the mother wonders if she was wrong."

"Okay, thanks. You can never tell in the beginning what's important."

For a moment the line was silent.

"Before your call, I'd never heard of Santa Rosa," Warringer said. "I Googled it. Looks like a nice town."

"Yeah, it's really a city now. Getting bigger all the time."

"You get many homicides?"

"Enough."

"Mostly armed robberies here. Last few years, we've had a real meth problem. Anyway, good luck with your investigation."

"Thanks again for your help."

"Glad to do it... By the way, maybe I don't need to say this, but with this mom of your victim, you're going to need kid gloves. Know what I mean?"

"Sure," Mahler said. "Kid gloves."

Chapter Fifteen

(i)

Coyle sat on a stuffed chair facing the two young women. He'd knocked on the door a few minutes earlier and roused them from bed. Now they slouched on a sofa, dressed in tank tops and flannel pajama pants, one rubbing her eyes and the other raking fingers through her hair. The forensic tech who had come with Coyle, Bailey Perkins, stood beside his chair.

The smaller of the two women asked, "Was Lisa really that girl they found in the park?" Her name was Molly. She had close-cropped hair and a shiny piercing on the side of her nose. She took a cigarette from a pack on the sofa and lit it.

"Elise Durand," Coyle said. "The victim was Elise Durand."

"She was trying to change her name to Lisa," the other woman, Kira, said. "She hated the name Elise and made us call her Lisa." She propped dirty bare feet on the end table, letting her tank top rise above her waist to show a roll of pale belly fat.

In the morning light pouring through a bay window, the room had a worn, partied-out look. Plates of dried pizza lay on the floor, empty beer cans balanced on the arm of a loveseat. A thick candle had melted over a coffee table, its waxen trail stabbed with cigarette butts. The walls were bare except for an area above the sofa where an Indian bedspread was stretched and pinned at the corners. The air smelled of stale smoke and garbage.

Coyle, who had prior experience being the first to tell a stranger that a relative or friend had died, watched the women's faces. They gazed back with weary boredom.

"How long did you live together?" Coyle asked.

"Six months." Molly shrugged. "We moved in last summer. Lisa was already here, with a girl named Jessica. When Jessica moved out, Lisa put a notice on the website for junior college housing and we answered."

"You're students?"

The girls nodded. Molly blew smoke out the side of her mouth.

Coyle looked up at Bailey. She was a few years older than the girls on the sofa, her dark hair pulled into a ponytail. She wore narrow, dark-framed glasses. Her arms were wrapped around the black shoulder bag she took to crime scenes. She studied the two girls intently.

"But Elise, or Lisa, wasn't a student, right?" Coyle asked. "She had a job as a graphic artist?"

"Yeah," Kira said. "She was, like, twenty-four. I think she wanted to be a student but didn't have any money. She was auditing a class at night or something."

"What else can you tell me about her?"

"I don't know," Molly said. "We didn't really hang. She was at work all day, and we were in classes at night. And she wasn't, you know, like us."

"How was she?"

"She was older," Kira said. "Dated older guys. In the beginning, we tried doing things together, clubbing, stuff like that, but it was super-awkward."

"In what way?"

"She didn't want to talk about the stuff we talked about. And we're drinking, like, Bud Light, and she's ordering twelve-dollar mojitos."

"When was the last time you saw her?"

"Sunday night," Molly said. "She was in her room. We didn't talk."

"When she didn't come home Monday night, it wasn't unusual?"

"Happened all the time."

"She didn't say where she was going?"

The girls shook their heads.

"Did she have a car?"

"Yeah, a Corolla," Kira said. "She always drove it to work."

Molly lowered her head and leaned forward. "Are you really a murder detective?"

"Homicide, yes," Coyle said. "Why?"

"I don't know, no offense, but you don't look like the ones on TV. They look different, more...tight."

"Tight?"

"Yeah, something like that. The clothes and the hair. You're more—"

"Loose?" Coyle offered.

"Yeah, I mean, no offense or anything. You're okay and all."

Looking up, Coyle saw Bailey smiling at him.

"Did Lisa have a boyfriend?" Coyle asked.

"A boyfriend?" Molly laughed. She trimmed her ash on the edge of a coffee mug. "Lisa was, you know...outgoing. Guys thought she was hot."

"Did you meet any of them?"

"Not really. They never came here."

"Do you know if there was one she dated more than the others?"

"I don't think she ever had just one," Kira said. "Anyway, all we saw was their cars. A couple weeks ago she got picked up out front by a guy in a Lexus. I mean, the guys we go out with can barely afford a car."

Coyle looked at his notepad. "What about three friends who might have been together with her—a white guy, an Asian, a Hispanic? Ring any bells?"

The girls shook their heads.

"So you don't know her boyfriends? I thought that was the kind of stuff roommates talked about."

"Not Lisa," Kira said. "At least not that way."

"What way was it?" Coyle asked.

"I don't know—it's weird talking about her now, after she's... gone." The girls looked at each other.

"What is it?"

"Lisa had this thing about guys and sex," Molly said. "She was, like, really into it."

"Oh, my God," Kira said. "I can't believe you said that."

"What?" Molly looked at Coyle. "It doesn't make any difference now, does it?"

"Why don't you tell me what you were going to say?"

"Lisa told me one time she made it with a guy for the first time when she was twelve. I don't know if I believed her, but it was, like, a huge deal for her. When she was out with guys, that was the first thing she thought about. She wore a lot of micros and fishnets. Slutty stuff. Maybe it was part of her bipolar thing, I don't know."

"Her bipolar thing?"

"She was, I don't know what you call it…uneven. Way, way up and then way, way down. I know she had medication, but she didn't always take it."

"When she was up, she was fidgety and talking all the time," Kira said. "When she was down, she wouldn't say anything for, like, two days. Sometimes I felt sorry for her, but it was weird."

"Did she have any girlfriends?" Coyle asked.

"Not that I know of."

"She was sort of close to Jessica, the woman who lived here before us," Molly said. "I can give you her cell number." She picked up her phone, scrolled through a list, and then held up the phone to Coyle.

Coyle jotted down the number and asked Kira to show them Elise's bedroom. It was the first of three on the apartment's central hallway.

Bailey went into the room alone and shot a dozen photos from different angles. When she was finished, she handed Coyle a pair of latex gloves and shoe coverings. "Boy," she said quietly, "when I'm murdered and my body's dumped in a park, I hope someone nicer than those two girls is around to remember me."

Coyle pulled on the gloves and coverings. "Give me a hundred bucks, and when you're murdered and your body's dumped in a park, I'll say I always knew you were the smart one."

"That's sweet, Marty, but meaningless coming from a loose detective." Bailey walked across the room to a chest-high dresser and opened the top drawer.

Coyle looked at the room's cluttered messiness, with clothing piled on the bed and scattered on the floor. He thought of its finality for the victim. Had she known she would never return, would she have left it differently?

He approached the nightstand, which held a lamp and a stack of four books. With one finger, he turned the books to read the titles: *The Collected Poems of John Keats, The Norton Anthology of Modern and Contemporary Poetry, Woman's Orgasm,* and *Lady Sophia's Rescue: A Regency Romance.* He remembered attending a memorial service for a former professor. A family member had read a list of the books from the professor's nightstand as if the titles alone were a reflection of the man's character.

"World's largest collection of thongs." Bailey reached her hands into the dresser drawer. "I'm almost positive my job description didn't say anything about looking through the underwear of dead people."

"It's not in the job description," Coyle said. "It's under Benefits." He picked up the books. The Keats volume was worn. Inside, the page margins were covered in a looping handwritten scrawl. He read part of a poem underlined in black ink: "Now, a soft kiss." Poetry always seemed feminine to Coyle. It made him uncomfortable. What was he supposed to think or feel? Should he think of a soft kiss from Adrienne? What was a soft kiss, anyway? What did the victim, the girl in the park whose head was crushed, think when she read this poem and underlined the words? Did it make any difference to her before she was killed? He closed the Keats and put it in an evidence bag.

On the nightstand a framed photograph hid behind a clock. It showed a man dressed in baggy trousers, shirt, and tie, standing at the edge of a field. The man's features looked like the victim's. Coyle put the photo in a separate evidence bag.

In the nightstand's drawer, Coyle found half a dozen prescription bottles with "Elise Durand" on the label: Haldol, Lithium, Risperdal, Depakote, and Paxil. He knew the first was an antipsychotic, the second a treatment for manic depression. He opened a bottle with the label torn off and showed it to Bailey.

She poured the contents into her gloved palm and counted four different kinds of tablets. "OxyContin, or synthetic heroin," she said, pointing to several hard, yellow pills. "These blue ones are Ecstasy. I don't recognize the others." She put the pills back in the bottle and dropped it into an evidence bag.

Coyle looked at the posters lining three of the room's walls: Tom Waits, a sweaty-faced female singer Coyle didn't know, an art print of a street café at night, and another of a woman lying beside a lake. He stared at the last poster, peeled off the tape, and laid the poster on the bed.

"Check out what I found in the sweater drawer." Bailey held up a plastic bag filled with a green, grainy substance, rolled tight, and bound with rubber bands. "Cannabis sativa. Blue Dream, if I had to guess. Not that I have any personal knowledge. By the way, why's stuff always hidden in the sweater drawer? Are sweaters some kind of high-security thing?"

"It's why I brought you, Bailey," Coyle said. "Only someone with your training could get past the sweaters." He turned to a handmade collage on the last wall. It was about three feet square, with words written in markers and pictures glued on. One picture was Keats, whom Coyle recognized from the book cover; another was an enlargement of the man in the nightstand photo. The words in marker were short phrases: "All I Want Is Boundless Love" and "Pray for the Grace of Accuracy." In the center was *"Ne M'oubliez Pas."*

"Know any French?" Coyle asked.

"Oui, monsieur." Bailey made a stage bow. "The department requires it of all new hires so we can infiltrate those new French gangs downtown. Once they opened that café on Fourth Street, it's been one baguette fight after another."

Coyle typed the words into a translation app on his phone. The translation read "Don't Forget Me." He pulled the collage off the wall, rolled it up, and put it beside the evidence bags.

"I do know one French phrase." Bailey stood in the closet

doorway, looking through the hanging clothes. "*Il y a une couille dans le potage*. My high school friend Andy used to say it all the time. It means something like 'There's a problem here,' but it translates as 'There's a testicle in the soup.' Fits almost any occasion."

Coyle walked across the room to a small wooden desk. On it lay a laptop and two small pieces of paper, with scribbled notes that looked like appointments. He put the computer and the paper in separate evidence bags. For a moment he watched Bailey search the closet. He thought of the way the roommates described the victim's oversexed clothes and unstable moods. She was pretty but overdressed and had mental issues. In her room he and Bailey had found poetry, prescription meds, and illegal drugs—all of it hidden from her roommates. *What did this add up to, and what did it have to do with her being killed?*

He left the desk, then turned and came back. With his right hand, he reached under the desktop and felt from one side to the other. In one of the far corners, he touched a hard object. Bending over, he saw something taped to the desk's underside.

He pulled on it and found, wrapped in tape, a black pock-etknife made of molded polymer. Coyle had seen one like it a few years before. He'd arrested a returning Iraq War vet on assault charges and found it in the guy's boot. The knife was a Microtech automatic. Coyle pressed a button near one end, and a three-inch, scalpel-sharp steel blade sprang out. The blade was covered in a dried, red substance.

Leaning over his shoulder, Bailey squinted at the knife. "What do you think the stuff on the blade is?"

"Probably exactly what you think it is."

"*Il y a une couille dans le potage*," Bailey said.

(ii)

"I wish you'd called ahead, before you came in." Craig Lerner sat behind a sleek, glass-topped desk. The sleeves of his pressed shirt were rolled to the middle of his forearms. He pointed Rivas to a black leather chair. "I could've saved you a trip. My attorney assures me the only way you can compel me to answer questions is by issuing a subpoena, and that requires a judge's order."

"He on retainer?" Frames stood across the room with his back to Lerner, peering at a row of wall-mounted documents.

"Who?" Lerner asked.

"Your attorney."

Lerner stared at Frames. "I understand your need to collect as much information as you can." He turned again to Rivas. "But I've already told you everything I know about Elise that bears on this case."

Frames snorted. "Everything that bears on this case."

"We have more questions," Rivas said, looking at his watch. He could tell Lerner was going to waste another five minutes jerking them around. He hated seeing this shabby side of people when they were backed into a corner. Sometimes he wondered if being around so much lying made him a liar. He found himself telling Eddie small lies about cases to avoid extra work. He even kept things from his wife, Teresa—not telling her how he dreamed of death.

"As business owners," Lerner said, "my partner and I need to follow certain professional standards as regards our employees…and former employees, so that our clients can trust their reputations to us."

"Trust? In advertising? You're kidding, right?" Frames leaned close to a shelf to examine the inscription on a star-shaped trophy.

Lerner ignored the comment. "I don't have to tell you what a small community this is, and how reputations can be—"

"Mr. Lerner, we're conducting a homicide investigation, and we're in a hurry," Rivas said quickly. "We need to ask you some questions. The sooner you answer them, the sooner we get out of your life and move on to someone else's life. When you take this attitude, it makes you seem—"

"Guilty," Frames said.

"Uncooperative," Rivas said.

"Whoa, whoa, hold it right there." Lerner pushed himself away from his desk. He stood, facing Rivas, who stared back at him implacably. "I don't appreciate this."

"How about if you sit down?" Rivas said.

"Is *he* going to sit down?" Lerner gestured toward Frames.

"Don't worry about him. Just sit down."

Rivas waited until Lerner was seated. The problem with secrets, he thought, is they pile up inside us and become another person living in our skin, like a second life that, after a while, we can't tell from our own. "Let's start with this," he said. "You told Detective Frames that Elise Durand was unpredictable. In what way?"

"We're in the image business. We have to be super-conscious of how we look to our clients. Our customers—wineries, banks, car dealers, doctor offices—are aware of their public image. Elise was a gifted artist, but she had some habits at odds with our office policies. She wore inappropriate clothing to the workplace. Very short skirts. Lingerie tops. And with the clients, she'd act out."

"Act out?"

"Make off-color jokes, flirt. When she was in one of her manic swings, we never knew what to expect."

"Did you talk to her about it?"

"Of course, but it was awkward for me…as a man and her boss. Usually, I had my admin speak to her. Anyway, my point is, I think she may have…come to the attention of men, and maybe that had something to do with what happened to her."

"What sort of men?" Frames crossed the room and sat next to Rivas. "Are we talking about one of your clients?"

"I don't know. I'm just speculating, trying to be helpful."

"Oh, great," Frames said, "*now* you're trying to be helpful."

Rivas took a photo from a file folder on his lap. "This is from Elise Durand's Facebook page. You know this man?"

Lerner looked at the photo without touching it. "No, I don't think I do."

"You're sure?" Rivas watched Lerner. It was almost over. Liars always give it up in the end. Just as one day Teresa would discover his dreams, just by looking into his eyes.

Lerner smiled tightly. "I just said so."

"We're going to take Elise's hard drive," Rivas said. "When we're finished here, you'll need to show us where it is."

"Is that really necessary? It has our client files. Don't you need a court order?"

"Do you want to go through that—with the publicity and all?"

"Publicity?" Lerner looked incredulous. "What publicity?"

"One thing," Frames said. "If we ask your admin if you were in Elise's cubicle this morning, what's she going to say?"

"I don't know. I may have gone there this morning. Why?"

"Because if you removed anything from Ms. Durand's hard drive, it would constitute obstruction of an investigation, which is a misdemeanor."

Lerner sank in his chair. "Shit, you guys are just going to keep fucking with me, aren't you?" He bit his lip and looked out the office window. "All right, look…that guy…the one in the Facebook photo, his name's Christopher Bennett. He's a client. He runs two dental offices, one here and another in Petaluma. We create print and TV campaigns for him. Elise did all the graphics. Apparently, Chris and Elise had a relationship. I didn't find out until…recently."

"A relationship?" Rivas asked.

"Whatever you call it. I don't know. I saw them in his car one time in the parking garage. They were…together…kissing. Sometimes Elise came back from lunch, and her clothes and hair were messed up. It was pretty clear what was going on. I should've addressed it, but there you are."

"Sounds like we need to talk to Dr. Bennett." Rivas stood to leave.

"I just want you to know that the reason I didn't say anything to you earlier is I'm sure Chris didn't have anything to do with this other…killing thing. He's a—"

"Dentist?" Frames said.

Lerner shook his head. "I was going to say family man."

Chapter Sixteen

(i)

Kate stood in the doorway to Mahler's office. She held out a wrapped sandwich. "Spiro's Greek Deli. The Number Seven. The Stroke Victim. Meat loaf and bacon on a soft roll, with purple onions, pepperoncini, whole-grain mustard. Extra salt. No goddamned lettuce. No frigging tomatoes. And no mother-fucking sprouts. Did I get that right?"

Mahler smiled. "How'd you get in here?"

Kate sat down in the chair that faced Mahler's desk. She put the sandwich on a pile of folders. "I bought a Number Three for Cindy in the lobby. She'll do anything for me, at least for the next twenty minutes."

She reached into a bag and took out a boxed salad. Her red-brown hair was longer than he remembered. With one hand, she pulled her hair away from her freckled face and looked at him. It was a gesture he had seen a thousand times.

"What?" she said. "Has it been that long?"

"A while."

"I'm the same girl, Eddie."

He nodded and looked down at his sandwich. He tore off the tape. "You hear what we got?"

"Whole city's heard what you got, Eddie. Even poorly paid attorneys like me. That's why I'm here. You forget to eat when you're on one of these things. Go on. You're allowed. I'll join you."

Mahler unwrapped the sandwich and took a bite. "Some things don't change," he said.

"Are we talking about me again?"

"Actually, I was thinking of the Number Seven."

Kate leaned forward. "How's the headache?"

"Is it that obvious?"

"Dark circles." Kate pointed under her own eyes. "Dead giveaway. Remember, we lived together for three years. Let me guess: a hundred milligrams of Imitrex and four hundred of ibuprofen every six hours, right?"

"More or less. Can we talk about something else?"

"Team doing okay?" Kate asked. "I hear you have two new ones. Steven Frames from the uniforms. Seems like an eager guy."

"We'll see. Long as he shoots the right people."

"And a young woman. Eden something."

"Somers. Yeah, she's smart."

"Martin says she's pretty."

"I guess."

"You guess?"

"She's just out of college, Katie. I'm her boss. You want to see my certificate in sexual harassment training? It's around here somewhere."

"You weren't that old when we were together."

"How about you? How's Roger? Still helping the one percent keep its money?"

"Roger's firm specializes in trusts and wills. It's what he does. You should talk to him sometime. He could help you do some planning."

"I don't think planning's where I need help."

"He's my husband, Eddie. He's not the enemy."

"If you say so."

"You always seem to forget." Kate frowned. "You're the one who left me. Not the other way around."

"I remember. I especially remember Sunday brunch. Shirred eggs with homemade salsa, sourdough toast."

"And two fingers of Alquimia tequila on ice."

"Good way to start the day."

Kate smiled. "As I recall, that's not the first thing we did to start the day."

Mahler smiled back. For an instant, his memory pictured Kate pulling away her hair. Her face, with its soft, brown freckles, close to his own, her eyes shut as she leaned forward to kiss him.

"Sometime," Kate said, "you're going to have to confront this thing and not make a joke about it."

"Let's not go there. Not right now."

"Why do you think your life's like this? Where do you think the migraines come from?"

"Did you show up to bring me lunch or give me a hard time?"

"It's not about *me*, Eddie," Kate said. "It never was. Your heart got broken two years ago, but not by me. I loved you. I always will. But you loved this work more than anything. That girl, the second one who was killed, she's the one who broke your heart. After her, you couldn't love this job anymore."

Mahler searched Kate's eyes. "Wow," he said quietly. "You *are* the same girl. Is that what you came to tell me?"

"I'm sorry. That was a lot all at once. It didn't come out right." Kate pushed at her salad with her fork.

They ate in silence.

"Why do you stay?" Kate asked. "Do you know? You're smarter than the people you work for, and you don't understand the ones who work for you."

"It doesn't feel finished. It's hard to leave when it's not finished."

"Oh, come on. It's never finished."

"Yeah, but it feels close sometimes."

"What do you want, Eddie?"

"What's that supposed to mean?"

"It's a simple question. My therapist says we're not grown-up until we can ask ourselves that question and honestly answer it."

"Your therapist?"

"Yeah, I'm seeing somebody. Don't change the subject. What do you want?"

"To catch the guy who did this girl."

"No. Apart from that, apart from the job. What do you *want*?"

"I have enough riddles in my life. I don't need another one."

"This is the important question. What do you want? And don't say something about getting rid of the designated hitter in the American League."

"I don't know. By the way, I don't want to get rid of the designated hitter. But, seriously, I don't know the answer. What can I tell you?"

Kate shook her head. "Did you really walk out of Truro's press conference?"

"I think so."

"Jesus, Eddie."

"The investigation's all that matters. We do it right, no one'll care about anything else."

"I know, and it'll be different this time. You'll get this guy."

"That's what Martin says. He doesn't think this one's Partridge."

"What do you think?"

"I can't talk about it."

Kate reached her hand across the desk to hold Mahler's. "Well, Eddie, you lead an unexamined life. But you're a detective at heart, and I'm glad I'm not the one you're after."

"Yeah," Mahler said. "Let's say that's true."

(ii)

(WEDNESDAY, 12:35 P.M.)

"The agony of the leaves." Tom Woodhouse poured steaming water into a porcelain pot. "That's what tea drinkers call the unfurling of dry tea." The retired detective smiled at Eden. They sat at a table on the deck behind his house.

"When I was on the job, I drank coffee," he said. "But after I retired, I tried tea. Now it's all I drink. Chinese black tea, called Keemun Mao Feng. Grows on the hillsides of the Anhui Province, between the Yellow Mountains and the Yangtze River."

He arranged a cup and saucer for Eden and one for himself.

Woodhouse noticed Eden looking at his hands. "Arthritis," he said. "More like claws than fingers, aren't they? Still work, though, mostly."

The old man poured milk into each cup and poured the tea on top of it. "Researchers at Loughborough University in the English Midlands found that putting the milk in first prevents the hot tea from caramelizing the milk fat and spoiling the tea's flavor. Only in England would someone actually study that."

He sat back in his chair and faced Eden. "But you didn't come here to listen to me talk about tea. I read the files you emailed—your analysis of the victims. You've made real progress. What do you need from me?"

"Anything you can tell me about Irwin Partridge. I understand you interviewed him more than anyone else."

"Yes, that was my sad privilege. He is not a likable man. Uneducated, incurious. But very quick mentally, the sort of intelligence that's mostly smart-ass. I'm sure he was, or is, capable of anything."

"You believed he killed Michelle Foss and Susan Hart?"

"No doubt, whatsoever. And from what you told me on the phone, that girl in Vallejo, Beth Hunter."

Eden looked at the neatly tended beds of white daisies and red mums bordering the yard. Some sense of beauty and order had survived Woodhouse's career as a homicide cop. "But we don't have any forensics that connect Partridge to the murders."

"No. He was careful, which probably means it wasn't his first time. He chose victims in circumstances where he knew he wouldn't be seen. I'd also guess he studied the setting and movements of people for days before the murders. Wore gloves, destroyed his clothes afterward. All that good stuff."

"According to the files, he was a suspect early on, for the first girl, Michelle Foss?"

"Yeah, he was in our records for an assault, where no charges were filed." Woodhouse drank from his cup. "But it put him on a short list of local guys to look at. At the time of the Foss murder, a woman riding a bike in the park said she saw a man standing on a trail that goes up to the water tanks where Foss was killed. Even ID'd Partridge in a photo array. But the witness was riding past him and didn't get a good look. And she got scared; I think she found out her ID was all we had, and she didn't want the responsibility."

"But you talked to Partridge?"

"I interrogated him." Woodhouse raised one finger. "What stood out for me was what he didn't say. Most guys in that situation tell you where they were at the time of the crime and deny their involvement. Partridge did neither until he was asked."

Eden picked up her cup and sipped the tea. "But you couldn't put him at the scene?" She hoped Woodhouse wouldn't interpret her questions as criticism.

"He was a delivery guy for an auto parts store. For some reason, the store didn't keep logs of his deliveries or where he was. We looked at the mileage on his car, but it was inconclusive."

"So not enough to hold him?"

Woodhouse shrugged. "No, but ultimately it wasn't our decision. It was the DA's call. Guy named Michael Nugent. At the end of his term. The year before, a case went south on him. So, for this thing, he told us he needed more evidence. Told us to go out and get something else. Of course, at the time, we didn't know the second killing would happen. Afterward, Nugent and the chief at that time, Frank Stone, hinted to their contacts in the press that the investigative team opposed holding Partridge after the first homicide. Unidentified source dropped Eddie's name. Said he choked."

"And in the second case, you had the shoe print on the victim's leg?"

"I thought it was worth something. The lawyers thought it was weak. It was partial and not a clear match to Partridge's boots."

Eden heard resignation in Woodhouse's voice. "Did you notice in the Foss and Hart murders, the cord was wrapped around their necks three and a half times?"

"Yeah. It's an odd pattern. Not a coincidence, I'd guess. You have any ideas about it?"

"I'm still working on it. You saw the cut on Susan Hart's lower back, the signature?"

"I did, although I don't think I ever knew what it meant. Didn't matter anyway. By then it was panic time. Nugent had us chasing our tails. We looked at Susan Hart's boyfriend, then a boy who lived on the street with the Foss girl. Next, it was a couple of locals with sexual assault charges. Then we had a gang shooting on the west side with a child victim. So that was the new big headline. Two years went by. Everyone forgot the girls in the park. Sometimes it happens like that."

"If we can tie Partridge to any of the signature killings," Eden said, "we might be able to link him to the others."

"What do we know about killers who use signatures?" Woodhouse seemed enlivened again.

"Extremely rare," Eden said. "One or two percent of all homicides."

"What else?"

"In their study of serial killings, the researchers Hawthorne and Weeks at the University of Chicago believe many signatures are—"

Woodhouse held up his hand and smiled. "Let's put aside the academics for one minute. I was raised a Roman Catholic. Served as an altar boy at Saint Anne's, down in the city. My church believes the killing of another human being is a sin. The malice of the sin is its violation of the supreme ownership of God over the lives of his creatures. Some killers, especially the deliberate ones, believe themselves to be God, and the ones who leave signatures believe it more than others. They sign their work like it was a creative act."

"It's an act of arrogance," Eden said.

"Yes, young lady, and that word *arrogance* is interesting, isn't it? Ninth-grade Religious Studies class. Fifty years ago, and I still remember it. Sister Anne-Marie taught us the Latin root—*rogare*, which means to ask or beg. *Rogation* is prayer. But *ar-ro-gance* is the inverse; it means to presume to not need prayer. What does that tell you? To not need prayer. That's the sort of killer we're looking for. But man, of course, is imperfect. He always makes a mistake, and that's where someone as smart as you comes in."

Eden stared at Woodhouse. He had the same intelligence as her FBI mentors. But he was gentler, too, and not possessed by the need to prove his indifference to the horror of the work. "But we still don't have any hard evidence."

"My late wife, Linda, was a spiritual person. Not a church-goer as such, but she prayed every morning before she started her day. After thirty-five years of police work, I found it difficult sometimes to believe in the grace of God. Linda had the faith, even after the chemotherapy. She told me once she believed the souls of homicide victims are at work to help cops like us to see what we need to know. You think that's possible?"

Eden blushed. "It doesn't feel like it today, Mr. Woodhouse. I guess I'm not sure where I'd go to find what they had to tell me."

"They come to you, Miss Somers. They come to you. According to Linda, we just need to have faith. You're still young. You can afford faith." Woodhouse looked at Eden. "But you've already seen something in another case, haven't you? Something dark, was it?"

Eden ignored the question and drank from her cup.

"As the newest member of Eddie's team, what do you think your contribution will be?" Woodhouse asked. "Each of us has a gift. What's your gift?"

"I'm not sure I have one. I was trained to look at evidence, that's all."

"That's a rare gift, believe me. You're different from the ones Eddie usually hires. When I see you, I think Eddie hasn't given up."

"I honestly don't know why Lieutenant Mahler hired me. He doesn't seem interested in my background."

"Oh, he's interested, all right. If he wasn't, he would have already reassigned you."

"He sure doesn't say much."

"The Susan Hart case did a number on Eddie. In this job, you see a good deal of loss, terrible things done to people, families who'll never be the same. But that case was different. Somewhere in there, I think Eddie forgot what his job was. Thought he was supposed to save people, not catch their killers."

Woodhouse held his cup close to his nose and smelled the tea. "But back to Partridge," he said after a moment. "My advice: follow where he's gone. Guys like him can't stop, once they start. Where's he gone the last three years?"

"He never left Santa Rosa."

"Sure, he's lived here, but where's he *gone*?"

Eden looked back at him. Then she folded her notebook and stood to leave.

"One other thing, Miss Somers," Woodhouse said. "I read your analysis of the ideal body type for all the victims. You realize you fit that, right? Indulge an old cop. Until this is over, keep your doors locked. House and car."

Eden smiled and realized too late he was serious.

He stared back. "Best to be safe, dear."

Chapter Seventeen

(i)

Frames stopped Rivas at the doorway of the interview room. "How do you want to do this? Maximization? Reid Technique?"

Rivas turned to face Frames. "How about we keep it simple? Craig Lerner said this guy was spending his lunch hour mussing up the victim's hair. Let's see where that ended up."

"No, really? Mahler gave me crap for the first Lerner interview. The second time, in Lerner's office, I was winging it. I didn't know the plan. I need to know the plan."

"What I said *is* the plan."

Frames raised both hands. "What is it with you guys and forethought? I'm just asking for some forethought. Is that such a terrible thing?"

As they entered the room, Christopher Bennett stood. He smoothed the front of his necktie and fastened the top button of his suit jacket. "I told the officer downstairs, if I'd known the young woman in the park was Ms. Durand, I'd have come in right away. I'm obviously happy to help." He smiled and sat down.

Rivas and Frames sat facing him across the table. "Dr. Bennett, it's standard procedure to record a conversation of this nature," Rivas said. "Do you understand?"

"Sure. Sure," Bennett said. "No problem."

Rivas switched on the recorder and noted the date, time, and the names of those present. "Before we start, do you understand that you're free to leave at any time?"

"Okay. Good to know."

"And, I need to ask if you'd like a lawyer present."

"Lawyer? Wow, that sounds serious. No, I don't think I need a lawyer. Not for what those guys charge. I honestly don't have all that much to say."

"All right. Let's start with how you knew Ms. Durand."

"Sure thing. Craig Lerner did ad buys for my dental practice for a few years. Last fall he suggested I refresh my website and Facebook pages for a bump in online traffic. We decided to shoot a couple videos about the innovative things I'm doing with dental implants. Anyway, Ms. Durand was the in-house artist on the project. She came up with the initial design for the home page and worked with the contractors."

Frames worried about his encounter with Rivas at the door. An instructor at the academy once said many older cops don't see themselves as teachers, and that anyone new to the job has to take the initiative to watch and learn. But how was he supposed to do that if he didn't know the plan? "So you met her at Mr. Lerner's company?" Frames asked.

"That's right."

"Where, exactly?"

"Where? You mean, in which room? In the conference room,

I guess. Or maybe in Craig's office. I don't remember. Is that important?"

"How many times?" Rivas asked.

"I really have no idea. I run a small business and take an active role in my advertising. So I'm, you know, always—"

"Did she ever come to your office?" Frames asked.

"My office? Why on earth would she do that? I told you, she just worked on the website design. From what I saw, she was a competent graphic designer. Most of my...contact...was with Craig."

"Did you go out to lunch with Ms. Durand?" Rivas asked.

Bennett shifted in his chair. "We may have. With Craig, of course. Working lunches, that sort of thing. I really don't understand what you want. Like I said, I didn't know her that well."

"Did you talk to Ms. Durand about things outside your ad campaign?"

"Small talk. Usual stuff. She seemed like a nice young woman. This terrible thing that's happened is—wait. I remember I talked to her one time about art. She showed me a few of her paintings. I'm no expert, but I thought they were pretty good."

Frames noticed how Rivas sat motionless and stared at Bennett. "Where'd that happen?" he asked.

"What do you mean? I have to say, these questions are odd. I don't really feel comfortable—"

"Did you have a relationship with Ms. Durand?"

"What?" Bennett said quickly. "What sort of question is that? No. God, no. Are you kidding? She was a young woman. I'm forty-two. I have a wife and children and a successful business practice. I'm an honest man."

"You were never intimate with her?"

"No, absolutely not."

"So you didn't meet her in your car in the parking garage across from Craig Lerner's office?" Rivas asked.

"I may have taken her to lunch a few times without Craig, if that's what you mean. And we probably took my car."

Frames studied Bennett's face as he had seen Rivas do. He noticed the tension around Bennett's eyes give way and a smile start to form. "So if you were seen on the parking garage's security camera having sex with Ms. Durand in your car, you're going to deny that?"

"Security camera? There's no—" Bennett sat up in his chair. "Okay. Hold on a second. This has now gone too far. It isn't right. You can't—I came in here to help you."

Bennett turned to Rivas. "Are you the one in charge? Can we turn that recorder thing off for one fucking minute? I have something to say."

Rivas looked back silently.

Bennett took a deep breath. "All right. But everything I say from now on has to be in confidence. This cannot be made public. You understand, it cannot be part of any…public record or whatever you people call it."

He tapped the table with the index finger of his right hand. "I did not do anything to hurt Elise. I swear to God. I could never hurt her."

"Was she going to tell your wife?" Rivas asked.

"No. It wasn't anything like that."

"What was it like?"

"We met in my car a few times and…made out. That's all it was. It was stupid and immature and a betrayal of my marriage."

Frames suddenly thought he understood Rivas's method: Keep your own body still. Watch the other guy's eyes and body language. Pay attention to each word. "You made out? What? Like teenagers?"

"Do I need to be graphic?"

"Did you have intercourse with the victim?"

"That's such a crude way to say it."

"Did you?"

Bennett looked at the tabletop. "Okay. Yes, but it wasn't anything serious. That's all I'm going to say."

"So Ms. Durand didn't think it was serious either?" Rivas asked.

"That's right."

"Did you argue with her?"

"Sometimes, sure. She was doing a lot of drugs. Oxy, some E. All sorts of stuff. I didn't think it was good for her."

Frames could hear a tone in Bennett's answer, explaining something obvious to the dumb Mexican. *Why do people always think cops are stupid?* Frames wondered. *Does their size make them seem less intelligent? Or, does the work look easy?* "When was the last time you and Ms. Durand were together?"

"A couple weeks ago. I don't remember exactly."

"We have the security camera tapes." Frames sighed. "We're going to find out."

"Last week. But for a few months now, we haven't been together as much. I think she was seeing another guy."

"Did she say who?" Rivas asked.

"No. I asked, but she wouldn't say."

"That must have pissed you off."

"A little, sure. She thought it was funny that I wanted to know. She made jokes about it."

Frames could hear Rivas coaxing Bennett, letting the guy throw himself over the edge. "But it wasn't funny to you, was it?" Frames said.

"I just wanted a straight answer, and the more I asked, the more games she played."

"Drove you crazy, didn't it? She was just a young girl."

"I was the one taking all the risks, with everything to lose."

"So last week was the first time you saw her in a while? What happened?"

"We talked. I said I wanted to see her. But she wouldn't... commit."

"Did things get a little physical?" Rivas asked. "You grabbed her, to get her attention?"

"No, I did not do that."

"She hit her head. It wasn't intentional. It just happened."

"No, I told you. I—did—not—hurt—Elise."

Something there, Frames thought. *Too much denial. How much more can we get from this guy before he asks for a lawyer?* "What kind of car do you drive?"

"What? A Lexus. Why?"

"How about your wife?"

"Lincoln Navigator. You haven't answered my question."

"You know anyone who owns a vintage Mercedes? Early sixties?"

"No."

"Where were you Monday evening?" Rivas asked.

"Monday? I was home. I had dinner with Lynn and the kids."

"All evening?"

"Yes."

That last bit was too quick, Frames thought. Bennett's eyes sought the safety of the wall behind them. "Your wife'll confirm that?" Frames asked.

"My wife? Is that really necessary?" Bennett tried Rivas but gave it up. "Okay. I went out later for...something."

"Something? What was it?"

"It's not important. I was gone for maybe an hour. I went out about ten and was back by eleven."

"Where'd you go?"

"It's not relevant...and you know what?" Bennett folded his

arms across his chest. "That's all I'm going to say. I want to speak to my attorney."

Frames watched Bennett sitting stiffly in his chair, as if bracing himself against an approaching wave.

Rivas pushed himself up and stood to face Bennett. "Tell your attorney to meet you here. And tell him or her we're seeking warrants to search your car, your office, and your home. You understand?"

"My home?" Bennett looked stricken. "Come on, guys. Between us, can you give me a little latitude here? Can I at least talk to my wife first?"

Rivas stared at Bennett and waited. "I need you to answer for the recording."

Bennett sat back in his chair. "Yes," he said softly.

(ii)

(WEDNESDAY, 3:00 P.M.)

They were in Thackrey's home in Dry Creek Valley, a half hour north of Santa Rosa. Thackrey sat in a leather chair, facing an open French door that looked out to the back lawn. He threw a tennis ball to the two dogs waiting on the lawn. "She was scared Monday night. Elise...she was scared."

Russell squatted on the floor in the middle of the living room, rubbing a section of the floor with a damp rag. "For good reason, as it turned out."

"When I picked her up after work, she argued about getting into the car. She knew something was up. She asked where you boys were, didn't want to be alone with me. She said, 'Please, Benny, can we be together some other time? I need to go home.' But I had some OxyContin, and I said she could have it if she got in the car."

"Anyone see you?"

Thackrey shrugged. "Doubt it. Nothing to see. Just a guy giving his girl a ride. By the way, what's that doing to the wood grain?"

"It's not recommended for hardwoods, if that's what you mean."

"Smells like hell."

"Oxygen bleach. Only thing that makes blood traces invisible even if the police use luminol. I cleaned the blood off the coffee table. Is that where she cut her head?"

"Hmmm. Made an awful sound."

"The problem is cleaning out the seams between the wood planks. If the cops remove the planks, they'll find traces. You're lucky the area wasn't larger."

"Yeah, lucky." The larger of the two mastiffs ran inside with the tennis ball. Thackrey threw it again.

"Where'd you pick her up, office or home?" Russell asked.

"Office. But out on the street, not in the parking garage. The garage has a security camera."

Victor joined the others, a large plastic trash bag in one hand. "It would help if we knew exactly where she was in here Monday night. I found her stuff in the guest bedroom and bathroom."

"She was everywhere," Thackrey said. "She was always everywhere. But the drugs made it particularly bad Monday night."

The other dog ran through the open door with the ball in its mouth and slid into Victor, who kicked the dog away with his foot. "Can't you keep these things outside?"

Thackrey took the ball and threw it out to the lawn again.

"The Oxy didn't calm her down?" Russell asked.

"She was too impatient to wait for it. In the car on the way home, I saw her swallow something else. She was supposed to be taking Depakote, but when she couldn't find it, she grabbed whatever was in the bottom of her purse."

Victor knotted the top of the plastic trash bag. "Speaking of medications, Ben, how're you and your Adderall getting along? Your pupils dilate any more, you'll qualify as an anime character."

Russell laughed. "Yeah, buddy, you know your right leg hasn't stopped twitching for the last twenty minutes? And I heard you throw up in the john this morning."

Thackrey turned to face the other two men.

Victor looked back at him. "You haven't slept since what? Sunday? You can't talk straight. You've been throwing that stupid ball for an hour. With that gun stuffed in your waistband, you're going to shoot your nuts off."

"You really think it's a good idea to be a junkie when the cops get here?" Russell asked. "Dial it back, Ben. It's for your own good."

Thackrey turned away and lobbed the ball to the dogs on the lawn. "Nothing's for my own good. Could you just finish cleaning up here?"

Victor shook out an empty trash bag. "Okay. What'd you do with the clothes you were wearing that night?"

"Already dumped. Trash pickup was yesterday. They're in the county landfill."

"Your shoes?"

"Jesus, yes. The shoes. Pair of thousand-dollar Johnston & Murphys. Speaking of clothes, what's that thing you're wearing, Victor?"

Victor raised his arms. "Called a kurta. Traditional Indian shirt. Very comfortable. Just the thing to wear when cleaning up after a murder."

"Very metrosexual."

"By the way, I checked the keystroke logger a few minutes ago. The cops identified the body as Elise. And they've talked to Craig Lerner, who knows you."

"Never met him," Thackrey said. The big mastiff returned the tennis ball to him.

"Doesn't matter. He knows you and will get around to mentioning it. They've also interviewed your girl's roommates and searched her apartment."

"Well, God knows what the cops'll find, but I was never there."

"You don't think Elise ever told her roommates about you? We finish here, Russ and I are getting on a plane."

"Where're you going?"

"Thailand. Place called Ko Lanta. It's an island off the southern coast."

"Let's get back to Monday night. Did you stop anywhere on the way home that night?" Russell asked.

"Straight home. When we got here, I put on some Sinatra and cooked dinner. That song 'I've Got the World on a String' came on, and I made her dance with me in the kitchen. She was still scared. She freaked out at first, didn't want me to touch her. Something about a dream she had. But I held her, and we danced. All around the kitchen. I taught her a couple swing steps, and I sang to her."

"Sounds magical." Victor rolled his eyes. "Can we dig the rounds from your gun out of the sheetrock in the living room?"

"Knock yourselves out. Not sure what difference it makes. I told you, Elise fired the gun, not me."

"Let's not give the cops too many story lines."

"Dancing with her, I remember thinking how smart she was. That webpage she did for DivingBell was like a lesson in color theory. The blue and the orange together, opposites on the color wheel, make the images pop. Everyone who sees the site, that's the first thing they notice."

"What about traces of her in your car?" Russell asked.

"Steam cleaned this morning. Nothing left but what I remember."

Thackrey leaned back in his chair. "That's what's so maddening. She could be wonderful. One night after Christmas, we had dinner with friends. Went to an Italian restaurant called Acquerello off Van Ness in the city. She entertained us for an hour. Told a story about how the English artist Turner added beeswax or something to his paints. Then she talked about a letter that Keats wrote. She knew things like that. When she was on, she was...glorious. So different from Reggie."

"Didn't save her from ending up like Reggie, though, did it?" Victor said.

Thackrey fired the tennis ball at Victor, who missed catching it and was nearly knocked over as the mastiff slammed into his legs to retrieve the toy.

When the dog returned to his side, Thackrey rubbed the top of its head. "But Elise was crazy, too. Crazy and messy. Nothing would change that—she was always going to be crazy. And we were wrapped up with each other, entangled, and I didn't know how to separate us. No matter what I did, we kept...being together."

Thackrey looked out the open door. "Odd, isn't it?" he said. "All the poetic wisdom in the world about falling in love, one soul finding another, but no poetry to help us know how to remove someone from our lives."

Chapter Eighteen

(i)

Coyle parked at an apartment building on the city's west side—the address for Jessica Alvarez, a former roommate of Elise Durand.

Alvarez, a woman in her twenties, answered the door. She showed Coyle through a corridor to a bright, uncluttered living room. The apartment smelled of new paint and carpets. They sat on opposite sides of a sofa.

"I'm still in shock," Alvarez said. She had designer glasses and wore a cotton plaid shirt and jeans. "I've never known someone who was murdered. It's...I don't know...scary."

Coyle saw wariness in the woman's eyes. He'd seen the look before and knew that he had brought this thing, this threat, into the room with him, almost like he was coated with a stain. His face and clothes now embodied for Alvarez another world from her own, a nighttime place she locked her door against—a dirty, ugly world where a girl's body was found in a park.

He nodded, as if he agreed that the murder of her friend was scary, as if he remembered his own innocence. He took a notebook and pen from his pocket. "We're hoping you can help us. Anything you can tell us about the victim."

"Elise and I were friends. Good friends. I think I was the only one allowed to call her Elise. She was trying to make everyone else call her Lisa."

"You shared a house for a while?"

"For about a year. I moved out to be with Greg. We lived at his old place before we found this apartment. But Elise stayed in touch. We were very different, and she had her problems. She was my wild friend. I guess I got to be a little wild by knowing her."

"What kind of problems?"

"Bipolar disorder. Huge highs, where she was off-the-wall manic. Then terrible depressions, where she'd cut herself. I picked her up at the ER once after she accidentally hit an artery in her ankle and almost bled out. That was, like, a year ago. I think lately she was trying to get a handle on that whole thing."

"How?"

"Medication, mostly, and therapy. She was seeing a psychiatrist named Bittner. She talked about that."

Coyle made a note.

"With Elise, it all went back to her dad. He was French. A classical musician, but I got the feeling he never really made it. She said he gave her the name Elise, after the Beethoven music. You know, the song 'Für Elise,' that kids play when they're learning piano? She said when she was little, the name made her special, but later she hated having to explain it. Anyway, when she was three, her father left the family. Like, packed up and went back to France or something."

"Was she in touch with him?"

"Not much. I think he wrote letters. She adored him, even though it seemed one-sided. She was like some of my other friends with divorced parents. After her father was gone, Elise got to make up who he was. He sent her books of poetry. When she talked to me about him, the poems got all mixed up with her father. She thought he wrote them, and she was always trying to understand what the poems meant so she could understand her father and why he left. She never got over his leaving. She was still a little three-year-old girl whose father left her behind. She was just alone and...lost."

Tears suddenly rolled down Alvarez's cheeks, and she wiped at them with the palms of her hands. She looked away from Coyle. Then something shuddered through her, and she bent over and wept with deep, heaving breaths.

Coyle leaned toward her but stopped. He had been taught a single, unalterable consolation: *I'm sorry for your loss.* The sentiment always sounded to Coyle like something tested by attorneys to be safe from misunderstanding or repercussion. No longer capable of imbuing it with sincerity, he had grown to hate the expression. But he also knew the dangers of touching a young woman alone in her apartment. He said, "I'm sorry... this happened."

The words came out in a whisper. He wasn't sure she heard him. He was no good at reassurance. He was the computer guy, too small and thin to represent any kind of protection.

After a while, Alvarez calmed. She sat up straight and ran fingertips across her wet cheeks. "I'm sorry about that. You're just doing your job. You must hate all...this."

Coyle shook his head. "Please take your time."

Alvarez breathed in deeply. "I'm ready."

"You were talking about poetry. We found a line of a poem written on Ms. Durand's leg."

Alvarez smiled. "She was always doing that. On her arm or leg. Or she repeated a line of poetry over and over. Some bit that meant something to her. There was one special line by a poet named Frank somebody: 'the catastrophe of my personality.' I'll never forget the way she said it. She was so…vulnerable, always close to falling apart."

"When's the last time you saw her?"

"About a week ago, but I spoke to her over the weekend. Sunday, I think."

"How was she?"

"She was excited about some paintings she finished."

"Did she talk about anyone she was spending time with?"

"Guys? With Elise, there were always guys. She tried to make herself available to men, and then when she got them, she was already looking at the next guy. Sometimes she became a caricature of the sexy girl because she didn't really know what it meant. She had this thing where she wore short skirts and low tops because she thought guys liked that look. But afterwards, after another date with another lame guy, she'd complain to me about how stupid men are." Alvarez smiled. "She told me once, even the smart ones are stupid."

"Was there one guy in particular?"

"I never met any of them, except this biker kid a long time ago. For the last six months, she was with an older man. He was married, which seemed like a total disaster. And lately she told me about this new guy. I think she was doing some free-lance work for him. She said he was really smart and had a lot of money. He made a fortune in computers or something, and now he doesn't have to work anymore. He has this big house with a bunch of rooms. And a couple of guys were always with him."

"Did you ever meet him?"

"No. I saw his car once when he picked up Elise at a bar downtown. It was this new silver thing. I don't know what kind."

"Do you remember the body type—SUV, sedan?"

"Sedan, four-door."

"And you didn't see the guy's face?"

"No, it was too dark."

"Do you know where he lives?"

"In the country somewhere. Must not be too far, because Elise would stay overnight and go to work."

"You don't know his name?"

"I don't think she said."

"How about the two guys who were always with him? Did she ever describe them?"

Alvarez shook her head.

Coyle watched her. He wondered at this woman with her neat clothes, new apartment, and self-sufficiency. How did she have a friendship with Elise Durand, a woman struggling to find her ground, who gave Alvarez a window into an unrestrained life—and a murder? "Do you know the married guy's name?"

"She called him Chris. Told me she was tired of being with a guy who wouldn't take her out in public. And she said he'd done this thing to her, and it was the last straw."

"What thing?"

"She didn't say. But I think he hit her. Last Tuesday I bumped into her at a bar downtown. She had something on her sweater, and I asked her what it was. She wouldn't say, but it looked like blood. It freaked me out. I was like, 'Is that blood?' She wouldn't answer me. She just laughed."

"You're sure it was Tuesday?"

"Yeah, Greg had to work, so I met up with Elise."

"Which bar?"

"Becker's. The other place she hung out a lot was the 1285 Club."

"Do you remember anything else she said in your last phone call? Any plans she had? Anything new in her life?"

"She told me this thing about a street buy."

"A buy? Drugs?"

"Yeah. Elise always did pills. Downers mostly, and some rave stuff—DMAA, that whole scene. Anyway, she starts talking about this buy she and her friends made. I was like...*whoa*. I mean, it sounded super sketchy."

"Did she say who her friends were?"

"No. I think she was protecting them."

Coyle gave Alvarez his honest face. "If you know, you can tell me. We don't care about the buy. But if it had anything to do with the murder, we want to know."

Alvarez looked back. "Honestly, I don't know."

"Was it local?"

"I don't know. But when you asked about anything new in her life, I thought of that right away."

"Did Elise happen to say where she was going or who she was going to be with Monday night?"

"Monday? No, I don't think so. Wait, I remember something else. She said she was breaking up with someone and was worried about how he'd take it."

"Was it Chris or someone else?"

"I don't know. She just said he was going to be pissed."

Coyle stood to leave.

Alvarez wiped her eyes. "I hope you get whoever this is. You probably see these things a lot. But Elise never hurt anyone. She didn't deserve this."

They never do, Coyle thought.

(ii)

Frames held up his phone for the rest of the VCI room. "This Christopher Bennett motherfuck is our guy. Just got a message. The evidence techs searched his car and found traces of blood on the front seat. Someone tried to wash it off but couldn't get it all out of the seams."

Coyle watched Frames waving the phone. "Do we know it's the victim's blood?"

"For chrissakes, man, they just got the car. But I fucking guarantee it's hers. It's like that scene in *Pulp Fiction*, you know, where Jules and Vincent have to clean the car because Vincent shot the guy in the back seat."

"What kind of car does Bennett have?"

"Lexus ES. White exterior. Leather seats and bamboo trim on the dash. Man, I love it when it's a guy with a car like that."

"So you figure Bennett strangles the victim in the front seat of his car, somehow cuts the back of her head, wraps the body in a blanket, drives to the park, and carries the body to the bench?"

"Why not? Guy's a dentist. They have strong fingers. Natural stranglers."

"But why's he do all that?" Rivas asked. "Why go all the way to the park? Take some balls to drive through town with a dead woman sitting next to you."

"Techs find any blood in the trunk?" Coyle asked.

Frames sighed. "I don't know. I told you they just started searching."

"What about the old, dark-colored Mercedes in the surveillance footage and the guy in the hoodie?"

"Maybe he had a friend and switched cars. I don't know."

Rivas leaned back in his chair. "Always risky involving a second person, and now you're moving the body twice."

"Maybe he knew about the surveillance camera," Frames said. "Didn't want his car seen."

"Nobody knows about the surveillance camera," Coyle said.

Frames looked back and forth at the other two. "But Alvarez said Elise Durand was afraid of breaking up with someone. This has to be the guy."

Coyle shrugged. "We don't know that."

"What? So now you think she's breaking up with two guys in one week?"

"Even if it's the victim's blood, we don't know it got there Monday night. Alvarez told me she saw blood on Elise Durand's sweater a week earlier, last Tuesday."

Frames turned to Mahler. "Help me out here, Eddie. Aren't we making this too complicated?"

Mahler, who had been leaning against his spot on the squad-room wall, straightened and moved to the center of the room. "Bennett has an hour unaccounted for Monday evening. Ten to eleven. When you asked him what it was, he called his lawyer."

"So, Sherlock, is an hour enough?" Coyle aimed the question at Frames. "Is it possible to meet up with the hoodie guy, switch the body, drive to the park, and get back home to kiss the wife goodnight?"

Frames shrugged. "Everything goes right, it's not impossible."

"What'd his wife say?" Mahler asked.

Rivas looked at his notepad. "Confirms he was gone at that time. Doesn't know where."

"Woman's definitely going through some changes," Frames said. "We start asking questions about her husband's affair, which, of course, is news to her. And then we get to the part about the victim, and she freaked. Kids are home from school in the next room. In three minutes, she's rethinking her life. Whole dentist-wife-thing down the toilet."

"We asked if she had a red blanket," Rivas inserted.

Frames waved his arms. "This insults her. Goes off on a riff about color schemes. A dead body is one thing, but a red blanket in her house—"

"I'll talk to Bennett once his lawyer gets here," Mahler said. "What else do we have?"

"We've got Arturo Peña's statement to the DA." Rivas read from the screen of his laptop. "In exchange for this information, the DA agreed to release Peña's cousin and give Peña immunity on the drug-dealing evidence that was part of his testimony. Peña says he was approached on Saturday night by four individuals who wanted to score some speed. Tall white man, an Asian, a dark-skinned male, and a white female. All well dressed. The female's height, weight, and hair color match our victim's. They drove up in a silver Jaguar sedan. The white guy was in charge. Peña described him as *gallito*, cocky. Had a semiautomatic in his belt that he made sure to show Peña. Bought five grams, paid with hundreds. As they leave, Peña heard one of them call the woman Elise."

"That matches what Alvarez told me about a drug buy," Coyle said. "And it also sounds like one of them might be the new boyfriend who drives a silver car and lives in the country."

"If these three are involved," Mahler said, "they could be the 'little men' our witness, Donald Michael Lee, saw. If one's Asian, he could've used the Cantonese word, *faideela*, that Lee heard."

Frames held up one hand. "Okay. A minute ago, you guys are jerking me around about the old Mercedes? How'd these guys get from a silver Jag to a 1960 Mercedes?"

"The uniforms are still processing the DMV search for the Mercedes owner," Coyle said. "Lot of phone calls."

Rivas went to the whiteboard. Across the top, the countdown to another possible homicide now said thirty-one hours. Rivas pointed to a timeline written in marker. "Here's what we know. According to Alvarez, last Tuesday, Elise Durand meets her at Becker's downtown and has something that looks like blood on her sweater. On Saturday night, our victim is with three men making a drug buy. According to the roommates, on Sunday night, she's home.

"Monday morning she drives to work. Security camera in the parking garage shows her arriving at 8:53 a.m. Her boss, Craig Lerner, and the admin confirm she's in the office all day. Lobby camera shows her leaving the building about noon and returning ten minutes later with some takeout. Admin says no one visits her all day, but she does receive phone calls. We're still processing calls received on the office line, but she could also have taken calls on her cell, which we never found. Martin's also going to go through her office hard drive to look for emails. Then at 5:40 p.m., the office lobby camera shows her leaving the building."

"So she leaves out the front door, not to the parking garage to her own car?" Mahler asked.

Rivas nodded. "That's right. Someone picked her up or she walked downtown. In any case, she left her car in the garage."

Coyle looked at his laptop. "Trish says the bruising around the cut on the back of the victim's head indicates that wound was made not by a weapon but by striking a sharp surface, probably post-mortem, after she was strangled. By the way, she also says the cause of death was compression of the larynx and fracturing of the hyoid bone by manual strangulation. The area and angle of the attack indicate it was administered from the front of the victim. No evidence of ligature marks, indicating no use of a rope or cord." Coyle looked up at Mahler. "So the cause of death is different from the girls two years ago."

Mahler looked back at Coyle for a moment. Then he walked across the room and leaned against the far wall. "Daniel, check to see if the victim's car has been towed to our garage. Martin, when you go through the victim's hard drives, look for anything on this boyfriend with the silver Jaguar. If she's doing freelance work for him, there's bound to be files with a name."

Mahler turned to leave and then called back for Frames. "Come on, hot shot. Let's see if your favorite suspect has a lawyer."

Chapter Nineteen

(i)

Eden stood in front of the apartment door as a woman opened it just wide enough to peer out.

"Detective Somers, Santa Rosa Police Department." Eden held up her badge. "Does Irwin Partridge live here?"

The woman gripped the door. "This is Win's place, but he's not here right now." She was short, with unevenly bleached hair. A thin scar traced a line above her left eyebrow.

Eden nodded. "What's your name?"

"Lorin Albright. I'm his girlfriend. What do you want?"

"Just routine. May I ask you a few questions about Mr. Partridge?"

"You have any papers that let you come in here if I don't want you to?"

"Papers? You mean a warrant? No, I'm not here to search your house."

"I guess it's okay." Albright let the door swing open. She turned and walked back into the apartment.

Eden followed her, entering the living room, a dark space with curtained windows and a stained brown carpet. A TV stood on a pedestal table at one end, playing an episode of *Law & Order*. Arranged around the TV were a high-backed sofa, two mismatched chairs, and a coffee table. The room was warm and smelled of mildew.

Albright sat on the sofa and picked up an already burning cigarette from an ashtray. She inhaled deeply, blowing smoke toward the ceiling. "Win's coming home soon. And just so you know, he doesn't like the police. He told me that. It would be real good if you weren't here when he gets home."

Eden made a space for herself on one of the chairs by pushing aside a pile of clothes. She took a pad from her jacket pocket. "I understand. Was Mr. Partridge home on Monday evening?"

"Most nights he goes out to drink. I watch the TV, and he doesn't like the TV."

"So on Monday evening, he wasn't at home? He was out... drinking?"

"I don't remember exactly, but I guess he was. That's what he usually does."

"And you weren't with him?"

Albright took another long draw on her cigarette. She blew out the smoke. "No. Mondays, there's the *Idol* program I like to see."

Eden wrote on her pad.

"What'd you just write? Are you writing what I say?"

"Just taking notes."

Eden wondered at the apartment's ordinariness. The sofa was covered in a print of faded dahlias. The wall behind the sofa held a framed winter landscape and a clock with a painted rooster. *Was this the house of a serial killer? What did she expect? Body parts on the bookshelf?* "When Mr. Partridge goes out, does he go by himself or with a friend?"

"Alone, I guess. He never says. I don't care for it myself. I worked at a bar for a while and saw enough of those people. On Fridays, Win and me go to Applebee's. The other nights I have my programs."

"Do you remember what time Mr. Partridge returned Monday evening?"

"I don't know. We don't keep track like that."

"Were you still awake when he returned?"

Albright drew on her cigarette and shrugged. "I think I was. I was watching the news, so it must've been around eleven."

"You're sure of that?"

"Pretty sure. What's this about anyway?"

Loud voices suddenly erupted on the TV, and both women turned to watch. Briscoe and Green were questioning a teenage suspect on a street corner. Green shoved the suspect against a wall, and Briscoe tried to restrain his partner.

Eden looked back at Albright. "It's important we understand where Mr. Partridge was that night."

"Are you trying to say he did something?" Albright jabbed her cigarette into the bottom of the ashtray. "Lady, you really ought to get out of here before he comes through that door. He'll be real mad at me just for letting you in."

Hearing the other woman's suspicion, Eden thought of her own mother. Madeline Somers of Ridgefield, Connecticut, lived under one guiding principle of upper-middle-class manners—other people's private lives are their own affair. Here was her oldest daughter poking into a couple's life. "Did Mr. Partridge say anything when he came home Monday night?"

"He said he saw the Giants game at the bar."

"What was his mood like?"

"His mood? How the hell should I know? You're just like Win said. He told me law enforcement has it out for him. They're always after him for something."

"How long have you known Mr. Partridge?"

"A long time. Twelve years or so. Win's an honest man. He has a job and works hard. He made a mistake years ago, is all. He told me all about it."

Eden looked at a poster on the living room's other long wall. It was a colorful, ornate print of a man sitting cross-legged, hands in his lap. "That's an unusual picture," Eden said.

Albright turned to look. "Creepy, if you ask me. But it's kind of a big deal for Win. Something called Kundalini. When Win got out of prison, a friend started him on it. Gives him power, Win says."

Eden wrote on her pad.

"Now what're you writing?"

"Just some notes."

"Listen, Detective whatever you are, I wouldn't be here asking all these questions and writing stuff when Win comes home. I already told you he doesn't like you cops. It's just the way he is." Albright walked to the door and opened it.

Eden stood. "I notice, Ms. Albright, you have an unusual accent, not like the other Californians I've met. May I ask where you're from?"

"Where I'm from? I live here."

"I mean originally. Where'd you grow up?"

For the first time, Albright smiled. "Oh, my family's from Fresno. That's where I used to live. My mom and grandma are still there, on Arden Drive. They grew up in Oklahoma, so that's why I talk like this, I guess. I go over to Fresno when I can. Holidays, things like that."

"Fresno? That's in the Central Valley, isn't it?" Eden stepped to the doorway and crossed under the threshold. Suddenly she remembered Tom Woodhouse's advice to follow where Partridge had gone. She struggled to calm herself. She smiled at Albright. "That sounds nice. Does Mr. Partridge go with you?"

"Win? Oh, sure. He loves it. Sometimes we go for a whole week."

"Really? When was the last time you and Mr. Partridge were there?"

Albright's smile disappeared. "I'm not saying anything else." She stepped back and slammed the door.

(ii)

(WEDNESDAY, 6:12 P.M.)

"My client would like to clarify his earlier statements," the lawyer said, addressing Mahler and ignoring Frames. A business card, slid halfway across the table, identified the lawyer as Thomas P. Stricker. Under Stricker's name, the card read "All Felonies and Misdemeanors. Over 20 Years of Aggressive Criminal Defense."

Mahler read the card without picking it up. He looked across the table. Christopher Bennett straightened his posture and ran his open palms down the front of a wool suit jacket. He imagined the man at the end of each day exchanging his starched white lab coat for a jacket. The two sides to Bennett's life: the clean, exacting efficiency of his practice and the indulgent leisure it afforded him.

Mahler had faced dozens of men like Bennett, and he could see in the man's eyes that the dentist's ordinary life had been flipped upside down. The confidence with which he spoke to his patients, advising of them of crowns and implants, was shaken. The picture of himself as husband and father had been readjusted. But Mahler saw something else, too. Unlike other men, who by now were recalibrating how to break the fall to the bottom, Bennett had something about him that looked frayed and lost.

Mahler turned on the recorder, identified everyone present, and noted the time. He opened a file folder in front of him with a transcript of Bennett's earlier interview. "What clarifications would your client like to make?"

Bennett took a deep breath and let it out. "I was in a relationship with Elise Durand. For the last six months, I saw her several times a week. Sometimes in my car and sometimes in a room at the Hyatt. We were…intimate. We had sex."

"How was that going?"

"How was it *going*?" Bennett shook his head in disbelief. "I was in love with her. Flat out. Like a kid. I told her. I told her I'd leave Lynn and marry her."

"But you didn't do that."

"I didn't know how. I didn't know where to begin."

"How did Ms. Durand respond?"

"She was all over the place. Up one day, down the next. She wanted to get married, then she didn't. She started asking for things. First a car. Lately, it was a house. Jesus, I offered to cosign a note for a condo."

Frames understood the flatness in Mahler's tone. If Rivas had been the teacher in the interrogation four hours before, Mahler was the Zen master. Mahler's questions were so plain and quiet they left all the air in the room for Bennett to fill. Each word was like a gentle hand at the suspect's back, urging him forward. Frames now pitched his voice in imitation. "But you didn't, right? What happened?"

"Last week she said she wanted to end it. Stop seeing each

other. I think she had another guy. Some man younger, richer. She didn't say that, but I could—"

"When last week did she tell you this?" Frames couldn't believe how much he sounded like Mahler.

"I don't know. Tuesday?"

"So it wasn't this Monday, two days ago?"

"No. I didn't see her Monday. I told you before." Bennett's shoulders fell. "Why do you people keep asking the same questions? You have the answers in front of you."

"What happened in your car?"

"I told you. We met there sometimes."

Mahler turned a page in the file. "We found blood on the front seat."

"Blood? That's not possible."

"Hold on, Chris," Stricker said.

Mahler closed the file and let twenty seconds go by. He could see the thing about the blood had surprised Bennett. The guy probably put some effort into cleaning the car seat, figured he had it whipped. Mahler saw no reason to tell Bennett forensics hadn't confirmed the blood was the victim's. Bennett just needed a few seconds to realize he wasn't getting out of this room like he thought he was. Mahler felt a weariness at the testimony he knew was to come.

"Dr. Bennett," Mahler said, "Elise Durand was murdered. We're investigating a homicide. Whatever you're trying to spare yourself you can forget. It's too late. The lies you've told your wife and yourself for the past six months are in the past. All I care about now is what happened. Your attorney here—"

"I hit her." Bennett blinked, surprised at his own words.

"Chris, listen to me," Stricker said.

"You hit Ms. Durand?" Mahler asked.

"Yeah. I didn't mean to. We were arguing, and she slapped

me. Hard. I wasn't expecting it, and before I knew it, I slapped her back. A slap, not a punch, but I hit her nose and it started bleeding. The blood got all over both of us. It was a mess." He looked at Mahler and, seeing no sympathy, turned to Frames. "I mean, my God, I've never struck anyone in my life."

Frames held his look. In the dynamic of the moment, he was the good guy, Bennett's friend. "It happens. What'd you do after that?"

"We stopped the bleeding, and we both calmed down. But she said she wouldn't see me anymore. She said it was over, done."

"*Did* you see her again?"

"No, I—"

"From last Tuesday to this Monday, you didn't see her?"

"I tried. I called. I went to Lerner's office, but she wouldn't see me."

Mahler leaned back in his chair. "Until Monday night."

"Until Monday night? No, Jesus, how many times—" Bennett closed his eyes.

"Dr. Bennett, we checked your phone. You called Elise Durand seven times Monday night." Mahler opened the file in front of him. "You also gave us a statement earlier. Concerning your whereabouts on Monday evening, you said, quote, 'I went out later for something. I was gone for maybe an hour. I went about ten and was back by eleven.' Your wife's confirmed this."

Stricker put his arm in front of Bennett. "I need to advise you, Chris. This is—"

"My wife? What'd Lynn say?" Bennett waved away the lawyer's arm. "What'd she say about Monday?" His voice was breathless.

"Lieutenant Mahler," Stricker said, "I'd like to request a moment alone with my client."

Mahler ignored the lawyer and addressed Bennett. "Did you see Elise Durand Monday night?"

"I repeat," Stricker said. "For the recording, Thomas Stricker, representing Christopher Bennett, requests—"

"I went to her house," Bennett said quickly. "I parked out front. I don't think she was there. Her car wasn't on the street where it usually is. I just sat there."

Frames waited a beat. "You didn't see her?"

Bennett looked down at the tabletop. "No. The lights were on, but I never went to the door."

"You were in your car the whole time?"

"All kinds of things went through my head. I was out of my mind. You can't imagine." He ran his fingertips over the table's surface, as if searching for something. Then he looked up. "Have any of you been in love with a woman? I mean, so, so in love? I thought about the color of her eyes, the way her hair smelled after a shower. And I couldn't stand it, couldn't stand her leaving me. I thought...I wanted to make her stop, to do something so she'd never go away. I wanted...I wanted—"

Mahler waited for Bennett's eyes to focus on him. "To kill her?"

"Yes...No. I don't know. But I didn't. I swear to God, I didn't. I did not kill her. You can give me a lie detector test. I left. I drove home." Bennett licked his dry lips. "It was late. Lynn can tell you. She was in bed, and I woke her up. I made love to her. I guess I was rough. Is that what she said? She yelled at me to stop, and I didn't. Suddenly, I heard her screaming...as loud as if—"

This time, Stricker reached out and held his client's forearm.

Bennett looked up, pleading with Mahler. "Can I see Elise? I never got to see her. Just for a minute? Ten seconds? I promise I won't touch her."

Mahler met Bennett's eyes without answering. Then he

announced for the recording that the interview had ended. He nodded at Frames, and as the two men left the room, Mahler looked back. Stricker had his arm around Bennett's shoulder and was leaning close to whisper.

Chapter Twenty

(i)

Mahler sat in a leather chair and watched Dr. Jeffrey Bittner slowly roll a black pen between his fingers. The doctor's office was a dark, high-ceilinged room on the second floor of a downtown Victorian.

"I don't know what I can tell you," Bittner said, "other than to confirm that Elise Durand was a patient in my psychiatric practice for some time."

Bittner was middle-aged, with gray hair and a weighed-down look. The bags under his eyes and the paunch falling over his waistline suggested that he was subject to more than the usual gravity.

Mahler shrugged. "I understand, but since we're in the middle of a homicide investigation, I'd appreciate anything you can tell me."

Bittner looked at his pen. "You know, of course, that by

California state law, patient confidentiality extends post-mortem. Besides, I'm not sure how information about the victim is going to help you identify the person responsible for her death."

"We're following a number of lines of investigation, and there's a chance she wasn't just in the wrong place at the wrong time, that her murder was...more deliberate. Anything you can tell me about her state of mind or who she might have spent time with would be useful."

Bittner looked thoughtful. "Of all my patients, Elise worked the hardest to heal herself. For her sake, I'd like to help you. Maybe I can talk in a general way. Are you familiar with bipolar spectrum disorder, or BSD?"

Mahler nodded. "Is that what used to be called manic depression?"

"It's now thought that the disorder involves more than two alternating conditions. Patients may suffer more symptoms of mania than depression, or vice versa, or may experience other psychotic behaviors between episodes. One subset of BSD is called Bipolar I, which involves one or more episodes of mania and one or more episodes of depression. Let's imagine an individual with this condition."

Bittner waited to see Mahler's look of assent. "The condition typically arises in adolescence. The manic episodes usually start just as feeling pumped up or having racing thoughts, then develop into all-out mania with impulsive behaviors and frenetic activity. Sometimes hallucinations. These periods are replaced by depressive intervals in which the individual loses appetite, is unable to sleep, and has thoughts of suicide. But it's not a simple back-and-forth. Manic episodes can last for two minutes or a week, and the individual can experience a dozen different types of mania."

Mahler made notes in a small pad on his lap. "How do you treat it?"

"Psychotherapy in combination with medication. The tricky part is finding which medication works for each patient. One individual might take mood-stabilizers like lithium or Depakote, in combination with antidepressants such as Elavil or Prozac. It usually takes a while to find the right mix."

"How does the condition change as the individual gets older, say, in the twenties?"

"Often it's worse. At that age, they're considered adults. Now they live on their own and set their own schedules. Some have substance abuse problems, which exacerbate their symptoms."

"So, if they were to take OxyContin or Ecstasy—"

Bittner shook his head. "It could have terrible consequences. Increase the highs and lows. Push them over the edge."

"So it might be difficult for someone with this condition to be in a relationship."

"A big threat for people with Bipolar I is high-risk behaviors, which can mean multiple partners, excessive sexual activity, or relationships with abusive partners."

"So apart from seeing a therapist and taking medications, how does someone with BSD deal with it?"

Bittner puffed his cheeks and let the air out. "Deal? It's more like a battle. A daily, even hourly, battle. You can't believe how hard this thing is. Sometimes it helps if they have something to focus all that manic energy on. Some consistent thing they can come back to, that can ride the ups and downs, and be an anchor for them."

"A thing? Like a hobby or interest?"

"It's obviously different for different individuals."

"So it could be something like reading? Say, poetry?"

"Reading's not so common because it requires concentration."

"But for the sake of an example, let's say it's reading. And let's say it's the poetry of Keats."

The two men looked at each other. "I told you, Lieutenant," Bittner said. "I can't talk about Elise."

"And I told you I'm investigating a young woman's murder."

Bittner pulled himself upright. "All right, look. I'll tell you something if it'll help. But none of this is simple. It's not like putting together a puzzle and finding a single answer. People with BSD like Elise often have trouble with boundaries, distinguishing between their thoughts and reality. Her father abandoned his family when Elise was three and rarely communicated with her. But he sent her a book of Keats poetry. Sometimes Elise believed her father *was* Keats and he was writing to *her*. What she thought or said about the poetry was not always connected to the real world."

Mahler waited. He was beginning to think the doctor had been right from the start—that he really couldn't say anything useful in identifying a suspect. He decided to give it a few more minutes. "Can you tell me anything she said about poetry?"

"Not specifically. But in our sessions, Elise was drawn to Keats because his poetry often articulates two conflicting ideas. For someone like Elise, whose life was trying to find balance between two behavioral poles, the poems had a profound personal message."

Mahler looked down at his notebook. "Does the phrase 'to take into the air my quiet breath' have a special meaning? We found it written on her leg."

Bittner sighed. "Elise often wrote messages to herself on her arms and legs. Because her world was spinning, she felt the need to remind herself of thoughts or ideas. In our sessions, she spoke about that particular line often. It's from a poem where Keats talks about yearning for death. Elise was definitely drawn to suicidal thoughts. But she resisted them, through therapy and medications."

Mahler could see sadness in the doctor's eyes. He wondered how success was measured in a world where the patients didn't have much of a chance. "Can you think why she would have written it now? Was she afraid of someone, or something?"

Bittner hesitated. "She was more fearful in recent sessions."

"Fearful of what?"

"She wouldn't say."

"We have evidence indicating that, at the time of her death, the victim was in the presence of three adult males and participated in a street drug buy. Did she talk to you about her male friends or a boyfriend?"

"She talked about a lot of men in her sessions, but it wasn't always clear if they were in her life now or in the past. I don't feel comfortable with this subject. Anything I say could be misleading."

Bittner looked at the forgotten pen in his hand. "Let me tell you what I do know. Lately, Elise talked about one thing over and over. It was something Keats wrote. Great artists, according to him, have a quality called negative capability, which allows them to live in uncertainties and doubt without searching for fact or reason. The purpose of poetry is not to work out the paradoxes but to accept the mystery. Elise's fear was that, in coping with her BSD, she'd lose that artistic quality, which was the only thing about herself she really liked."

"So, if she got better, she'd lose her art?"

"More or less. I'm not saying it was true. It's just what Elise believed. Something or someone was definitely pushing her to the edge these last few weeks."

"With all due respect, isn't it a long way from pushing her to the edge to taking her life?"

"It's not for me to say, Lieutenant," Bittner said. "If she was abusing drugs, as you've implied, she might act out in a way that could be threatening to those around her—and at the same time make her more vulnerable."

"But what's that got to do with a murder investigation?"

Bittner tossed the pen onto his desk. "That's your job, isn't it? But since you're asking me, I'd say she was afraid of someone who was smarter than her other boyfriends, someone who was trying to exert his will over her."

(ii)

(WEDNESDAY, 8:30 P.M.)

They sat on matching Adirondack chairs on the deck behind Thackrey's house facing the lawn. Light from the windows behind them shone across the lawn all the way to the meadow. The dogs slept together at the end of the deck.

"'Night,'" Thackrey said, "'making all things dimly beautiful.' Elise taught me that line."

Russell handed a joint to Victor. "Is that from *Cyrano*? Little late in the game to be quoting the neoromantics, isn't it?"

Victor took a deep hit from the joint and let it out. "Also a little late to think that night can make all things dimly beautiful. It's time for Russ and me to leave before the law gets here."

Thackrey leaned back in his chair. "This thing's all so boring and second rate. I don't want a cop intruding in my life, poking around my house."

"Unavoidable now, I'm afraid," Victor said. "We've cleaned up what we can. Turned all the binary choices from ones to zeros. Paid back all the debts you said we owed. But we're improvising. It's sloppy, spur-of-the-moment stuff. We're bound to make a mistake."

Russell nodded. "And your friend wasn't exactly the model of discretion. Probably left a trail that leads back to you."

Thackrey turned to face his friends. "You know what I hate? People who solve mysteries, figure out puzzles. It's derivative. The real creativity is *making* the mystery, not solving it."

Victor studied the burning end of the joint. "Can't dispute your logic, Benjamin. On the other hand, you did kill a young woman. Actually, two, if we're keeping count—Girlfriend One and Girlfriend Two. Society tends to frown on that. One of the ancient boundaries."

"What're you saying?"

"Matter of time. Local coppers'll be out here in a couple days, three at the outside. You might want to contact Armand, see if he can recommend a good criminal attorney."

"I don't want Armand involved in this. He's got his fingers in my business as it is."

"I should point out, we're all in this together," Russell said. "For Vic and me, it's called principal liability. Same penalty under California law."

Thackrey poured pills from a small container onto his left armrest, picked up two, and swallowed them dry. "Don't get ahead of yourselves."

Russell played with the touchscreen on his iPad. "Let's see what the keystroke logger has on the VCI investigation."

Thackrey looked up at the night sky. "Before you two make judgments about the messiness of this, you should know the drama I've been exposed to. When Elise was in one of her manic binges, she went shopping. I was with her once when she bought five hundred dollars' worth of art supplies—brushes, paints, canvases. All excited about some project. She never took the stuff out of the bags when she got home."

Victor smiled. "As I remember, you said you liked her energy."

"One time we drove nine hours down to LA just because she wanted to have breakfast at Nick's Café. You know that place in Chinatown where the cops eat? Then we turned around and drove back. Me doing a hundred on Interstate 5, her asleep in the back seat. Eighteen hours, door to door."

"You told us, you met this new fun girl. You used the word *spontaneity.*"

"Then there were the down times, when I found her on the bathroom floor, cutting her ankles. Blood smeared everywhere, and she's dabbing at the cuts with a Kleenex. Or she drives up here at four in the morning, pounds on the door, and wants me to give her a bottle of OxyContin. 'Just give it to me, Benny, and I'll go away. I'll swallow them all and be done. You won't have to worry about me. I promise I won't take them until I get home. No one will know it was you.'"

"Water under the bridge now."

Russell bent close to his tablet. "Something here you ought to see, Ben. VCI talked to a former roommate named Jessica Alvarez, who told them Elise was dating a guy who made money in computers and drove a silver car. And the meth dealer we went to see, Arturo Peña, said he saw three men fitting our description with your girlfriend last Saturday."

Victor took a long toke from the joint and put it back in the ashtray. "Sounds like the boys in blue will be here sooner than later. Good luck with that, Ben."

"What makes you think I'm the one they arrest?" Thackrey pulled the gun from his waistband and laid it on the armrest. "How about if I shoot you two right now? I say you killed Elise. Your car's the one driving into the park. You threatened me, and I shot you in self-defense."

Victor faced Thackrey. "You're not going to do that."

"Really? You know that? What do I have to lose?" He picked

up the gun. "I could put a round in each of you before you stood up."

Russell leaned forward. "Okay. Let's calm down. What do you want, Ben?"

Thackrey looked to the end of the deck. "We need to do something with the dogs."

"Petey and Oscar? What do you mean?"

"Dog hairs on the blanket that we wrapped around Elise are going to help the cops trace the murder back to me...to us."

"So you shoot them," Victor said, "and bury them in the meadow."

Thackrey shook his head. "I'm not killing them."

"Wow. Good to hear you draw the line somewhere. We could take them to Mendocino and leave them."

"I'm not doing that either." Thackrey walked to the end of the deck and sat next to the dogs. He was still carrying the gun.

Russell watched him. "The cops are going to find them if you don't do anything."

Thackrey smiled. "All right, then. Why don't we give them to the cops?"

"What're you talking about?"

"If they're bound to find the dogs, let's turn them over."

"You mean drive up to police headquarters and drop them off?"

"No, take them to one of the detectives' houses. Or, better, put them in one of their cars."

"You do know that's stupid, right?"

"Unlike everything else we've done for the past twenty hours?"

Victor looked down the length of the deck at Thackrey. "I'm not doing this. We've already done the three things you wanted."

"What three things?" Thackrey asked. "I'm a coder. What makes you think I can count?"

"I can. We're done, out. You want to shoot us, go ahead."

Russell stood and faced Victor. "I'll do it. What do you want?"

"Are you crazy, Russ?" Victor shouted. "He's playing us. This is all a joke to him."

Russell sat on the arm of Victor's chair. "It doesn't matter. I'll do it. I owe him."

"You owe him what?"

Russell put a hand on Victor's shoulder. "Four years ago. Remember? I was ready to off myself. Ben helped me. He was the only one. I wouldn't be here if it wasn't for him."

"It'll never stop. You know him. It'll always be something."

"It's okay. I'll help him." He looked up. "What do you want, Ben?"

Thackrey scratched the head of the dog nearest him. "Put the dogs in the girl's car. What's her name? Eden Somers. No, wait. We'll do something with the girl later. The dogs go to the ex-Marine, Frames. I assume you can get into the police parking lot?"

"Probably," Russell said.

"And into the cop's car? Without being seen?"

"Yeah. We hack the keyless lock."

"You two are idiots," Victor said. "So you put the dogs in the guy's car. So what? What's that achieve?"

Thackrey smiled. "It's all about *how* you put them in the car. Suppose we give them some juice? If there's one thing I know, it's how to stay awake."

"You mean speed? They'll tear us apart."

"Not if we sedate them first. Then we give them speed. They'll be little time bombs."

"You want us to do all this? Why? What do we gain by it?"

"How the fuck do I know? The Marine gets a surprise."

"It's pointless. It's nuts."

"We'll do it," Russell said quietly. "Then we leave."

"Sure," Thackrey said. "Then you leave. Fly off to Thailand, or wherever you're going."

Victor snorted. "While you get a head start."

"Oh, I'm not leaving yet," Thackrey said. "I've got one more task of my own."

"What's that?"

"I'm going to find my way into Lieutenant Mahler's house."

"You're kidding."

"Not at all. I'll bet you I get in and out before he finds me."

"What on earth for?"

"Because I can. They invade my privacy, I invade his. Anything, boys, to fuck with their minds."

Chapter Twenty-One

(i)

Tom Woodhouse parked his Honda and walked back toward Mahler's car.

As Mahler watched, the retired detective moved with a slow, uneven gait. *Knees gone to hell.* But even in Tommy Woodhouse's prime, quickness had never been his gift. It was something else.

Mahler remembered a 10–66, suspicious subject call, years earlier, when a junkie with an Oakland Raiders neck tattoo suddenly lifted a Ruger from a hoodie pocket. Mahler could still picture how Tommy stood, two feet from the junkie, not moving at all—three cop guns drawn behind him, calmly talking, minute after minute, voice barely above a whisper, until the kid handed him the gun.

The old man climbed into the passenger seat. "Okay. I'm here. You going to tell me why we had to meet in a car instead of my living room?"

"It's better this way."

They sat in the dark. Even three feet away, Mahler could not see Woodhouse.

"This the book club you always talked about?" Woodhouse asked. "How's that plan of yours to read all of Thomas Hardy's novels in order? Start with *Far from the Madding Crowd*, wasn't it, all the way to *Jude the Obscure*?"

"It's...something else." Mahler leaned across Woodhouse and reached into the glove compartment. He removed an object wrapped in a towel and laid it on the console. As he opened the towel, the glove compartment light revealed a darker glow—the barrel of a handgun.

Woodhouse looked down without touching the gun. "I saw lots of guns on the job, Junior. I don't ever need to see another one."

Mahler clicked off the light. "It's a Browning 22 with a suppressor. I found it at a crime scene a few years ago and never logged it into the system. Brand-new. Unregistered. Never been fired. Serial number filed off. Doesn't exist."

"Clean gun. So what?"

"I decided to kill him. Irwin Partridge—I've decided to kill him." As he spoke, Mahler breathed in relief. He'd meant to take his time and gradually come to this admission.

Woodhouse snorted. "Partridge? You're kidding, right?"

"He goes to the Tap Room on Santa Rosa Avenue every weekday night except Friday. Gets home about ten. Parks in a carport behind the apartment."

"You actually checked this out?"

"The carport's lit by two fixtures. I remove the bulbs before he arrives."

"What if someone sees you?" Woodhouse asked.

"No windows face the carport. Most residents are older. By that time they're inside."

"At least that's what you hope."

"When Partridge drives up," Mahler said, "I put two in his head. No one finds him until morning, unless his girlfriend comes looking for him." Mahler could see it in his mind. Partridge's car approaching down the alleyway, slowing, and pulling into the same space. The engine shuts off, the headlights go out. Walk out of the shadows, raise the gun, wait to see Partridge's face turn.

"Is the car window up or down?" Woodhouse asked.

"Doesn't matter."

"The hell it doesn't. Window up, he's harder to see. Makes more noise, too."

"I'll play it by ear," Mahler said.

"That's what the dumb ones say." Woodhouse shook his head. "Where's your car?"

"A parking spot a block away. I walk in and out."

"Someone can see you."

"There's no one around. I've been there a dozen times."

"A dozen times? Are you serious?" Woodhouse took a deep breath. "What about the sound? That suppressor isn't like on TV. It'll still make a sound on a quiet night."

"It's a 22. It's not that loud."

"You'll have brass on the ground."

"I'll pick it up."

"What happens with the gun?"

"I take it apart and dump it." The entire exchange made Mahler feel far from himself, as if he was describing someone like him, but not him.

Down the street, a man stepped out on his porch and lit a cigarette. Mahler imagined being that man. He pictured the family left behind in a living room around a TV, while he came outside to be alone for a few minutes.

"I can't believe we're having this conversation," Woodhouse said. "How'd you get so stupid so fast? It must be some kind of record."

"He's going to walk again, Tommy. Maybe he didn't do this latest girl, but he did the others. And we've got nothing."

"You sure about that? What I hear, your Detective Somers is working on a few things."

"We don't have evidence."

"So this is your answer? You'll get caught."

"How? Tell me. It's dark. No one else there. The gun's got no forensics." Mahler rewrapped the gun and put it back in the glove compartment.

"Anyone know you took it from the crime scene?"

"No, I was alone."

"What about the gun's owner?" Woodhouse asked.

"Dead. I took it before the techs got there."

"Can it be traced to a dealer? There'll be a bill of sale."

"Not without a serial number."

"You'll get blowback on your clothes."

"I'll throw them out."

"What if someone walks up while you're doing it? You shoot them, too? A hundred things can go wrong. Partridge sees you and drives away. You miss. You hit him and don't kill him. He falls on the car horn."

"That won't happen," Mahler said.

"It could. Haven't you sat across the table from a hundred idiots who thought what you're thinking? They always screw up. You'll screw up."

"That's just it. They don't always screw up. Look at Partridge. We never found a single piece of direct evidence. He killed those girls, maybe more, in daylight in a public park."

The smoker dropped his cigarette on the sidewalk and

stepped on it. The man leaned back and looked up at the night sky. Mahler wanted to be him, looking as far into the sky as he could.

"Guess who's going to be lead investigator?" Woodhouse said. "You are. You'll have to pretend not to know what you know. A hundred chances to say something wrong."

"It's not that complicated."

"Rivas and Coyle, and this new smart one, Eden Somers, will be on the case, too. They know you want this guy. What's your story going to be? Where were you at the time of the killing, Lieutenant Mahler?"

"I'll be at Tristan's every night," Mahler said, "watching a game at the bar. That night I'll leave my spot at the bar at nine thirty and go to the can. Be back by ten fifteen."

"You're screwed. You'll spend the rest of your life in prison, with every dirtbag you sent there."

Mahler shrugged. "But Partridge'll be dead."

"Can't argue with that. But what if you're wrong? What if he's not the guy? Then what? It's okay because he's a worthless piece of shit?"

"Come on, Tommy. You know he's the guy."

"Maybe, but that doesn't give me the right to kill him. What gives you that right? Because you're a cop? Because you have the skills?"

"Because I saw the girls."

"I saw them, too. And forty others. Still doesn't give me the right. After this, you'll never look at suspects the same."

"So what? You think we're different?" As he said it, Mahler realized he didn't believe his own words. He knew he wouldn't kill Partridge, never wait in the dark with his gun, never see the fear in Partridge's eyes. The failure of his plan brought a new sadness. He saw, too, the shame of talking it out in front of

Woodhouse. Whatever happened, this would be between them. Down the street, the man gazing at the stars was gone.

"You need to quit this job, Eddie. Retire. Get out. Leave it all to someone else."

"Yeah, maybe." Mahler was too tired to think. He looked at Woodhouse in the dark. He wished he could see his face. "You going to give evidence against me for this?"

"No." Woodhouse opened the door. "Far as I'm concerned, our little confab here never happened. This whole deal is about *your* destiny, Eddie, not mine. Read your Thomas Hardy."

Woodhouse climbed out of the car, then leaned back inside. "Besides, if you're really as smart as you think you are, you'll find Partridge when he's got his own gun, in public, in front of witnesses. Then, Mr. Clint Eastwood, you put two in the SOB's head."

(ii)

(WEDNESDAY, 10:42 P.M.)

Eden looked up as Mahler appeared in the interview-room doorway. "Okay if I work here?" she asked. "I needed to spread out." She opened her arms to indicate her stacks of papers that covered the tabletop.

Mahler entered the room. "Just don't leave things here if you go out." He sat on the edge of the table. "Tell me about Partridge."

"We know he lived in Vallejo from 2004 to 2006. Worked at a company called Mare Island Rigging as a rigger, tying loads for long-distance haulers."

"How do we know that?"

"Detective Jermany of the Vallejo PD found the apartment

complex where he lived." Eden shuffled through the papers. "The apartment manager confirmed the dates of Partridge's rental, and the rigging company faxed over an employment history. Beth Hunter was killed March 11, 2005. Coroner puts the time of death at about 5:30 p.m. I talked to the Mare Island foreman, who checked timecards and confirmed Partridge was working that day. The shift was from seven to four. Partridge would've been in the yard until at least four."

"How far away's the park where Beth Hunter was found?"

Eden ran a finger down the page. "Six miles, freeway and surface streets. Fifteen minutes in traffic."

"So he had enough time." Mahler nodded. He was still shaky from his meeting with Woodhouse. He forced himself to focus on Eden's words.

"The other thing is, the rope the company uses for rigging might be a match for the width and pattern of the marks on Beth Hunter and the two girls killed later here in Santa Rosa."

"Might be?"

"Detective Jermany got a sample and measured it. But he sent it for lab analysis to be sure."

"Is it the kind of rope the company had in 2005? And is it the only rope they use?"

"Yes, it's the same as in 2005. The foreman said it's not the only one, but it's the most commonly used. He said Partridge had access to it, and employees drove their own vehicles in and out of the yard without security."

"Okay. So that gets us closer. Can we connect Partridge to the murder? What about the crime scene?"

"Beth Hunter's body was found in Dan Foley Park, a sixty-acre public park in Vallejo." Eden flipped through the pages. "It's got a lake, community center, picnic areas, baseball and soccer fields, and a playground. Similar to our Spring Lake Park."

"Where was the body?"

"Marshy area near the lake." Eden pulled out a map and pointed to a spot on the lake's perimeter. "Beth Hunter went to the park four days a week to meditate. Always at five p.m. Always took a bamboo mat and thermos of tea. Sat in the same spot, on a flat bar of land that extends into the lake, so she could face the setting sun. The gate guard was familiar with her routine. When she didn't return as usual and he saw her car in the lot, he went looking. Found her body and called the Vallejo PD at 6:45 p.m."

"What about physical evidence at the site?"

"Not much. The victim was strangled with a cord, like the victims in Santa Rosa. Same pattern of overlapping around the neck. Same signature cut at the base of the spine."

Eden looked up. "By the way, I went to see Partridge's girl-friend, Lorin Albright, like you said. On one wall of their apartment was a picture of a man in a pose for something called Kundalini. It seemed an odd choice, so I looked it up. Kundalini is an Eastern religious practice. Translates as 'serpent' and refers to sexual energy wrapped in three and a half coils in the sacrum bone at the base of the spine. The cords on Foss, Hart, and Hunter were wound three and a half times, and the victims had a small cut at the base of the spine."

Mahler stared at Eden. "Wow. That's good work, detective. Really good work. So we know Partridge has some sick thing going on with this Kundalini when he kills the girls."

"Yeah. I mean...maybe."

"But we still don't have—"

"I know, any direct evidence connecting him to the murders. So...getting back to the Vallejo victim. No other marks on the body or clothes. No usable evidence on the ground near the body. The theory is, the killer came out of tree cover. Behind the victim. Plenty of tall brush to shield him from view."

"And no witness evidence of Partridge in the park at the time of the killing?"

"No." Eden shook her head. "If anyone saw him, they didn't come forward. The circumstances fit the same pattern as the girls in Spring Lake Park. Beth Hunter came to the park regularly. Partridge would've been able to study her movements and plan his attack."

"Any security cameras in the park?"

"The gate has a camera. The Vallejo PD checked the film, but a lot of cars are exiting the park at that time of day—games finishing, concessions closing, people going home to dinner. Partridge was driving a 1999 white Mazda pickup, according to the rigging foreman. So Jermany's checking tapes for that vehicle."

"What do you think of Jermany?"

"Seems conscientious. Case file's in good shape. He was willing to help when he found out why I was interested."

"Did he have any other ideas?"

"No, but I do." Eden spoke now without any prompting from the paperwork. "I started wondering if Partridge might have left any DNA when he made those signature cuts. No one looked in the original examinations. We'd have to exhume the bodies."

"Susan Hart was cremated. You'll have to talk to the coroners here and in Vallejo about the others. It requires a court order." Mahler pushed himself off the table to leave.

"Sir, I think I found something else."

"In Vallejo or here?"

"Neither. In Fresno."

"Fresno?" Mahler sighed. *Where was this going?*

"Wait. Just listen. I talked to former Detective Woodhouse."

"Tom, I know." Mahler thought of the retired detective in the car an hour earlier, swearing himself to secrecy.

"And he said we should look where Partridge has been the past three years."

"Partridge lives here."

"But he's made visits outside the area."

"To Fresno?"

"Lorin Albright told me she's from Fresno. She said Partridge goes with her when she visits home."

"When? Do we have dates?"

"Albright wouldn't say. But Partridge moved to Santa Rosa in September 2006 and met Albright about that time. So I'm looking for similarities in female homicides from December 2006 to now."

"So how many homicides are we talking about?"

"Thirty-seven."

"Thirty-seven?" *Christ, what a world.*

"Yes, sir, thirty-seven."

"Big number."

"Yes, sir."

"And ViCAP has no record of a similar case in Fresno?"

"No, but it might have been missed."

"So you're looking through thirty-seven separate cases?"

"Well, yes. But I can sort them by ideal victim type and geographical location, like I did before. I just started and—"

Mahler sat down and gestured with one hand to silence Eden. "When your application came in, I read your thesis and that FBI report on the Highway 60 serial murders. The FBI thing—all 246 pages, and how many endnotes?"

"A lot. They require details be included as endnotes for future investigators. So I ...643."

"That's right, 643. Another big number. I didn't read all of those, but it was good investigative work. I understand the Missouri and Arizona state police are reopening the cases and that—"

"Sir, I don't think—"

"You found new things: the discrepancies in the Arizona medical examinations, the suspect's statement in that Tennessee traffic stop that no one else noticed, the girl who survived a similar attack in Texas. And just now, in this case, that whole Kundalini thing. Like I said, it's really terrific work."

"I just want to—"

"But right here, right now, Detective Somers, you're not writing a paper or on a two-year FBI contract. You won't get a grade or a bump in government pay scale. Behind this...stuff...are dead girls. Not photos in a file. Real people with families and a life. We have to make choices. If it's like the last time, we've got twenty-six hours to find our killer. We need to follow evidence we already have. We don't have time to look at thirty-seven new homicides that may or may not mean anything."

"Lieutenant Mahler, sir, I'm trying—"

"Your best shot is to keep working with Jermany and see—"

"...to find direct evidence of—"

"Do you understand what I just—"

"STOP IT," Eden suddenly shouted. "PLEASE...STOP."

For a moment, they faced each other without speaking. A phone rang in another office. Mahler felt the migraine rise once more, its starting point behind his eyes.

Eden looked down at the tabletop. "Sir, I'm sorry. Lieutenant Mahler, sir, I'm sorry. I'm sorry I raised my voice. But...you don't listen to me."

Mahler watched her face redden.

Eden met his eyes again. "I understand what you're saying. I know...these girls... These girls are dead. Give me some credit. I know...*that.*" Her voice shook.

He saw her eyes fill and her face tighten against the emotion.

"You can write me up for disciplinary action for the way I

just spoke to you. But I want you to know that…that I can…do this job." She looked at him defiantly, even as tears rolled down her cheeks.

Mahler stood silently. Eden turned away, wiping at her face. The black thoughts came back to him—that he would never arrest Partridge, that nothing he said to the ghost of Susan Hart would make her alive.

"Do you even *know* what your job is?" Mahler asked. "Do you *know* why we're here? No one cares that you figure this out, that you know how it happened. They don't give points for that. What they want is for it not to happen again. Most of the time we come in after the worst is done, when it's too late. And the people there aren't glad to see us. The rest of the time, we're just janitors for the dirt no one wants to know about. We catch some jerk and take him off the street. And we fail there, too. But failure in this job isn't like any other kind. When you screw up, when you fail to keep people safe, you never forget. Whatever else you achieve, whatever distractions you find, whatever else…is in your life, it never—balances—out."

Mahler walked to the doorway. "Do what you want, but do it fast," he said as he left the room.

Chapter Twenty-Two

(i)

Bailey stood in the evidence room behind a table covered in plastic evidence bags. "Obviously we're still processing these things."

Mahler and Rivas faced her across the table. The room was windowless and dark, lit only by a shop light over the table. Mahler looked past Bailey, to the far wall. Beside a desk piled with file folders, a figure sat alone in the dark. Leaning away from the shop light's glare, Mahler saw it was Eden.

Bailey pulled on latex gloves and handed sets to Mahler and Rivas. "First things first. Dusting the victim's bedroom gave us only her prints and one other set. Turned out to be a roommate's. Nothing of interest on the sheets or in any of the clothes."

She pointed to the tabletop. "This is everything we got warrants for. It includes everything Marty and I brought back from the victim's apartment and that Steve and Daniel found in her cubicle. Marty still has the hard drives from the victim's laptop and office computer."

Bailey picked up a plastic bag with a small knife in it. "Marty found this little number taped under the victim's desk. Pretty serious knife. Microtech UTX-70. Retails online for $250. It's an OTF model, which means the blade comes out the front. Two-and-a-half-inch blade, powder metal steel, scalpel sharpness. Blade and handle contain traces of the victim's blood type. Trish says the evidence of healed cuts on the victim's ankles, feet, and forearms, apparently self-inflicted, is consistent with this kind of blade."

Rivas took the bag from Bailey and turned it over. "What's she afraid of? Why's it taped under the desk?"

"Shame." The word came from Eden, still sitting in the dark. Rivas looked across the room and nodded.

Bailey pointed to an evidence bag filled with pill bottles. "Prescription meds, with and without prescriptions. Antipsychotics, antidepressants. Whole bunch of painkillers— OxyContin, Demerol, Vicodin, Percodan, Percocet, Valium, even some morphine."

"Jesus, where'd she buy them?" Mahler ran his fingers over the bag.

"Honestly?" Bailey shrugged. "Any high school parking lot."

Bailey gave Mahler a framed photograph in a plastic bag. "This was on the victim's bedside table. On the back side is a handwritten inscription: 'Saint-Jean-de-Côle, 1983.' It's a small town in the Dordogne, in southwestern France. The man in the picture is probably Sebastien Durand, the victim's father. The Keats book, which I'll come to in a minute, has the same inscription and a note that says, '*votre père aimant*,' or 'love, your father.' You can verify that, of course, when you talk to the victim's mother."

Mahler pressed the plastic tight against the photograph and studied the image. "She had her father's eyes."

Bailey waited for Mahler to finish. "Sir, I'm not sure how the rest of this applies to your investigation, but maybe it gives you a sense of the victim." She looked back and forth at Mahler and Rivas.

Mahler put the photograph back on the table. "Just show us."

Bailey held up the art poster. "This was on the victim's wall. It's a copy of a painting by a nineteenth-century artist named John Everett Millais. It shows the character Ophelia from Shakespeare's *Hamlet* lying on her back as she drowns in a river."

Mahler leaned closer. "What's written at the bottom?"

"'As one incapable of her own distress.' It's a line from the play as Ophelia's dying. From other evidence, the phrase matches our victim's handwriting."

Bailey picked up a second, poster-sized paper. "This collage appears to have been made by the victim. In the center is an enlargement of the framed photo of her father and a black-and-white drawing of the poet John Keats. The inscription, *Ne m'oubliez pas,* means 'Do not forget me.' At the bottom are two lines of poetry. I did a web search on them; they're from poems by Frank O'Hara and Robert Lowell. I printed out copies of the full poems."

Rivas took the collage from Bailey. "The former roommate, Alvarez, said she thought the victim's depression was caused by her father's abandonment. These words she's written here...she didn't want her father to forget her."

Mahler looked over Rivas's arm at the collage. "Explains the picture of Keats, too. The psychiatrist said the victim sometimes believed her father was Keats and was trying to communicate with her through his poetry."

"Which brings me to this." Bailey picked up a small book

inside a plastic bag. "This is a collection of Keats's poetry. It's marked up with colored highlighters and ballpoint pens. Almost every page has highlighting and things written in the margin."

Bailey removed the book from the bag and flipped the pages to show the others. "It's got literally hundreds of handwritten things—comments, cross-references to other poems, and lots of questions. See—here she highlighted the line 'awake for ever in a sweet unrest,' and she's written next to it: 'What makes it sweet?'"

Mahler turned several pages. "Anything else stand out?"

"Yeah, this." Bailey pointed to one page. "See that number written in red? In eight places throughout the book, different numbers appear."

"Some kind of code?"

Bailey smiled and looked into the darkness at Eden. "Maybe. Eden helped me with this. Each number is next to a line of poetry about the same subject—death. See? 'For if thou diest, my Love, I know not where to go.' And, 'I have been half in love with easeful Death.' Not surprising. Keats was apparently obsessed with death."

"Is there any pattern?"

"First we copied out the lines and put them in numerical order to see if they meant something. But they didn't make sense—they were just random lines. We tried isolating the first letter in each line, low number to high number, high to low. Then we thought of something. Actually, it was Eden's idea. You should tell them."

Eden rose slowly and joined the others at the table. "I don't know if it means anything or if it's right. But I thought the victim was a young woman who was probably not familiar with sophisticated encryption. Maybe it's something simple. At boarding school, we used a code where each letter in the alphabet is numbered. A is one, B is two, and so on. We used it to write numerical messages to each other in class."

Bailey laughed. "My friends and I did the same thing. Must be a middle-school-girl thing. Anyway, if you take the eight numbers in the order that they appear in the margins of the book and match them to the corresponding letters, you get a word: *thackrey*."

Mahler looked at her. "So what's that?"

Bailey shook her head. "We don't know. It could be a place— there's a small town in Canada with that name. Or a thing. A 'thack' is part of a roof."

"Or a surname," Eden said. "It sounded familiar, and then I remembered there's this guy down in Silicon Valley named Benjamin Thackrey. He's some kind of startup genius who's become a celebrity. Martin would know the name. That would fit with what Jessica Alvarez told Martin about Elise dating a man who made a fortune in computers. And he could be the one Dr. Bittner described as being smarter than Elise's other boyfriends."

"Another thing," Eden continued, "in several places, Elise circled the word 'queen' and wrote 'murder' in the margin. I don't know what it means, but it might turn out to be something."

"She's trying to tell us something," Mahler said. "What was that quote she wrote on her leg?"

Eden looked at him. "'To take into the air my quiet breath.'"

"Yeah." Mahler remembered Susan Hart telling him that breathing would be important in this case. "She knew her killer was going to strangle her. Peña said she looked like she knew she was going to die." Mahler held up the book. "She's trying to tell us with this."

Mahler flipped through the pages. As he looked at the inside back cover, he said, "What's this?" He held the book close to the hanging lamp and ran his fingertips over the endpaper. "Something's inside."

Bailey watched him. "I didn't notice that."

Leaning close, Eden pointed to the top edge of the endpaper. "The paper's been cut and repasted."

Bailey went to the desk and returned with a camera, a knife, and a pair of tweezers. She took photos of the endpaper from three different angles. Working carefully, she inserted the knife blade into the endpaper, ran it along the top edge, and peeled back the paper. With the tweezers, she reached inside and pulled out a single sheet of folded stationery. Inside were several handwritten lines. Bailey slipped the stationery into an evidence bag, pressed the seal, and spread the document flat for the others to read.

Someday, my love, you'll take into the air my quiet breath.
And once your hands have finished their business around
my neck, wrap me in something warm and carry me then,
my lost angel, to the water and lay me down, to sink and
fade to the next world.

Mahler looked up at Bailey. "Is this the victim's handwriting?"

Bailey shrugged. "I'm not an expert. But it's like the other handwriting."

Mahler turned to Rivas. "Tell Martin to look on the hard drives for any reference to someone named Thackrey. I want you and Eden to call the victim's employer, what's-his-name, Craig Lerner, and the others—Christopher Bennett, the roommates, Jessica Alvarez. All of them. See if any of them knows this name."

Eden stepped back from the evidence table. "We can't talk to Bennett. He's got a lawyer."

"Okay. For Chrissakes, talk to the lawyer."

Rivas held up his hands. "Come on, Eddie, it's after midnight. A lot of these people—"

"So what? What is it with you two? This is a homicide. You want to wait for permission? Wake them up. Wake them all up. I want an answer in thirty minutes."

When Bailey had retreated to her desk and the others had left the room, Mahler picked up the evidence bag with the handwritten note. He read the lines through and saw again the victim lying on the park bench, her lips parted as if she were about to speak.

(ii)

(THURSDAY, 12:10 A.M.)

A noise came from the back of the car as Frames shifted into fifth. He turned down the Dave Matthews. Clutch slipping? Too far back. Universal joint? Does a Dodge Charger even have a universal joint?

Alone in the fast lane, running at seventy, Frames backed off the accelerator. He didn't want to get rung up on the empty freeway by a highway patrol unit looking to make its daily numbers. He felt the release of getting out of the office, on his own time, moving fast. He figured fifteen minutes to reach his apartment in Rohnert Park, another twenty to take a shower and microwave a chicken potpie. Back in the VCI room by one thirty at the latest.

The noise again. A deep grinding from higher in the car's back end, not the undercarriage. He accelerated to see if speed changed the sound. It stopped but immediately returned, this time two different grindings, both much louder, echoing off the car's interior.

Heart pounding, Frames looked ahead. No exit for a couple miles. He needed to pull over and call for a tow. He downshifted to fourth.

Suddenly a powerful scratching came from behind the rear seat. *Fuck, was someone in the trunk?* His skin turned to ice. He tried to twist around enough to look toward the noise, but the space was dark. He pulled out his Glock. "Hey, who's back there?"

Grinding and scratching blended, faster and louder. He checked the road, then turned around again. The rear seat, which was not far away in the Charger, shook violently. "Police officer," he shouted. "I'm a police officer."

Just get the fuck off the highway. In the passenger-side mirror, headlights hovered a quarter mile back. Reaching for the shifter, he remembered the Glock in his hand. He put the gun on the passenger seat and downshifted to third, swinging the car into the middle lane. At fifty in third, the rpms roared. He picked up the Glock, hand trembling.

In the rearview, he saw the back seat bend forward, rocking wildly.

Where was his phone? Left front jeans pocket. He'd never get it out!

This time, as he turned around, the head of a large animal burst over the rear seat—a thick, square face, mouth open and growling.

Frames flung himself away from the animal, his left hand wrenching the steering wheel. The Charger lurched as the car behind came up fast and blared its horn. He glanced over his shoulder at the road and swerved into his own lane as the other car flashed by.

The animal wedged itself through the seat top and broke forward. Its rumbling snarl filled the car. Frames frantically shielded his face. In the dark, he couldn't see what the thing was.

He looked at the road, then back at the animal. It was closer now. He could just make out a dog's short, black muzzle. The body was compact and muscled, under a smooth coat. Some kind of bulldog or mastiff. The animal's claws tore at the seat's steel frame and foam stuffing. The dog growled again, then let out a short, explosive bark. It stretched toward Frames.

Could he shoot it? The angle was bad, and in an enclosed car, the bullet could bounce around.

All at once, the dog burst forward. Its jaws grabbed Frames's right forearm, teeth digging into flesh. Jerking in pain, he squeezed the trigger on the Glock and fired a bullet that blasted out the passenger window. He heard himself screaming, "Fuck! Shit. Fuck. Shit."

With the animal's head six inches from his face, Frames could see its eyes were frantic and wild. The animal was shaking. Something was wrong with it. The body smelled of wet fur and urine.

The dog lunged forward again, aiming for the dashboard. Its front paws ripped across the console, jamming the shifter into second. The tachometer redlined as the engine let loose a deafening squeal. Frames braked to cut the speed and tried to pull his arm free to reach the gear knob, but the dog's teeth sank further into his forearm and locked tight.

He felt the slipperiness of the blood under his shirtsleeve. Past the dog, his right hand still gripped the gun, his fingers unable to let go. The wind whistled through the open passenger window.

He looked at the road. Two lanes to reach the shoulder. In the passenger-side mirror, the high, bright headlights of an eighteen-wheeler rushed toward him. He accelerated to get ahead of it. The car now at eighty in second gear, the engine shrieked like a giant metal wire stretched tighter and tighter.

Frames pulled into the next lane. The truck's air horn blasted, its tires skidding. The Charger flooded with the truck's lights, and as he looked back into the blinding glare, Frames saw another animal leap from behind the rear seat. The second dog, a twin of the first, tangled with the hind legs of its mate, and they growled and kicked at each other.

Frames looked ahead and pulled the car right to race along the paved shoulder, out of the truck's lights. The truck roared past, its horn shrieking, and buffeted the Charger in a giant wash of air.

The second dog fought to get around the first and pull free of the seat frame.

Then Frames thought of it: the pepper spray, the OC, left over from the Peña raid. Rivas had given it to him, and he'd put it…where? On the floor of his own car. Driver or passenger side? He lifted one knee to brace the steering wheel and reached with his left hand under the seat. First nothing—then he felt it. He raised the small canister of pepper spray and held it against the steering wheel. His fingers found its trigger.

The effort turned the car. The passenger-side wheels fell over the pavement edge, forcing the car to straddle asphalt and gravel. He braked, but the car shook as half of it raced across the rough ground at sixty miles an hour. Without looking back, he swung his left arm over his right and shot the OC behind him, just as the second dog broke free. The spray hit the animal in the face. It leaped back onto the first dog, throwing both dogs onto the car's passenger side. Their weight flung the car farther off the shoulder. Frames felt the rear tires now digging through dirt and grass.

He grabbed the wheel again, heard something crack, and saw a signpost, sheared off by the bumper, sail over the roof. He aimed the OC at the dog crushing his arm. The jet squirted into the animal's eyes. The dog yelped, jerking back its head and releasing Frames's arm.

The OC seared Frames's arm wound and burned his eyes. The car dipped, weightless for an instant, and plunged down a grass embankment. Rough ground flew at him through his blurred vision. The car shuddered like it was coming apart. He pumped the brakes as the car hurtled down, then rocketed up the bank's other side. Too late, he saw the chain-link fence. Jamming the brakes, he hit the fence, and just before he lost consciousness, he watched the windshield spray toward him and felt the airbag explode into his chest.

Chapter Twenty-Three

(i)

Mahler sat alone in the ER waiting room, his head tipped against the top of a sofa. The hospital corridor was quiet, the ceiling lights dimmed. A TV screen mounted on the opposite wall soundlessly played cable news—a suicide bomber in Pakistan, cars aflame, people running in the street. He closed his eyes.

"When I graduate from college, I'm going to marry Ron Morrow," Susan Hart said. As usual, the dead girl waited for him, confident he would arrive.

Here we go, Mahler thought. "The kid you were dating? The one we investigated for your murder?"

"Yeah, that one," Susan Hart said. "You and Tom Woodhouse were hard on him, holding up the crime-scene photos, telling him it was his fault. But you didn't find anything, did you?"

"No. He was scared. Seemed kind of young."

"Of course he's young. That's why I'm going to wait until we get out of college. I want him to grow up before we get together."

Mahler wondered at her certainty. "I waited. Look what good it did me. Divorced two years later."

"You were older, just not grown up. Besides, she was wrong for you, nothing in common."

"We knew how to do one thing really well."

"But it wasn't enough, was it? Ron and I never had sex. We'll be good at it."

"Do we have to talk about this?"

Susan Hart laughed. "You started it. Come on, Eddie; you're forty-three."

"In the interrogation, Ron was afraid to say anything about your relationship." Mahler was relieved to change the subject. "Probably thought he'd look guilty."

"Of course he did. For months we're dating, and he's having all these teenage-boy fantasies about me. Then I'm dead, and he's got two old farts, you and Tom, asking him creepy questions."

"But I could tell from his embarrassment he liked you."

"That's because you're the great and wonderful detective." Susan Hart put a hand on his arm. "I used to think about Ron when I was running. You run seventy-five miles a week, you have a lot of time to think. The big thing on your mind, of course, is pain. I got tendinitis in the Achilles—hurt like crap. But the rest of the time, you think about...things."

"Isn't it distracting?" Mahler asked.

"For you, maybe. But I'm a girl. We can do two things at once. In my runs, I imagined what Ron and I will say in our wedding ceremony. I don't want the usual stuff—some lame-ass poem by Shelley or Shakespeare that everyone's heard a hundred times. I mean, look at those guys. Shelley eloped with a sixteen-year-old schoolgirl. Shakespeare left his wife behind in Stratford when he went to London. What do they know about marriage?"

"My ex-wife had one of her bridesmaids recite 'You're My Best Friend' by Queen."

"Yeah, and look how that worked out." Susan Hart's voice turned serious. "No, I want each of us to write an original poem. If Ron can say how he feels, he'll know who he is. You can't go through life being a kid, Eddie, not knowing who you are."

Mahler opened his eyes. He watched Coyle sit on the sofa facing him and put two coffees on the table. The men looked at each other silently.

Massaging his right temple, Mahler wondered if he had spoken any of his dream conversation out loud and if Coyle had heard it. What would Coyle, or any member of the VCI team, make of his talking to a dead girl?

Mahler reached for a coffee. Breaking open the plastic top, he wrapped his hands around the cup. "Steve's okay. They gave him Percocet, so I don't think he's feeling anything."

Coyle looked up at the TV screen, where firemen sprayed water at burning cars. "You see him?"

Mahler nodded. "Dog bite on his forearm. No stitches— they're leaving it open to drain. Filled him with enough antibiotics to give him the runs for a week. X-rays showed cracked ribs. Bruises on his chest from the airbag. Glass cuts on his face. Could have been a hell of a lot worse."

"He say anything?"

"Said he just made the last payment on the Charger."

Coyle opened his coffee and drank. "Car looks like it was hit by a tank. According to the tow truck driver, it was a miracle Steve came out alive."

"What do we know?"

"DA's office is taking over the investigation because it's an assault on a law enforcement officer. Paul Eckel's in charge, and it's all on hurry-up. Looks like the dogs attacked Steve inside the car while he was on the freeway. According to blood tests, the dogs were injected with liquid amphetamine—speed. Must have been shot up after they were shoved in the trunk, or it was a time-release deal. Lab estimates at least a hundred milligrams. By the time Steve got in the car, the animals would have been higher than shit."

"And how'd they get there?"

"Someone broke into the trunk. The dogs clawed their way from the trunk through the back seat. Crazy, right?"

"Jesus. Who thinks of this stuff, and why take all the trouble? Steve in some kind of shit outside the job we should know about?"

"Daniel's checking a few personal things in our young friend's life, but get this: Bailey sees the dogs, and the first thing she says is, the hairs look like a match for the hairs on our victim's blanket. We haven't had time for a lab analysis or anything, but—"

"What're you saying?"

"Whoever did our park victim decides to get rid of the dogs and at the same time—"

"Come after us."

They stared at each other.

"Who the fuck is this?" Mahler asked. "Partridge?"

"First off, we're talking about two individuals. It would have taken a couple of strong adults to get the dogs in the trunk. And maybe someone smarter than Partridge. Eckel's looked at the gate over at the Brookwood lot, where Steve parked his car. The doers broke through the gate with something more sophisticated than bolt cutters. Must have been a keypad reader to reproduce the numerical code. Same guys managed to remotely overheat the circuits on the parking lot's surveillance camera, so we don't have pictures."

"You're kidding? What kind of people know how to do that? How'd they get into the car trunk?"

"Wasn't a crowbar. I've seen talk in online chat rooms about hacking keyless locks. My guess, that's what happened here. Whoever these guys are, they're technically skilled."

Mahler massaged his temple again. "Psychiatrist said the victim was around someone smart. Have we located Benjamin Thackrey?"

"Not yet. He owns several houses in the Bay Area—Los Altos and San Francisco. I haven't found anything local. No record of a Thackrey paying county property taxes. But I'll keep looking."

"By the way, while I was poking around online, I came across a few interesting things about this guy. I'd heard of him. He was a sort of celebrity in high-tech circles. And I remembered he'd been involved in some trouble a few years ago. Thackrey was single and incredibly rich. Which made him an eligible bachelor. So he's into the whole San Francisco party scene. At some point, that scene includes a trust-fund girl named Reggie Semple. Old San Francisco family, but the girl's a train wreck. Serious coke habit and a taste for bad boys. One night she gets into a cab in Pacific Heights and is never seen again. SFPD investigates. The father offers a reward, but the woman disappears, and no one's charged with anything."

"And Benjamin Thackrey?"

"Was her live-in boyfriend. But San Francisco Homicide couldn't find any direct evidence to connect Thackrey to the disappearance. And after the Semple investigation, Thackrey kept a lower profile."

"We've got to find this guy."

"I'm working on it." Coyle drank his coffee. "By the way, with Steve out, we need some help. We can't wait around."

"I was thinking of bringing in Tim Frost from Gang Crimes."

Coyle held up one hand. "Rivas and Frost got into it a few years ago when they arrested that guy Quintero. Something about lost evidence. Still bad blood there. How about Ken Holland from Narcotics? Been around a while. You won't have to tell him what to do. And I heard he wants to come over to us anyway."

"The kid who wears a stocking cap all the time?"

"He's good on his feet. Solid arrest record. He and Steve are buddies. Might take some of the sting out of his replacement."

Mahler saw the TV screen had changed to a battlefield scene from Afghanistan. "Where're Eden and Daniel now?"

"Office. Why? You think we need to watch our backs?"

"Not a bad idea. I put an officer outside Frames's room. Daniel knows what to do. One of us'll need to watch out for Eden."

"You still giving her a hard time?" Coyle asked.

In his mind's eye, Mahler saw Eden's face a few hours earlier, fighting back tears. "She say something to you?"

Coyle shook his head. "I just read her notes on the Partridge stuff in Vallejo. It's good, especially for a new kid."

"Yeah. It's...promising. She's smart enough. But she puts her head down, doesn't see what's around her."

"Who's that sound like, Eddie?"

"I never dug in like that. The research shit. Not to that extent."

"Not the academic stuff. But the deep-in-the-weeds thing. That's who you are. And I know you. You can't help thinking something's coming out of all that work, can you?"

"We'll see if any of us survives the shitstorm that's coming if we catch another homicide up in the park."

Coyle took his coffee and stood. "You staying?"

"Yeah. The nurse said Steve won't sleep much. I want to see if he remembers anything else... You okay?"

"I just wanted to thank you, Eddie, for letting me do more of the field stuff—interviewing the roommates and Jessica Alvarez." Coyle heard himself stumbling over the words and realized he had never before directly addressed his assignments with Eddie.

Mahler saluted him with his coffee cup. "No problem. But now you're out there, don't let down your guard."

Mahler watched Coyle walk into the corridor and saw his right hand lightly touch the spot on his belt where his gun was strapped.

(ii)

(THURSDAY, 3:07 A.M.)

Returning from the break room to the VCI office, Eden remembered her laptop was still open to the last file she read—a Google search on Eddie Mahler. A few minutes earlier, the office had been empty. Now Rivas was there, walking past her desk and glancing at her laptop screen. She watched until he looked up and met her eyes.

Rivas smiled. "Find what you're looking for?"

Eden's face reddened. She walked back to her desk. "I'm not sure what I was looking for. Just trying to understand what makes him tick, I guess."

Rivas sat next to her. "Probably won't be in any online search."

"It doesn't matter. I think the two of us are pretty far apart right now." Eden closed the laptop.

"We've all got stories, Eden," Rivas said. "You work here, you might as well know Eddie's."

"I didn't mean to pry."

"You're a forensic psychologist and a cop. Makes you

curious." Rivas leaned back in his chair. "Eddie's father was a big-shot defense lawyer in San Francisco back in the seventies and eighties. You might have heard of him—James David Mahler."

"Oh, yeah. I read about him in college. Handled some famous case, right?"

"Eventually, but he started small. Made his bones defending little guys. Then he's named public defender for a homeless man named Michael Becker accused of killing a Swedish tourist who wandered into the Tenderloin at night. Eddie's father proves the lead homicide investigator fabricated evidence. It's a huge deal. National news."

"Didn't it expose corruption in the SFPD?"

"That's right. It's a whole political thing. After that, James David becomes a high-profile attorney, specializing in cases of the downtrodden versus law enforcement. In another big case, he defends two African Americans accused of killing a police officer."

"He was, like, a fixture in San Francisco, wasn't he? Did Eddie grow up there?"

"No. With his public exposure, Eddie's dad doesn't want his family in the city. So Eddie lives in Santa Rosa with his mother and his older sister, Diane. Mother dies when the children are young. They essentially grow up parentless. The kids resent their father for abandoning them. Both of them act out. Diane was one of the top middle-distance runners in the county, but she hooks up with some lowlife and starts shooting heroin. Eddie gets into fast cars, some weed."

"One happy family."

"Money and prestige don't always protect you, Eden. Anyway, one night Eddie's stopped for speeding, mouths off to the cop. The cop shoves his head onto the car hood, breaks Eddie's nose. He knows that if he tells his father, his old man will bust the cop and sue the department. If Eddie hates the cop, he hates his father more. Eddie doesn't say anything, but he never forgets that moment, the way the cop treated him. The officer's anger and the anger it planted in Eddie."

"And he still became a cop?"

"I'll get to that. After high school, Eddie goes back East to Princeton. Start of his second year, Diane relapses. OD's on smack and dies. Back in town, Eddie meets the cop who first arrested Diane when she was sixteen. They spend some time together while Eddie's dealing with his grief. Turns out this cop kept track of Diane after that arrest. Got her into Narcotics Anonymous, arranged for sober-living housing, made sure she stayed with the program. When she disappeared from the housing, the cop went looking for her in the neighborhood, talked to people, block after block. Eventually found her body behind an empty garage downtown."

"What happened to Eddie?"

"Finishes Princeton. Goes into the Army, picks the Rangers— mainly to piss off his father. When his tour ends, he comes back here. Joins the department, works the streets in a uniform— which is obviously his old man's worst nightmare. He marries a beautiful young woman, VP of marketing at a winery. After two years, she can't decide if it's worse when he doesn't talk about his work or when he does. Eddie makes detective, spends a year in Narcotics, but I think it had too many memories of Diane. Gets reassigned to VCI. After three years he heads the unit."

"So it's all about his father?"

"You're the psychologist. You tell me. I'm just a tired, old cop who's wasted his life trying to understand why one dirtbag in this town thinks it's a good idea to stab another dirtbag. I've also raised two boys, but that makes me more a philosopher than a psychologist." Rivas shook his head.

"From my time being around Eddie," Rivas continued, "I think what's inside him is something else. Eddie sees two sides of law enforcement. He sees guys who work in the community, like the cop who arrested and then tried to help Diane. Then there are the head-bangers, like the one who slammed Eddie into his car when he was a kid. Eddie's all the time trying to work it out, how to do the job. That last kind of cop makes him skeptical of force, critical of some tactics. And it makes him, let's say, unpopular among some fellow officers."

"Which probably has repercussions for him."

"You bet. Fast-forward to the Foss and Hart homicides in the park two years ago. Big cases for this town. We worked the Foss killing as hard and fast as any I've seen. And we were close with Partridge."

"Tom Woodhouse told me the DA declined to indict. Then after the Hart murder, the DA and the chief blamed VCI, and Lieutenant Mahler, in particular, for not holding Partridge."

"Yeah. It was the usual thing. Once Susan Hart's killed, everyone's looking for a goat. People in the department who don't like Eddie decide it's time to score some points. Hart's father reads one of the press stories. Eddie shows up at the funeral, and he's asked to leave by two of the victim's uncles."

"It's like a public humiliation."

"Big-time. Worst part was Eddie starts to actually believe it's his fault. He didn't do enough, fast enough. Eddie goes to a dark place for a while. Starts drinking at lunch. Breaks up with his girlfriend, Kate Langley. Gets migraines. Makes even more enemies in the department."

"So why's he stay?"

"He's good at what he does. Listen, Martin and I would follow Eddie anywhere. Someone in my family is in trouble or, God forbid, killed, the only person I want to investigate is Eddie."

"Yeah, I get that."

Rivas stood and stretched. He looked at Eden. "So, now you've heard it, you like that story? Not a lot of laughs, is it?"

"No. No, it's not. But thank you for telling me." Eden quietly opened her laptop to stare at the empty screen. As Rivas walked away, she said, "By the way, whatever happened to that cop, the one who helped Eddie's sister, Diane?"

Rivas stopped at his desk. "Became a detective here, retired now." He turned to face Eden. "I think you met him—Tommy Woodhouse."

Chapter Twenty-Four

(i)

Mahler looked out the window of the VCI room and watched the scene in front of the police station. The sky was dark and wet with fog. A streetlamp made a pool of light beneath the window. A white sedan drove past, then a Safeway truck. On the sidewalk a homeless man walked a bicycle, black trash bags tied to the frame and handlebars with bungee cords.

Rivas joined Mahler beside the window. He held out a newspaper. "You see this?"

The headline read "Investigators Stalled in Park Homicide." The first three paragraphs quoted Police Chief Truro, who admitted his department had no suspects in the homicide of Elise Durand but was following several leads. The story went on to say the police were concerned about the potential for a second homicide seventy-two hours after the first killing, as happened two years ago. Extra patrols were assigned to the park.

Rivas waited for Mahler to finish reading. "That part about several leads come from you?"

"I send him reports every couple hours," Mahler shrugged. "We haven't talked."

"Word is, he wants to take you off the case."

"I'll bet." Mahler turned and looked at Eden. "The victim's mother is coming in at nine thirty to ID the body. We'll talk to her then."

Eden nodded. "What about Bennett? Is he no longer a suspect?"

"He's not our guy."

"Based on what?" Eden asked.

"Intuition. I don't see the guy having the state of mind to transport the victim's body to the park. The DA could charge him with obstruction, but as far as this case is concerned, we're back to square one."

Rivas sat at his desk in front of an open laptop. "Yeah, the techs didn't find any blood in Bennett's car trunk. But the first report came in on Elise Durand's car. Victim's prints, plus one other set we're trying to track down. Clothes, pills. Oh, and a bag of dog biscuits."

"Did our victim own a dog?" Mahler asked.

"Not that we know of," Coyle answered without looking up.

Mahler watched two cars drive east, then saw a car approach from the opposite direction. It pulled over in front of the police building. The car idled in the No Parking zone.

"The DA's investigator, Paul Eckels, emailed me some early stuff on Frames's accident," Rivas said. "They recovered his Glock. One round missing. Also found a canister of pepper spray Frames used on the dogs. No prints on the trunk of the car or on the lock outside the parking lot. Eckels says this doesn't look like a random thing. Someone went after Frames. He figures they might try again."

Mahler looked at the street. "Eckels is a smart guy. He's probably right. Someone connected to this homicide is coming after us." A pickup drove into view and maneuvered around the idling car.

Coyle turned in his seat to face Mahler. "Eddie, I went through the victim's computers. On her office hard drive, I found traces of files that had been deleted but not wiped clean. All from one folder. I'm trying to see if they can be recovered from the cloud. The home laptop had art files for a company called DivingBell. Craig Lerner says it's not one of his clients, so the work must have been a freelance project that the victim was working on. DivingBell's a startup in San Francisco. Something to do with search engines. Benjamin Thackrey's not involved, according to their website and filings."

"Call them," Mahler said. "See if they know Thackrey and what our victim was working on."

Eden pointed to the whiteboard. "Whatever happened with the DMV search for that vintage Mercedes on the park's security film?"

"Working on it," Coyle said. "Patrol found two owners of that model in the Bay Area. Ruled out one. The other's an individual named Victor Banerjee. We're looking at him and trying to get an address."

Mahler watched the idling car. The headlights were on, the windows closed. A small vapor stream came out of the exhaust. By the light of the streetlamp, Mahler could see the car was silver, and by body shape and the taillights, he knew it to be a Jaguar.

Without turning from the window, Mahler said, "Eden, Steve has a pair of binoculars in his top drawer. Could you bring those over here?"

"By the way, Eddie," Coyle said, "I'm getting some strange messages on my computer. The guys in IT think we've been hacked. I'll let you know." He scrolled through a file. "I also called Los Altos PD and asked them to check Thackrey's residence there—place was empty."

"What's the make on his vehicle?"

"Jaguar. 2018."

Eden handed Mahler the binoculars, and he focused the lens on the car windows. A figure was visible in the driver's seat. Mahler moved the lenses back to the license plate. "What's the number on that registration?"

Coyle leaned close to his screen. "7KRJ508."

Mahler refocused the lenses. The trunk lid cast a shadow over the plate face.

Rivas joined Mahler and Eden at the window. "You want to go down?"

"Yeah, the two of us." Mahler put down the binoculars and turned to Eden. "The car moves before we get there, call patrol, and have them pull it over. Assume the driver's armed."

In the first-floor lobby, Mahler slowed Rivas with a hand on his arm. "Take the passenger side."

They approached the car from behind. On the driver's side, Mahler held his Sig Sauer behind his thigh. Badge in his other hand, he tapped on the window. "Santa Rosa Police," he yelled.

The window came down partway, and the driver's face turned toward him. Mahler waved the badge and registered: White male, early thirties, business suit.

"Santa Rosa Police," Mahler repeated. "Put your hands on the steering wheel."

The driver spoke into a cell phone. "Hold on. Something's happening." He put his hands, still gripping the phone, on top of the wheel.

Peering inside, Mahler checked the passenger seat, and back seat, and saw they were empty.

"What's your name?" Mahler shouted.

"What is this?" the driver said. "I just pulled over to take a call."

"What's your name?"

"John Ledger. What's this about?"

"Is this your car?"

"Yes. No, my wife's. Diana Ledger."

Mahler opened the car door. "Keep your hands where I can see them, and step out of the car."

As Ledger turned and stood on the street, he saw Mahler's gun. "Oh, man, wow. Look, I really just stopped to answer my phone. I don't know what—"

Rivas came around the back of the car to where Ledger stood with his hands raised, the phone still in one hand. Rivas put his Sig in his holster and patted Ledger for weapons.

A tinny voice came out of the phone in Ledger's hand. "John? John? Are you there? I can't hear you."

Ledger looked back and forth from Mahler to Rivas.

Mahler holstered his gun and waved for Ledger to lower his hands. "Let me see your license."

The license identified the driver as John Ledger, with an address in Santa Rosa. The plate number was different from the number registered to Benjamin Thackrey in the DMV database. Mahler returned it to Ledger. "You know this is a No Parking zone?"

"Yeah, but—"

"But what? You thought it doesn't apply to people who are busy?"

"No, it's just that it's…early."

Mahler shook his head and turned to follow Rivas around the back of the car.

"That's it?" Ledger called after him. "You're not going to apologize?"

Mahler walked silently away. No, he thought, at least this once he wasn't sorry.

(ii)

(THURSDAY, 9:44 A.M.)

Mahler quietly greeted Carol Durand as he and Eden entered the interview room. She sat stiffly behind the table and looked toward Mahler without meeting his eyes. Despite her stillness, something was alive in her presence, as if whatever made her rigid was vibrating inside.

Mahler introduced himself and Eden. "Thank you for coming all this way, Ms. Durand. Did you have any trouble finding a place to stay?"

Durand shook her head.

Mahler waited a beat to see if she would speak. "I understand you've had a chance to identify your daughter...Elise."

"My ex-husband gave her that name," Durand said softly. "After the Beethoven piece. Sebastien only cared about one thing: music. He thought if he named his daughter Elise, he would care about her."

"It's a pretty name," Eden said.

"When she was a little girl, she'd hum 'Für Elise' to herself. Over and over, because she knew it drove me crazy. When she grew older, she hated people bringing up the song—as if she'd never thought of it and they were the first to tell her. Sometimes, when we'd meet someone, a new teacher or a parent of another child, and they'd say something about the song, Elise would pretend she didn't know what they were talking about."

Mahler leaned forward. "When was the last time you spoke to her?"

"She called two weekends ago. She mostly talked about her job. Said they really liked her."

"Did she say if she was having any problems?"

"Problems?"

"Outside her job. With friends or a boyfriend?"

"My daughter always had problems, Mr. Mahler. Elise was bipolar. After Sebastien left, she was a handful. She ran around the house, playing one game after another. At parties, she scared the other children and wasn't invited back."

Eden opened her notepad. "What about recently? Did she talk about any difficulties in her life the past few weeks?"

"No, as long as she remembered to take her medicine, she didn't have any trouble."

"What was her mood in that phone call? Did she sound worried?"

"She was excited and talked too fast. She had medicine for that, too. When she was a little girl and got too excited, she'd sit in one place to calm herself down. She'd rock back and forth and say the same thing a hundred times. Anything that rhymed. 'In an old house in Paris that was covered in vines lived twelve little girls in two straight lines.' Again and again, until you wanted to scream."

"Another witness told us that Elise seemed fearful lately," Mahler said. "Did she say anything to you about something she was afraid of?"

"No, but she wouldn't want to worry me. I was never afraid someone would hurt her. I thought she'd hurt herself. When she was eleven, she cut herself. She bought penknives and cut her wrists. Sometimes too deep, and I'd find blood in the bathroom sink. When she was fourteen, we were arguing about something at the dinner table. She took a steak knife and jabbed half the blade into her thigh." Durand's voice cracked. "It was a long time ago."

"Do you remember anything else she said in that phone call?" Eden asked.

"No. I should have written it down. Elise had a beautiful voice." Durand looked at Mahler. "Did she say anything before she died? Did she speak to you?"

The question caught Mahler off guard, so far was it from the reality of the victim's homicide and discovery by the police. For an instant, he remembered leaning close to the dead woman on the park bench and imagining her voice. "No...no, she didn't."

"Do you know where Elise was Monday night?" Mahler asked.

"You mean *that* night?"

"Yes, that night."

"No. I hadn't spoken to her since that last call. On Sunday she sent me an email with a photo of a new dress." Durand took out her phone and poked its screen. She turned it toward Mahler to reveal the victim in a pale blue dress. Elise Durand smiled at the camera.

Eden pointed to the phone. "Did she send any photos of her friends?"

"I can look. I don't think so."

"Did she have a boyfriend?"

Durand sighed. "My daughter never knew how to act with boys. She was...too friendly."

"Was she seeing anyone lately?"

"She said this one boy liked her. According to Elise, he was rich and could buy her anything. I teased her, you know, and asked if they were serious. She said she didn't think it would work out. There was something wrong with him."

Mahler nodded. "Something wrong?"

"She never told me what it was exactly, but I thought, the way she spoke, it was drugs. Don't ask me why. Something about him being different."

"What was his name?"

"She didn't say. She was always very private that way."

"Did she mention someone named Benjamin Thackrey?" Eden asked.

"Is he the one who did this thing?"

"We don't know. We think whoever did this had friends. Did Elise ever mention this boy's friends?"

"As a matter of fact, she said he was always with his friends, and she didn't appreciate that."

Mahler watched Durand. "Did she talk about a work project for a company called DivingBell?"

"No, I'm sorry. It's a funny name. I'd remember if she did."

Mahler waited a moment to see if Durand would say more. Then he said, "I believe that's all the questions we have. If you think of anything else, please call us."

"Can you let me know when I can take my daughter home? I want to have her in Pennsylvania near me."

"Yes, ma'am. As soon as we can."

Durand leaned toward Mahler. "Elise wasn't a bad girl. She tried hard to do the right thing."

"This wasn't Elise's fault, Ms. Durand," Mahler told her. "We're going to find who did this."

Carol Durand looked at Eden. "She missed her father. My husband, Sebastien, didn't want a family. He gave Elise her name and books of poetry, and then he left. He hated a child's noise—the crying. He was very sensitive to sounds. He liked only beautiful sounds in the house. He'd say, 'Carol, *chérie*, can't you take her outside?' He wanted to be a composer, but he didn't have the talent. He had other jobs, tending bar, pouring drinks, where he learned to be an alcoholic. He was a disappointed man. I disappointed him. Elise disappointed him. Everything disappointed him."

The room fell silent.

Mahler stood to leave. "Thank you for speaking with us, Ms. Durand. We appreciate your taking the time."

"You look familiar, Mr. Mahler." The woman looked up at him and smiled. "I think Elise mentioned you. Did you know her?"

Mahler smiled back and shook his head. "No, I'm sorry. I didn't."

Durand reached across the table and took Mahler's right hand in her own. "When I saw Elise just now, lying in that room, she looked so neat and still. Not at all hurt. I wanted to thank you for taking such good care of my daughter."

Mahler looked down at the spot where the woman held his hand. He felt her squeeze his fingers. "I'm sorry," he said. "I'm sorry for your loss, Ms. Durand." He gently pulled away.

For a moment, the woman's hand hung suspended in the air, and Mahler wondered if he should reach out to hold it again. But she slowly settled back in her chair, and he watched her recede into herself once more.

Chapter Twenty-Five

(i)

(THURSDAY, 12:08 P.M.)

A balding, red-faced man stood behind the table in the interview room. The visitor, who wore a wrinkled shirt and baggy corduroys, held a large envelope in one hand.

Coyle peered at the name tag pasted on the man's chest. "Rushton Tyndale?"

"Rushton Allan Tyndale," the man said. "37 Rolling Oak Crescent, Santa Rosa."

Coyle sat at the table and waved Tyndale into a chair opposite him. He covered his mouth to mask a yawn. Except for a nap on the sofa in the break room, he'd been awake for two days.

"At the outset, you ought to be aware of my legal status," Tyndale said. "I'm not, strictly speaking, a native of your country. Born in Dorking, south of London. Studied maths at Oxford. Got into electronics, of all things. Washed up on your shores in the nineties to work in the chip business—semiconductor, not potato. In any case, I was naturalized in 2003, so for better or for worse, I'm subject to the laws and regulations of this municipality and nation."

Coyle struggled with Tyndale's accent. He took a deep breath to wake himself. "I understand, Mr. Tyndale, you have some information regarding the murder of Elise Durand?"

"That's correct. I would like, Inspector Coyle, to make a clean breast of it. Full disclosure."

"We're not called inspectors in this country—wait a minute. What did you say? Full disclosure? This information involves yourself?"

"I'm afraid so."

"In what way?"

Tyndale raised one hand. "I'm not entirely familiar with your protocol. But I've seen the *Law & Order* once or twice, so I know you and I are meant to start with a kind of informal to-and-fro, a sort of rough bargaining."

"We don't actually—"

Tyndale raised his hand again. "However, before you *book* me, I'd like to make one request—that I be allowed to serve my sentence in a facility as close to Santa Rosa as possible. My wife doesn't drive, you see, and it would be a hardship on her if she were to have to travel great distances to visit me."

"That's not really a matter—"

"And I have something to trade." Tyndale tapped the envelope on the table in front of him.

"How about if we start with the…clean breast?"

Tyndale nodded gravely. "I'm a photographer. Hobbyist, not professional. Although, mind you, I have sold a number of snaps here and there." He winked at Coyle.

"My passion is birds. I've been a birder since I was a lad. Here, I like Angel Island and Goat Rock. Terns and finches.

Taken over my life in some ways. My wife complains I spend more time at it than anything else."

"What exactly did you—"

"Yes, quite right," Tyndale said. "Terrible habit of waffling. Long and short of it is, I've been entering your Spring Lake Park before the official hours of admittance. Well before, truth be told. I climb over a fence on Channel Drive, at three or four most mornings. I have a seasonal pass, of course, so it's not a matter of avoiding the fee. The issue is really the timing, if that's not to put too fine a point on the matter."

Tyndale looked at his hands. "The thing is, the best time for sightings is just at dawn. If I wait until the park opening, I can miss the shy ones, the ones that hide in the reeds and bushes. By setting up my camera in the dark, I can shoot at first light."

"Mr. Tyndale," Coyle said, "is your disclosure that you've been entering the park before the gates open?"

"That is the bare fact, yes."

Coyle sat back in his seat. "All right. As much as that's a violation of the park regulations, it's not a matter for city law enforcement. You can speak to the Sonoma County Parks Department. I believe you pay a fine."

"Really?" Tyndale blinked. "The posted warnings are worded quite sternly and would lead one to believe—"

"But what exactly does this have to do with the murder of Elise Durand?"

"Quite right, Inspector. To the point. Tuesday last, I was in the park before dawn. Over the fence on Channel Drive as usual and found a spot near the Discovery Center to set up my cameras. I was after a pine siskin. Do you know it? Small bird, streaky brown body, bright yellow markings on the wings. Winter bird, not common here. Often mistaken for a house finch, but as I'm sure you're aware, the adult siskin has a slenderer bill and—"

"Mr. Tyndale." Coyle raised his arms in frustration.

"Yes, yes, of course. Important to stay on track. The thing is, I took some photos you fellows might be interested in." He opened the envelope, removed a dozen eight-by-ten prints, and slid them across the table to Coyle. "I shoot an appalling number of pictures, no matter how hard I try not to. These digitals seem to encourage excess. Half the time, I don't even bother reviewing them until I'm back home. I took this series before it was light. Just setting up the camera, not even looking in the viewfinder."

Tyndale pointed to the left edge of the top photograph. "I intended to shoot the northern side of the hill just there. I'd seen a siskin in the manzanita the night before, and I was hoping to be ready for it at daybreak. But when I set the camera on its stand, it must have been pointing at the bench where you found that poor woman. This morning, when poking around the early frames, I saw these chaps off in the background, and I thought they might jolly well be something the authorities would want to see."

Coyle stared at the prints. The pictures were dim and grainy but showed three individuals carrying a large object. In successive photos, the figures climbed down the hill to the bench, where they placed the object, visible in the final photo as a body wrapped in a blanket.

Coyle realized he had stopped breathing. He looked up to Tyndale.

"I can tell by your expression what you're thinking," Tyndale said quickly. "Why didn't the bloody man just use the 70 millimeter lens at F/2.8? The other lens was in his kit, after all. Fair point, indeed. But, if you'll allow me, I think I can make a case for the 300 at F/5.6. I was anticipating the lighter sky behind the hill and above the trees—"

Coyle held one of the photos in front of Tyndale. "Mr. Tyndale, did you, in fact, *see* these individuals in the park?"

"No, no, Inspector. You misunderstand. The motor on the Nikon D4 shoots eleven frames per second, on a wireless remote shutter release. I assure you, my attentions were on the position of the stand and preparing my lens case. I was otherwise employed."

"And they didn't see you?"

"Good Lord, I hope not. What a diabolical idea."

"Did you post these images online? Have you shared them with the press?"

"No and no. I came directly here."

Coyle pushed back his chair and stood. "We'll need the original memory card."

"Quite right. Time is, as they say, of the essence." Tyndale reached into the envelope and handed Coyle the memory card. "Perhaps your lab boys can find something I missed in the images."

"Thanks for your help," Coyle said as he ran out of the room.

"If it's not too much trouble," Tyndale called after him, "might I ask that you put in a good word with the Parks Department on my behalf? First offense. Best intentions. The quality of mercy. That sort of thing—"

(ii)

(THURSDAY, 1:00 P.M.)

Mahler stood by bracing himself against the side of the toilet stall. His throat ached from vomiting. He kicked the flusher and leaned against the metal wall. The upstairs men's restroom at the police station was silent, and he knew he was alone. He breathed deeply, eyes closed. His equilibrium stopped swimming. For now, he was done being sick.

This was a predictable stage in his headache: high dosages of pain medication, leading to nausea and vomiting.

Mahler pushed open the stall door and walked slowly to the sink. He found the can of Coca-Cola he'd left on the counter. He took a mouthful, rinsed, and spat it out. Then he drank the rest of the can.

In the mirror he saw his ghostly, pale skin and, under his eyes, the black circles that Kate noticed. Dilated blood vessels just beneath the skin caused the darkness. "Raccoon eyes," migraine sufferers called them.

As bad as it was, this was not the longest or worst headache. Once, when he lived with Kate, a migraine had lasted two weeks. In the last few days, he hated the smallest things she did: the wordless tune she sang to herself while she dressed, the ritual searching for keys at the bottom of her purse, tapping of her toothbrush on the sink's edge, the Hank Williams ringtone on her cell. Listening to it from under the ice pack on his forehead, he wanted every molecule of her body somewhere far away.

Mahler turned on the water and cupped his hands in the hot stream. He splashed his face and slowly massaged his eyes.

A year earlier, a migraine had started at night while he lay in bed. He had seen an aura, the bright, sparkling lights of a migraine scotoma, as he had Tuesday night in the interview room with Dorothy Knolls. But that time, a year ago, as he blinked and watched the lights swell and fade, he had seen something else, a figure in the darkest corner of his room—crouched, wings folded, head raised to stare at him—an angel.

The restroom door opened. Chief Truro walked in, wearing his Class A uniform, with dark shirt, black tie, and navy jacket. Seeing Mahler, he stopped, still holding the door. "I was looking for you."

Mahler felt the chief taking him in, seeing him bent over the sink, his face dripping with water. He straightened, letting the water fall onto his shirt, and faced Truro. "Tell me something, Chief. Do you believe in an afterlife? Do you think we're spirits?"

"Lieutenant Mahler…Eddie, you can't go on like this. You need to go home."

"You must believe in something, don't you? Or do we just end up underground, buried with animal bones—mixed with birds, mice, and cats—stranded forever between the tree roots and the dirt?"

"You can't lead a team this way. The investigation's getting away from you. You're no longer able to protect your own officers. We got lucky with Frames. The city's out there waiting for the other goddamned shoe to drop."

"The problem is, there's so much counter-evidence in our work. What kind of God permits the things we see?"

"A story's going around that you and Rivas pulled your weapons on a motorist in front of police headquarters. Social media'll get hold of that. You're not doing yourself any favors."

For the first time, Mahler looked at Truro. "We had cause to think the car might be the suspect's." He looked away again. "I want to believe. Sometimes I think I do."

"I've seen your file, Eddie. You've handled tough cases. The Macias thing where the father cut his children's throats. The drive-by shooting that killed the little girl on the west side, where you tracked down the shooter in Arizona. I want to help you preserve the way you'll be remembered as a police officer, Eddie. People in this department respect you. You need to think about your reputation, what you'll be left with."

No matter what else happened, Mahler thought, what he'd be left with was a dead girl talking to him whenever he was alone.

"I've come to let you go, Eddie. Effective immediately.

Officially, it'll be retirement. I'm bringing in Tony Call from Gang Crimes to head VCI. Interim basis at first, see how he works out. I've already written the press release."

The words jolted Mahler. He wanted to launch himself on Truro and tear at this uniform. But he put both hands on the edge of the sink and felt his weariness. Then he yanked a string of paper towels from the dispenser and wiped his face. "We have photos of the killers."

"What? Who are they? Can you ID them?"

"We don't have an ID yet, but we will." Mahler tossed his paper towels in the trash. Looking at himself in the mirror, he smoothed down his hair.

"And when were you going to let *me* know? I've got a press briefing at three."

"The photos just came in from a witness in the park. The lab's trying to find a way of getting more detail in the images. I'll let you know when we know."

"A witness? You have a witness?"

"Not exactly. I'll put it all in a report." Mahler walked up to Truro and waited for him to move out of the doorway.

"This doesn't change anything," Truro said. "You're still finished. You're no longer leading this investigation."

"Really? We could have another homicide any time, and you want to have a new guy getting up to speed?" Mahler stepped around Truro. "This time, it'll be on you, Truro, not me."

The two men looked at each other. "You've got twenty-four hours to make an arrest," Truro said and walked down the hall.

Chapter Twenty-Six

(i)

Eden stood beside the entrance gate of the employee parking lot and watched a dozen uniformed officers approach as they came off shift. In the middle of the pack, she spotted Gina Cipriani and Bob Pace, the officers who'd helped two days earlier with the telephone tip line. They were laughing as they walked. Then Cipriani looked ahead, past the other officers, and met Eden's eyes.

When they reached Eden, Cipriani nodded and smiled. "Detective Somers."

Eden nodded back.

"Something else come off the tip line?" Cipriani asked. "I hear we ID'd the victim."

"No, it's…not that." Eden waited.

Cipriani turned to Pace. "Give me a minute. Girl stuff."

Pace shrugged and turned into the lot.

They watched Pace walk down an aisle of vehicles and disappear behind the cars. Eden was aware again of Cipriani's height and broad shoulders. She found herself looking up at Cipriani's face. "I'll try to make this quick. I know you're headed home."

"How's the case?"

Eden hesitated. "It's...still there. I need to ask you about Fresno."

Cipriani's face tightened. "What about it?"

"On Tuesday, you said you worked a homicide tip line when you were on the job in Fresno."

"So?"

"This is about Sandra Avelos."

Cipriani gave a low whistle. "You sure you want to do this?"

"On April 18, 2017, two days after Easter, the body of Sandra Avelos was found in Roeding Regional Park in Fresno. Twenty-one years old. Five feet seven inches. Strangled with a cord. Unusual pattern—three and a half times around the neck."

"I'm familiar with the case."

"No physical evidence at the scene. The investigators talked to a former boyfriend and a jogger in the park at the time of the murder. But in the end they had no leads. No arrest was made. She was one of seven female homicides that year, the only one strangled."

"What's this have to do with anything?"

"I'm not sure."

"You're not sure? Really? And yet you came all the way out to the parking lot to see me."

"It may be connected to the girls killed in Santa Rosa two years ago."

"I'm waiting to hear why I'm standing here listening to you."

"The Fresno medical examiner found an anomaly on Avelos's body—a two-centimeter cut at the base of the spine. It wasn't related to the cause of death. The ME made a note in the file, and everybody forgot about it."

"So what are you accusing me of?"

"The two girls in Santa Rosa and another in a park in Vallejo had the same cut. It's called a signature. It's left there by a serial killer. One particular serial killer."

Cipriani rested her hands on the top of her duty belt. "Are you trying to say something to me, Detective Somers?"

Eden could see Cipriani coming apart. Some instinct arose in Eden to help her. "Why're you so up in my face about this?"

"None of your business."

"I'm trying to get some information."

"No, you're not."

"Calm down. I phoned the Fresno PD and spoke to the investigator on the Avelos case, Lieutenant Sandoval. I told him about the signature. He said I should look at a transcript for the tip line on the case."

"Do you know what you're doing?"

"He wouldn't tell me what it was. He's faxing me a copy. He told me to read the transcript and get back to him."

"You're in over your head, you know that? This is not how you treat a fellow officer."

"When he found out I was in Santa Rosa, he said I may as well talk to Gina Cipriani, who worked the tip line and is now working for the Santa Rosa PD."

Cipriani stepped close to Eden. "I'm going to say this thing once, since you're young and new to law enforcement and obviously don't know how things are done. I shouldn't have to, but I guess someone thought it was a good idea to give you this job, even though you don't know what the fuck you're doing."

Eden fought the urge to back away from the larger woman but couldn't move.

"This is a small department in a small town." Cipriani stuck a finger in Eden's breastbone. "Word gets around about this, the way you treat me, you're going to have a *real* hard time with the uniforms. You work with Eddie Mahler, you start to behave like him, and you'll have everyone lined up against you. That what you want?"

Mahler's name triggered something in Eden. Suddenly his voice sounded in her ear. "I'm investigating the murders of three girls whose bodies were dumped in a park, and I don't give a fucking shit about your code or whatever this is." It came out before she could stop herself.

"You freaking little princess." Cipriani looked down at Eden. "We weren't officers, you'd be on the ground right now."

Eden stared back. "Well, at least, for once, you remember what your job is."

Cipriani pressed her lips together. She slowly turned away and walked into the parking lot.

Eden watched Cipriani make her way between the cars. "What're you afraid of?" she whispered.

(ii)

(THURSDAY, 6:30 P.M.)

Rivas sat at the kitchen table, finishing Teresa's salad—part of his wife's efforts to help him lose weight and lower his choles-terol. He watched her across the room, working at the sink. He remembered his Aunt Malena saying, "When you get older, Danny, love looks different. It's still there, if you're smart or lucky, but now it's in her eyes, or a joke between you, *un chiste,* or the food you make for each other. The trick is to see what the love is in your life and not to expect what it isn't."

"Should I take some *posole* to Steve?" Teresa asked without turning around. "The hospital food's probably not very good. Do they let you bring food to patients?"

"You can try. But he'll probably get out tomorrow."

Teresa looked over her shoulder. "Really? The way he's hurt?"

"You know him. All that macho Marine stuff."

Heavy feet sounded on the stairs, and Alex bounded into the kitchen. Rivas looked at his sixteen-year-old son and the mass of shaggy black hair that fell to his shoulders. Teenage boys all went through a phase where they became a single part of their body—in this case, hair. Alex leaned against the table. "Mom told us what happened to Frames. She said someone may be coming after you guys."

Rivas glanced past Alex to his wife.

"What?" Teresa shrugged. "I'm not supposed to tell my sons? This is about them, too."

"Can I get the Glock from the upstairs safe?" Alex asked. "I know how to use it. You took me to the range, remember?"

Rivas shook his head. "No, absolutely not. You'll shoot your brother and tell me it was the gun's fault. You're not registered to use it, you're underage, and you're not trained. You need more reasons?"

"So what do you want us to do?"

"I talked to one of the uniforms, Hector Mendes. You remember him? We went to his daughter's *quinceañera* last year? He's going to drive by in his unit a couple times a day. You and your brother keep your eyes open. You see anything, you call 911 or Hector. I gave your mother his number."

"I'd feel better if I had the burner."

"The burner? Really?" Rivas smiled. "Go do some homework. You might be too stupid to be my son."

With Alex gone, Teresa sat at the table. "Do you know who these guys are, the ones who put the dogs in Steve's car?"

"We have a name. Martin might have a photograph of one of them."

"So you're getting closer?"

"It's hard to know. These things don't always follow a straight line."

"If they could break into Steve's car, can they break into yours or mine?"

Rivas sighed. "These guys are smart. But I don't think they'll do the same thing twice."

"What's Eddie say?"

"Eddie? Eddie may be irrelevant. Truro's trying to replace him."

"Really? In the middle of an investigation? Isn't that kind of unusual?"

"Who knows? The rest of us don't know what goes on behind the scenes."

"Would you stay if they brought in someone else to run VCI? Eddie's the one who recruited you from Gangs."

Rivas shrugged. "Someone new might clean house. Each year goes by, I don't know why I'm still in Investigations."

"You know everyone in the county who's been in and out of the system."

"These days it's more about databases. The other guys are always on their phones. I don't even know what they're looking at."

"Tom Woodhouse said you have an instinct for interrogations."

"I'm definitely not the kid anymore. They've got Frames for that."

"So is it time to take the package and leave?"

"I've got two more years for the full package. We can't afford for me to go early. We took a hit in the recession. The house isn't worth as much, and we've got two college tuitions coming up."

"I don't care. I'd be happy if you were doing something that didn't involve people trying to hurt you."

"It's not that bad. This thing with Frames is an exception."

"What about that officer killed last year, Ray something?"

"Fessler. Narcotics. Something went wrong undercover." Rivas pushed back his chair. "I've got to go back to work."

Teresa struggled to smile. "I'm not going to worry about you, Danny. You know that, right?"

"I know. You have your limits: 'The human heart has only two chambers, Daniel, and you gave me two boys to love.' I'm on my own. Besides, anything happens, the death benefits are pretty decent. Pay for the boys' college, get yourself the Boxster convertible you always wanted, the red one."

"No, silver."

"All right, silver. You'll be good in silver, your hair blowing in the wind." He looked across the table and saw her eyes fill. He reached out and held her hand.

"Remember when you started?" she asked. "I said, don't say you'll be safe, don't make me promises you can't keep."

Rivas squeezed her hand and smiled. "No promises, *mi cariño*. No promises."

Chapter Twenty-Seven

(i)

(THURSDAY, 7:02 P.M.)

Thackrey picked up his vibrating phone. "Thought you'd never call."

"We're a little busy. Vic's destroying anything that could be traced to us. We're leaving in the morning. You should, too. Where are you?"

"Residence of one Edward Mahler."

"Oh, fuck. You really did it?"

"Yeah. I'm sitting on the floor in the master bedroom, north by northwest." Thackrey took a drink from the bottle beside him and tasted the sharpness of the cold beer.

"Any trouble getting in?"

"Not much. You'd think a cop would expect the worst. But he's got a middle-grade alarm system. Magnetic sensors on the doors, front and back. Glass-break sensors on the windows."

"Motion sensors?"

Thackrey drank from the bottle again. "Nope. Like I said, middle-grade. The guy must not have any shit worth stealing."

"Are you drinking something?"

"India pale ale. Found it in the fridge."

"Jesus, Ben. You didn't fuck with the wires on the outside box, did you?"

"No, I did not, because my little hadji friend advised me not to. The keypad is beside the front door. I did a search on the brand name and found it requires an alphanumeric password with at least eight characters. Used a password-capture software to get the pass code."

"You are taking precautions, right?"

"Gloves and disposable shoe covers like we used on our last endeavor. Should I have a condom pulled over my head?"

"So apart from breaking in, what's your plan?" Russell asked.

"I'm leaving the lieutenant some music in my late friend's name. I downloaded it to his sound system and patched a remote to my phone. Untraceable, of course. Beethoven's 'Bagatelle in A Minor.' Catchy little number."

"I thought your girlfriend hated that thing."

"I'm beginning to think I never understood that girl," Thackrey said. "Waiting for your call, I remembered something. A few weeks ago, I woke up at 2:00 in the morning. Elise wasn't in bed. I walked around the house and found the patio door open. The deck and the yard were empty. I was about to give up when I heard Petey barking in the meadow.

"Elise stood in the tall grass with the dogs. Just stood there. Naked, her gown a few feet away. She was facing the vineyard, but she must have heard me. 'I dreamed you killed me, Ben,' she said. I told her she needed to cut down on the OxyContin. She was doing two eighties every couple hours. Off-the-charts shit.

"She turned around with this funny look. 'In the dream you

made me dance, and you killed me. At first I thought you'd save me. But now I can tell you'll kill me.' I asked her why I'd do that. She laughed. She said it was because I'm smart, because I know how to do everything. 'You know how to kill me.'"

Russell sighed. "She was crazy, Ben. I think we all saw that."

"That's just it. Maybe she wasn't. She knew I was going to kill her because of what she heard about Reggie. But she didn't run. Why would she do that? Why would anyone do that?"

"I hate to change the subject, but shouldn't you be leaving, Ben?"

"No. I'm staying until this guy Mahler comes home."

"Are you serious?"

"Yeah. It's really the point of it all."

"How do you even know he'll show up?"

"That's the sweet part. I found the alarm control panel in the front hallway. On the main menu, I went to user settings. In case of a break-in, the default is a call to the alarm company. On my cell, I downloaded an app called Alarm Remote. Then I added my cell number to the alarm as a remote control."

"Not traceable, right?" Russell asked.

"The usual spoofing."

"So what happens?"

"When I'm ready, I bypass one of the alarm zones. That triggers an error message. I set the preference for error messages to signal owner."

"Suppose he calls the company or sends someone else there?" Russell asked.

"Then I'll deal with it. But my guess is, he's a macho do-it-yourself kind of guy. After you boys put the dogs in the other cop's car, he'll be curious. If he's downtown, once I trigger the alarm, he'll show up in eight minutes."

"You know where you'll be and how to get out?"

"I'll stay here. The bedroom has two doors—one to the living room, the other to a utility room that goes out the back door. I'll choose the one he doesn't."

"What if you guess wrong?"

"Well, that'll be a problem, won't it? That's why I brought the gun."

(ii)

(THURSDAY, 7:45 P.M.)

Mahler waited beside Eden's car on the second floor of the downtown parking garage. He'd arranged with Coyle to keep an eye on her for the night.

From the stairs came the sound of someone climbing. Mahler was about to call Eden's name but stopped. A figure reached the top step and paused. It was Irwin Partridge.

Mahler watched Partridge position himself behind a beam with a view of the stairwell.

Quietly pulling out his gun, Mahler aimed across the garage at Partridge. The gunsight covered what he could see of Partridge's head. He fingered the trigger.

It's a sign, he thought. *Do it.* For an instant he imagined the scene unfolding: his finger pressing down, the Sig kicking, the shot echoing, Partridge falling. Over. Done. Just like that.

Light steps echoed in the stairwell. Mahler saw Eden reach the landing and look toward her car.

"Hey there, Chiclet." Partridge was behind her in a dark corner of the stairwell.

Eden turned around to face him.

He smiled. "Now, if I killed those girls in the park, you'd be in a pretty bad spot right now, wouldn't you?"

Mahler watched Eden feel for her gun.

"You really think you have time for that, darlin'?" Partridge shook his head. "Unsnap the holster, pull out the gun, flip off the safety, hold that big, old weapon of yours with both hands? All before I get there? You that sure of yourself?"

Eden hesitated. Her hand rested on top of the gun. "Are you threatening a police officer?"

"Am I? Here I thought I was just talking."

"You're a person of interest in a homicide investigation, confronting me in a threatening manner. I'd be justified in shooting you."

"Really? You've done this before?"

From thirty yards away, Mahler watched them, his gun leveled on Partridge's head and one finger near the trigger.

Eden unsnapped her holster and took out her Glock.

Partridge stepped forward again, raising his hands, palms out. "Apparently, I'm unarmed. Not even a cord in my pocket to wrap around your long, white neck, like the girls in the park."

"What makes you think they were killed with a cord?"

"I think we all know they were killed with a cord, don't you? You're not going to be stupid now, are you? I like it so much better when you're smart."

Mahler listened. He could see Eden's command of the encounter and felt no need to intervene. Something about Partridge's voice held him. *What was he up to?*

Eden raised the gun and, bracing the handle with two hands, pointed it at Partridge. "Are you here to confess to the killings?"

Partridge took another step closer. "Oh, Chiclet. That's not what you really want, is it? No, I think it's going to end another way."

"Stay where you are."

"I came here tonight with a—let's call it a suggestion. I hear you visited my friend, Lorin. She's a pretty little thing, but sometimes she gets confused. I hold you responsible. So I'm here to tell you politely to stay the fuck away from my girl and my apartment."

At these words, Mahler felt a flash of recognition. The sensation came over him without his understanding. He remembered Woodhouse once saying sometimes with a hopeless case, he'd get a feeling of an opening even before the facts arrived. It's as real as the world, Woodhouse said.

Two days earlier in the interview room, Partridge had momentarily lost himself, peering at Eden like a prey animal. Now it was Eden again. But it was different. *What was it?* Without knowing why, Mahler lowered his gunsight from Partridge's head.

"Lorin Albright's part of our investigation," Eden said. "We can talk to her any time we want."

"Well, you *can*, but you shouldn't." Partridge stepped within ten feet of Eden. "Not if you don't want to get hurt. You're young and smart. Nobody wants you to get hurt." With his hands still raised, Partridge wiggled his fingers and smiled.

In an instant Mahler understood. *The guy's scared. The son of a bitch has never been scared. But now he's scared.* Mahler let out a breath he didn't know he was holding. *Table's turning,* he thought.

Mahler stared at Eden, standing now with her gun raised. *How had this young woman done what he had failed to do for two years?*

Mahler walked forward, gun in hand. "It's time for you to leave, Irwin."

Partridge's focus moved from Eden to Mahler. "Lieutenant Mahler. What do you want?"

"You remember where your car's parked, Irwin?"

Partridge looked back to Eden and winked. "We're not done, Chiclet. You want to watch your step."

Eden waited for Partridge to disappear down the stairwell. Then she turned and crossed the garage floor to Mahler, shoving her gun in its holster. Suddenly unsteady, she leaned against the car. "Not sure I could have shot him."

"You did the right thing." Mahler rested one hand on her shoulder.

"Did you hear him? He knows the girls were strangled with a cord."

Mahler shrugged. "His lawyer'll say he guessed. The important thing is, he's worried about Lorin, and maybe that Kundalini thing. Whatever you're doing, it's getting to him." Mahler put his gun away.

Eden looked at him. "How long were you there?"

"A while."

"You knew he wasn't going to strangle me?"

"I wasn't certain, but an academically trained investigator on my team told me Irwin Partridge's preference for killing is in a public park."

Eden managed a weak smile. "Why'd you come here in the first place?"

"Looking after you, Detective Somers. From now on, none of us goes out alone."

Mahler's cell went off. He fumbled for the phone, swiped his thumb across the screen, and stared at the image. Then he looked up. "Someone's just broken into my house." He was already running toward his car.

Chapter Twenty-Eight

(i)

"Tell me again what your phone message said." Eden braced herself as Mahler's car accelerated around a corner. They were tacking across town, on the quickest route to his house.

"Alarm trip. Time-stamped 7:21."

"Shouldn't it go straight to the alarm company?"

"Yeah. Usually goes to the Florida office. Automatically called in to the PD here. This time it didn't."

"Why?" Eden asked. "Why would it do that?"

"I don't know. But after what happened to Steve, I want to look myself."

As they approached his address, Mahler pulled to the curb three houses away and shut off the engine.

Eden looked down the street. "No car out front."

Mahler shrugged. "They could've parked behind and come down the hill on the back side."

"You see anything out of the ordinary? I could call it in and have patrol up on the street behind your house."

"No, let's just go. We'll call it in once we get inside, if we have to. Leave your gun in your belt until we get to the house. I don't want to scare the neighbors."

They walked quickly down the street and into the drive at Mahler's house. Along the far wall of the garage, they took out their guns.

"Go around the front," Mahler whispered. "Look for signs of a break-in. I'll do the back side, and we'll meet here."

Without waiting for an answer, Mahler crouched below the window line. He ran to the left of the house, while Eden moved to the right. A minute later they met again at the garage. "Doors locked," Mahler said quietly. "No broken windows."

"Same for me."

They stood together, each holding a gun, catching their breath.

Mahler leaned toward Eden. "I'm going in the back door. Stay here and watch the front. Stop anyone coming out and call patrol."

At the door, Mahler shoved his gun into his holster, unlocked the deadbolt, and eased open the latch. He slipped off his shoes and walked to the kitchen in his socks. Taking out his gun again, he sat on the floor.

He closed his eyes and slowed his breathing. From an open window in the hallway, he heard the wind blowing through the oaks in the backyard and, closer, the refrigerator's machine hum.

Mahler remembered training for night patrols at the Army Ranger school in Georgia twenty years back. Sitting alone in the dark at the base of a tree, waiting for the other patrol. One, two hours at a time. The instructor was a scary guy named Wills, who had spent three tours in the jungles of Phuoc Long.

As far as he could tell in the dark, nothing in the kitchen was moved. But now Mahler sensed something. *What was it? A sound? A smell?* Whatever it was, he knew what it meant: someone else was here. *Where were they? Living room, dining room, bedroom?* The first two rooms were open and exposed. If their places were reversed, he'd choose the back rooms. *How many guys? More than one? No. It would be one.* Every lesson learned in Ranger school told him so.

He unconsciously squeezed the Sig. He let his hand relax and stilled his mind. From the office came the sound of a ticking clock.

He thought of Wills again. Guy had a Zen about combat patrols. He heard Wills's voice in his ear: *What do you know about the other guy?*

Not a smash-and-grab kid, Mahler thought. *Whoever this guy is, he broke into the house and got past the house alarm, and somehow reprogrammed it to bypass the alarm company. He knows my cell number.*

Why'd he do that? Wills asked.

He wants me to come, Mahler thought.

Now that you're here, what's he want?

To find him.

What's that tell you?

He's ready. Sitting on the floor of one of the back rooms, holding a gun, just like me.

Who has the edge? Wills asked.

He does. He can sit there all night, waiting for me.

How do you change that balance?

Go to him, Mahler thought. *Make him move. Assume he's in the last bedroom, the master. The room has two doors: one down the hallway from the living room, the other through the back utility room. No matter where the shooter is in the bedroom, the first doorway exposes me to a clear shot. Also, if I go that way, there's a chance I drive him out the back door, where Eden can't see him. The second doorway has some cover, and I force him into the hallway and the front door.*

Mahler stood. He walked quickly out of the kitchen, through the dining room, to the entrance to the utility room. He stopped at the doorway's edge. He scanned the space around him. Then, holding the Sig in both hands, he swung into the utility room. The space was darker than the rest of the house. His eyes adjusted, and he could see the room was empty. Again, nothing seemed to be moved.

In the darkness, he listened. Wind blew against the window.

Stepping carefully across the utility room, he found the bedroom door closed. He turned the knob and stepped away from the doorway. He listened for a sound. Someone standing? Steps toward him? A slide pulled back to chamber a cartridge? It was silent.

Had his instincts been wrong? Had the intruder left? Was the house empty?

Mahler touched the trigger of the Sig. Then he crouched and ducked into the bedroom. The space in front of the bed was empty. He stared across the room, into the black at the far end. The darkness unfolded, revealing shapes and surfaces. He saw something beside the window. A figure bent over? As his eyes adjusted, the thing turned into a chair. Everything appeared unchanged.

He stood still, his gun aimed ahead, listening.

Where is he, Ranger? Wills asked. *You can't see him, but he can see you.*

Mahler blinked at migraine hallucinations dancing across his vision. He swung to the left and looked behind him into the farthest corner. Nothing.

With each passing second, his fear grew. Where was this guy?

Suddenly, something caught his attention on the floor, ten feet away. A small, upright object. He didn't remember anything there when he'd left the house two days before. A step closer, he could see it was a bottle. He stared at it in wonder. Someone had been here.

There's always a reason, Wills said. Why'd he put it there?

Could it be wired? Rigged with explosives? He felt with his hand for a trip wire. He slowly reached to the bottle. He touched it, tipping it over. The glass clattered to the floor and rolled slowly under the bed.

He realized he was holding his breath. He breathed deeply. In the same instant Mahler heard a sound—a footstep down the hall. He swung his gun to the door. Nothing could be seen in the darkness.

As he jumped out of his crouch, the room swam. He staggered to the doorway and looked down the hall. Empty. His body flat to the wall, he crept to the study. He waited and listened again.

A sound came from the living room. So soft, at first Mahler felt it must be his imagination. Something metallic. No, music. A single piano. Bright, quick, high notes. A familiar melody. What was it? He rushed to the archway entrance to the living room.

He looked into the dark. Ahead of him were still, black shapes. He stared into them, looking for something out of place, moving. A faint light shone through a space in the curtains and played along the floor, climbing the bookshelf.

All the while the music softly played. Short piano notes, the same repeated phrase. Had the intruder turned it on? Had he, Mahler, inadvertently set a timer in the sound system?

The music grew louder, first filling the room, then blaring, until it vibrated the speakers. Mahler felt the piano keys hammering inside his head. The sound swelled the pain of the migraine throbbing behind his eyes. He braced himself against the wall to keep from falling to the floor.

From the back of the house came another sound, something moving. Mahler pulled away from the wall and raced across the living room, through the dining room and kitchen. At the back entrance, he found the door open.

Mahler looked into the dark backyard and heard someone running ahead of him toward the woods. As he jumped down the back steps, he saw Eden sprinting across the lawn. He wanted to call to her to take cover as she ran, but she was gone in the darkness. Running after her, he stopped at the edge of the woods and took cover against the trunk of an oak. Without his shoes, his socks were wet and cold. Ahead someone crashed through the underbrush. Behind him the music still blared from the open door.

He turned away from the tree and began running through the woods, the headache pain weighing him down. He heard a car engine start at the top of the hill and knew that by the time he climbed the hillside, the car would be into the switchbacks rising through the neighborhood. He could call for a patrol car, but he did not have a description to give dispatch.

Eden appeared out of the darkness, breathing heavily. She bent over, bracing her hands on her knees. "One male... Tall, maybe six feet... Light-colored sedan... Couldn't get the plate."

She straightened up and fell awkwardly forward into Mahler. He caught her and let her head rest against his chest. For a moment they stood together while she caught her breath. Neither of them spoke. From the house, the music slowly faded. In the silence, he let her go, and they walked back through the darkness.

(ii)

Entering Hyde's, Mahler found Tom Woodhouse at the bar. The retired detective must have noticed him come in the door, but Woodhouse's face gave nothing away.

When Mahler sat next to him, Woodhouse put down his drink. "You look even crappier than usual, Junior. Have a beer."

"Can't, old man. I'm out there saving the city."

"Sorry. I forgot I'm sitting next to a hero." Woodhouse raised his hand toward the bartender, a young woman in a black blouse and trousers, wearing narrow-framed glasses. "Sydney, please bring Junior a coffee—black and strong enough to dispel the forces of evil."

Mahler looked around the room. The rest of the bar was empty. Only one table was occupied. "Not exactly a cop's bar."

"This place has everything a great bar should have," Woodhouse said. "The absence of TVs. The faint scent of the roasted meat on the menu tonight. The couple at the table behind us, who haven't stopped looking into each other's eyes for the last thirty minutes. And most of all, Sydney here." The bartender put a mug of coffee in front of Mahler. "Sydney knows how to make the perfect gimlet: half gin, half Rose's lime juice—the way Terry Lennox drinks them in *The Long Goodbye*, the greatest American novel. Her only fault, other than extreme youth, is a delusion that Pabst Blue Ribbon qualifies as beer."

Sydney smiled. "Long as you believe that's my only fault, Tommy."

As the bartender moved away, Mahler said, "I didn't take you away from your cooking shows, did I?"

"No, I was sitting alone in a dark room, waiting for Eddie Mahler to call. How's the headache?"

Mahler blew across the top of the coffee. "Coming and going." As if on cue, bright flashes of light streaked across his line of vision.

"Yeah?" Woodhouse looked at Mahler. "These days, I'll bet mostly coming."

"We're a little busy down at the shop."

"And I heard you and the new chief are like brothers. That didn't take long, did it? You ever get along with anybody your whole life?"

"Let me get back to you on that. This afternoon he gave us twenty-four hours to make an arrest."

"Are you that close to making one?"

"No idea. You know how it is."

"Also heard about Steve Frames. Pretty rough."

"How'd you hear that?" Mahler sipped the coffee.

"I have friends in the department."

"Better friends than me?"

"They're all better friends than you, Junior. Speaking of which, how's young Detective Somers?"

For an instant, Mahler remembered Eden falling into his arms an hour earlier. "Fine. Why'd you ask?"

"Because she strikes me as a good investigator. Have you told her how good she is? No, you wouldn't. You're probably just making her life hell."

"Why would I do that?"

"Because you didn't get what you needed when you were three years old?" Woodhouse shrugged. "How would I know?"

"The worst part is, after she talked to you, she decided to investigate a homicide in Fresno."

"Fresno? I didn't say anything about Fresno."

"No, but she's found a case there with similar evidence."

"I've got to hand it to you, Junior—you're a brave man to hire someone smarter than you. By the way, you have a leaf in your hair. Trying out a new look?"

Mahler pulled a dry leaf from the side of his head. "Must have come from my backyard. Someone broke into my house tonight."

"Take anything?"

"Don't think so. Left something. Classical recording of a tune called 'Für Elise.'"

"The name of your victim? Someone screwing with you?"

Mahler drank his coffee. "That's what it looks like."

"So?" Woodhouse asked. "Why'd you call me?"

"I need you to keep an eye on Partridge."

"Seriously?"

"Yeah. He approached Detective Somers tonight. Threatened her. Told her to stay away from his girlfriend. I don't trust him."

"Since when did we *ever* trust him?" Woodhouse held up his glass to study the ice cubes. "I'm too old to sit in a car waiting for a jerk-off like Partridge to do something stupid, and this will seriously cut into my flirting with Sydney."

"We all have to prioritize. You told me that."

"Probably sounded smarter when I said it. Tell you what, Eddie. I'll do it. Not for you, but because I admire your Detective Somers."

"It's an honor working with a man of principle," Mahler said. "Remember, Partridge knows you, so you'll need to be a little—"

"Okay, I'll be a little. You want to teach me how to do this now?"

"Maybe you could wear that ugly Giants cap of yours. I hear it's what the homeless are wearing this year."

"What'd you want to know?"

"Where he is, where he goes, day and night."

"Tall order."

"I'll record *Wheel of Fortune*, so you don't miss anything. You own a cell?"

"That one of those things you talk into?"

"Call me when he moves."

Mahler slid a piece of paper toward Woodhouse. "Here's his home and work addresses."

"Am I supposed to eat this after I've read it?"

"I'll leave it to you, Tom. You always were a man of discretion."

Chapter Twenty-Nine

(i)

The team fell silent as Mahler walked into the VCI room.

"We didn't know where you went," Rivas said.

Looking chagrined, Mahler moved to the center of the room. "Sorry. I should've called you. I had to see a friend."

Ken Holland, the detective transferred to replace Frames, sat at the extra desk. The young detective was dressed in flannel shirt, jeans, and wool cap. Mahler nodded silently at him and turned to Eden. "Did I leave you stranded?"

"No, no," Eden said. "One of the units drove me back to my car. We just got the first report from the evidence techs on the break-in at your house. No signs of tampering on the entry alarm. The intruder must've used a passcode reader, like on the gate at City Lot 2, where Steve parked his car. Also no finger-prints on the doors, the sound system, or the bottle. Bailey says we might get DNA off the beer bottle, but it'll take a few days."

"Anything stolen?" Rivas asked.

Mahler shook his head. "I don't think so."

"So this wasn't a robbery?"

"Doesn't look like it."

"What does it look like?" Coyle asked.

Mahler considered it for a moment. "Hard to know. Some sort of stunt, maybe."

"Was it just one guy?"

"Only one came out the back door. Male. We couldn't get close enough to see him. He ran up the hill behind my house and got into a car. We didn't get a make on the vehicle."

Holland came forward. "Wait a minute. This guy was actually *inside* your house when you arrived?"

"Yeah," Mahler said. "He was there."

"You surprised him?"

"We don't know."

Eden tapped at the screen on her phone. "I don't think so. Bailey spoke to the alarm company. They're still running diagnostics, but they claim the alarm didn't malfunction. It was hacked. That's the only way the sequence could happen. Someone reprogrammed the alarm to call Eddie instead of the alarm company. So this guy was waiting for us."

"Can we get a trace on the cell?" Mahler asked.

Coyle shrugged. "We're working on it. But if the guy was smart enough to get in the house and hack the alarm, he probably used an untraceable phone or spoofing software to block the trace."

Holland raised his arms. "Guys, guys. I know I'm new to this, but do you hear yourselves? You're saying some bright guy takes all this trouble to bypass the house alarm, break into the house, drink a beer, and then hack the alarm to call Eddie. I mean, fucking come on. What's the point?"

"Same as the dogs in Steve's car," Rivas said. "To screw with us, show us how smart he is."

Holland rubbed his wool cap. "And tell me again, how do we know it's connected to the park homicide?"

"The music," Eden said. "The intruder put a song called 'Für Elise' on Eddie's sound system."

"Was it playing when Eddie arrived?"

"No. It came on as the intruder was leaving."

"We think he controlled it remotely," Coyle said. "Probably through his cell."

"Can we trace anything on the recording?" Mahler asked.

"No, it's a generic download. No digital fingerprints. Could have come from anywhere."

Mahler looked across the room at the team and took a deep breath. "By the way, I've already told Daniel and Eden, but the rest of you should know. The chief has given us until one tomorrow afternoon to make an arrest."

"Are you serious?" Coyle asked.

"I'm afraid so."

The room fell quiet. Mahler turned to face a new display of photo enlargements taped side by side on the wall beside the whiteboard. In sequence, the photos showed three men carrying the victim's body to the park bench, then climbing back up the hill. "What do we have on these photos?"

Rivas joined him at the display. "We showed the photos to Peña. He confirmed seeing these guys with the victim Saturday night." Rivas pointed to one photo. "According to his earlier testimony, the guy in the front is the Asian, the guy in the middle is dark-skinned, and the last guy is taller and white."

Mahler peered at the photos. "The faces of the first two are pretty clear. If we can ID them, we can put them in the park with the victim's body. This last guy—can the lab do anything on the resolution?"

"Not according to the techs." Coyle sat back in his chair. "Something about the image lacking information. Anyway, the photo was taken in the dark, and the camera lens was focused on the foreground, a few hundred yards away. But we do know the Asian is also the hooded guy in the surveillance film taken at the park gate. Analysis of that film showed he was five feet four and left-handed."

"The middle guy's about the same size," Eden said. "So these are the 'little men' the homeless guy talked about."

"Maybe this dark-skinned guy isn't Latino," Rivas said. "Maybe he's East Indian. The owner of the vintage Mercedes in San Francisco you're trying to track down is named Victor Banerjee."

Holland tapped one of the photo enlargements. "See this thing? On the Asian guy's jacket?"

"It's a shadow," Rivas said.

"No, that's what I thought, too. But look—it's in all the photos, no matter which way he's facing." Holland picked up a black pen and circled the shape in each photo. "Look. Here and here and here. It's something on the jacket. A picture or a letter."

"It's like a ball with a line coming out the top," Eden said.

Coyle bent close to his laptop. "I've seen that somewhere else." He swiveled the screen toward the others. "Yeah. Look, it's the logo the victim had on her computer. It's that startup down in the city—DivingBell."

Mahler walked back to Coyle's desk. "So, up to now, we *were* looking for a connection between DivingBell and this guy Thackrey, the name in the victim's book of poetry. But maybe the connection's with one of his friends. What'd the company say when you called?"

"I only asked about Thackrey, and the company's representative said Thackrey was not associated with them."

Mahler looked across the room to Rivas. "Daniel, you and Ken go down to the offices of this startup first thing tomorrow. Ask about Victor Banerjee and the Asian guy with the hoodie."

"Speaking of these guys," Coyle said, "get this. Remember this morning I said I was getting weird messages on my computer? The IT guys did some poking and figured out someone hacked my fucking computer."

"When?" Eden asked. "How? Someone came in here?"

"Yesterday," Coyle said, "and, no, they didn't come in here. They did it remotely, from well...anywhere. Probably broke through the city's online firewall."

"Oh, man," Holland said. "What happened to the days when we just walked around and shot the bad guys?"

Rivas laughed. "Really? In what universe?"

"The thing is," Coyle said, "whoever hacked me planted a keystroke logger on my operating system."

Mahler rolled his eyes. "Martin, what's that mean, in English?"

"It means they're tracking literally every keystroke I type and intercepting what we're doing."

"Who is it?" Mahler asked. "Can we trace it?"

"They covered their tracks. But if I had to guess, I'd say it's those guys." Coyle pointed to the photos on the wall. "The same ones who put the dogs in Steve's car and broke into your house."

"Can you remove this...keystroke logger thing?"

"Yeah, but instead I thought I'd leave it there and screw with them. From now on, I'm using this new computer, with different online access, for the investigation."

Mahler gestured again toward the photographs. "What about Thackrey? Is this Benjamin Thackrey? Have we found him yet?"

Coyle looked at his screen. "Maybe. When Thackrey was

questioned in the disappearance of Reggie Semple, one of the online articles mentioned a law firm called Walker and Prince. In the Sonoma County tax records, I found a property in Dry Creek Valley with that name listed as the owner. On Chiott Road. Eight thousand square feet. Fits the description Alvarez gave us."

"All right." Mahler looked at Eden. "Let's go pay a late-night visit to Mr. Thackrey."

The phone rang. Rivas picked it up and listened. When he turned to the others, his face looked stricken. "Something's been found up in Spring Lake. It's a mannequin made to look like a homicide victim."

(ii)

(THURSDAY, 11:18 P.M.)

Mahler and Rivas took the western entrance into the park. Two units sat on the shoulder at the gate, lights flashing. A uniformed officer leaned toward Mahler's window. "Down near the boat launch."

At the end of the parking lot, they found three more units. A cluster of uniformed officers stood beside the forest's edge. Yellow caution tape was strung across the entrance to Fisherman's Trail. Mahler parked his car and walked slowly toward the uniforms. In the middle of the group, Mahler saw Hadley, the park guard, from two days earlier.

Hadley held a notebook and a large flashlight. "This isn't part of our route. It's not wide enough for patrol. We take the road through the picnic area to the West Saddle Dam." He pointed up the hill.

"All right." Mahler watched him. "You've covered your ass. Tell me what happened."

Hadley looked at this notebook. "About twenty-two hundred, Office Templin and I saw a vehicle near the boat ramp and lights moving on Fisherman's Trail. We immediately left our station and came down here."

Hadley glanced up to see if Mahler was listening. "At the parking area, we observed an older-model pickup truck driving at a high rate of speed out the west gate. We called 911 and reported it. Officer Templin and I proceeded on foot onto Fisherman's Trail. About two hundred yards inside, we found the...thing. It was covered with a tarp. At first we thought it was a body. But when we opened the tarp, we saw the mannequin. We called 911 again and secured the scene."

In the group of officers nearby, Mahler recognized Sergeant Ray Alcott. "Ray, you know what happened with the BOLO?"

Alcott approached Mahler. "Yeah. We had two units at the park—one at the Violetti Gate on the east side, the other at Oak Knolls on the south side. Both responded. Looks like the truck went into the neighborhood. We're going street by street now. Copter's on the way."

Mahler nodded. "How'd they get past the gate?"

"Busted the deadbolt," Alcott said. "Idiots probably used a sledge. On the way out, their truck hit the gate and left some paint transfer."

Across the parking lot, Mahler saw Bailey climb out of the evidence van.

"I can show you where the mannequin is, if you like," Hadley said.

Mahler took the flashlight from him. "Stay here."

Hadley gestured toward the caution tape. "This trail follows the lake's edge to the loop road. It's where they found the girl two years ago."

Mahler looked into the dark woods. "I know where it is." He

ducked under the yellow tape and waited for Rivas and Bailey to join him. On the trail, Mahler took the lead, shining the light ahead and stepping carefully around rocks and tree roots. At a point where the trail veered abruptly away from the lake's edge, he saw a manzanita fronting a wide patch of flat earth. A dark shape lay in the center of the clearing. Mahler shone his flashlight past the bush and onto a blue plastic tarp. At its top edge lay a mass of brown hair.

Mahler paused, aiming the light around the tarp.

Behind him, Bailey pointed to indentations in the dirt. "Footprints on the near side."

Mahler stepped aside. "Get some pictures."

Bailey went closer. The others waited while she shot a dozen photos from different angles.

Next, Bailey took a small flashlight from her jacket and approached the mannequin, stepping around the footprints in the mud. She pulled on latex gloves and put her equipment case on the ground. Then, kneeling close, she shined her light where the hair protruded from the tarp.

The flashlight's beam caught the long, straight strands of a woman's wig. Bailey looked behind her at the others. No one spoke.

She peeled back the tarp to reveal a life-size fiberglass mannequin. The thing lay facedown, unclothed. The torso was smooth and pink-colored. Its limbs were flung out stiffly on either side. A sticky red paste was smeared over the back.

Bailey backed away. "Who the heck does this?"

"Take pictures." Mahler blocked her path. "Process it—all of it, footprints, prints on the mannequin and tarp."

Rivas looked at Mahler. "You think these are the same guys who went after you and Steve? They're fucking with us again?"

"No." Mahler handed him Hadley's large flashlight. "Those

guys wouldn't have broken the lock at the gate and left a mess like this."

Mahler looked into the impenetrable darkness of the trees, struck again by how everything could appear normal and then fifteen steps down a dirt path it all came back, a blackness so dense you could lose yourself.

Susan Hart would come out of the trees soon—young and shy in her shorts and sweatshirt, drawn to their voices from the place on the trail where the killer had left her.

He thought of how little power the dead have.

He took a breath and waited. Closing his jacket, he shoved his hands in his jeans pockets. Homicides on television never got it cold enough, lonely enough.

He thought of Susan running her fastest time in Santa Cruz in the dark. What had she meant? He distrusted the darkness, knew what it harbored.

The work on the mannequin unfolded a few feet away in a cone of dim light—Rivas holding the flashlight, while Bailey moved slowly across the surface of the plastic skin with a brush and jar of latent powder. It was an echo, a farce of their real work to solve three homicides.

He suddenly felt all the tiredness he had ignored for the past three days. Every part of him, down to his bones, ached from exhaustion. Then he knew he didn't want to be there any longer.

Mahler tapped Rivas's shoulder and gestured behind him. Then he walked alone back on the dark trail toward the parking lot.

PART III

Chapter Thirty

(i)

Mahler hung his shirt on a hook in the men's restroom. He washed his face and took shaving cream and a fresh razor out of his kit. His cheeks and chin were smeared with foam when Rivas came into the room.

"How'd you make out last night?" Rivas asked. "I heard you picked up the guys who left the mannequin in the park. Three of them, was it?"

Mahler ran the razor across his cheek and dipped it in the sink water. "Yeah, the copter spotted the truck six or seven blocks from the park. One of the geniuses was passed out in the front seat. The other two were hiding in a backyard a block away. All three had jackets for small shit: drug possession, public intoxication."

"You talk to them?"

"If you can call it that. They were pretty wasted. Said they smoked some crack and thought it'd be funny to plant the man-nequin. The DA's charging them with obstruction."

"Truro there?"

"Yeah," Mahler shrugged. "He was there. He's doing a press conference at nine. Bailey get what she needed?"

"Fingerprints, shoe prints, even some fibers. More than enough. Is the forensics team letting you back in your house?"

Mahler felt his newly shaven skin with a fingertip. "After lunch. They're still looking at the type of hacking used on the alarm system."

"You're welcome to shower at our place. Teresa's at work all day."

Mahler smiled. "Thanks. I'm okay for the time being. Anyway, Eden and I are headed up to Dry Creek in a few min-utes to talk to Thackrey."

"So, are we going to meet the chief's deadline? Do we have enough to charge Thackrey?"

"No. Arturo Peña ID'd him in a drug buy with the victim two nights before. But that doesn't connect Thackrey to the homi-cide, and Peña makes a terrible witness. Only other evidence is Thackrey's name in the victim's book of poetry and the note about someone killing her. I've written a search warrant for his house and vehicle. Maybe we get lucky and find a judge to sign it."

Mahler finished shaving.

Rivas handed over a paper towel. "Your headache any better?"

"The pain's still there and some...side effects." Mahler looked at Rivas silently, as if considering something. He wiped his face with the towel. "You okay partnering with Holland for the time being?"

Rivas shrugged. "It's fine. We're going down to the city to talk to the owners of this company DivingBell. See if we can confirm the IDs of the suspects and get a line on their addresses."

Mahler smoothed his hair and reached for his shirt. "Interesting to see how Holland handles himself in the field. Martin thinks he's a good fit."

They walked down the corridor to the VCI room. Holland stood at the whiteboard, peering at the victim's timeline. "So, Eddie, can we discontinue the seventy-two-hour countdown? No actual body was found last night, right? Don't we have to admit the Elise Durand homicide isn't the same as the ones two years ago?"

The room fell silent. Rivas, Coyle, and Eden watched Mahler slowly move across the room to Holland. "No victim's been found in the park, but that doesn't mean one isn't there."

"Come on, Eddie, the evidence's different for this one." Holland pointed to the photo enlargements taped to the wall. "That's not Partridge carrying the body. He's not our guy."

Mahler smiled. "You sound awfully sure for someone who just came on the case."

"I'm looking at the evidence."

"Partridge's not our guy for this one. But until I see something different, I say he's the one who did the girls two years ago, and I don't think he's finished."

Eden stood and walked to the whiteboard. "I agree. Last night when you were in the park, I did some more work on the victim in Fresno, Sandra Avelos." She pointed to a new photo. "This is her. Strangled in a public park in April 2017, two days after Easter. Killer used the same type of cord and strangulation pattern as the earlier Santa Rosa and Vallejo victims. Same signature cut at the base of the spine. Partridge's girlfriend says he went with her to Fresno for the major holidays."

She faced the others. "But there's something else. The medical examiner found blood on the tail of the victim's blouse."

"So what?" Coyle said. "The killer cut her, right?"

"Only it wasn't Avelos's blood. The doer must have accidentally cut himself."

"Wait. What? Is it a match to Partridge's blood type?"

"It's his type. But it's O positive, same as forty percent of the general population. By itself, it's not conclusive. If we had Partridge's DNA, we could run a test that would tell us one way or the other."

Mahler peeled the Avelos photo off the whiteboard and examined it. "I hear the Fresno PD sent you something."

Eden nodded. "Yeah. It's a transcript of a phone call on their homicide tip line the day after the killing. Caller says on the night of the Avelos homicide her boyfriend came home and beat her. Then he forced her facedown on their bed and used a knife to cut her lower back. The call was anonymous, and the Fresno investigators weren't able to track it. Probably a prepaid phone. I'm still looking for something in the transcript to make an ID."

"How about Elise Durand?" Mahler asked. "What're we missing?"

Rivas pointed to the timeline. "We've still got a huge hole in the sequence. Security camera at the victim's office shows her leaving the building, without her car, at 5:40 p.m."

"Then comes the huge hole," said Coyle.

"Yeah. What we know is, eleven hours later, at 4:02 a.m., the surveillance video at the Violetti Gate shows a hooded figure dismantling the lock on the gate. Then, according to the timestamps on Tyndale's photos, the three men carry the victim's body to the bench from 4:09 to 4:18 a.m. The video shows the car driving out of the gate at 4:23 a.m."

Coyle raised his hand like a kid at school. "We do know a few other things. In the missing eleven hours, according to the autopsy, the victim eats an expensive meal and swallows a shitload of OxyContin and quetiapine. She fires a gun, someone strangles her, she cuts open the back of her head, and she's wrapped in a red blanket. All in a location we haven't identified. In the company of a person or people we haven't identified."

Mahler stood in the center of the room. "Eden and I are going to talk to Benjamin Thackrey this morning. We should know more after that."

Holland pointed to the whiteboard. "It looks like we also know our victim ends up in the trunk of a vintage Mercedes, which may or may not be owned by someone named Victor Banerjee, who may or may not live in San Francisco."

"Speaking of Victor Banerjee," Coyle said, "I did some searching online and found pretty much nothing. Which is strange, right? With social media and online everything, it's not easy to disappear. If I run a search on any of you on Facebook or a few other sites, I'll find something."

Holland laughed. "Some of us more than others."

"So what's it mean?" Rivas asked. "This guy's not online?"

"I think," Coyle said, "it means Mr. Banerjee wants to be invisible and has the technical expertise to do it. The only thing I found was a three-year-old newsletter for a Muay Thai dojo in Oakland, which lists V. Banerjee as a competitor."

"What the fuck's Muay Thai?" Holland asked.

"Chinese martial art. Close combat. Short, quick punches. Leg-kicks below the waist. Think Bruce Lee."

"Did the newsletter have an address or photo of the competitors?" Mahler asked.

Coyle shook his head. "By the way, when you talk to Thackrey, don't mention Banerjee. I'm using the keystroke logger to make them think we're following other leads. In fact, ask him if he was in Fresno in April 2017."

Holland motioned for Rivas. "We should get on the road. We

might learn something about Banerjee from this tech startup place."

As he passed Mahler, Holland turned. "I talked to Frames. The hospital's releasing him. He's still in pain, but he's able to get around. I promised to keep him up to date. He said he wants to talk to the boys who put the dogs in his car."

Mahler nodded.

"Sorry about that thing earlier. I have to say what I think."

Mahler waited a beat. "Everyone who comes through VCI thinks he's right the first day. Gets harder the second day."

(ii)

(FRIDAY, 9:35 A.M.)

Mahler and Eden found Thackrey's address in Dry Creek Valley. A narrow, paved drive zigzagged up a grassy slope to a sprawling, one-story house. The building sat on a hillside, on the western side of the valley. In front of the house, a windbreak of Italian cypress bordered a green lawn.

A tall, dark-haired man opened the door. Mid-thirties, he wore a black shirt untucked, faded jeans, and leather clogs. He smiled at his visitors. From inside the place came the sound of Sinatra and the Sands Hotel, Vegas, 1965.

Mahler held up his badge and introduced Eden and himself. "We're looking for Benjamin Thackrey."

"Ben Thackrey. What's this about?"

"We have a few questions about Elise Durand. May we come in?"

Thackrey frowned. "Ah, Elise. Poor girl. Sure, come on through."

They followed Thackrey down a marble-tiled corridor into a

large living room filled with morning sunshine. A floor-to-ceiling glass wall and French doors looked out on a lawn. Beyond that stood a meadow and then a vineyard, where straight, trellised rows stretched the width of the valley.

Thackrey waved his guests to a white leather sofa. He pointed a remote to turn off the sound system. "I was just having a coffee." He held up his mug. "Can I make you a fresh one? Sumatran, low acid?"

Mahler and Eden declined.

Thackrey drank slowly from his mug and looked at Mahler. "I read an online account of Elise's murder. Terrible thing. I understand this might be related to earlier killings in the park? Serial killer, is it?"

Mahler shook his head. "We're still looking at the evidence. Tell me, Mr. Thackrey, what was your relationship with the victim?"

"Elise? Interesting. I hadn't thought of her as a victim until now. I guess you'd say that, for a time, she and I were involved romantically."

"For a time?"

"Yes, but for all intents and purposes, it ended."

"How did it end?"

"How does it ever end?" Thackrey smiled at Eden. He sat with his legs crossed. His right foot held a clog by the toes and rocked quickly up and down. "We grew apart. Elise was very attractive, obviously. But she was less mature than the women I usually see. And she had a...drug dependency."

"A drug dependency?" Mahler asked.

"Downers mostly—OxyContin. But really anything she could get her hands on. It's sad to witness an addiction taking over someone's life. I don't mean to be critical, given what's happened, but she needed more of my time than I was able to spare."

"Was the decision to end the relationship mutual?" Mahler asked. "Did you and Ms. Durand argue?"

"Nothing of consequence. We just stopped getting together."

"When did you last see Ms. Durand?"

"A while ago. Two, three weeks."

Behind Thackrey, a large abstract oil painting hung on the wall. A bright red slash stabbed across a white canvas. Eden pictured Elise coming toward her from the kitchen, sitting beside Thackrey. *Had she been killed in this room? Had her body lain on the floor?*

"We have a witness who saw you with Ms. Durand last Saturday night," Eden said.

Thackrey sipped his coffee. "Really? Well, that's awkward, isn't it? And what does this witness say Elise and I were doing?"

"Buying five ounces of meth."

"You're kidding, right? Methamphetamine? Do I look like the sort of person who would buy meth?"

"Please answer the question."

"I was not with Elise on Saturday night, and of course, I was not buying meth."

Mahler, who had spent years in rooms with liars, found himself admiring the smoothness of Thackrey's lies. "Where were you?"

"I don't remember. In the city, I think. I had dinner."

"Where?"

"Perbacco's on California Street."

Eden wrote in her notebook. "Can someone corroborate that?"

"I was alone. I had the stracci."

"So you'd have a receipt, or an online record of the transaction?"

"I'm not comfortable giving you access to my accounts without a subpoena."

"What about Monday evening, say, after five thirty?" Mahler asked. "Where were you?"

"Here, by myself."

"Did you make any phone calls that would back up your statement?"

"I don't remember. Why would I have to back it up?"

"Do you own dogs?"

"Dogs? That's an odd question. But, no, I'm not really a fan of animals. I have a number of fragile antiquities I'm rather protective of." Thackrey pointed at a cabinet across the room. "That marble sculpture of Artemis the Hunter is from the second century. Worth two million."

Mahler watched Thackrey's shaking leg again and then looked at the man's eyes. *What kind of shit was this guy on?* "Nervous, Mr. Thackrey?"

"Of course I'm nervous. I'm being interrogated by police officers about a murder. What about you? You keep blinking. What's that about?"

Mahler wondered if Thackrey's shaking leg was tuned to a beat inside his head, keeping time to music only he heard. "How about last evening around seven? Where were you?"

"Last night? You know, I'm getting pretty tired of this. I was here. I'm always here. And I was alone, with no one to 'back me up,' as you say."

Mahler imagined asking, *Were you inside my house last night?*

"Besides, what difference does it make where I was?" Thackrey said. "Wasn't Elise already deceased by that time?"

"It was a…related incident."

"A related incident? That makes it all clear."

"Were you in Fresno in April 2017?"

"Good God. Fresno? 2017? You people have the strangest

way of questioning someone. No, I was not in Fresno in April 2017." Thackrey laughed. "And anyone who says I was is a liar."

"Do you own a firearm?" Mahler asked.

"A gun? Do you have any idea how insane this is? I'm a Stanford grad. I built startups that are on the Nasdaq. I live in wine country. Why would I have a gun?"

"Do you own a firearm?"

"No, I do not."

Eden, who had been quiet for the last few minutes, spoke up. "I understand you were questioned two years ago in the disappearance of Reggie Semple?"

Thackrey lowered his coffee mug and peered at Eden with new interest. "That's correct. I was questioned."

"And Ms. Semple was never found. Is that right?"

"I believe so. I haven't followed the news."

"You were dating Ms. Semple at the time of her disappearance?"

"Dating? Wow. I haven't heard that word in a long time. Yes, I was in a relationship with Reggie for a while. I believe she was seeing other men as well." Thackrey put his coffee mug on the table in front of him. He frowned. "I'm not sure what my relationship with Reggie has to do with events here in Sonoma County."

"Did Elise know Ms. Semple?" Eden asked.

The question brought silence to the room. Mahler, who had risen from the sofa in expectation of leaving, stood still.

Thackrey's right foot stopped rocking. He looked back at Eden. "*Know* her? Of course not. How do you even imagine that happening? I haven't seen Reggie in years, and when I did, it was down in the city. I met Elise up here in Santa Rosa. Different worlds."

"With you in common."

"With me? Yes, I suppose—although I don't know what you're implying by that."

Thackrey faced Eden as she stood. He smiled. "I must say, Detective Somers, you don't have the usual personality of a police officer."

"What personality is that?"

Thackrey glanced at Mahler. "Smugly moralistic."

"I don't find those sorts of generalizations hold true."

"Is that right? I only meant you seem a bright young woman. I never associated intelligence with law enforcement."

"Maybe we'll surprise you."

"Maybe you will. I'm not an expert on the matter, of course. I'm just an engineer who happens to be good at writing code. It's a binary occupation, one thing or the other."

"But that's not all you do, is it?"

"Isn't it? Perhaps we can chat again. In the meantime, I hope you'll take care. Intelligence is a...rare gift. But in your line of work, I would think it's equally important to know when you're close to danger."

Eden looked back and met his eyes. "What makes you think I don't know?"

Chapter Thirty-One

(i)

"What kind of place is too good for a Starbucks?" Rivas came out of the coffee shop on the corner of Howard and Third in San Francisco's South of Market district. He maneuvered around a crowd of pedestrians waiting for the light and turned his back against the chill, damp wind blowing down Third.

"Six bucks for a small." Handing one of the coffees to Holland, Rivas yelled above the roar of a jackhammer across the street. "Something called Ethiopia Sidamo."

Holland smiled, opening his coffee. "This is what the world looks like when high-tech money takes over, Rivvie. Different scene back in the eighties when my dad was on the job here. Then it was bathhouses, leather bars, junkies shooting up in the doorways. Now it's the Digital Renaissance. Hipsters and posers. Skinny jeans and designer glasses in every sidewalk cafe."

Rivas took the top off his coffee and watched a cyclist change lanes in front of a Muni bus. "Man, I feel like a fish out of water. Where the fuck are we going?"

Holland looked at his phone. "End of the next block. By the way, I texted Frames on the drive down. Told him we're close to the boys who put the dogs in his car. Thought he'd want to know."

The offices of DivingBell were the ground floor of a renovated, century-old stone building. The entrance was etched with the company's logo—a windowed canister, with a chain rising upward—which the detectives had seen on Elise Durand's computer. Entering, Rivas and Holland stepped into an empty lobby. Their attention was immediately drawn to a glass door on the left side, with a view of a cavernous space where tables of computer workstations spread across the floor and an army of Holland's hipsters stared at screens.

A large, blank television hung on the lobby wall in front of the detectives. Cheery musical notes sounded, and an earnest-looking woman with a mass of curly hair appeared on the screen. She seemed to be sitting behind a desk in a bare room. "Good morning, gentlemen," she said. "May I help you?"

Holland held up his badge. "Police. Here to speak with the owner."

"The owner?" The woman frowned. She repeated the word as if it were in a new language. "I'm not sure *who* that would be."

"Okay, darling. Your top cheese. Whatever his or her title is."

"Yes, sir. Do you have an appointment?"

Holland grinned. "No, sweetheart. We don't make appointments. It's about a murder."

The woman on the screen blinked and shifted in her seat. "I'm sorry, sir. Did you say murder?"

"That's right. Homicide investigation. We have a few questions. Quick chat, and we're out of your hair." Holland turned toward the glass door. "Through here?"

The woman jumped up. "Sir, sir. You can't go inside without an escort. Please wait for Monica." She looked down and tapped at a computer tablet. "You'll be meeting in...Nebraska."

Holland looked back at the screen. "Sorry. What?"

"Nebraska. Third room on your right. Monica will show you."

Thirty seconds later, a woman in jeans and oxford shirt arrived on the other side of the glass and lifted a plastic card from a lanyard around her neck. The door emitted a metallic buzz and swung open.

"All right if we bring these?" Holland held up his coffee. "Won't contaminate anything?"

Monica giggled and led Holland and Rivas through the company's workspace. The room was filled with conversation and ringing phones. The interior walls were painted in bright primary colors. Redbrick pillars rose to a fifteen-foot ceiling featuring exposed ventilation ducts and electrical conduits. Farther inside, they came to a row of glass-walled conference rooms, labeled Illinois, Michigan, and Nebraska. Monica gestured toward the open door of the last room. "Enjoy," she said and walked briskly away.

Inside the meeting room, Holland and Rivas took seats at a polished oak table. The cheery musical notes sounded from another TV screen on the wall, and the curly-haired woman appeared again. "Ms. Palmer and Mr. Keegan will join you shortly." The screen went blank.

Holland drank his coffee and looked around the room. "You suppose they can hear us?"

Rivas shrugged. "How can they? We're in Nebraska."

A minute later, a man in a flannel shirt and cargo pants led an attractive woman into the conference room. "Josh Keegan," the man said, "VP for Operations, and this is April Palmer, in-house counsel." He put business cards in front of the detectives while the two of them sat on the opposite side of the table. Keegan's short, black hair was moussed into peaks like cake frosting. Palmer sat stiffly in a trim, dark suit.

Rivas saw Keegan take in Holland's wool cap.

"Sorry for the delay," Keegan said. "Major launch coming up. All-hands teleconference in"—he consulted his cell phone—"exactly twelve minutes."

Rivas took a folder from his lap and laid it on the table. "We'll make it quick."

Keegan nodded, reading something on his phone.

"We're investigating the murder of Elise Durand last Monday night in Santa Rosa."

"What's that have to do with us?" Keegan still looked at his phone.

For an instant Holland imagined grabbing Keegan's phone and snapping it in half. "We believe two individuals associated with this company were involved in the homicide."

Keegan looked up, smiling. "Really? I'm sorry, officers, but this is a sixty-million-dollar startup. We're building a new tool for search engines, and our first major launch is in three weeks. The people out there are working twenty-four seven and don't have time to—"

Rivas removed from his folder a piece of paper bearing the company's logo. He slid it across the table. "Elise Durand, our victim, designed this."

Keegan glanced at the logo. "I'm not involved with marketing collateral. I work mostly with the teams writing code. You'd have to speak with—"

Holland leaned forward. "Let's keep it simple. We just need to locate the two men."

"Who are they? We have many employees from the North Bay."

Rivas took out the photo of the three men in Spring Lake Park. "We're trying to identify these men. We believe two of them are Benjamin Thackrey and Victor Banerjee. The third is an Asian male."

Keegan whistled. "Benjamin Thackrey?"

"You know him?" Rivas asked.

"Obviously. Guy's a legend. But Ben Thackrey wouldn't be involved in this."

Rivas suddenly saw how out of place the black-and-white homicide photos were on the table of this brightly lit conference room. What did the couple across from him, or the people in the workspace beyond, know about murder? Their lives and their busyness were based on the illusion that they weren't inches away from a stranger reaching out and taking their life.

Keegan pulled the photo close. His face paled. "It's a little difficult to see anything in this picture."

"So you don't recognize them?"

"I didn't say that. What's that...thing?"

"That *thing* is the body of Elise Durand," Rivas said.

Keegan shoved the photo to Palmer. He held up his hands. "Look, guys. I don't mean to sound uncooperative. But in the digital age, privacy is the new frontier. And this company has a commitment to preserving the privacy of employees and customers. It's right here in our original mission statement." Keegan ran a finger across his phone screen and held it toward Holland. "Third bullet. Commitment to ensuring the privacy of personnel and users."

Palmer straightened in her chair. "I think what Josh is saying is, this company requires a subpoena before revealing any information about its principals, staff, or investors."

Holland smiled. "A *subpoena*?" He gathered the photo and the logo and put them back in Rivas's folder.

"That's correct. It's standard administrative procedure in circumstances such as this. You'll find the same thing at other companies."

"Standard administrative procedure?" Holland gestured outside the conference room. "Lot of people working here." He pulled his phone from his pocket. "Here's the other way we do this. I go to a chat room at the *Chronicle* or *Wired* and say two individuals at DivingBell are under suspicion as accomplices in the murder of a young woman whose body was found dumped in a park in Santa Rosa."

Rivas turned to Holland. The detective gave away nothing in his expression.

Keegan's phone rang again. He angrily jabbed at it. He stood and faced Holland. "You can't come in here and bully us into giving you private information."

Palmer touched Keegan's arm. "Josh, I think we might consider a different course of action."

At that moment Monica knocked on the conference-room door and pointed to her watch.

"I've got to do this telecon," Keegan said.

Palmer interrupted him. "My thought is, in the present circumstances, our fiduciary responsibilities take precedence over the privacy issues. It's in the best interest of this company to submit to legal authority and identify the individuals and their addresses. We can file an objection ex post facto and cite the exigency of the request."

Keegan pulled his arm away from Palmer. "Whatever," he said. "The launch slips, and this building'll be empty in two days." He pushed past her to leave the room.

Palmer tapped her computer tablet and turned it to face Rivas and Holland. "The individuals in question are not principals or employees of this company, but they were among the original angel investors. Their names are Victor Banerjee and Russell Tao. That's their address. We have no information for Mr. Thackrey."

Rivas wrote the address in his notebook, and the two men stood to leave.

"What will it do?" Holland asked.

Palmer held the conference-room door open. "What will *what* do?"

"Your product. What will it do?"

Palmer smiled. "What they all do. Change the world."

(ii)

(FRIDAY, 10:10 A.M.)

When Gina Cipriani appeared in the doorway of the VCI room, Eden looked around her for help, but for the moment, she had the place to herself. "If you're here to make a disciplinary report to my supervisor, Lieutenant Mahler's not here."

"We need to talk." Cipriani spoke quietly.

Holding up a finger, Eden led the way to the interview room and closed the door. They sat to face each other across the table.

Cipriani shook her head. "I hated girls like you in high school."

"What's that supposed to mean?"

"Good grades. Pretty girls who got dates."

Eden smiled. "Wow. That last part was definitely not me."

"The only way I get along as a cop is to be as hard and tough as the guys. Even then they don't respect me. They look at me and figure I'm butch."

"Law enforcement doesn't attract the most sensitive men."

Cipriani shrugged. "Anyway, I'm not here to talk about that.

I came here to tell you about Fresno. I never really caught on at the PD there. The department had a few women before me but not many. Command tolerated us but didn't offer any support. I was fair game for the guys in the field. Practical jokes, sexual threats. At first I thought it was initiation stuff, but it went on and on."

"Did you file a complaint?" Eden asked.

"For what? A female officer before me filed a complaint and got a load of shit. I went along and kept my head down. But when the thing happened with the Avelos case, it was the last straw."

"What exactly happened?"

"Sandoval sent you the transcript from the tip line?"

"I read it, but why don't you tell me." Eden took out a notepad and pen and leaned forward.

Cipriani stared at the tabletop. "After the Avelos girl was found, the department opened a homicide tip line. On the second night, I'm working the phone. After midnight I get this call. Female. Young. She's crying, out of breath. It's somewhere outside, traffic in the background. And the girl's...scared. That's the thing that stuck in my head, even weeks later. How scared she was. That's what you don't get in the transcript."

"Go over what the girl said."

"She said the night of the Avelos murder, her boyfriend comes home and starts acting weird. He's excited, can't sit still. She asks him what's wrong, and he says to shut the fuck up. She tries to say something, and he lets loose. He gets her facedown on the bed and tears off her blouse. Then he takes out a knife and cuts her. Once, at the base of the spine."

Cipriani looked up at Eden. "The medical examiner told us about the cut on Avelos's body, but that information wasn't public. No one outside the department knew. So I hear this girl talking about the same kind of cut, and I think, shit. I ask her to repeat it so I'm sure. And she says it again. The way she says, it's at the *bottom* of her back."

"But according to the transcript, she doesn't give you her name or the boyfriend's name, right?" Eden wrote quickly on the pad.

"No. She's obviously scared. Scared of him, of what he'll do. So all I can think is, keep the caller talking, calm her down, develop trust. But she starts crying again. I'm asking for the location, saying we can have a unit there. I ask the boyfriend's name, but she says the guy's going to kill her. I ask her name. I ask that three times. But she doesn't answer. That's all she says."

"Yeah, I saw that," Eden said. "Then she hangs up?"

"There's some ambient sound. Something, I don't know… cars going by. After that she hangs up. The whole thing is seventy-three seconds. I remember because we went over and over it. We couldn't trace the call."

"So you didn't get any names?" Eden tapped her pen on the table.

"No, and that's just it. It's the whole point of our job, right? After the call, I get funny looks from other officers. Turns out, the investigating detectives figure it's my fault I didn't get the names. If the guy kills again, or the girl on the phone turns up dead, it's on me."

Eden leaned back. "So when I come to you yesterday, you figure I'm blaming you for the girls here in Santa Rosa."

"Something like that."

"You realize I'm not, right? Anyway, the girls in Santa Rosa were killed *before* Avelos."

"Yeah. I get that."

"But tell me, is there anything else you remember about the call? What was the girl's voice like?"

"She had that Okie accent some people in Fresno have, but nothing unusual. Believe me, I went over that transcript a hundred times. No unusual words or expressions. No details. No... nothing."

Eden nodded. "I didn't see anything either."

Cipriani raised her hands in futility. "I don't even know why I'm telling you this. No matter what I do, it's going to come back on me all over again, in *this* friggin' department."

"No, it won't. I won't let it."

Cipriani hunched over the table. "You can't promise that. Why would you even say it?"

Eden met her eyes. "You're right. I'm sorry. So why *did* you tell me?"

"Last night, I'm home alone, thinking about what you said. How you got under my fucking skin."

Eden forced a smile.

"Sorry," Cipriani said. "It's true. Anyway, I go through the call again in my mind, and I remember something I must have blocked from my memory. At the very end of the call. I'm asking the girl questions and waiting to hear her voice, and she doesn't say anything. So I stop talking for a few seconds and wait. But there's another sound, after the traffic sounds. Another voice— not the girl's. It was too faint for the transcriptionist to hear, and I forgot it because the voice wasn't the girl."

"What was it?"

"A man's voice. Or, at least at the time I thought it was a man. Maybe it didn't happen at all and I imagined it. I don't know."

"Wait. It was a man?" Eden moved forward, on the front of her chair.

"Yeah. A man."

"Could you recognize anything about the voice?"

"That's just it. He only says one word. It was a name: Laura."

"Laura?"

"Yeah. Someone said it. Laura. Or maybe Lauren. I mean, who the fuck cares, right? It's just a first name. We don't have anything else." Cipriani spread her hands on the tabletop and stared at them.

"Could it have been Lorin? With an 'o'?"

"How the Jesus fuck do I know? I just said I could barely hear it. What difference does it make?"

Eden reached across the table and grabbed one of Cipriani's hands. "You on shift?"

Cipriani looked down where Eden was holding her hand. "No. I'm off 'til Sunday. Why?"

"I want you to meet Lorin."

Chapter Thirty-Two

(i)

"Where are you now?" Russell's voice came out of Thackrey's phone.

Looking out the driver's-side window, Thackrey could see leaves blowing across a wet parking lot. He was tired—finally. The police interrogation had drained the last of his energy. If he could just close his eyes, he would sleep for days. Thackrey held his phone in his fingertips. "Outside a condo in Santa Rosa. Waiting for someone."

"Jesus, Ben, are you buying more shit?"

"No...it's something else. The cops were just at my house."

"What? From VCI?"

"Yeah, the one called Mahler. The boss. Something's fucked up with that guy. He's got this...weird thing about him." Up close, the cop had surprised Thackrey. The guy had a dangerous raggedness that made him seem capable of something irregular.

"What kind of weird thing?"

"Like he's sick. Or, he did a couple lines of coke before he came in."

Russell sighed. "Maybe that was the drugs in *your* head."

"No, I'm serious," Thackrey said. "The other thing, I'm looking at him, and I'm thinking, 'Fuck, man, I was inside your house last night.'"

"Does *he* know that?"

"Maybe. I could see he's thinking about it. The other one was there, too. The girl."

"Detective Somers?"

"Eden Somers. That girl's playing some games." Thackrey saw her face again, refusing to smile.

"Are you on crank right now?"

"I don't remember. What difference does it make?" Over the last few hours, reality had become unreliable for Thackrey. His memory surprised him, with flashes too vivid for a dream—a woman he recognized, digging her nails into his arm, screaming like a wounded cat.

"What'd the police ask?" Russell said, trying to keep Thackrey on a linear path.

"Usual mangled syntax. What was your relationship with the victim? How do you have a relationship with a victim?"

"What'd you say?"

"I said I was involved. Anyone who came within ten feet of Elise was involved. The cops know about the drug buy Saturday night. That dipshit Peña must have talked."

"I think we knew that was going to happen."

"They asked if I have a gun," Thackrey said. How had he remembered that? He was amazed at this single fact floating to the surface.

"We must have left some residue on your girlfriend's right hand. Where's the gun, anyway?"

"It's not at home, if that's what you're worried about. By the way, the questions weren't all depressing. We had a few lighter moments. Mahler asked me if I own dogs. 'Do you own dogs, Mr. Thackrey?' The way he said it was funny."

"Hilarious. You didn't laugh, right?"

"Of course not."

"So you were calm?"

"I'm always calm. But it was strange. Detective Somers was sitting on the sofa with her feet in Elise's blood. All she had to do was to look down."

Hearing himself, Thackrey wondered if the part with the blood was real. It sounded real.

"Did they ask about Vic and me?" Russell asked. "Did it sound like they ID'd us?"

"Not a peep. Maybe you guys lucked out and you've got some more time."

"Maybe. The keystroke logger shows they're investigating a murder in Fresno."

"Yeah, they asked me if I was in Fresno in 2017. It was bizarre."

"So nothing about DivingBell?"

"Nada. Maybe they're not as smart as you think. At least not all of them." Thackrey remembered Eden asking him about Elise and Reggie. For a moment he thought of telling Russell but decided against it.

"Did it sound like the cops know what happened to Elise?" Russell asked.

"What did happen?" Thackrey leaned against the headrest and stared out the windshield, his mind thrown back into the terrifying story. Fragments of memory mixed themselves with the nightmares he'd been having, so it felt like picking his way through fractured glass. "I remember cooking dinner, Elise and I eating at the kitchen counter. I look at her and I can see the Oxy going off inside her head. She does that zombie thing. Barely talking. Hair hanging in her eyes. Finally she looks at me and says, 'When I'm dead, I want you to wrap me in a blanket and put me in the water.' Where did she get those ideas?"

"You told us that."

Did he already tell them? It seemed impossible. "She wanders off. I think she's asleep in the bedroom. I'm not feeling well. So I take all the Adderall and snort five or six lines of the new shit."

"In hindsight, probably not the best idea."

"Next thing I know, she has my gun. 'I'm going to kill you,' she says. 'I know what you did to that other girl, and I'm not going to end up like her.'"

"What'd you say?"

He couldn't remember, but details weren't important anymore. "I try to calm her down. I say I'll help her. But she tells me I'm not her father."

"What about the gun?"

"It's heavy. She can't hold it straight. All of a sudden it goes off. Boom. Then two more times. It kicks, and the rounds end up in the wall. She starts crying and drops the gun."

"That's when you should have left."

Thackrey looked at his phone and considered the thought. He tried to remember driving away. Had he left? No. He saw himself standing in the living room with Elise. "I stayed. I put on her favorite song—Sam Cooke singing 'You Send Me.' She's like a little girl now. She wants to be held. We dance in the living room without any lights. Back and forth in front of the sofa. She's humming along. I tell her she'll be okay. We hold each other in the dark, barely moving. The song's on repeat. It goes on and on."

Each time he remembered, something different flew at him. Now, alone in the car, he held up his hands against what was coming. "But all the speed I snorted is going through me like a truck. My head's spinning. I keep it in as long as I can. Then my whole body's...rushing. I think I'm having a stroke. I don't know what's happening. All of a sudden, she's fighting me. 'Take me home,' she says. 'Take me home.' Over and over. I try to touch her, but she's like this thing coming apart in my hands. I grab her hands...neck. She digs her nails into my arm. She's crying, making this terrible sound. I think: This is what I've always hated. How uncontrolled she is."

Had he screamed out loud just now or only remembered it? He looked outside again and watched leaves floating in a puddle. "She falls backward." Thackrey spoke quietly, his voice hoarse from screaming, or imagined screaming. "One minute I've got her. The next, she hits her head on the corner of the table and blood's everywhere. The song...it's unbelievable...the stupid music's still playing. I lie down and cradle her head. For once in her life, she's still."

"Which is when you called us." Russell's disembodied voice coming out of the phone startled him.

"Yeah...that's when I called you." Thackrey put his hands on the steering wheel and saw their innocence.

"Ben, listen," Russell said. "You need to do something. Call Armand. He's got lawyers."

"I don't know. The thought of being in that office...listening to the way he talks—"

"You don't have a lot of choices, Ben."

Thackrey looked across the parking lot and saw the street number and the building's darkened windows. Story over. "I don't need a lot of choices—I just need one."

(ii)

Susan Hart sat in the chair that faced Mahler's desk. "What is it this time?"

"I was thinking about your ponytail," Mahler said. "You were the youngest. Just twenty, right?"

"I still am twenty."

"Your father talked about the things you won't get to do."

"What's to stop me? You asked me once what I want. You know what I want? To breathe again. To take a long, full breath and feel it in my lungs."

"I can't help you with that."

"You keep blinking." Susan Hart leaned forward and peered at him. "What's wrong with your eyes?"

"The migraine affects my vision. Someone's coming to help me."

"Good," she said. "You know, I never saw the guy who killed me. Did I tell you that? I stopped to catch my breath, and he came up behind. It's usually the best part of a run. You've got the high of your run, of being spent. Except for that time—"

"We figured that from the footprint patterns."

"I heard him, though. Voice like he had a snake for a tongue. 'You should be more careful.' That's what he says as he's squeezing the cord around my neck. 'Bitch,' he says. I always hated men saying that word, and it was the last thing I heard."

"This time we'll arrest him."

"It won't change my murder, will it? I'm not coming back. This…with you…it's not living in the real world."

"I get that."

"You remember that Dickinson poem where she says our death makes a short, potential stir? My death wasn't my own."

"It's my fault we didn't get Partridge."

She looked down at her hands. "I hated that my death was with that man…and you."

"With me?"

"After I died, you were always there, wanting something."

"You're right."

"I like you, Eddie, but I don't want to be stuck here with you. Saying the same things over and over."

"Is that what we do?"

"It's better when we talk about other things or we don't talk at all."

"So it's changing?"

She smiled a thin, wan smile. "You are, Eddie. I'm dead, remember? This is you. Each time you think of me, it's different."

A knock sounded on Mahler's office door. He looked up to see Kate standing inside.

"Your message said to come over." Holding her briefcase, she shifted back and forth. "It said urgent."

He glanced at the empty chair opposite him. Susan Hart never hung around for company. "Close the door, Kate. Please."

"What is it, Eddie? Come on."

"Close the door."

Kate pulled the door shut and looked at her phone. "I'm due for a court appearance in forty-five minutes. What do you want?"

What did he want? It was the same question she asked the last time. He never knew what he wanted. Or, rather, he did—to have her come into his office while he replayed the fantasy of changing their last argument two years ago. He would retrace his steps all the way back to her apartment and awaken to her kissing him in bed. The impossibility of it washed over him, an unexpected grief. He took a deep breath. "I can't see."

"See what?"

"Remember when we were together, and I got migraines? I had those things in my eyes?"

"The dead spots? You called them something—"

"Scotoma. That's what's happening now."

"So what do you see?"

"A bright light. Growing and moving across my eyes. It's like…flickering."

"It's there now?"

He blinked and looked. For an instant he saw her, gripping her purse strap—a familiar sign of impatience. She was always smarter, quicker, three steps ahead. He remembered the sexual energy of having all that intelligence waiting for him. "The light was there a minute ago. It alternates with this other thing. Like a blind space I can't see through. The space blocks out the middle of my sight."

"Shouldn't you go to the ER?"

"I don't have time. Truro's given us a deadline to make an arrest. We've got two and a half hours."

"So, you're kidding, right?" Kate pulled her hair away from her face. "Deadline or no deadline, you can't see, and you're driving a car?"

"We're close to the end on this investigation. I can't stop."

"You have a suspect in the Elise Durand homicide? You can make an arrest?" She was suddenly a lawyer again, all business.

"I can't say any more. But we're close."

Kate rechecked her phone. "In that case, I have to go. Why'd you call me?"

"I wanted to talk to somebody…you."

"Now I remember why we're not together." Kate sat in front

of Mahler, in the chair Susan Hart had left two minutes earlier. "How much medication have you taken? When was the last Imitrex?"

"Couple hours." Mahler spread pill packages on his desk. "I've taken two hundred milligrams today."

"Take a hundred more and another four hundred of the ibuprofen."

"You want me to OD?"

"You want to be able to see?"

Mahler cut apart the packages and swallowed the pills.

"Drink some black coffee," Kate said. "I'll get a cup from the break room."

Mahler heard the parental tone in her voice. She was taking care of him. If he needed any confirmation of how far they were from their old intimacy, it was there in her solicitude.

When Kate returned, she put a paper cup in Mahler's hand.

Mahler tasted the coffee. "You're going to miss your appearance."

"I texted Pat and asked her to take care of it."

"Who's the client?"

Kate shrugged. "It's not that interesting."

He felt trapped by the pain of being with this Kate, who no longer loved him and who reminded him of what he had lost— both wanting her to leave and needing her to stay. "Tell me," he said. "Just sit there a minute and tell me."

"Okay. Peter John Fenton." Kate settled back in her chair. "Appearance before Judge Barron. Room 105J."

"Barron? I hope your Mr. Fenton has friends in high places."

"My Mr. Fenton has six friends every morning. His problem is, he drinks them for breakfast and then gets in his car."

"Let me guess. Third DUI."

"Fourth. Few years ago, this guy has his own tax preparation business. How do you screw that up, right? Somehow he manages it. Apparently his charm alone isn't enough to save the marriage. The unemployment runs out, and his wife leaves him for sunnier shores. Takes the kid *and* the dog. To Mr. Fenton, all this looks better when he's half in the bag. Which brings us to an appearance before Barron."

Mahler drank more coffee. "This how you imagined your career when you were a first-year at Hastings?"

"Life's a hoot, isn't it?" Kate stood. "I should go. How're the thingies in your eyes?"

Mahler blinked and stared at his desktop. "Better."

His phone buzzed. He held it at arm's length to read a text from Eden. He stood. "We might have a new break in the Partridge case. I've got to run, too."

Kate paused in the doorway and turned back toward him. "You still talking to her, Eddie?"

"Who?" He saw Kate weave in and out of his vision.

She smiled. "Come on, Eddie. You've got two girls in your life. I'm the other one."

"Sometimes. Not as much."

Kate pointed to his phone. "You'll arrest him now. It'll end."

"Yeah," Mahler said. "Or at least it's nice to think so."

Chapter Thirty-Three

(i)

Rivas and Holland drove Spear Street through San Francisco's South Beach, each intersection revealing a right-hand view of the Embarcadero waterfront one block away. At mid-morning, the street lay in a dark canyon of tall buildings. The area had a cold, lonely beauty. When they found the block they were looking for, the wide sidewalk was empty but for a dog walker and a young mother pushing a stroller.

Rivas checked the address. In front of them stood a high-rise condo, occupying half the block. He double-parked and put a police ID on the dashboard. Climbing out, he bent backward to look up. A forty-story glass building rose to the sky, its upper floors gleaming in the morning sun. "Fuck," he said.

Holland joined him on the sidewalk. "Yeah. Fuck is right. I just sent Frames the address. He asked me to keep him up to speed."

They walked across a patio to the building's lobby, where a concierge stood at ease on a green marble floor. "Good morning, gentlemen. Welcome to Empyrean Towers. How may I help you?"

Holland held up his badge. "We're going to 3711. You don't need to announce us."

The concierge straightened and raised his chin. "Sir, it's Empyrean policy to announce all guests."

"Your choice, Ace." Holland shrugged. "You ring them before we get there, and we'll come back and charge you with obstruction."

The concierge's eyes widened. He gestured toward the elevators. "First one's the express to the upper floors."

The elevator leapt upward with a suddenness that seemed to lift the men off their feet. When the doors opened to the thirty-seventh floor, Rivas and Holland found the entrance to 3711. They took out their guns. Rivas looked at Holland and pressed the doorbell. The door opened, and a young Asian man faced them.

"Santa Rosa Police." Rivas waved his badge. "Are you Russell Tao? I have a warrant for your arrest."

Russell nodded silently and stepped backward.

"Put your hands where I can see them."

Inside the apartment, music played. Wilco singing "Far, Far Away."

Holland pushed past Rivas into the living room, where another young man was on his knees beside an open suitcase.

Holland stood in front of him, Glock in hand. "Victor Banerjee? Santa Rosa Police. We have a warrant for your arrest. Let me see your hands and stand up."

Holland waited while Victor stared back at him and slowly rose from the floor.

"Where on earth is Santa Rosa?" Victor asked.

When Rivas took over, Holland checked the rest of the con-dominium. He returned a minute later, shaking his head.

Holland patted down Victor and Russell. He removed their cell phones, handing one to Rivas and putting the other on the kitchen counter. Then he cuffed their hands behind their backs and pushed them onto the sofa.

Rivas read the two men their Miranda rights. When he fin-ished, he took one of Rushton Tyndale's prints from his pocket and held it toward the men. "Recognize yourselves?"

Victor peered at the photo. "Is that supposed to be us?"

Holland smiled. "That your defense? Might want to work on it." For a moment, he turned from the men to look out at the wide vista of the city and the bay. "Quite a view, gentlemen. It's like you're on top of it all."

Russell looked at him. "We *are* on top of it all."

"But it's a long way down."

Rivas tucked the photo back in his pocket. "You didn't expect us so early, did you? One of our guys found your key-stroke logger."

Russell mugged surprise. "I don't know what you're talking about."

"You want to tell us what happened?"

"I thought you already knew," Russell said.

"Tell us now, before lawyers get involved. Might help your case."

Victor smiled. "We'll wait for the suits."

Holland studied the sixty-inch TV screen, which was divided into nine pictures, each showing a webcam feed from a room in the house. In the living-room picture, he could see himself looking at the screen. "You need a security system inside your house?"

"You never know," Victor said, "when the riffraff might show up unannounced."

Rivas faced him. "Where's your Mercedes, Mr. Banerjee?"

"My Mercedes?"

"1959. License 9AKR321. Registered to you. We have a photo of it entering the gate at Spring Lake Park the night of Elise Durand's murder."

Victor shrugged. "Basement parking garage."

"Why don't you show me?"

Holland stepped close to Rivas. "You want to call for a couple units from the SFPD before you do that?"

"Be a little complicated now," Rivas said.

Holland nodded. "Up to you."

Rivas guided Victor by the shoulder. As they turned to leave the room, Rivas saw Victor and Russell exchange a look. Rivas called back to Holland, "Keep your boy in front of you."

Holland patted the top of Russell's head. "This guy? He'll be fine."

Rivas and Victor left the apartment and walked down the corridor. On the elevator, Rivas tapped the button for the basement garage and stepped behind Victor. The doors closed. Rivas felt the whoosh and the floor drop out from under his feet as the elevator descended. In his ear, his grandmother suddenly whispered, "Ready now, Danny?"

Her voice unnerved Rivas. Did Victor hear it? He leaned against the elevator to steady himself. Then, as if in a dream, he watched Victor drop his shoulder against the control panel, tripping the emergency stop. The car lurched. Off-balance, Rivas reached out blindly. Victor dodged under the detective's outstretched hand and kicked into Rivas's lower leg, snapping it like a dry stick. Rivas sucked in a sharp breath and fell against the elevator wall. Victor swung his elbow and struck the bridge of Rivas's nose, breaking bone and flinging Rivas's head backward. Shifting his weight, Victor swept a foot against Rivas's heels, collapsing the detective onto the floor. Rivas lay still, his face covered in blood.

Victor jumped toward the fallen man. Sixty seconds or so before security personnel noticed the stopped elevator.

Ten already gone.

Hands cuffed behind him, Victor reached into Rivas's pockets for the keys. By feel, he awkwardly inserted the metal shaft into the keyhole and released the cuffs.

Thirty seconds.

Victor removed his belt and wrapped it around Rivas's legs. He yanked it tight.

Forty seconds.

He pulled his phone out of Rivas's front pocket, tapped at the phone screen, and found the websites for the building's security cameras.

Fifty seconds.

The elevator display showed they were on the twenty-ninth floor. On his phone he located the security camera for the hallway on the twenty-ninth floor. It was empty.

Sixty seconds.

Victor switched off the emergency stop and opened the elevator doors. Grabbing the belt, he hauled Rivas off the elevator. Just before the doors closed, he saw a small pool of blood on the elevator floor. Too late.

He dragged Rivas down the hallway to a utility closet. Using a passcode reader app, he unlocked the door. Inside the small room, Victor heaved Rivas against a floor polisher. Rivas groaned. His broken leg was bent under his body. Victor removed his belt from Rivas and fastened it around his own waist. Unsnapping the detective's gun from its holster, Victor jammed it into his waistband behind his back. Finished, he climbed over Rivas and closed the door.

As Victor turned away from the utility closet, he noticed a young woman coming toward him from the end of the corridor. She was texting as she walked. Victor smiled and nodded. "How's it going?" The woman didn't look up.

At the elevators, he stood with his back to the wall to hide the gun. He waited until the young woman took an elevator down. Victor took the next one up.

On the thirty-seventh floor, he opened his phone to see the condo webcams. He flipped through images until he reached the living room. He saw Detective Holland lying still on the floor. Russell was not in view.

He tapped the screen to call Russell's cell. The phone rang four times and went to voicemail.

Victor went back to the webcam screens for the other rooms in the apartment: kitchen, dining room, master bedroom, guest bedroom, office.

All empty.

Where the fuck was Russell? He stared at his screen.

Did he leave the apartment? Why didn't he answer his cell?

Victor checked the webcam screens for the remaining rooms: Guest bathroom empty. Laundry room empty. Balcony.

The image for the balcony was missing.

(ii)

(FRIDAY, 10:57 A.M.)

Eden led Gina Cipriani up the stairs of the apartment complex, where they found Lorin Albright on the third-floor landing smoking a cigarette. Eden watched Albright's attention focus on the larger, uniformed officer.

"This is Officer Cipriani," Eden said.

Albright took a deep drag, blowing smoke out the side of her mouth. "You bring her along to arrest me for something?"

"No. We have some questions."

"What if I don't answer? You going to have this one lay a beating on me? Win says you people like to beat on folks."

Defiance flashed in Albright's eyes, the practiced toughness of someone used to getting hit. But Eden saw something weak in the gesture, too, and the surrender waiting behind it. She recognized in Albright's face, old at thirty, and in her ragged, half-bleached hair, the woman's sadness, her concession to what she had learned to be her place in the world. "The last time I was here, Ms. Albright, you said you're from Fresno and you go there on holidays to visit your mother and grandmother."

"What of it?"

"You said sometimes your boyfriend, Irwin Partridge, goes with you. Is that right?"

"Sometimes. Win and me go lots of places." Albright flicked her cigarette ash against the railing.

"We want to ask you about Fresno," Cipriani said.

"I didn't do nothing."

"That's not what this is about."

"Can we go inside and talk?" Eden asked.

Albright lifted her chin. "Tell me what you want right here."

"It's about a young woman who was killed in Fresno in 2017. Sandra Avelos."

"I don't know anything about that. I'm not going to talk about it, neither."

"She was strangled. Her killer was never found."

"I got nothing to say."

"Day after the murder, the Fresno police set up a phone tip line for the public to call in information."

"So?" Albright dragged again on her cigarette.

"The following night a young woman called the tip line and said she had information about the killing. She told the officer her boyfriend came home the night of the murder and was acting funny. He was wild and angry."

"You're making this up," Albright said.

"The caller said her boyfriend hit her and cut her with a knife."

"I don't know anything about this. You all have no right coming here and talking to me like this."

"The cut was a single mark at the bottom of her back. The caller told the officer her boyfriend cut her there. She was afraid of what he'd do."

Cipriani stepped toward Albright. "I'm the one you spoke to. I was the officer on the line."

Albright looked up at Cipriani with confusion. "That...thing was in Fresno, not here."

"I was a police officer in Fresno then. I was on the tip line that night. You spoke to me."

"How'd you know it was me?"

"We didn't," Eden said. "Until now."

"You shit-bastards." Albright threw her cigarette down to the parking lot. "All you cops. You're shit-bastards."

"Tell me what your boyfriend did that night," Cipriani said. "He's involved in other murders. You know that now, right?"

"I don't have to tell you nothing."

"The mark he cut on your back, the same mark was on Sandra Avelos," Eden said. "It was on two girls killed here in Santa Rosa and one in Vallejo."

Albright backed away from Eden. "Those things weren't my fault. Don't make it sound like they were."

Eden could see the woman's fight was gone. "All right. But you need to tell us everything you know. Right now."

"Win'll find out," Albright said. "He'll know I told you. He said if I opened my mouth about him cutting me, he'd off me. He knows things. Even if I don't say, he looks at me and knows things."

"Then come with us," Cipriani said. "We'll take you someplace safe."

"He'll find me, wherever I go. Win finds girls. That's what he does."

"We can get a court order," Eden said. "Do you know what that is? A judge'll sign a piece of paper that says you have to tell us what you know. And you'll have to let a medical examiner see your back. If you refuse, you'll go to jail."

"He was drunk. He said he made a mistake." Tears rolled down Albright's face. "He didn't mean to kill that girl. He said... if I told anyone he'd kill me, too. I didn't know where to go or who to tell. I called that night, but then he found me. I lied to him. I was so scared. Every day I was scared. He said he'd choke me like that girl and put my body somewhere my mom would never find it. My body'd be alone in a hole. Nobody would ever know."

Cipriani bent close to Albright. "He's not going to hurt you. You understand? We're going to get you somewhere safe, and we're going to arrest your boyfriend. But you have to tell us what you know."

Albright wiped her arm across her nose. "I'll tell you, but I won't be safe. It don't matter where you hide me or where you lock him up. And he'll come after you, too." Albright looked at Eden. "He don't like you. He told me."

At the words, Eden felt herself stiffen. She took a breath. "We're going to arrest him, Lorin. He won't bother anyone."

"It won't never be over with him," Albright said. "Never. There's ones he's killed the police don't even know about. When it comes to killing a girl, Win's smart. He's smarter than all of you put together."

Chapter Thirty-Four

(i)

Victor ran down the corridor of the thirty-seventh floor, past the front door to his condo, to the end of the hall and the rear entrance. He tapped his phone and looked at the webcam feed for the space just inside the rear entrance, a laundry room. It was empty. He scanned his keycard in the lock and stepped inside.

Moving noiselessly across the small room, he stopped at the inner door and listened. Music played inside the condo— Imagine Dragons, blasting "Radioactive." He pulled Rivas's gun from behind his back and flipped off the safety. In his other hand, he held the phone. The webcam feed showed the next room, the master bedroom, was empty.

Victor silently opened the door and walked onto the bedroom's thick carpeting. The vertical blinds on the floor-to-ceiling glass windows were turned to reveal a view of blue sky and the top of Renaissance Tower a block away. He remembered the first time he had looked out this window. Cressida, their boozy Realtor, giving them the pre-bid tour. "Here's what you'll see, boys, when you wake up each morning," she said, with a sly wink at the sleeping arrangements. The view from the window was like looking out of a plane. Some days Victor stood in front of the glass for half an hour, watching the clouds change, following one car after another on Mission Street.

On the bedside table, Russell's coffee mug sat with his own teacup, left there an hour earlier—a lifetime ago. Was their plan unraveling? If the cops showed up, he and Russell had agreed to escape if they could. Packed bags and fake passports waited in the living room. Flight from SFO to Bangkok. Be on the beach in Ko Lanta in two days.

He could run now. Back down the elevator to the car. But where the fuck was Russell? He felt the urge to call out for him, but some caution warned against it.

Looking down at his phone, he saw the webcam feed for the living room. The cop Holland was lying still beside the sofa. The rest of the room was empty.

Victor walked into the living room. The sofa had been pushed a few feet from its usual spot, the chair beside it overturned. Signs of a struggle. He examined the cop. Holland was breathing but unconscious. A red welt was visible on his forehead; a path of dried blood ran under his nose and across one cheek. Victor pictured Russell's head kick, a sudden backward spin that Holland saw too late.

Imagine Dragons were on to "Demons." Victor tried to listen for other sounds. He thought of turning down the music but decided to let it play.

Any moment Russell would call and say he was in the Mercedes, engine idling on Spear, telling Victor it was time to go.

On his phone Victor viewed the dining room, guest bedroom, and office. All empty.

Victor raised his gun and walked to the kitchen. He leaned over the counter to see into the room's blind spot, the galley space in front of the stove and refrigerator. Nothing.

He checked the time. Twelve minutes since he'd left Rivas's body in the utility closet. *How long before someone found the cop or he regained consciousness? How long before someone noticed the blood on the elevator floor?*

Victor looked back the way he had come—through the living room, where he and Russell had spent fifty grand decorating to impress their guests. A lot of good it did now. Soon the cop on the living-room floor would regain consciousness, and Victor would have to make another decision.

The emptiness of the condo was a puzzle. He remembered Ben, sitting behind his own house in Dry Creek Valley two nights earlier, saying how much he hated people who solved puzzles. The real creativity was in making the mystery, not solving it. Fucking Ben. Why had they helped him? All he cared about was showing how smart he was.

Suddenly, Victor saw something. At the far end of the kitchen countertop lay Russell's phone. He stared at it. *Why was the phone there?* Russell never went anywhere without his phone. At least now he knew Russell would not be calling.

Only one part of the condo remained to check—the balcony. Victor walked to the balcony door and looked at his phone. The webcam feed for the balcony was missing. It had happened once before during a rainstorm, when the wind dislodged the camera's wiring.

Victor shoved his phone in his pocket and reached for the door handle. He felt tired. The nights without sleep, the things they had done—all of it settled on him.

He pointed his gun ahead of him and opened the door. A cold wind blew across the waist-high glass wall. The curving superstructure of the Bay Bridge was visible in the distance and, across the bay, the low hills of Oakland.

Russell stood in the corner of the balcony, bracing himself against the wall. The wind whipped his hair and billowed his shirt. He faced Victor but didn't speak. His eyes were open wide, frozen.

The moment Victor stepped toward Russell, he felt the tip of a gun barrel pressed against the back of his head. "Right about now," a voice behind him said, "I'll bet you're thinking, 'Who–the–fuck–is–this?'"

Victor looked straight ahead at Russell watching him. "First things first," the voice instructed. "Let's put that gun on the floor so no one gets hurt."

Victor bent slowly. He placed Rivas's Sig on the balcony floor and stood up. The man behind him kicked the Sig out of sight. The whole time, the gun barrel remained pressed against his head. "Now, to answer your question," the voice said, "I'm the asshole with the Charger, the one where you put the two dogs. Remember that?"

"I don't know what you're talking about," Victor croaked. His mouth was dry.

"Dogs on speed," Frames said. "Funny stuff. We all had a good laugh about that one, didn't we?"

Victor felt Frames lean close. "But now, bright boy, it's time to be serious for a minute. Your friend Russell and I were just discussing whether it's better to be shot trying to avoid arrest or take your chances jumping off this balcony. I told him any dope can be shot, but how many times in your life do you get to jump off the thirty-seventh floor? I mean, how do you really know you can't fly?"

"You won't shoot us," Victor said, trying to sound firm. "We're unarmed."

"Seriously? Man, you were armed until ten seconds ago. So was your little buddy. That means I have guns with your prints. Besides, Russell showed me how to disconnect the security camera out here. So who's to know? It's you, me, and the fucking seagulls."

Frames's voice in Victor's ear was dead calm. "But before we watch Russell over there test the laws of gravity, I've got another question for you, bright boy. Since you're carrying a gun belonging to Sergeant Daniel Rivas, I have to ask, how is he?

"Reason I'm asking, sport," Frames said, "I'm trying to decide where to put this gun when I pull the trigger. See, if Rivas is just unconscious, like, say, Kenny Holland back inside there, I'm going to put the end of this gun between your legs and shoot your balls off. Trust me, you're not going to need them in prison. But now, if Rivas is dead, I'm going to leave the gun where it is and pull the trigger. I'll be honest with you. You take the Glock's caliber and being this close up, the round's going to set your hair on fire going in and make a hole the size of a baseball on its way out."

The gun barrel pressed harder against Victor's head. "So let me ask you again, bright boy. How's Daniel Rivas?"

(ii)

(FRIDAY, 11:28 A.M.)

Mahler drove into the parking lot of Creekside Apartments. A police unit was parked at the base of the stairs. A tall female officer stood next to a young woman and two other uniformed officers. At the far end of the lot, Eden sat in her car.

Mahler parked beside Eden and climbed in next to her. "That Lorin Albright?"

"Yeah." Eden stared ahead. "The female officer is Gina Cipriani, the one I was telling you about. Albright gave up Partridge. Told us about Sandra Avelos, the girl in Fresno."

"She knew Partridge killed her?"

"Partridge told her. Said it was a mistake...an accident. Told Albright he followed Avelos in the park. Got angry she wasn't cautious. Wanted to show Avelos how vulnerable she was, but when he put the cord around her neck, she fought back. According to Partridge, the whole thing was Avelos's fault."

"What'd Albright say about Partridge cutting her own back?"

"After he killed Avelos, Partridge went back to Albright's mother's house. The mother and grandmother were watching TV in the living room, and he found Albright alone in her bedroom. She asked him a few questions about where he was, but to Partridge, this sounded like an interrogation. He hit her on the side of the head with a closed fist. She lost consciousness. When she woke, she was facedown on the bed and he was on top of her. He cut her back, like the women he strangled."

Mahler raised his eyebrows. "He did all this with mom and grandmom in the next room watching TV?"

"Apparently. But at some point, Partridge had enough awareness to know he couldn't kill Albright without being discovered. He told her about Avelos and said she's next if she tells anyone. He said he'd find her wherever she hides."

"She believed him."

Eden nodded. "She believed him."

Mahler studied the group across the lot. His migraine had eased. The scotoma was gone. But he knew the relief was temporary. "We'll need to get her full testimony," he said.

"What'll happen to her?"

Mahler shrugged. "Depends what she tells us."

"Can we arrest Partridge now?"

"I sent Martin to do it as soon as I got your call," Mahler said. "He's making the arrest where Partridge works, a big box store called Brenners, off the freeway. Couple more units'll be behind him."

"You know Partridge's there?"

"I've had Tom Woodhouse keeping an eye on him. Since last night."

"Tom? Why since last night?"

"After we met Partridge in the parking garage, I wanted to keep track of him."

Eden studied Mahler's face. "You mean after he threatened me?"

"Okay, yeah, after he threatened you."

"Would you have done that if he threatened Martin or Daniel?"

"I don't know. Maybe. The point is, Detective Somers, you're the one who pissed him off, because you worked the case."

"Yeah, Albright just said Partridge would come after me."

Mahler shrugged. "See what I mean?"

"Why didn't you tell me about Woodhouse watching Partridge?"

"I don't know. I should have."

They watched Cipriani help Albright into the unit.

"I'd like to assist with Partridge's arrest," Eden said.

"It's not necessary. Martin's got it. Like I said, more units are on the way."

"You don't trust me after the way I pulled my weapon in the garage?"

"Nothing to do with that. If anything, I trust you more. You did this." Mahler gestured toward the unit across the lot. He felt the smallness of his answer. *Should he tell her, as Woodhouse suggested, how good an investigator she is—how she had broken through the Partridge case?* He couldn't get the words out of his mouth.

"What about Thackrey?"

"Rivas and Holland are in the city, arresting Victor Banerjee and the other suspect from the park photos. My guess is, those guys'll turn on Thackrey once they're in cuffs. We just need to wait for the call before we go back to Dry Creek to pick up Thackrey. I have an arrest warrant for Thackrey and a search warrant for his house. We might actually meet Truro's deadline after all."

"Can I go with you?" Eden asked.

"Not much to do. We put him in cuffs, read him his rights. He asks for a lawyer."

The unit with Cipriani and Albright drove out of the parking lot.

Eden turned to Mahler. "So this is it? It's over? The thing with Partridge and the girls two years ago?"

Mahler looked at her. "We get Partridge, it's over."

"You told me Wednesday night all the public wants is that it doesn't happen again. Putting Partridge away does that, right? He won't kill another girl."

"Mostly."

"Mostly?"

"Stuff like this doesn't go away. You have homicides in a small town, people don't forget."

"You mean the family?"

"The family, the community, the officers involved."

Eden watched Mahler. "But our finding the guy makes it less painful, doesn't it?"

Mahler looked out the window. "Doesn't bring back the

girls. But, yeah, things change. Over time, memories definitely change."

They were both quiet.

"I keep thinking—" Eden said. "Lorin Albright lived with Partridge for more than a year after the Avelos killing. Shared a bed. Had sex."

"She thought she couldn't escape," Mahler said. "Staying was better than running."

"I want to think I'd run."

"Maybe she wanted to. But fear's a real thing. Makes people believe all sorts of stuff. We're all afraid of something, Eden."

Eden heard him use her first name. Her face reddened. "There's something I wanted to tell you the other night when you were talking about my thesis and my FBI work. When I was in college, writing that paper, I had this experience. I don't know how to—"

Mahler put his hand on her arm. "Hey, listen. Stop. Okay?"

"I need to tell you."

"I know, but another time. Go home now and get some sleep. It's been a long week. We'll have lots of time to talk."

Eden drew a long breath. "Sure," she said. "Lots of time."

Chapter Thirty-Five

(i)

Frames sat on a kitchen stool, watching the EMTs, Tomas and Jesse. The two had arrived with a gurney and knelt now on either side of Holland. Frames admired their efficiency. Tomas bent close to Holland, while Jesse examined the head wound. "Can you hear me, Ken?" Tomas asked. "Can you open your eyes?"

Holland grunted, and Tomas repeated, "Can you hear me, Ken?"

Jesse's phone buzzed. He read a text. "Your colleague on the twenty-ninth floor is conscious. Concussion, broken nose, and possible broken fibula. He'll survive. Off his feet a while."

"What's a fibula?" Frames asked.

"Bone on the lateral side of the lower leg." Jesse pointed to his own leg. "Breaking it would hurt a lot."

"Really?" Frames studied Victor, who sat handcuffed beside Russell on the sofa a few feet away.

Frames pulled out his Glock and laid it on the kitchen counter. "So Tomas, my man, how're you guys at treating gunshot wounds?"

"Depends." Tomas looked up. "Where's the wound?"

Frames shrugged. "I haven't decided."

"Beg your pardon?"

"Never mind. Just…letting my mind wander."

From the floor, Holland yelled, "Fucking motherfuck."

"Signs of intelligent life," Frames said.

"Your friend here took quite a blow to the back of his head," Jesse said.

Frames leaned on the bar to look down at Holland. "There're worse places to hit him. I've never seen him without the stocking cap. Good to know there is a back to his head."

"Well, he's got a large lump there now." Tomas laid a blue ice pack under Holland's head. "Can you hear me, Ken?"

"I've got to go," Holland shouted.

"Suppose the gunshot wound was to the chest?" Frames asked.

Tomas smiled, in on the joke now. "Not much for us to do really. Usually fatal. Chances are, you hit the lungs, the heart, major artery."

"Sounds promising. How about the abdomen?"

"Lot of plumbing. Always a danger of bleeding out before getting to surgery."

"So many choices."

"What happened to you?" Tomas pointed to the glass cuts on Frames's face.

"Car trouble." Frames looked at Victor and Russell. "Right, gentlemen? You two have anything to say? You've already been Mirandized."

Russell and Victor exchanged a glance.

"Wait for the lawyers," Victor said.

Frames put the gun back in his holster. "Suit yourself. Whatever happens with Thackrey, you boys'll be charged as accomplices in the murder of Elise Durand."

Russell shook his head. "She wanted to be laid near the water. Ben thought we had to do that."

"Wait for the lawyers," Victor repeated.

Frames shrugged. "We've also got you for assault on a police officer, with what you did to Rivas and Holland there. And don't forget the dogs in the car. DA might call that attempted murder."

"You don't have any evidence connecting us to the dogs," Victor said.

"Sure about that? Tell us what you know. It might help your side of things."

"What do you need? You've got the photo in the park."

"Tell me about Thackrey," Frames said. "If he's like every other mutt, he's going to roll on you the minute we pick him up."

"That's just it," Russell grimaced. "Ben's not like every other...mutt."

Victor sighed. "Russ, this cop's playing you. He doesn't have any authority to use what you say."

"I think I gave Ben everything I owe him." Russell faced Frames. "Okay, here's Ben Thackrey. Graduates Stanford in three years. Starts a company called StreetBox—grows 600 percent in two years—sells it for forty million. Starts another company, BluFish. Runs a public offering in the middle of the 2002 recession, when no one is putting money anywhere, finds a pool of investors. That's where Vic and I come in."

"You worked for him?" Frames asked.

"Work?" Russell laughed. "We're running fifteen, twenty hours a day. Sleeping on cots in the break room. Pizza for breakfast. But it's worth it to be around Ben. He's in his element. He's this kid, literally a kid, in front of a roomful of programmers, drawing diagrams on a whiteboard. He's got…vision. The product launches massive. Everybody wants a piece. Three years in, and the company's got fifteen hundred employees, offices in Milan, Beijing, Mumbai. But Ben's bored. Makes one call to Yahoo and sells the whole thing. Turns twenty-four, he's worth four hundred million. Flies us to Macao for his birthday."

"I get it, the guy's rich."

Russell shrugged. "The thing is, it's not really the money. Ben's fun to be around. He can make stuff. You say, it'd be cool if we could do something, a couple days later he has a program. It's like he invents his world. And he could be the sweetest, most generous guy in the world. Four years ago, he helped me out of depression. Literally kept me alive. I owe him everything for that."

Holland looked across the room, focusing on Frames. "What the fuck?"

Frames saluted him. "Russell here coldcocked you. Take a few minutes. It'll all come back."

"So here's a question." Frames sat back on his stool and looked at Russell. "How'd your boy Thackrey get from doing startups to carrying a dead body through a park?"

"After BluFish, there're more companies—NetPort, Stinger, Drift. All of them hit big. At some point, Ben's no longer just an entrepreneur. He's the face of something. People in Silicon Valley discover it's good to have Ben on your side. He's invited everywhere. He's a celebrity, known for just being Ben Thackrey."

"That's when women play a larger part in his life. Thackrey always dated beautiful girls, even at Stanford. Once he becomes a celebrity, he moves in a new orbit. He meets wealthy women, a lot of them smart in their own rights. But Ben's easily bored. He's already smart. Why's he need more smartness? He's always looking for something else. Something he can't find. He's addicted to adrenaline. He's like a shark moving through the water, picking up women, dumping them.

"He has enough money and enough status that he throws things away. He drives cars until he's tired of them, literally leaves them by the side of the road. He furnishes houses and condos and never lives in them. He lives in a disposable world, casting off things when he doesn't want them anymore.

"Then he meets Reggie."

"Reggie?" Frames asked.

"Reggie Semple. She was famous for a while." Russell adjusted himself on the sofa, trying to get comfortable with his hands cuffed behind his back. "Youngest daughter of Gregory Semple. Old San Francisco family. Reggie grew up in Hillsborough. Had her coming-out at the Cotillion Club in 2008."

"Are we getting to Elise Durand?"

"Be patient. Reggie's at loose ends. Spends a year at USF, drops out. Tries modeling but finds she can't keep appointments. What she likes are parties. That's where she meets Ben—private party in Pacific Heights. The girl's flat-out gorgeous. She and Ben are attracted to each other. But she's a loose cannon. Big fan of Hangar 1 on the rocks and never says no to coke or weed. And she's got other boyfriends besides Ben. Guy named Tyler Morris, son of another old-money family and full-time heroin addict, and P. J. Weston, a new forward for the Golden State Warriors."

"I love the Warriors," Holland shouted.

Jesse held the cold pack against Holland's head. "Take it easy, Ken."

"For a while Reggie and Ben are a couple," Russell said. "She moves into his place in Los Altos. But she's gone a lot. Ben figures she's doing other guys, and she is. Photos show up on Instagram of Reggie partying with Morris or Weston or a dozen other guys. A story goes around about an abortion. When Ben and Reggie are together, they go at it pretty hard, the full ten rounds. He hits her, she hits him back. They come to our place, and Reggie has a bruise on her cheek or a split lip. They break up, get back together, break up, get back together. Then she's gone for good."

"Where'd she go?" Frames asked.

"You never heard this? She's gone-gone. Like, disappeared. Morris watches her get into a cab outside his place in Pacific Heights, and she's never seen again. San Francisco cops can't find a record from a cab or an Uber of a pickup at that location. Her father offers half a million for leads. The cops question her boyfriends—Morris, Weston, even Ben. Morris is too strung out to know anything, and his family hires the best lawyer in the city. Ben has an alibi—he was seen at a party that night seventy miles away in Healdsburg. The cops figure the whole thing has something to do with Reggie's heroin habit. In the end, Reggie Semple just falls off the face of the earth."

Frames leaned forward. "So why's this a story?"

"Because Ben's different after that. He's got this thing… this—"

"Look," Victor said, speaking for the first time.

Russell turned toward him. "Yeah," he said. "First time we saw him after that weekend, we knew he did it. No doubt."

"He killed this woman, Reggie whatever?"

"Semple. Yeah."

"And *he* knows *you* know?" Frames asked.

"Sure, but he also knows we're not going to do anything about it. And something changes in his head. He kills this woman and doesn't get caught. It's like he crosses this great divide where rules don't exist. After that, he falls in love with risk-taking for its own sake."

Holland listened to Russell. "I remember you. You're that guy."

Russell stared back at him. "I'll take your word for it."

"Then Ben starts doing drugs. Big-time," Victor said. "He always did weed and coke, but now he needs something to keep him on his toes, in case you guys come after him. He discovers Modafinil and mixes it with Adderall. But Ben always wants more. He empties the capsules, grinds the contents into powder, and snorts it. He's got no job, no responsibilities. He does sixty...a hundred and twenty milligrams a day. Pretty soon he's mixing Adderall with crank. With the drugs, he figures he can beat anybody. He can beat you cops at murder."

Frames sat up straight on the stool. "Then he meets Elise Durand?"

"Yeah, something about Elise captures him. She's different from the trust-fund party girls. She has ideas, gifts. She understands philosophy, poetry, art in a way that Ben doesn't. But she's also impulsive, unpredictable. Ben says when he's with her, it's like watching a foreign film without subtitles."

"So why's he kill her?"

Russell and Victor exchanged a look. "Technically, that was my fault," Russell said. "One night we're all high on some new ganja. Elise and Ben get into a fight. I say something like, 'Careful, Lisie. Ben's girlfriends disappear.' Elise doesn't get it right away. But the fucking Internet being what it is, a few days later she figures it out. And Elise being Elise, she has to say something. She can't help herself. She asks Ben if he killed Reggie. He tells her to fuck off. But she knows Ben did it. And now Ben knows she knows."

Frames nodded. "And, unlike you guys, he can't trust her to stay quiet."

"No, he can't. After that, she knew he was going to kill her. She just waited for it. The weird thing is, I think he actually cared for her. He felt something for her he hadn't felt for other women."

"And Ben held us responsible," Victor said. "Because of Russ's slip of the tongue. In his mind, it was our fault he had to kill her. So he made us help him take Elise's body to the park."

Russell turned to Victor. "We talked about leaving. We should have left."

"And the dogs in my car?" Frames asked.

Victor shrugged. "What dogs?"

(ii)

(*FRIDAY, 12:33 P.M.*)

Coyle drove slowly down the center lane of the parking lot at Brenners Home Improvement looking for Tom Woodhouse's white Honda. The retired detective had called to say Irwin Partridge was inside the store. Coyle would meet with Woodhouse and then wait until two more units arrived before going inside to make the arrest.

The parking lot was full of shoppers, everybody getting a jump on the weekend. Woodhouse's car was supposed to be parked near the back of the center lane, but Coyle didn't see it. Wondering if he misinterpreted the message, he took the next lane, and then the one beside that. Twice he spotted the tops of white vehicles, but they turned out to be different models.

Coyle called Woodhouse. No answer. He stopped and surveyed the parking lot. Doing the arrest in this crowd was going to be a nightmare. Behind him, a driver blared his horn.

Coyle parked in the No Parking zone in front of the store. A unit pulled up beside him. Sergeant Dave Dietz rolled down his window. "You find Woodhouse?"

Coyle shook his head. "We need to do this low-key, or it's going to be a mess in there. I'll talk to the store manager and locate Partridge. Once I have eyes on him, I'll call you."

Dietz nodded. "Siefert's on his way."

Inside the store, Coyle found the manager, a stocky, red-faced man.

"What d'you need Partridge for?" he asked. "We're a little busy right now."

"Police business."

The manager consulted a clipboard. "He's supposed to be in Kitchens, last aisle. But on a day like this, he could be anywhere. You want me to call him to the office?"

Better not to tip him off. "That's okay. I'll find him."

Coyle made his way through the congested checkout lines and turned into the last aisle. He passed a couple arguing about sinks and a contractor balancing an oven hood on a shopping cart. Midway down the aisle, he saw a clerk in one of the store's green vests. The man was a hundred feet away, back turned. Coyle walked quickly, unconsciously touching his Glock.

As Coyle reached the clerk, the man turned around to reveal himself as a twentysomething kid. The kid stumbled backward. "Whoa, man, take it easy."

"You seen Partridge?" Coyle asked.

"*Ir*-win?" The clerk said the name mockingly. "I think he was here a few minutes ago, but, like, who knows?"

Coyle walked the next aisle, past displays of kitchen cabinets. He peered around for another green vest. None in sight. He called Woodhouse again. No answer.

Don't screw this up.

He saw he was on aisle Sixteen. He decided to make his way methodically down each aisle.

Fifteen. Fourteen, Thirteen.

Dietz called. "You found him? You need us to come in?"

"No. Just hold on."

At Twelve, he approached a woman in a green vest demonstrating a power drill to a young couple. "Have you seen Irwin Partridge?"

She shrugged. "Break room an hour ago. He's around."

"You all wear the green vests?"

"We kind of have to." The clerk stared at Coyle. "Why do you want to know?"

Coyle showed his badge.

The woman turned away from the couple. "Irwin wears his vest over one of those insulated jackets. He works out in the storage shed and gets cold."

Coyle ran to the next aisle and the one after that, scanning the length. On aisle Seven, he saw a green vest at the far end, partially covering a black insulated jacket. Coyle watched the clerk stack PVC pipe on a shelf. He imagined walking down the aisle, taking out his gun halfway, waiting until he was behind the clerk to say Partridge's name. *Should he call Dietz?*

Suddenly a hand was laid on his shoulder. Coyle jumped. Turning, he found an elderly shopper. "I'm looking for clocks."

Coyle shook his head. When he looked back down the aisle, the green vest was gone. He ran the length of the aisle, a sprinter in a maze, past shoppers and carts. At the intersection of a crossing aisle, he slammed into a customer, knocking the man backward into a display of spray paint, cans clattering to the floor.

By the time Coyle recovered, the green vest was gone. Coyle looked toward the dark storage shed. He moved slowly, until he saw the green vest facing a rack of metal fence posts. When he was ten feet away, Coyle raised his gun and shouted, "Police. Put your hands where I can see them."

The green vest continued pulling metal posts down from the rack. When Coyle moved closer, he saw the earbuds the clerk wore. He pulled the man around. It wasn't Irwin Partridge.

"The fuck you do that for?" the clerk shouted. Then he saw Coyle's gun. "Who are you?"

Coyle held up his badge. "I'm looking for Irwin Partridge."

"He's not here. He left." The clerk's eyes stayed on Coyle's gun.

"What do you mean, he left?"

"What do you think I mean? He drove away. Here, I'll show you."

The clerk led Coyle to the shed's loading dock, which had a view of the parking lot. "Irwin goes to his car to smoke. Nissan 240Z. Puke green. Always in the last space, first row. See. It's not there now."

"When'd he leave?"

"I don't know. Few minutes ago, I guess. What'd you want him for?"

Coyle ignored him.

"We done?" the clerk asked, louder.

Coyle nodded. He holstered his gun and called Dietz, giving him a description of the Nissan. Then he called Mahler. "I'm at the store. Partridge's gone, and I can't find Woodhouse. He's not picking up."

"Send a unit to Partridge's apartment," Mahler said. "I doubt he'll go there, but he might. If he tried to call his girlfriend and she didn't answer, he'll be suspicious."

"Where're you?"

"On my way to Thackrey's place in Dry Creek. The two guys in the park photo, Banerjee and Tao, gave him up. Frames called me."

"Steve's there?" Coyle asked.

"Long story. Look, if Woodhouse isn't at the store, he must be with Partridge."

"So what do I do now?" Coyle asked.

"Put out a BOLO, and keep trying to reach Woodhouse."

For a moment neither man spoke. Then Mahler said, "You better call Eden. Partridge's girlfriend said he's got a thing for her."

"She's not with you?"

"No. I...told her to go home. Just call her." Mahler hung up.

Coyle dialed Eden's cell. It rang four times and went to voicemail. Coyle stared at his phone.

Chapter Thirty-Six

(i)

Driving up the hillside to Thackrey's house, Mahler saw two patrol cars near the front door. As he neared, he noticed a pair of officers standing in front of the vehicles—Ted Bursick and Brian Hoenig.

Bursick, a tall man with close-cropped hair and wraparound sunglasses, stepped forward. "No answer on the door. No car in the garage."

Mahler climbed out of his car and walked to the door. He rang the bell and waited. No response, so he turned the doorknob. The door opened. He turned to the other officers. "I've got warrants."

Hoenig shrugged. "You're the boss."

They stepped inside, guns drawn. "Santa Rosa Police," Mahler called. "Benjamin Thackrey, we have warrants for your arrest and to search the premises." He led Bursick and Hoenig down the corridor, weapons extended. In the living room, they split up to search different rooms—no sign of Thackrey. Three minutes later, they gathered in the living room and holstered their guns.

"Now what?" Bursick asked.

Mahler watched the officer check out the large painting and wondered what he made of the bright red gash slicing down the white canvas. "Let's have a look around."

Hoenig reached into a pocket for latex gloves. "What're we looking for, Eddie?"

"Any evidence of where he went and whether he's coming back."

Bursick headed for the guest bedrooms; Hoenig, the office.

Mahler entered the master bedroom, where floor-to-ceiling windows faced the vineyard. The bed was made, the room clean. He checked the two bedside cabinets—both empty. A walk-in closet was only half-filled.

In the marble-tiled bathroom, Mahler caught a glimpse of his face in the brightly lit mirror. His eyes were still dark, an echo of his afternoon migraine.

Back in the bedroom, Mahler could imagine Thackrey emptying and wiping down the room. In a day or two, the techs might find whatever the cleaning had overlooked—chemical traces, fibers. But for now, the room had been stripped of both crime-scene evidence and all traces of Elise Durand's life. It was as if the victim had been literally erased from the space.

Who is this guy? If he's so smart, why'd he kill someone? Why didn't he run before this? More important—where's he gone? What am I missing?

Mahler shook free of his thoughts. He went back to the walk-in closet, facing a rack of dark shirts and black suit jackets, and ran a hand across the top of the hangers. As the clothes turned to his touch, he spotted a bright color. He flipped back and saw a tiny bit of yellow rising above a jacket pocket. He squeezed it between two fingers and pulled.

A woman's yellow silk scarf.

The scarf had a border of tiny flowers and smelled of perfume. Mahler imagined Elise Durand tying a knot in front, turning before a mirror, her fingertips tracing along its border close to her neck. He smiled.

I'm still here.

Mahler dropped the scarf into an evidence bag and went back to the living room.

Bursick was waiting for him. "Quite a house. Three guest bedrooms, home theater, pool house, wine cellar. Must have five hundred bottles. But nothing to say where this guy is. What'd you find?"

Mahler raised the evidence bag. "Scarf—might be the victim's. The room's cleaned out."

"You know something, Eddie?" Bursick asked. "You do this often enough, you get a sixth sense. You ever feel that? My gut says this guy's in the wind."

Mahler checked the empty spot on the cabinet top where earlier in the day Thackrey had pointed out the expensive sculpture. "Yeah. He's gone."

Hoenig came from the office, holding a small box. "I didn't find a map of downtown Buenos Aires like they do on TV. But I did find something else. These guys were in a desk drawer. Nine-millimeter hollow points. Two more boxes in the drawer. Weapon's not there, so our boy probably has it with him."

"Okay. I get he's gone," Bursick said. "But why doesn't he lock the door?"

Mahler shrugged. "Because he's not coming back."

The three men stood silent for a moment.

"Put out a BOLO on his car," Mahler said. "2018 Jaguar, silver, plates are in the system. And notify the airports. He's been on the move for at least an hour."

Mahler called Frames. "Steve, see if the two suspects there received any texts or calls from him in the last hour or so. I'll wait."

He walked to the glass walls overlooking the vineyard. Rows of grapevines ran straight across the valley. He remembered reading how vineyard managers use GPS technology to map out fields for perfect alignment. His thoughts followed the trellis rows to a vanishing point at the base of the low hills to the east. Little about this case had gone as he'd expected. *There's something here. What am I missing?*

"Eddie?" Frames's voice sounded on his cell. "No calls or texts in the past hour. But Thackrey called Russell Tao two hours ago. Said he was meeting someone."

"Who? Where?"

"According to Tao, Thackrey didn't say, and neither of these guys knows. Something else, though. These guys just told me Thackrey killed Elise because she knew he murdered a woman named Reggie Semple in San Francisco two years ago."

"Yeah. We knew SFPD questioned him about the murder. The connection to Elise Durand explains why Thackrey acted surprised when Eden mentioned it to him this morning. Look, if Thackrey tries to contact his friends, call me."

Mahler called Coyle. "Where are we on Partridge?"

"No word on his car, and I still can't get through to Tom. I just got a call from the unit that went to Partridge's apartment. He's not there. You think Partridge spotted Tom and ran?"

"I don't know. Why isn't Tom calling us? I told him to let us know if Partridge moved."

"You get Thackrey?"

"He's not here. The house's empty."

"Eddie, Eden's not answering her cell either. I tried three times. If Partridge is going anywhere, it might be to Eden. He knows she worked the evidence on his girlfriend. You want me to go over to her place?"

A new wave of pain pounded behind Mahler's eyes. *Was this slipping away? Both killers were gone. The evidence and leads were fading. Was it happening again?*

"Eddie, you there?" Coyle asked.

"Yeah. Look, I have an idea. Go to the park. Partridge'll be there."

"Spring Lake? Why?"

"He'll go back. Eden said his pattern is to kill in the same kind of place every time. If he's pressured, he'll go back to the park. Drive to the west parking lot, below the campground. If you see his car, take Fisherman's Trail, down near the boat ramp."

"What about Eden? Partridge's a stone killer. He kills girls like Eden, and you said he's got a thing for her."

"No. Go to the park. Partridge'll be there."

"You want to take him, Eddie? He's your guy. You've been after him for two years."

Mahler heard the words "your guy" and felt them register. A few hours earlier he might have jumped at the chance of personally arresting Partridge. But something had shifted. Maybe it was Susan Hart telling him that Partridge's arrest would not change her death and her not wanting to be stuck saying the same things over and over. Maybe it was already done between Partridge and him.

"It's okay," he said. "You go."

"You're sure he'll be at the park? If we're wrong—"

"Just do it." Mahler tapped the screen to end the call.

Coyle's voice hung in the air. *If we're wrong—*

(ii)

(FRIDAY, 1:00 P.M.)

Eden unlocked the back door of her condo and entered the kitchen. Except for a brief shower two days earlier, she hadn't been home since Tuesday morning. With the shades drawn, the room was dark and smelled of something rotten. She flipped on the light to look around. After the events of the last three days, she was surprised at the normalcy of her home.

Driving home, she'd thought of the cases' ending. *How was she supposed to feel? How did the rest of the VCI team feel? She should have a sense of accomplishment. They identified the killer of Elise Durand and found evidence to convict Irwin Partridge. So why did she have a sense of something left unfinished?*

Eden kicked off her shoes without unlacing them and walked across the kitchen in her socks. She turned on the countertop TV. When she pulled out the tie, her hair felt dirty and greasy. She removed the holster and gun and put them on the kitchen table. Emptying pockets, she found her cell phone and saw a missed call from Coyle. She hadn't heard it while she was driving. She reached to call him back but stopped to watch a breaking news story on the TV about a bank robbery in southeast Santa Rosa.

She opened the refrigerator door to investigate the source of the room's rank odor. In front of her, prominently on the middle shelf, sat an opened bottle of pinot grigio. The culprit for the smell was probably beside the wine—a milk carton past its due date. Or, the yellowing celery stalks, jammed in a glass of water in a forlorn attempt at restoration. Or, the brown-topped guacamole on the shelf below. She would deal with them later.

For now, she took out the pinot, found clean stemware in the cabinet, and poured herself a glass. The wine was cold and brought back memories of the first time she had drunk pinot grigio. It was the summer between junior and senior years in college when she and her friend Leslie spent three weeks in the Umbrian hill towns of Italy. One warm night they stayed outside Spoleto and bought bottles of chilled wine at a market. As they sat in the hotel's stone courtyard, two Italian boys rode past on motorbikes. A few minutes later the boys returned. They were shy and spoke little English. They offered to take the girls for a ride. When Leslie declined, Eden invited the boys to share their wine.

They sat around the hotel's shaky metal table—the taller boy, Giovanni, next to Leslie, and the other one, Ludo, beside Eden. At first, they spoke using hand gestures and Eden's untested sophomore Italian. Then they broke off into two separate couple conversations.

Ludo had long black hair and dark eyes. He was twenty, studying to be an engineer. Eden had struggled to keep up with his Italian. He spoke with a lilting accent and called her *E*-den.

They drank glasses of the cold wine. The name, pinot grigio, Ludo said, meant gray pinecone. He demonstrated how to hold the glass under her nose and smell the flowers and citrus. Eden loved the wine's cold, green flavor. After the third glass, she stopped trying to translate what the boy said and imagined his words to be an ancient lyrical poem.

Giovanni took out his phone and played Italian pop songs. He stood and gestured with his arms, inviting the girls to dance. *Ballare*, he said, taking Leslie's hand. *Ballare*.

Ludo and Eden danced with one arm around each other, their right hands holding a glass of wine. Ludo taught her to raise the glass, so he could see her beautiful face. *Bel viso.* He leaned close so she felt his soft hair on her cheek. He gently kissed her neck. She laughed and felt herself in a wonderful familiar dream.

Ludo paused in their dance. He kissed one ear and whispered the only English words he knew, taught by a visiting nun. "Montan-a," he said. "Col-or-a-do." Eden giggled at the boy's silliness. But she heard the earnestness in his voice as he spoke the words slowly, musically, syllable by syllable. Intoxication wrapped her in a cloud. His words became a happy dizziness.

Then Ludo drank from his glass and kissed her slowly on the lips, and she tasted the wonderful cold wine in his kiss.

Now in her kitchen, Eden remembered the music and the dance. It was a time, maybe the last time, when she could remember herself as a person without regrets. Holding the glass above her head, she closed her eyes and began to sway, alone, in front of the refrigerator. She moved in a small circle in her socks, round and round, humming one of the Italian songs to herself and remembering Ludo's hair softly brushing her cheek.

Suddenly an image played across her mind—something wrong in the last few minutes. *What was it?*

She stopped dancing and opened her eyes. She went back over everything in order: unlocking the back door, the empty kitchen, her shoes, the TV, her cell phone, the message from Coyle. She had forgotten to call him back. But that wasn't what was wrong. Her mind raced on: the TV screen, the wine bottle, the milk carton, the celery, the rotten guacamole—

Wait—the wine bottle. When she had last seen it on Tuesday, the bottle was two-thirds full, *above* the label. Now it was just a quarter full, *below* the label. She remembered this clearly, remembered telling herself how much she had to enjoy when the investigation was finished. How could the level be lower? She had been gone for three days. No one else had a key to the apartment.

Eden looked up at her right hand, still holding the wineglass above her head. Past that, across the kitchen, she saw her gun lying on the kitchen table.

Then she heard a faint sound in the living room. Cloth rustling? She turned toward it.

With the blinds closed, the room was dark, but she heard something. A glass? She stared wonderingly through the doorway to the living room. The light switch on the reading lamp clicked on.

A man sat there, watching her.

His legs were crossed, a clog on the right foot dangling from his toes. A wineglass stood on the table. One hand held a gun.

Benjamin Thackrey.

Chapter Thirty-Seven

(i)

(FRIDAY, 1:05 P.M.)

Coyle drove through the entrance to Spring Lake Park, tires skidding on the loose gravel. *Was it only four days since they had been here to discover the body of Elise Durand?* He waved his badge at the guard hut and accelerated down the park road and across the west parking lot. Near the bottom of the lot, he saw Partridge's Nissan and Woodhouse's Honda and, farther on, Tom Woodhouse standing beside Fisherman's Trail. Coyle jumped out, leaving his car door open.

"Where's Partridge?"

"Already on the trail. I was going after him."

"Jesus, Eddie was right." Coyle pulled out his Glock.

Woodhouse smiled. "Eddie told you to come here? Good for him."

They walked quickly onto the rocky path, Woodhouse struggling to keep up with Coyle.

"I couldn't call you," Woodhouse yelled to Coyle. "Fucking battery on my phone died."

"I figured," Coyle called back. "Partridge's panicking. He must've figured we have his girlfriend and enough evidence for an arrest."

At a dogleg in the trail, Coyle slowed to see around the corner. Partridge wasn't in sight. "What's he wearing?"

"Black jacket. Jeans."

"You see a gun?"

"No."

They ran together again.

A couple walked toward them. Coyle shoved the Glock behind his back and held out his badge. "Did you pass a man in a black jacket?"

"Just now." The woman nodded. "About a hundred yards back. He was talking to someone."

Coyle bolted past the couple, aware he was leaving Woodhouse behind. Around another corner, he saw Partridge in a clearing, with a young woman in a sweatshirt and running shorts. They stood on a muddy spit at the shallow edge of the lake. The woman faced Partridge, hands on hips.

As Coyle raced forward, the woman noticed him. In the same instant, Partridge pivoted behind her, looping a cord around her neck and pulling it tight.

Partridge and the woman instantly became a single, wild creature—at one end, Partridge kneeing his victim's back, all his weight on the rope ends, at the other end, the woman, arms wheeling helplessly in the air.

Coyle ran, gun leveled. "Police. Let her go."

Without a clean shot, Coyle shoved his gun in his belt and threw himself onto Partridge, tearing at the man's hands, prying away first one finger, then another. But the cord, fastened around Partridge's wrists, held. The force of it threw the woman's head backward, thrusting her chin in the air.

Coyle pounded Partridge's face, over and over, bloodying his nose. He looked back but couldn't see Woodhouse. As Coyle shifted, he slipped forward, tumbling with the pair and knocking all three of them into the shallow water.

The woman's head submerged, the cord still wrapped around her throat. Her head whipped frantically from side to side.

Coyle seized her sweatshirt and pulled her partway out of the water. But Partridge further tightened the cord, squeezing it into the woman's neck.

Over his shoulder, Coyle sensed someone running toward him. Then Woodhouse's arm slammed a gun handle onto Partridge's head.

Partridge's body went slack, and Coyle shoved the weight away from him. He pulled the woman's head out of the water and unwound the cord from around her neck. Her body was heavy and still. Curling his arms under hers, he dragged her to dry ground and laid her faceup.

She wasn't breathing. Coyle knelt beside her and, with one hand, pinched her nostrils. He took a deep breath and put his mouth over hers. He blew in. He did it again.

Coyle felt his own exhaustion and the coldness of his wet clothes.

He blew into the woman's mouth.

He heard Woodhouse drag Partridge out of the water.

He blew again, now aware of people watching.

After his fifth breath, the woman coughed and opened her eyes. Coyle hoisted her into a sitting position and held her while she coughed and vomited. Her face was pale, her eyes struggling to focus.

"My name's Martin Coyle," Coyle said. "I'm a police officer."

The woman breathed heavily. Water dripped from her hair down across her face. Her sweatshirt was soaked, her bare legs scratched and smeared with mud.

Behind her, Partridge said something to Woodhouse. The side of his head was wet with blood.

The woman turned to see Partridge. The cord, still wrapped tight around his wrists, lay across his body.

Two hikers helped Woodhouse to his feet. Gun still leveled at Partridge, Woodhouse told the hikers to call 911. In front of the onlookers, a teenage boy took photos.

The woman tipped back her head and closed her eyes. Red, crisscrossed bruises marked her neck. For a moment, with her eyes shut, she looked like the dead girls in the forensic photos.

Heaving a breath, she opened her eyes.

Coyle watched her eyes blink and focus on him. They stared, as if seeing something new.

"Good," he said softly. "Good."

(ii)

(FRIDAY, 1:10 P.M.)

Thackrey pointed to the chair beside him. "Let's talk shop."

Eden sat on the edge of the cushion. Her hand trembled as she put the wineglass on the table.

Thackrey smiled. He took her hand and ran a thumb slowly across its back. "You know why I'm here?"

"Because I said the thing this morning about Reggie Semple." Her voice was a whisper.

"You were testing me, weren't you? Well, guess what? You were right. Unfortunately, it's not always a good thing to be right."

He let go of her hand and sat back on the sofa. From his pocket, he took a pill bottle. He unscrewed the cap and poured several into his mouth. "How'd you know?"

Eden tried to gauge Thackrey's attention level. His eyes darted around the room. Was he alert or just processing the pills? She imagined jumping on Thackrey, ripping the gun from his hand. An even bet had her rising from the chair and being shot in the stomach. "When we went through Elise Durand's things, we found a book of Keats poetry. She wrote lots of stuff in the margins. But one note puzzled me. Three times, where the word 'queen' appears, Elise circled it and wrote 'murder' in the margin."

"Elise loved her poetry."

"Then when we ID'd you, I saw an entry in your file. The San Francisco homicide detectives questioned you at the time of Reggie Semple's disappearance. Reggie's short for Regina, which means *queen*. Elise must have found or heard something that convinced her you killed Semple. You had to kill Elise because she knew. I wasn't sure until this morning in your house. When I said that thing about Reggie, you stopped smiling for the first time."

Eden watched Thackrey's crossed leg jiggling up and down as it had earlier that morning. "Someone'll find the evidence."

Thackrey looked up at the ceiling, his eyes studying something there. "That's just it. There is none. Since you enjoy puzzles, I'll tell you this one. I hired a gypsy cab in the Mission District. A Honduran national named Javier Griffin. Señor Griffin was a great admirer of cash. I paid him a thousand dollars to call the residence of Tyler Morris and pick up Reggie. She and her boyfriend were so strung out on smack, they didn't question a cab showing up. Griffin brought her to me, asleep in the back seat. I paid him another thirty thousand dollars to disappear."

"We'll find him," Eden said.

"Good luck with that. After he left, I injected Reggie's bony ass with a veterinary tranquilizer called xylazine. Like putting a cat down. I weighted her body and sank it in the bay. Then I donated Griffin's cab to a salvage yard in Fremont, where it was crushed and sold as scrap. Poof. Gone. Why does anyone think murder's so difficult?" Thackrey picked up his wineglass and sipped, his eyes dark.

Eden watched him drink the wine that held her memories. Her anger rose. The image of Reggie Semple floated across Eden's mind. She saw the dead woman's dress pulled up in the back seat of the gypsy cab. She suddenly felt furious. "Elise was different from other women, wasn't she?" Eden said. "She was smarter than the party girls and, like you, she was a risk-taker. She had a wild streak, an exuberance, that showed in her art, without the cushion of your money and the fear that lived in the back of your own soul."

"Elise was flat-out crazy."

"Oh, sure, but you couldn't kill her right away, could you? You had to, but some feeling got in the way. You needed to talk yourself into it. Reggie was easy, but Elise—"

"And where do you fit into all this, Detective Somers?" His voice was cold now.

"I'm the cop you saw coming, the one you're taking all that speed for."

Thackrey stood and pulled Eden up beside him. "Come on. Let's do this right."

Thackrey took Eden's hand and led her to an open space in the living room. Eden tried to pull away from him, but he held her hand tightly. When he put his arm around her, the gun pressed against her lower back.

Eden saw his eyes nervously following her.

Thackrey pressed Eden's body close to him. "Tell me, Detective Somers, in your nightmare, how do you see yourself killed? Strangled like the girls in the park, choking on your last breath? Or another way?" He tapped his gun against her shoulder. "A bullet? The American way?"

Eden glimpsed something different across the room. As it appeared, she saw Thackrey register the change in her eyes.

Thackrey swung around. Eddie Mahler stood in the doorway twenty feet away. His Sig Sauer was braced in his hands and pointed straight at them.

"Put the gun on the floor," Mahler said.

Thackrey smiled. He slowly ran the tip of his gun through Eden's hair. "I'll put it down in a minute, Lieutenant Mahler. First, you're going to watch as I shoot your girl here."

Chapter Thirty-Eight

(i)

Mahler leveled his gun at Thackrey. The pair paused in front of him, Eden in front, Thackrey behind.

Thackrey smiled. "You're early, Mahler. Detective Somers was just about to die."

Tiny lights flashed in Mahler's field of vision. He tried to blink them away. "There's no play here, Thackrey. A dozen units are on the way."

"Spare me your threats."

Mahler watched Eden and Thackrey as they turned in a circle. Thackrey's left hand clasped Eden's fingers. His right hand, holding the gun, pressed her lower back, pushing her into him.

"Step away from her, and put your hands where I can see them." As Mahler watched them, the shadow of a scotoma slowly formed, blocking the center of his vision.

"Shall I make it easier for you?" Thackrey swung Eden until

he was in front of her. "Clean shot now, Mahler. Of course, you still have to worry about the bullet going through me and into Detective Somers. Or, you might miss me altogether and hit her."

In Mahler's eyes, the couple disappeared for an instant behind the scotoma before they came out the other side.

Thackrey continued moving until Eden was in the front again. "From what I've read, Lieutenant Mahler, you're a screwup. Can you handle this?"

"This isn't a game, Thackrey."

"Isn't it? Before you arrived, your pretty detective was telling me about my relationship with Elise Durand. It was somewhat insulting, but maybe she can help you. Tell me, Detective Somers, what do we know about Mahler?"

Eden looked fully at Mahler. She remembered her hostage training. Stay calm. Don't hurry. Make eye contact with the rescuing party. Try to establish a line of communication outside the hostage-taker's awareness, so that you and the rescuing party know what you're planning.

Thackrey pressed the gun against her back. "You think I'm kidding?"

"Lieutenant Mahler suffers migraine headaches," Eden said quickly. "Research shows migraines can be a psychological sign of the need for retreat. In this case, the body's way of coping with work pressure."

Thackrey laughed. "Nail on the head. What everyone remembers about Eddie Mahler is he screwed up and a girl was killed."

Eden stared at Mahler. She felt as if she and Mahler were communicating on a new level. "But memories change over time."

"You mean people forget."

"No. It's not forgetting. Memories change. We understand events in a new way. We go on after a mistake. We think we'll be a hero in our own story. Sometimes we aren't."

"You're quiet over there, Mahler," Thackrey said. "What's wrong?"

Eden could sense the connection with Mahler ending. "One other thing. According to Lieutenant Mahler's service record, he's fired his weapon twice while on duty. Both kill shots. Which means when he shoots you, you'll be dead."

Thackrey pulled Eden toward him so their faces were inches apart. "Think so? Maybe he'll miss and kill you." He swung Eden around. "Come on, Mahler, take your shot. It's simple. It's like a program code, a binary choice. Yes or no. On or off. Her, then me. You can handle that, can't you?"

Mahler turned his head to keep the moving couple in the good corner of his vision. The rest of the room remained a wavy, moving blur.

Thackrey stopped moving and stared at Mahler. "Wait a minute. Something's wrong. You can't see, can you? I noticed something odd about the way you tipped your head when you came to my house."

In Mahler's field of vision, the scotoma began to vibrate and move.

Thackrey leaned close to Eden. "You're screwed, Detective Somers. Your boy here can't see to shoot. You need a different hero."

As the pair swung around again, Mahler found them in his vision. He caught a glimpse of Eden looking directly at him with the signaling posture every law enforcement officer learned. The next time, as Thackrey began his turn, Eden gripped the hand that held hers and swung it hard into Thackrey's face.

The blow stunned Thackrey. He let go of Eden for a second,

swaying. Regaining his balance, he raised his gun. Before he could shoot, Mahler fired three times.

The bullets exploded into Thackrey's body and opened like flowers on his chest. He looked down, searching for something. Then his legs weakened. He fell backward, hitting the coffee table on his way to the floor.

Mahler rushed across the room, his Sig still leveled on the fallen figure. He pulled the gun from Thackrey's fingers and laid it on the table out of reach. Holding Thackrey's wrist, Mahler felt for a pulse. When he found none, he let the arm fall beside the dead man's body, where dark blood had begun to pool. The room was suddenly still, as if death had extinguished sound and left behind a hollow, empty space.

(ii)

(FRIDAY, 1:35 P.M.)

In her move to strike Thackrey, Eden had fallen to the floor. Now she crawled on her hands and knees across the room until she reached a corner and couldn't go farther. She sat there, crouched in a tight ball.

Mahler returned his gun in its holster. He walked to Eden and knelt next to her. When she looked up, he noticed red stippling across her forehead. He reached with his sleeve to wipe it off.

"Oh, God." She ran her fingers over her face and hair. "Is it gone?" Mahler nodded.

"I don't want him on me." Her body shook. "Did you get it?"

"It's gone." He held one of her hands. "It's gone."

Eden looked across the room. "I didn't think it would be like that."

"No. It's not what you expect."

"It happened so fast."

"It's over. You did the right thing."

"The blood smells," Eden said. "It's like something—"

"Metal," Mahler said.

"Yeah, metal." Eden took a deep breath and let it out. "Was Thackrey right? Are you having trouble seeing?"

"Yeah, one of my migraines."

"But you saw me?"

Mahler let go of her hand and sat beside her. He didn't want to think about how close it was. "I saw you."

"How'd you know to come here?"

"Thackrey's friend Tao told us about Reggie Semple. I figured Thackrey might try to get to you after that question you asked him this morning about Semple and Elise Durand."

For a moment neither of them spoke. The room was dark. They looked across to where Thackrey lay—only his legs visible, splayed where he had fallen.

From outside came the sounds of patrol cars arriving.

"I can't do this work." Tears welled in Eden's eyes. "I was wrong when I said I could."

The footsteps of other officers sounded behind them. Turning, Mahler held up one hand. "The shooter's down," he called to them. "Give us a minute."

When the others retreated, Eden said, "I'm no good at it." She wiped at the tears.

"You helped solve the cases, Detective Somers."

"I should quit. It'd be better for you."

"For me?"

"You could hire someone more like Frames."

Mahler smiled. "I'm not sure I could handle two Steve Frameses. Besides, I may not have a job. Chief Truro said he was replacing me."

"On Wednesday night, when you said I don't know what this job is, you were right. I don't."

"I didn't mean it."

"No. You were right. You remember my college thesis?"

"Sure. The Highway 60 serial killer."

"When I started that research, I wasn't sure what was important, so I read everything. Witness statements, interview transcripts, investigators' files, medical examiner's notes."

"I remember the appendices."

"But something happened. That's what I wanted to tell you this afternoon. One night in college I read the Arizona ME's report on the cause of death for one victim. You know how the girls were murdered?"

"Suffocation, wasn't it?"

"The suspect, Albert Jory, put dirt and grass in their mouths and noses. Then he taped their mouths closed. They aspirated on dirt." Eden's voice cracked. "The Arizona ME wrote a full page on one victim. He said before the victim blacked out, she tasted dirt. The Arizona surface soil, according to the examiner, is alkaline. He said it would have tasted chalky and coated the tongue."

"We see and hear terrible things in this work, and it affects people in different ways. I've seen it before. You'll get through it."

"I still have the panic attacks. I've been on Ativan for two years."

"The department has counselors. We can get you help."

"I don't know what this work is, how far to go. I can't help opening the door and looking in. I'm like Elise—the way she couldn't stop asking Thackrey about Reggie. After I read the Arizona report, all I could think of was the dirt in that girl's mouth."

Mahler saw Eden waiting for an answer. "Someone as arrogant as Thackrey thinks all cops are the same," he said. "If the chief lets me keep my job, I need different kinds of people on my team. I need a guy like Danny Rivas, who can see two gangbangers and tell which one's got a nine-millimeter behind his back. Or, someone like Frames, who does the right thing in a split second. Someone like Coyle, who can find stuff in a database. And someone like you—"

"Who can't stop doing research? Why'd you recommend me to the chief, anyway? You knew I flamed out at the agency. The only thing on my résumé was a failure."

"No," Mahler said, "the failure was the agency's for not backing you up. What you did was to get inside the victims better than anyone else. That's why I wanted you here. Remember, with every homicide, all we've got at the start is the victim."

"You want me to keep working for you?"

"I don't know what kind of a cop you'll be, Eden," Mahler said, looking into her eyes. "A murder investigation is about looking at what's there. You're good at that, one of the best I've worked with. But cases are also about everything that's left out—all the things we don't know, all the questions we have. It takes time to see how to live in that world. You need to learn your craft. Hang around guys like Rivas. Have a beer with Tom Woodhouse, and let him bend your ear about the cases he worked."

"And you?"

"Me? I'm not that old."

"What about the terrible things we see?"

"Part of the job. You have to find your own way with it. Listen to the victims. They'll tell you how far to open the door."

Eden looked at Mahler to see if he was serious. "The victims talk to you?"

Mahler shrugged. "Did I say that?"

Read on for a sneak
peek at the next

Violent Crime

Investigations Team

mystery!

Chapter One

(i)

Annie never saw Paul drive away, her husband getting smaller and smaller until he was a speck on the horizon. Instead, all of him, every unlucky molecule, suddenly vanished, like those characters on *Star Trek* dematerialized by the transporter.

The ingredients, the essence, of Paul Behrens departed—his sad face, that daily uniform of Oxford shirt and khaki trousers, the sound of his Nikes on the kitchen floor, the stale paper smell he carried around with him the last few years, which was like putting your nose close to the pages of an old book. Just like that, those things no longer existed where Annie was. Here, then there. Although it was not a there she could actually name.

The way he left shouldn't have mattered, at least not more than the fact of his leaving. But somehow it did. It seemed aimed at her, like something she wasn't smart enough to get.

Annie could picture it. Paul full of his English teacher thing, using a literary reference to explain his departure. It would take five minutes because there would be a book or play she'd never read, and he'd have to tell her about it—like she was a slow student. He'd start by saying something about the cat in *Alice*, and Lewis Carroll's writing style, and she'd stop listening after the first twenty seconds.

That, of course, became a problem later when the police had questions. For more than a year, Annie had been in the habit of not listening to Paul. She was a kind of expert at it. Her superpower was envisioning him across the kitchen table or on the other side of the family room, hearing the sound of his voice with its puking sincerity, all of it locked in her head, without being able to tell you anything specific he said.

The first thing Annie did remember about the day Paul left was that moment when she was lying on the sofa in the family room and heard her phone ping. She was covered in an afghan, still wearing her nurse's scrubs from the previous day's three-to-eleven shift. With the blinds closed, it was impossible to tell the time. The house was quiet and dark. Paul had already left for his job. Jesse and Claire were off to school.

Her head was pounding, her mouth dry. *Did she drink a whole bottle of Zinfandel before she fell asleep?*

She found her purse on the floor and dug out her phone. 8:32. Her brain immediately did the math: six hours' sleep. On the home screen, she saw a text message from Jennifer Steeley, the principal at Brookwood Middle School:

> Paul didn't come in. Not answering cell. Called sub.
> He OK?

Oh, Christ. He's home after all.

Annie threw off the afghan and walked through the kitchen to go upstairs. On the table were the remains of the kids' breakfast—cereal boxes and dirty bowls—and beside them her empty bottle. That last bit was a classic passive-aggressive message from Paul: I'm not going to hide it for you.

Going up the stairs, she felt through her cotton scrubs that her panties were missing. Her fogged brain drew a blank. Then she remembered the night before, leaving them on the back seat of the car. Shit. *Had Paul seen them?*

At the top of the stairs, Annie noticed the open door to the master bedroom and braced for a confrontation with Paul. But the room was empty. The bed on his side was mussed, pajamas thrown on the bedspread.

Annie headed back downstairs and opened the door to the garage. Paul's silver Elantra was gone. On the rear seat of her own Camry, she found her panties and stuffed them in her pocket.

Back in the kitchen, Annie rooted through a cabinet for a bottle of Advil. She washed down two tablets with a full glass of Sauvignon Blanc, poured another half glass, and sat at the table.

The empty Zinfandel bottle stared back at her across the table. The label was an artsy painting of a vineyard. $9.95, screw cap. Annie remembered the clerk in the supermarket wine department. Thirtyish, kind of cute, with that unshaved, not-quite-a-beard thing guys were doing these days. She smiled, found herself flirting, asking about the tannin-to-alcohol balance, or some shit she'd read online. He looked into her eyes and wasn't fooled. He reached to the lower shelves for one of the "value bottles."

Annie dialed Paul's cell. It rang three times before his voicemail clicked in. There was her husband's deep, earnest voice. "Hi. This is Paul. Sorry I missed your call. Leave me a message and—" She clicked off.

She found the number for Jennifer Steeley on her phone and tapped it. The time was 8:45. Busiest time of day for a principal.

Steeley picked up on the second ring, talking over the noise of a crowded hallway. "Hey, Annie. Thanks for calling back."

"Yeah. Got your message. Sorry about that."

"It's okay. We found a sub. Remember Penny Freese? Taught seventh-grade history before her first kid?"

"Good. Good. Glad it worked out."

"Part of the job. Is Paul okay?"

"I'm sure he's fine." Annie took a deep breath and tried to think how to start. "He's—The thing is, I'm working second shift these days and get home late. Sometimes we don't see each other for days. I didn't talk to him before he left this morning." *What business was it of this woman that she and Paul weren't sleeping together?*

"No problem, Annie. Really." Steeley's voice sounded impatient to end the call. "If he could just let me know how long he'll be gone and where he left his lesson book."

The buzz from the Sauvignon Blanc kicked in after she hung up. Annie refilled her glass and took it to the living room. She opened the curtains to look out on the backyard.

If Paul isn't at work, where the fuck is he? She thought of her father-in-law, recovering from chemo and staying with Paul's sister.

She clicked on the number. "Hey, Beth. It's Annie. This too early?"

"Yeah, right. No, honey. We've been up since four."

"Sorry to bother you, but is Paul there? We missed each other this morning, and he didn't show up at school. Just trying to track him down."

"Nope, not here. My experience is—and you probably know this, too—the guy's driving somewhere. Mister Careful never picks up while he's driving, even on Bluetooth. Try again in a few minutes. Tell the jerk to come by tonight for dinner. Dad wants a word. I'm making burgers."

Annie hung up and tried Paul's number again. This time she heard the phone's ringtone coming across the room, from her husband's briefcase lying beside the recliner. She crouched next to it and clicked open the latches. Paul's phone lay atop a pile of student assignments. She turned it off and stared at it. He never went anywhere without his phone.

Beneath the student assignments lay her husband's lesson plan. *How could he teach the day's classes without his plan?* Under the lesson plan was a sealed manila envelope with no address. She felt something inside the envelope and tore it open. Out fell a thin, multicolored friendship bracelet—the kind teenage girls tie around their wrists. Attached to one end of the bracelet was a tiny plastic red heart. She shook the envelope, but it was empty. No note, no letter.

Annie dug deeper through the briefcase, not knowing what she was looking for. At the bottom, she found a photo. As she picked it up, she froze. She held it away from her body like an object arrived from another world. Without thinking, she crushed the photo, squeezing so hard her fingernails cut her palm. Then she shoved it into the pocket of the scrubs and pushed down until her fingers felt the silk of the panties crumpled at the bottom.

(ii)

(WEDNESDAY, 8:45 A.M.)

"No one's good at surveillance," retired homicide cop Tommy Woodhouse once told Frames. "It's like saying you're good at putting your pants on. You're there to see something. The tricky part comes when that something isn't what you thought it would be."

Frames sat alone in the front seat of an unmarked Malibu. He was on temporary part-time loan from Violent Crime to the Narcotic Investigations Team. His car was parked in a residential section of Roseland, on the opposite side of the street and a few doors from a lime-green stucco rented by Lucia Cervantes. The narcotics team wanted surveillance on Cervantes, known to be the girlfriend of a street dealer named Jorge Lopez. A week ago, Lopez was identified as the supplier for a thirty-eight-year-old user who suffered a fatal overdose. After the OD, Lopez disappeared. One of the team's snitches said Lopez might show up to visit Cervantes.

In four days, Frames had seen Cervantes three times—twice when she emerged to drive to Safeway for groceries, and once when she watered the dying roses along the front fence. She was a small woman with straight, black hair who wore, on all three occasions, tight-fitting spandex workout suits. Watering the flowers, Cervantes stood in one spot for five minutes, smoking a cigarette and aiming the spray at the top of the plants. Halfway into it, Frames fought the urge to climb out of his car, walk down the street, and tell her what his grandmother had drummed into his head: water the plant base, not the blossoms.

On this latest shift, Frames passed the time by making a mental list of everything that hadn't changed since he arrived: no one in or out of the house, no lights on, window shades unmoved, no sound from inside the house, roses dead as the day before.

"What do you suppose she does all day?" a voice asked in his ear. Wiggins.

The other half of the surveillance team—Wiggins and Buckley—sat in a Ford parked across from Cervantes's driveway. Connected by wireless mikes, the three men had begun the surveillance observing a strict no-chatter policy. Wiggins ended the policy on the first day.

"TV," Buckley said. "Most people watch TV."

"All day? How do you watch TV all day?"

"Look on the roof. She's got the Dish. 190 channels. Other night, I turned mine on, and there was a soccer game from Albania."

"So you're saying she's inside there right now watching Albanian soccer?"

Buckley sighed. "No. That was an example. Are you familiar with normal conversation?"

"You know what I'd like right now?" Wiggins asked.

"Really? We're going to do this again?"

"One of those ham croissants from that place downtown. Don't tell me you couldn't eat one right now?"

"Sure," Buckley said. "We'll have it delivered to the car. What could go wrong?"

"How about, you, Steve-O? You hungry?"

"No," Frames said. "And remember how I asked you not to call me that?"

For Frames, the most frustrating part of working with Wiggins was not that he talked incessantly but that he had beaten Frames to it. Frames was known in Violent Crime as the talker. It was his signature. But here Wiggins had been first off the mark and grabbed the play. Now, with the earpiece, it was like Wiggins had gotten inside Frames's brain. Or, had become his brain.

"Okay. De-tec-tive Frames, tell me this. What's the longest surveillance you've been on?"

"This one," Frames said. He wanted to say any surveillance with you would seem longer.

"Really? I had one last year that was ten days. How about you, Buckminster?"

"2012. A whole month."

"You're kidding. Department had the budget for that? Hey, Frames, somebody said you were a jarhead. Anything this boring in the Corps?"

Frames debated not answering, but he knew Wiggins wouldn't give up. A few weeks earlier, Frames had seen an anonymous list on Twitter. Five most irritating SRPD officers. Wiggins was number three. Frames had never met numbers one and two, but he was impressed two officers were more irritating than Wiggins.

"Guard duty. Fallujah. First Battalion, Third Marines." Frames remembered the adrenalized mindset of Iraq. "Stood all night in a doorway of the house where guys in the platoon were sleeping. Had to be on your toes. Local paramilitary came out after dark."

"Nothing like guys coming to kill you to keep your eyes open, right?"

In an instant, Frames felt the M16 in his hands and smelled the decaying bodies in the desert night air. "That's just it," he said. "There were always lots of sounds—dogs barking, gunfire on the perimeter—but not much to see. From where I stood, the only light came from a window a block away." He saw the little square of light again at the end of a dark street.

"I couldn't look inside, obviously, but I kept myself awake imagining the family living where that light was. Father, mother, couple kids. Going about their normal life in the middle of a war zone. Every day you had bodies in the street, helicopters just over the housetops, bombs going off. But this little family went on with life. I made up this whole thing. The father drove a taxi. He met his wife when they were teenagers. The boy was the oldest, just starting to read. The little girl was afraid of the gear the American soldiers wore."

"At night, the father told a story before the kids fell asleep. The story was always about a beautiful flying woman. She was, the father said, as beautiful as their mother, and she flew through the air and rescued the people of the city. Every night was a new story of rescue."

When Frames finished, the mikes were silent. "That's what I imagined anyway," he said.

"That's what you thought of?" Wiggins said after a few seconds. "In fucking Iraq? You are one weird dude, Steve-O."

"Hey, Wiggins." Frames let his head fall back on the top of the seat. "Do you think if I came down there and pounded your ass, there's any chance you'd stop calling me that?"

"Wait a second, boys." Buckley suddenly serious. "We've got somebody on the move. One. Two of them. Running fast."

Frames sat up and peered down the street. He couldn't see anything. "Where?"

"Back of the driveway." Buckley spoke quickly. "It's Cervantes. And somebody else. Male. Six feet. See them?"

Frames stared ahead. A hedge blocked his view. "What're they doing?"

"Looks like Cervantes is trying to get away from the guy." Wiggins this time. "Wait. The guy's got something in his hands. Poles."

"Poles?"

"Or, sticks. Let me get the scope."

Frames still couldn't see anyone. He heard Wiggins's scope bang against the window glass.

"Oh, shit. They're swords."

"Wait. What?" Frames yelled. "Did you say swords?"

"Yeah. You know, like a pirate."

"You see them, Frames?" Buckley breathless. "They're fucking behind us, on your side, turning into the street."

Frames leaned close to the windshield. He could see Cervantes now racing toward him down the sidewalk. Bathrobe open, hair flying, face wild with fear. Behind her a man with a sword swinging in each hand.

Frames pulled the Glock from its holster. He let Cervantes run past. Then, opening the car door, he leveled the gun at the approaching figure. "STOP. Police."

The figure kept coming. He was close enough now that Frames could see the guy's shaved head, bare chest, and heavily tattooed upper arms.

"STOP," Frames shouted again.

With the man nearly in front of him, Frames fired a shot and saw it hit the man but not slow his approach.

"Frames, Frames." Wiggins yelling in his ear.

Buckley on the radio: "David 12. Shots fired. 418 Greenwood Avenue. Code three medical."

The man lunged with the right-handed sword over the top of the car door. Frames shielded himself with the door and fell backward inside the car. Thrown across the driver's seat and console, Frames fired again and missed. The attacker thrust the sword through the doorway. The blade sliced into Frames's calf like a hot poker.

Half a block away, the Ford's engine roared.

The attacker ripped the blade out and came at Frames again—this time with the sword held in his left hand.

Frames steadied his gun and fired three times. The rounds hit the man in the chest.

The Ford screamed down the street, skidding to a stop.

The attacker fell, slamming onto the doorframe and landing on Frames's legs. The man lay still. Frames saw his own arms extended, frozen in place, blood sprayed across his fingers, the tip of the Glock nearly touching the top of the man's head.

Outside, the flash of Wiggins sprinting after Cervantes. Then Buckley filled the car doorway, yanking the swords out of the dead man's hands. "Frames, you hurt? You need help? You okay?"

Frames looked at the other officers without really seeing them. He felt the dead man's weight and sweaty skin on his legs. The body was large and soft, and seemed to be settling, as if the man had crawled inside the car to fall asleep.

"Yeah," Frames said. "Yeah. I'm okay."

ACKNOWLEDGMENTS

My gratitude goes to the whole team at Poisoned Pen Press and Sourcebooks who enthusiastically embraced this book from the start and supported me in its publication. Special thanks to my editor, Barbara Peters, who brought to bear her long experience in this genre and who provided smart editing and counsel. I'm also grateful to Robert Rosenwald for first reading the book and to Diane DiBiase, Beth Deveny, Anna Michels, Jenna Jankowski, and Leyla Parada, who patiently steered a first-time author through the publishing process and helped me keep my feet on the ground.

I would like to thank my longtime critique group, who read the book from the start: Andy Gloege, Thonie Hevron, and Billie Settles. They taught me to add more and cut in just the right places. Without them, the book would not be what it is today.

Thanks also to my early readers: Chris Baker, Sean Cotter, Robert Digitale, Brian Fies, and Carol and Robert Sanoff, who generously read a rough draft and whose comments helped greatly.

I must thank David Rintell, who prodded me to keep writing,

who read a copy of the novel on a coast-to-coast flight when he was supposed to be preparing a business presentation, and who had a fateful conversation on behalf of my book at a wedding reception. Thanks also to Gayle Shanks for making a connection for an author she never met.

I am indebted to retired Santa Rosa Police Lieutenant Tom Swearingen. Tom read the story and answered my questions with the unique experience of a police officer who actually worked on the SRPD VCI team. No, he's not Eddie Mahler or any of the others, and he's obviously not responsible for any errors or exaggerations in the portrayal of the team. To quote the English novelist Kate Atkinson, "All mistakes are mine, some deliberate." I was also given great insight into the officers and practices of the Santa Rosa Police Department by the terrific Citizen Police Academy course given by the SRPD.

Finally, thanks to my wife, Meg McNees; my daughter, Chelsea Weisel; and my son-in-law, Steven Turner, who listened to me talk about this story for years, who went with me to look at tall buildings in San Francisco, who explained painting and coding, who kept me from being arrested when I asked a police officer too many questions about security cameras in a park, and best of all, who encouraged me when I needed it most. This novel is for you.

ABOUT THE AUTHOR

Photo by Rob Martel

Frederick Weisel has been a writer and editor for more than thirty years. *The Silenced Women* is his debut novel. He lives with his wife in Santa Rosa, California, and is at work on the second novel in the VCI series. You can check out his website at frederickweisel.com.